BERKLEY TITLES BY JAMES ABEL

White Plague
Protocol Zero
Cold Silence

COLD SILENCE

JAMES ABEL

BERKLEY
New York

BERKLEY
An imprint of Penguin Random House LLC
375 Hudson Street, New York, New York 10014

ISBN: 9780425282984

Berkley hardcover edition / July 2016
Berkley premium edition / June 2017

Printed in the United States of America
1   3   5   7   9   10   8   6   4   2

Cover art: Artwork by Studio Liddell for aareps.com; *Red fused liquid* © Svetara/
Shutterstock; *Biohazard symbol* © Miguel Angel Salinas Salinas/Shutterstock
Cover design by Anthony Ramondo
Interior art: *Deserted area* © by Anastasia Koro/Shutterstock
Book design by Kristin del Rosario

PROLOGUE

===

I'LL NEVER GET OUT OF HERE ALIVE, THOUGHT TAHIR KHAN.

He backed away from the peephole in the Boca Raton penthouse apartment, as the quiet knocking on the front door continued. Across the room, bright sun flooded in through floor-to-ceiling sliding glass doors that faced the blue Atlantic, dazzling and still, twenty-four stories below. In early January, seventy-degree air washed in from the balcony and he heard the ocean, vaguely, insistent as a hiss.

Khan looked around wildly, as if somehow, magically, an escape hatch would appear in the walls. But all was as it had been when he rented his hideaway. The place was costly but ugly and generic; hospital white walls and matching floor tiling, curving Naugahyde couch wrapped toward a giant TV. Bright lime green cushions topped wrought iron furniture. The same generic pastel beach paintings hung in a thousand rental condos from Key West up the East Coast, to New Jersey. Still life conch shells. Wind ruffling dune grass. Six-year-old children in bathing suits, wielding plastic pails.

Khan was tall and stick-thin and he wore a black short-sleeved tropical shirt with a yellow once-festive and now sweat-soaked orchid pattern. He had underdeveloped muscles, soft hands, and big eyes. He thought, Call 911 for help? If I do that, I'll be arrested.

"Hey!" the friendly voice called through the door. "I know you're in there. Open up. I just want to talk."

Khan peered through the peephole again and saw, magnified, like two spread fingers, air tickets, and then the tickets moved away and the smiling face was back, features exaggerated by the lens, ratcheting up his terror.

I'm trapped. I'm finished. He'll kill me, he thought.

He'd taken a bus here, because cheapo bus lines accepted nontraceable cash, changed his name on the lease, to Phillip Zahoor, and paid a pile of hundred-dollar bills up front for three months, plus a hefty damage deposit. He'd barely left the apartment for the last two weeks.

But they always found you. They tracked you down. They used computers and satellites, databases and old-fashioned footwork. It had been stupid to try to leave. He should have shut up and gone along and batted away his doubts.

"How did you get past the guard?" he called out.

Knock-knock-knock. The thin door looked as if it was caving in with each impact, however slight.

Fucking Florida construction. Fucking South Florida–quality work. South Florida, where planned obsolescence meant concrete spalled months after being poured, roofs leaked in storms, doors were as sturdy as on Hollywood sets.

Appearance was everything. Quality was a joke. The voice sounded close, male, soft, and intelligent.

"Guard? I didn't see a guard."

"I'll call security if you don't leave, Orrin."

No answer. Then, as if the man felt hurt, "Aw, what do you want to say that for? And why'd you leave anyway? After four years? Things are finally about to pop, Tahir!"

Tahir Khan was a twenty-six-year-old ex–biology grad student from Pakistan, still legally in the United States, although he'd withdrawn from the State University of New York at Albany. Family abroad. Cold sweat flowed from his bald head, shaved two days ago, and ran down his face, where he was trying unsuccessfully to grow a beard. It coursed past his glasses and down his ropy neck and sprouted inside his armpits. His throat was closing. He couldn't breathe. His head pounded. He'd heard the expression "knees going weak" but had never, until now, experienced it, and he wobbled backward from the door as if, any second, it would crash in. First thing on getting here, he'd called a locksmith to come, to install a deadbolt, and the hearty American voice on the phone had promised, "You betcha! We'll come today!" *But no one had shown up.* "Our guy got a flu. Sorry, sir." *So Khan tried a second place.* "We can come next Friday. Is Friday okay?"

Friday was tomorrow.

Now the voice came again through the door and it was patient and soft but inside the patience was something dark. The voice was Midwestern, reasonable on the surface. It was confident. "If I wanted to hurt you, I could have done it last night at the fish restaurant. Or this morning when you walked on the beach, Tahir."

Tahir felt hope stirring. "You were in the restaurant?"

"You ordered mahimahi. Me, I prefer lobster. With butter. And lots of dark beer."

Tahir risked the peephole magnifier again, saw Orrin's plain and forgettable face. There was absolutely nothing memorable about the man. He seemed composed of a collection of bland features. Height just short of normal. Face, almost round but not, nose, one of those computer-generated combos showing common features of humans, two holes for breathing in a functional pasted-on knob. He was a genetic mix of average. You could see him straight on and forget him if a breeze distracted you. The skin was tanned. His tropical shirt, worn loosely, featured a racing cigarette boat pattern. The baseball cap said MARLINS, *as it did on ten thousand people walking around here. The left hand held up Delta tickets again. Orrin's smile looked genuine. It always did. But Tahir had seen the kind of damage the man could do. The doughy body was an illusion.*

"See? One ticket for you. One for me. What are you going to say if you call the police anyway? You know what they will do to you? Open the goddamn door and let's go."

Tahir considered it. His two-bedroom penthouse sat above a concrete patio on the beach side, three blocks from the inland waterway in the west. At this height, any tourists walking on the beach would be beyond earshot if he screamed, and his next-door neighbor, a snowbird psychiatrist from Manhattan, was away for the weekend at his daughter's wedding on Long Island.

Tahir thought, I should have gone back to Pakistan.

Tahir was in Florida for the first time and the only human being he'd had contact with here for more than five minutes had been the real estate agent. I need to rent something today, he told the man. He'd paid cash at Best Buy, for a TV, which he'd sat staring at for days, waiting with dread for the BIG NEWS to break, the thing he'd been working on. Cash in the supermarket, where he'd stocked up on food. Cash to the cabbie who'd brought him here.

No motel for him. No lodging where he had to sign a registry book, even with a false name, because handwriting could be tracked. He'd been drilled on techniques. The people looking for him would check hotels and motels. They'd bribe desk clerks. Watch security tapes. Send phony tourists to sidle up to other guests and start conversations. They'd sit in cars in front of hotels.

So after he rented this place, other than a daily walk on the beach, to keep from going crazy, or that one restaurant meal, he'd stayed inside and watched TV. Sometimes waiting for the BIG THING, sometimes just eyeing mindless fluff: Judge Judy. Wife Swap. *Anything to keep him half sane as he tried to figure out what to do next. Tahir Khan had become one more anonymous figure trudging the Florida tide line, watching porpoises offshore at sunrise, and other fins, bigger ones. Less-benign life looking for something smaller to eat. Tahir among the handful of sleepless retirees, young lovers who had been up all night making impossible promises, sunburned tourists giving one last longing look at a beach before boarding the plane back to gray Newark or Pittsburgh. And among them, one fugitive, running from the biggest mistake of his life.*

The plan had been to sit here for a few weeks, get distance, and decide when to try to get out of the country and sit out the disaster that was about to begin.

But now the doorknob turned and Orrin Sykes somehow just stepped into the apartment. How could he have a key? The private security guard downstairs was "here twenty-four hours a day," the rental agent had promised. Khan had pushed it, demanded, "What happens if someone gets past security?" and the beefy guard behind the desk had laughed, nodded at video monitors showing elevator interiors, and said, poking his chest with pride, "Ex-ATF," as if that guaranteed that no intruder, no stranger, not even a ninety-year-old cripple would pass his station without proper ID.

But Sykes was a ghost, and now the man stood just ten feet away, same distance as the phone. For an instant Tahir flashed back to a film he'd seen in freshman biology class, too many years ago. It had been called Animal Camouflage. It had featured creatures—a certain frog, a moray eel, a crab—all of which looked beautiful, and rarely moved, and then with sudden shocking aggression would lunge. A tongue would flick out. A mouth would open. Whatever life form had been innocently feeding nearby a moment before would be gone, and the killer would be sitting there again.

"Come on, Tahir. Pack a bag. Let's go home."

"Really?"

"What do you think, I'd hurt you? You're valuable."

He started to feel relief. The sweat flow dissipated to a trickle. Was it possible? He began to babble, as he moved backward, toward the bedroom, toward his ratty suitcase in the back closet, all the time watching for Orrin to lunge.

"I didn't tell anyone. Who would believe it, right?"

Sykes nodded. "You had doubts."

"I admit I thought about calling a reporter. Or the FBI. I did. I considered it. But I didn't do anything. I just wanted to get away. For a little while. To think."

"Think."

"Everyone needs time to think."

"I know I do," Sykes agreed, nodding.

The bedroom lay down a short hallway from the living room, and the walk gave Sykes a view of all the other rooms in the condo. Kitchen, empty. Bathroom, empty. Guest bedroom, empty. Master bedroom.

"No one really here," Sykes said.

"I told you that."

"I was just checking," Sykes said.

Tahir opened the mirrored sliding closet door with shaking hands. He reached up for his suitcase. He actually felt Orrin move before, it seemed, the reflection did in the three mirror panes. Tahir did not have time to turn. In the mirrors three meaty arms circled three skinny throats and three Tahirs were lifted bodily off the carpet. There was an awful cracking sound and he watched his head spin around. Orrin's face remained expressionless.

In a freshman biology class at SUNY, Tahir had heard a professor say once that after a human being is killed, the brain keeps functioning for a few more moments. Now his brain processed that he was being carried back into the living room, and that he was hanging over the patio railing. Wow, I am dead, he thought, falling, the concrete flecked with shiny mica, its squares forming a chessboard, the empty squares coming up fast.

ONE

LIONEL NASH'S PLEA FOR HELP WENT UNANSWERED BECAUSE I could not reach my ringing satellite phone. My hands were occupied, gripping the steel fuselage in back of a C-130 Hercules, to keep me from sliding out of the plane. One engine had failed but the other three held altitude. I was strapped by bungee cord to the wall, six hundred feet above southern Sudan, as the big transport went semivertical, nose up, rear ramp open. I heard, over ringing, the high-pitched scream of wind, and the prop engines. Through that open door, I glimpsed six thousand starving Dinkas below, waiting for our life-giving cargo of Kansas-grown grain to fall.

There had been some mechanical problems over the last couple of weeks when it came time to release food. I'd insisted, against Eddie's objections, on riding in back today to see if I could find the snag. It had been small.

I'd fixed it. *Drop the food and let's go home*, I'd told the three-man crew up front.

The ringing stopped as we hit drop-angle. Not many people had my number. That the phone was ringing meant there was an emergency. In this part of the world, that could mean any number of things.

It could be a government attack on rebels. Disease. Aid workers injured. The whole continent is a basket case.

I was the only person in back; no seats here, just the steel cave, and centering it, a track on which sat wooden pallets piled with 110-pound burlap sacks, filled with sorghum. From the outside, our blue UN markings were supposed to protect us if Sudanese MiGs showed up. Sometimes precautions worked. Sometimes rebels or government troops shot at relief planes. Sometimes planes—rattletrap workhorses to start with—failed and fell to the savannah below.

The phone began ringing again.

Below, men, women, and children had been waiting for food for days, sitting on their haunches, a silent crowd an eighth of a mile deep. Some had walked a hundred miles to reach the huge field, an arbitrary rectangle of grass. Looking up at us was a sea of hungry faces smeared with chalky dung powder, natural protection against sand flies. Twelve thousand eyes watched this afternoon's lone contribution to the bucket brigade of aid planes feeding four hundred thousand Africans at the junction of Kenya, Somalia, and Sudan, amid drought last year, flooding this year, and a thirty-year-old civil war.

Gravity did the job. The bags began to slide down the track, sluggish at first, then faster, food going down a gullet. The palettes and sacks tumbled out to separate and drop like bombs toward the veldt, where UN food monitors kept the crowd and a crew of TV journalists from running onto the drop zone, for a better shot, or for the food.

Last week a news show host from Copenhagen had done just that, stupidly had run onto the field to be on camera when the sacks hit the ground. Too late, she realized the bags were falling directly toward her. She tried to run, but her high heels snagged and a bag smashed her legs, and Eddie and I helped to amputate them back at the base.

She'd been airlifted home, a twenty-five-year-old blond beauty who had only weeks before appeared in Scandinavian magazine ads, and now would be fitted with artificial legs, who had considered Africa a form of entertainment or career advancement, and had come to see that it represented a more basic role than that.

What happens here threatens the world.

The ringing started up again as the plane stabilized and the remaining inboard port engine coughed. We limped toward home. I answered and went still, shocked when I heard who was calling. I'd thought today's mission was over. But what was starting would turn my world—the whole world—upside down.

MY NAME IS JOE RUSH AND I'M A MEDICAL DOCTOR, ALL RIGHT, BUT also a retired Marine colonel who occasionally goes back on duty to do jobs for my old unit in D.C. My records have been sheep dipped, given selective truths. Kid from a Massachusetts town, that part is true, as is the ROTC training and Parris Island and later assignments in Indonesia, the Philippines, Iraq. Marksman, the file says, capable of running a field op. True. Forty-one years old. Divorced by a wife who got tired of secrecy. I live alone now in the town where I grew up and I advise the Wilderness Medicine group at Harvard two days a week on medical work in "difficult" areas of the world. The file looks complete, to an outsider.

But the death of my fiancée eighteen months ago isn't there, nor is the fact that, when summoned, I still run a two-man bioterror team comprised of myself and my best friend, Major Edward Nakamura. My secrets from even my bosses are certainly not there either. That I wake sometimes from dreams of strangling one man and watching another die, frothing at the mouth, in a foreign private hospital, run by a foreign security service. Sometimes when I open my eyes from those dreams, I feel a presence in the room. Not a consciousness. Not a ghost. I don't believe in that. So I'm unsure what is there, in the room with me. Memory? Blame? Rage? Regret?

My feeling when I lie awake those nights in my isolated home in Massachusetts, and wait for dawn, is complicated. It's not guilt. I did what had to be done. Not fear, because I don't care if something beyond our earthly comprehension is really there. "It's vigilance," Eddie once said. "You concentrate on what you need to do to protect others."

But Eddie is an optimist. He always thinks things will turn out right.

Once waking, I thought I saw a small green glow in the corner of my bedroom. But later I decided I probably didn't see it. Or it was the reflection of a headlight passing on the dirt road. Or an afterimage from rubbing my eyes. I'm a doctor. I'm a scientist. I hunt diseases and believe in facts. I don't believe in little glowing lights. Or in religion. Or certainly, anymore, in a benevolent God.

Wilderness Medicine is in the file, too, and it was the official reason that Eddie and I were in Africa, thanks to a secret agreement our director—back in Foggy Bottom—made with Harvard. Wilderness Medicine is a new field, the art of getting fast care to patients in remote parts of the earth. Sometimes they are explorers or adventurers who have been injured in the Amazon, or the Arctic, or the deep sandstone canyons of Utah. A sea snake–bitten *National Geographic* photographer in Micronesia. A farmer dying from a new, resistant malaria in Peru. WM patients tend to be the very rich, who use the wilderness as playgrounds, or the very poor, who lack even basic medical knowledge or care.

"But Wilderness Medicine also includes disaster relief, rapid response to hurricanes, cyclones, earthquakes, outbreaks," Admiral Galli, the director, had explained when the agreement was signed. "Officially, you're going to Africa as relief doctors. You'll work out of the giant aid base in northern Kenya. You'll treat locals and aid workers. Vaccinations. Health classes. Diet. You'll be based at the junction of three countries."

"And unofficially?" I'd asked as the three of us sat in Galli's townhouse office, walking distance from the White

House, where we mapped outbreak games or war or terror scenarios like the one that had brought us to Africa.

The admiral frowned. He's a small man, sixtyish, a former Coast Guard hero. We've been through so much that we sometimes address each other more like friends. He's one of the few people left in Washington Eddie and I trust.

"Joe, there have been some disturbing reports coming out of East Africa."

"What reports?"

"For two decades we've anticipated that if a bio-attack comes on U.S. soil, it will be in some recognizable form. Anthrax. Ricin. Bad stuff, but at least a form we know."

I felt a chill. "Something new has appeared?"

"Threats, Joe. CIA warning. That an Islamic splinter group is trying to develop a new kind of bioweapon, somewhere in that cesspool."

"Why go to the trouble to come up with something new, with so much other stuff out there?" Eddie asked. "Hell, someone must have stolen or bought half of those old Syrian germ stockpiles by now."

"Because, the rumor is, if this new thing hits, nobody will associate it with an attack. It will be considered a natural outbreak. So no reprisals. *Rumor* is, the perpetrator will not claim credit, just allow panic to spread. They'll step in later, after massive damage is done."

"Who started the rumor?"

"The origin is Nairobi."

"Who is the perpetrator supposed to be?"

A frown. The admiral went to his window, gazed out at happy, strolling American U students. State Department workers disappeared into the Metro. "That's the problem. ISIS? Al Qaeda? They've both expanded in Africa. Truth is, no clue."

Eddie said, "That's helpful."

"And the new bioagent? What are we looking for?" I asked.

Washington implies order: streets in a grid, stoplights that function, the Capitol dome that symbolizes—if not cooperation—at least some form of dominance over enemies. But our unit lived in the world of negative possibility. If the public knew what we'd stopped in the last two years, three hundred million Americans wouldn't sleep at night. The unit hunted down other people's nightmares. At night, we handled our own, and on our own.

Galli looked unhappy. "All we hear is, some group's scooping up diseases. Look, the newest splicing equipment is small and easily available. We face three generations of well-funded bad guys, trained in our own schools. Forget any technical gap. Science-wise, we're equal. The *rumor* is, they are close to coming up with something. So let's hope it's just one more false thread that won't pan out."

"But if they're there, find them," Admiral Galli said. "If they've come up with something, obtain it, destroy it."

"And the people?"

"Why even ask? Stop them. Kill them if you have to. Either way, get it done."

"LIEUTENANT RUSH? IT'S LIONEL NASH. REMEMBER ME?"

I froze, hearing the name over the sat phone. I'd been wobbling down the empty fuselage toward the cockpit. I had not heard from Lionel Nash in years.

He's one of my old Marines.

The Hercules pitched and I grabbed the wall for balance. "Lionel? How are you?" But then something else hit me. The voice was too old to be him. My old Iraq crew would be in their late thirties or early forties now. But on my sat phone I heard an old voice, sick or half strangled with disease. A ninety-year-old throat cancer victim. A man with terminal emphysema; the wheezing of a smoker struggling to get words out, who would soon require an electronic voice box to aid plain speech.

"Remember . . . me, Lieutenant Rush? Well, you're a colonel now, I hear."

"Of course, Lionel."

How did he get this number? And do I remember him? I'll never forget him, or what we all found in Iraq.

The voice tried to be calm, but I heard panic beneath the surface. "We're sick, sir. Over half of us. Sixteen dead. *Hassan* won't let us bury them. He won't let us leave. He took our phones and then gave me this one back and said make one call. I'm sending you a picture. *Hassan* thinks we brought the disease here with us."

"How did you find me, Lionel?"

"I called your base from our field camp. I'm with the

SUNY Albany East Africa project, sir. I'm an associate professor. I went back to school after the Marines. I'm a geologist now."

"You're out of the same base I am?" I was confused. Eddie and I bunked in an aid camp, not a science camp.

He coughed. The cough went on. "No, I'm at a satellite camp in the bush. We started out at your base."

"Is there a doctor with you?"

"She died two days ago."

"Do you recognize the illness?"

He wheezed out, "It's eating us away."

"Lionel, who is Hassan? Who won't let you leave?"

"He heads the clan fighters who surrounded us. They're afraid they'll get sick if they come close. They were arguing whether to kill us or let us call for help. Hassan told me two doctors can come. But only two. My feet . . . my face, sir! Oh God!"

He sounded like he was strangling. He got out, "We're just across the border from you. In Somalia, sir."

"*Somalia?*" This was getting worse by the second. Sudan was bad but at least only two sides were fighting there—rebels and government. In Somalia there had to be at least ten factions, all shifting allegiances constantly. Clan against clan. Muslim fundamentalists against seculars. Bandits against everyone. Pirates on the coast. There was no official government anymore. All forms of higher order had collapsed. To enter Somalia was to cross the line into a patchwork of fiefs where order came from AK-47s, allegiances shifted on an hourly basis, and wandering bands of refugees were followed by lions or hyenas who ate stragglers at night. It was the worst place on Earth— medieval Europe, back in century twelve.

"What are you doing in Somalia, for God's sake?"

He calmed a little. I'd diverted him from his symptoms. "First expedition allowed in, in a decade," he said with what might have been pride under other circumstances. "For fifteen years scientists have been afraid to come here. The work is important. We're dating sediments. We paid off the clan for safety . . ."

I thought, *That didn't work so well.*

Lionel said, "Our work will help determine the age of human remains found in East Africa."

"From wars, you mean?"

Lionel said, "No. Of the first humans. People who walked the earth a million years ago. If we can date the sediments, we can date the remains."

"Lionel, tell me your symptoms."

"Didn't you get the photo I sent, sir?"

"Send again. Meanwhile, list symptoms."

His voice was so broken up that I had to strain to hear. His gravelly babbling sounded as if his throat was closing up even as he spoke. "The tingling first. Redness."

"What kind of redness?"

"My feet. They don't work right anymore. My face. My fingers! Oh God!"

I was in the cockpit now and the three-man crew— private contractors from Dallas—stared at me, eyes wide.

"Lionel, do you have a fever?"

"I . . . I don't think so."

"No? No one? Everyone is sick but *no fever*?"

"Maybe a little. I'm not sure. My face, sir. In the mirror! I'm sending another photo now."

I checked. Nothing came in. I switched to another subject. "Which clan area are you in?"

"*Hawiye*. Aidids," he said, which started my pulse pounding. Somalia was bad enough, but Aidid was as bad as you could get. Lionel had named the faction that fought U.S. troops in 1993 in Mogadishu, killed twenty-nine, and turned "Operation Restore Hope" into "Operation Flee." Our guys had been trying to arrest the clan leader of the Aidids. Instead, they left with their tails between their legs, and U.S. corpses being dragged through the streets.

Lionel and his grad students had been fools to go in there, and the State Department fools to let them go, but that was not the proper subject at the moment. "Tell me more about your face, Lionel."

His cough degenerated into a high-pitched series of barks. Or was it laughter?

"Lionel?"

"Throat . . . closing. Numb. Fire. Burned. The salve doesn't help. Those two nuts in tent four won't stop chanting. End times, sir. Cathy Luo says it's end times."

"Lionel, concentrate. Are you saying you were burned by fire? Or your hand burns? Which one is it?"

A moan. I felt his despair in a wave washing out of the phone. "We're gargoyles, man. Just damn gargoyles."

"*What?*"

"Like on Notre Dame."

"What are you talking about?"

"In the mirror, sir! I saw it. I did. I saw a gargoyle!"

"You think you saw a *gargoyle*?"

"My wife, Amy! My kids back in Albany!"

Hallucinations, I added to the list. *Throat closed. Possible nerve damage in feet.*

Lionel shouted, "I'll kill those grad students in tent four! *Shut the fuck up!*"

I tried my soothing doctor's voice and then my Marine colonel voice to keep him focused. He'd been a tough soldier, a brave nineteen-year-old. But he was a professor now, probably softer. He'd gone back to school and gotten a degree and pursued his old interest in rocks. I had a mental glimpse of Lionel—Iraq War One—advancing beside me down a long, concrete tunnel, chem suit on, goggled eyes huge. Alarms roared around us and visibility was almost zero from smoke. Suddenly small figures rushed us, and Lionel opened fire with no hesitation. Completely mastering his fear.

Now, more than two decades later, he must have held up the phone so I could hear the chanting outside. I heard, faintly, other voices. Male voices.

> *And the Lord sent his prophet,*
> *To walk among the people*
> *And the prophet smote all evil*
> *On that great and fearful day.*

"Lionel! Come back!"

"Shit, shit, I'm not going to see Amy and the kids again, am I?"

I stared at the phone and suddenly another thought hit me. *Is this really Lionel, out of the blue? Or is this a trick to lure us across the border? It wouldn't be the first time that a foreign journalist or op got pulled in.*

"Hey, Lionel! Remember that photo of your dad's sheep farm you used to show around? Remember those German shepherd attack dogs your uncle raised?"

A pause. I heard his labored breathing, in and out. He said, "Shepherds? No, sir. It was cattle, not sheep. Rotties, not shepherds. *It's really me.* Hassan will tell you our coordinates. He says only one small plane can come. No troops. No weapons. Bring medicines. You need to land exactly where he says. He's listening in. Hassan?"

Through Lionel's wheezing another voice broke in, deeper and unaccented. As generic as a California radio host. "Hassan Farrah Dir here, Dr. Rush. If you bring more than two, we will shoot. If we see a drone, we will burn these people. Treat them or evacuate them. My brother is sick, among your scientists, inside that camp! He is a cook for them. Help him."

"You know I can't evacuate more than a few survivors in a small plane."

The voice remained steely. I tried to remember facts about the *Hawiye* clan. They were Sunni Muslims. They had fielded many Somali military and religious leaders. Hassan said, "We want your government to know we had nothing to do with this sickness. We don't want it used as an excuse for attack. Americans get worked up. You need someone to blame. Your people and mine, there is bad history. What has happened here has nothing to do with us. See for yourself. Call me back when you know the plane you will come in, so we do not shoot at it. And, Doctor?"

"Yes?"

"Bring many protective clothings. Bring a short-range radio system. I wish to listen to everything you tell each other while you are here."

He gave me coordinates. And hung up.

Is it a trap? Are these the people the admiral sent us to find?

Lionel's photo came through ten minutes later. But it was gray and grainy. I couldn't see a face, just a shape, which looked swollen. The photo was useless. I stared at the odd shape.

I PUNCHED IN EDDIE'S SAT NUMBER. BELOW I SAW NO ROADS, JUST grassy savannah, meandering footpaths, a bombed-out village composed of a dozen mud-wattle huts. We skirted the edge of the Sudd, the largest swamp in the world. Biggest crocodiles on Earth. Worst diseases. An immense land-locked maze of black water rivers, mud islands, brackish air, and festering diseases and everything, animal and vegetable, swollen with rain in January, when it should have been dry. Walk into the Sudd and just about every life form within a hundred yards turns toward you, sniffing, watching, thinking: *Get it!*

The sky, in this longer-than-usual rainy season, bulged with immense gray-black clouds, pressing in on the plane like mountains, granite, solid matter. The pilot flew by sight, not instrument, squeezing the big transport through narrow slot canyons of light, slim spaces between cliff-clouds, as if the clouds might actually rip the wings off the plane.

Eddie answered from our tent lab, where, he said, he was analyzing blood taken from villagers from Thiet who had contracted leishmaniasis, an ulcerating disease caused by protozoa. The organism enters the human bloodstream in the bite of a sandfly. I told him to take a break and order up one of the base's small planes, one equipped with the ability to conduct conference calls by satellite. The Gates Foundation had two. I told him to stock the plane with antibiotics, antivirals, biokits, biosuits, and neck-mike radios with multiple headsets.

"Somalia? Are you out of your mind? Call Washington."

"I'll do it from the air."

Eddie turned sarcastic. "That's a little late, isn't it? And this Hassan guy *listened in*? Come on, Uno. Lionel called under duress. He's a hostage. We go, *we're* hostages. Call the admiral and find out about Hassan."

"Later. In and out," I said.

"Uno, I didn't argue when you ordered that Hercules to keep going when the engine died, and I didn't when you treated that potential Ebola case without protection last week."

"It wasn't Ebola and I could see that."

"You didn't know that for sure at the time."

"He needed attention, Eddie."

"One, since we got to Sudan, you've put yourself in every hazardous situation possible. It's reckless."

"Not now," I said as the Hercules topped a rise, and

the sprawling aid camp came into view, a mass of semi-permanent dirt streets, a mile-square grid of compounds run by international aid groups . . . sleeping, warehouse, and garage tents, prefab Quonsets, rising smoke from a hundred cooking fires and a dozen dining tents. There was a single paved runway and, camped a hundred yards away, a side camp of two thousand Turkana nomads, who had taken up residence near the now twenty-year-old aid city that had sprung up in the bush.

"Now is *exactly* the time," Eddie said. "*You didn't kill her.* You saved five thousand lives and even the President said so! I don't care if you won't talk about it. *I'll* talk about it until you see a shrink, and deal with it instead of working your ass off, burying yourself in the woods, and leaping at every dangerous assignment that comes our way."

"This is about Lionel, not me. One of our old guys!"

The pilot brought us down the runway past wrecked planes that had never been cleaned away—a sixty-year-old Air Manitoba Douglas that had dropped an engine, a vintage Fokker whose malaria-ridden pilot lost control during a shivering attack, a 1976 Tri-Star that had flown so long without maintenance that the port wing sheared off. The sides of the runway were a gauntlet of shattered steel, a mechanical graveyard, where planes went to die.

Eddie said, "Some guys get to your point, they put an M4 in their mouth. You hope someone else will do it."

"The *Hawiyes* promised us a pass."

"The *Hawiyes promised*? Black Hawk down? Copters blown up? Our guys . . . corpses . . . dragged through the streets, and crowds celebrating? *Those* guys promised?"

I snapped, "Then stay here, Dos."

"Right. Like I'll really do that."

Private contractor soldiers with M16s patrolled the base to deter theft. The compounds were operated by Irish Relief, Red Crescent, Red Cross, UNICEF, Doctors Without Borders, World Vision, World Without War, World for Christ.

The warehouse tents we rolled past contained tons of food, medicine, jerry cans for gasoline, clothing, soap, aspirin, and tax write-off donations from corporations: canned water from a Milwaukee beer company, crates of out-of-style trousers from a Minnesota clothing company, forty-year-old plastic eyeglass frames from Chicago, vegetarian cookbooks, donated baseball cards, toothpaste, art supplies, vitamin C pills, canned tuna fish, shoelaces. Antibiotics next to air fresheners. Syringes beside bathroom mats. One box filled with vital supplies, the next with something ridiculous.

"Eddie, this illness may be what we're here to find. So get the plane. And don't call Washington yet."

Eddie and I have been buddies since college. He's a savage fighter and a fiercely loyal friend and the annoying flip side of his faithfulness is his unshakable need to watch my back at all times.

"Yes, sir," he snapped.

I hung up.

We powered down within view of hundreds of Turkana men and women around a bonfire, even during the day, jumping up and down and singing the same song that had kept me awake last night. The comely women wearing multicolored bead necklaces. The tall men holding long, thin, iron-barbed spears. Up and down, up and down, working themselves up. So many people that the piston-like pounding of bare feet raised a dust cloud.

The song, in my mind, served as an anthem for this upside-down place, revenge central, anarchy incarnate.

The four words were, *Who stole my goat?*

Big emergencies start small.

This has nothing to do with Karen, I'd insisted to Eddie. *I know what I'm doing.*

Sixty minutes later, we were in the air.

TWO

═══════════

I GREW UP AS FAR AWAY FROM AFRICA AS YOU CAN GET, IN THE small Berkshire town of Smith Falls, Massachusetts, on a cracked two-lane rural road ten miles south of the Vermont line. We took for granted our small but well-stocked general store, our late-model cars that worked, and food so plentiful that health problems came from eating too much of it. We had solid roofs over our heads and schools that stayed open. We trusted the state cops who drove past each day, especially since some were our relatives. We resided in an area that magazines identified as a tourist destination, not a world trouble spot: the Berkshires, where you could take a road trip to see the bright red leaves in October, pick fresh apples, hear the Boston Symphony play outdoors at Tanglewood, dine in restaurants rated by the *New York Times*.

Not that I did that. I was a *townie*, and Smith Falls was an old mill town, where my ancestors—immigrant Welsh coal miner great-great-grandfather and his immigrant Norwegian peasant wife, who met on a steamer—worked at a textile mill. By World War Two, my family was making uniforms for the U.S. Army. By the Grenada invasion, the mills had closed, moved to Honduras, and Rush family members were the plumbers and carpenters for the second-home owners who showed up in the Berkshires each June, and went back to New York or Boston in September.

I found our calm life boring, our July Fourth parade, Christmas sing-alongs, and backyard barbecues stifling. Safety was for old people. The small homes, mowed lawns, and blink-of-an-eye main street felt suffocating. I thrilled to commercials showing U.S. Marines storming ashore to rescue Americans in trouble, guarding our nation against foreign attack. I wanted to be one of the few and the proud, so I studied hard and won an ROTC scholarship to the University of Massachusetts. After I left, I did not look back.

I married my college sweetheart. I thought my life was on track. What a fool I was.

Then one day during the first Iraq war, Eddie and I and other soldiers including nineteen-year-old Lionel Nash stepped down a long subterranean tunnel and into a world more terrifying than anything we'd imagined. We'd found a hidden lab, and in it were monkeys being infected with the world's worst death agents: plague, anthrax, Ebola. The doctors had evacuated and left the animals cuffed to operating tables, or stuffed into cages, screaming and crying, substitutes for the human beings that Saddam's planners hoped to one day infect.

When we emerged back into the sunlight, we were changed men. That lab sent Eddie and me to medical school on the Marine dime, and made us experts on toxins. The desert, the rocks and starkness, had excited Lionel Nash in a different way, sent him to school, made him a geologist.

Now was he leading us into a trap?

THE DECEPTIVE THING ABOUT TECHNOLOGY IS THE WAY IT MAKES the world seem smaller. The world is not really smaller, but by eliminating mental distance, our devices deceive us into thinking the person on the other end is exactly like us. Somalia is sixteen hours from Washington, just like Minneapolis if you drive. So people who fly around the world begin to think that the difference is small between Washington and Somalia.

Hey, let's all sit down and talk and we'll see our differences are minor, and you'll see things my way.

Big mistake.

"In other words, Colonel, you waited to alert your director until you thought it would be too late to stop you from going." The man on my laptop screen sneered.

Eddie and I were the only passengers in a twelve-seat prop plane entering Somali airspace, but at the same time we were in a meeting in Washington, where it was 6 A.M. Something was wrong back there. My call had summoned the admiral from a meeting, but why was he in a meeting so early in the day? When I'd forwarded him the grainy photo Lionel Nash had sent, he'd put me on hold, and three minutes later I was startled to see the whole group.

Eddie leaned over and slipped me a note. *Look at the water pitchers. They're in the Situation Room.*

In each square on-screen, looking back, was a tense-looking member of the President's Advisory Committee on Bioterror Preparedness. I'd addressed the group a few times, during war games at the Center for Strategic and International Studies on Rhode Island Avenue, designing scenarios—anthrax attack, food contamination, rail hit.

The committee met rarely, and these meetings, which were theoretical, never occurred before noon.

Frank Burke—glaring at me now—was the committee head, a high-profile presence in Washington and a study in contradictions, who "doesn't like you, to say the least," the admiral had told me. The Assistant Homeland Security Secretary was an ex–police commissioner of Dallas, a forty-seven-year-old ex-Congressman and tough fireplug with a unique background—off-the-charts IQ, forest ranger parents, Interpol experience, most decorated cop in Texas history. He often made the *Post* social pages, which covered his penchant for squiring around famous actresses, his leadership in Capitol Hill prayer meetings, his fancy dress boots, and his belief, reported in the *Washington Post* during confirmation hearings, that evolution was "just a theory that I don't believe in. I believe in the Lord."

Burke had tried to get our small unit moved from the Defense Department to Homeland Security. He disapproved of having an ex-Coastie running a bioterror group. "You're a sailor, not a warrior," he'd told the admiral. He'd also tried to get my contract canceled, twice, and failed.

"You're the kind of man I would have kicked off my police force," he'd told me once, in a men's room, during a war game break. "I saw your file. The real one. Some guys work for the right side for the wrong reasons. That's you, Rush. You've tortured. You *strangled* someone. You deny it?"

"No."

"Well, use my committee as cover to hurt people—even guilty ones—and I don't care that the President protects you. I'll bury you in Leavenworth and you'll never get out. You'll never even get a lawyer. You get it?"

Overhearing the remark, Eddie had said, "He's honest at least."

Frank Burke was the probable heir of the agency when the current head's resignation took effect a month from now. He was shorter than average, but had the presence of a large man—with broad shoulders; a powerful-looking shaved head; a fancy handlebar mustache, jet-black and not dyed; and an aggressive walk. He was a compulsive consumer of lime-flavored hard candies. It was as if they exercised his jaw.

"I went in right away because I thought speed essential, sir," I lied to Burke now.

Burke made a mocking sound in his throat.

The instrument panel told me that our plane had crossed into Somali airspace, but no markings below indicated this. No troops or fences. No roads or villages.

The savannah looked the same down there—soaked and misty—as it had five minutes ago. There were some thorn trees. We passed over a large lake churned up by a herd of pinkish animals—hippos. There was the sense of rushing into a vacuum, being sucked—or suckered—forward by fate.

I said, "Sir, if the committee is in session, is there a problem at home?"

"Not your concern."

"Sir," I persisted, aware that the admiral was trying, with his eyes, to get me to shut up, "I'm unclear why an incident in Africa concerns the bioterror committee. Is there something I need to know?"

"No."

"Are you ordering me to turn around?"

Burke tended to consider himself the smartest guy in the room, which, I had to admit, he often was. And the committee—set up after a sarin scare in Sacramento two years ago—was an interagency group with a direct line to the President in the event of a bioterror incident, *but at home, not abroad*.

Burke told me now, "We could have sent in drones to look the place over before you put yourself in jeopardy."

The pilot of our small twin-engine 1978 Cessna 421 Eagle was named Farhan, which, in Somali, means "happy," which he was not. Our Doppler radar screen glowed bright red, which meant bad rain and wind ahead, and the plane began pitching violently as a sudden storm pummeled us at fifteen thousand feet. The ground disappeared.

"Drones won't work, Frank. Cloud cover," said Admiral Galli, on Burke's left. Trim and weathered, the hero of the most recent Gulf oil spill had sparse gray hair, youthful clear blue eyes, and a deceptively calm manner. He, too, was furious that I'd not called him right away. But he wouldn't mention this in front of the others. He's that way.

To Galli's left, on-screen, was Chris Vekey, thirty-four, from Emergency Preparedness. The former major in the CDC Epidemic Intelligence Service was a public health expert whose job in the event of a bio-attack was to help coordinate containment. She was a petite, voluptuous brunette with blue-black hair cut to the neck, framing a cupid face. Mouth a lovely bow. Part Irish, part Cherokee. She'd formerly tracked TB outbreaks in low-income Vietnamese immigrant neighborhoods, then joined the Gates Foundation Africa anti-malaria effort, then rejoined government. An ex-teenage mom from Alabama, she'd been stripped of her high school valedictorian title when she became pregnant. She never revealed the father's identity. She worked her way through Auburn U, then Yale School of Public Health. She was still single, soft-spoken but tough, and Burke had an avuncular weakness for her because, like him, she'd come up the hard way. She was the most intoxicating-smelling woman I'd ever met. She and her teenage daughter lived in a converted spice warehouse in Northwest D.C. The odors had permeated their apartment. She smelled of cinnamon, vanilla, tropical islands. Between her gorgeous face, fit body, and smell, she turned heads wherever she went. You could sense the animal inside her. It made her gray business attire seem as sexy as bathing suits, Eddie said.

"She has a crush on you, One," Eddie would say. "I like her."

"Me, too, but not in that way." This was a lie. I was strongly drawn to her. I would never act on it.

"All guys like her in that way."

"Then talk to them."

Chris broke in. "Colonel Rush has to go in and you know it, Frank. We have Americans on the ground who need help."

"Chris, you have a big heart." Burke sighed, but he didn't tell me to turn around. He was probably realizing that since I'd gone in without permission, I'd be blamed if things went sour. He'd get credit if they worked. If he stopped me, and U.S. scientists died, Frank would be on the hot seat. Frank would have to explain the lapse. Not me.

His slow smile told me that he did not appreciate being manipulated. I couldn't care less. I was still trying to understand why the committee was in session.

The admiral asked me now, "Do you have more photos?"

"No, sir."

"Dr. Nash's face looks swollen, but you can't see features," said Chris thoughtfully.

"It's not the same thing," insisted Frank Burke.

I thought, *The same thing as what?*

"Well, it certainly *looks* swollen the same way," said the next face in line, Dr. Colonel Wilbur Gaines, from Fort

Detrick, Maryland, where the Army had its bioterror labs. Gaines, the top-left-hand face, headed disease tracking and was in his late forties, with light brown skin, thick short hair, and round, clear reading glasses on a red string around his neck. He got along well with Burke.

"I agree it is a stretch, Frank, but we need a better photo."

Burke said, "Can we blow this shot up, make it clearer?"

"No."

"Can we ask the sender to resend?"

"I can try."

Left to right, box to box, as in a high school yearbook, I saw Ray Havlicek, FBI, Chris's ex-boyfriend, who still carried a torch for her and would head up domestic investigations in the event of attack; Celia St. Johns, CIA, in a tent dress, a sixty-two-year-old onetime Cold War Mata Hari, who looked more like a bag lady these days, and who, considering her appearance—brown tent dresses, wet wool smell, mustard stains, stringy matted gray hair—had to be really good at her job, or know secrets, to still represent her agency at this high level.

Next was Lester Ormand, FEMA, emergency food and med-aid, a natty man who looked more like a Wall Street lawyer, and Carla Vasquez, forty-nine, White House liaison with governors of all states. Carla was a third cousin to the vice president, and a former big fund-raiser from Miami.

"Perfect social life for you," Eddie liked to say. "All work. At least someone calls out for food."

If Chris spoke for compassion, the next speaker represented urgency. Ray Havlicek, forty-nine, was an ex–college sprinter from the University of North Carolina, still lean and fit, the son of an FBI agent who had arrested Rajneeshee cult members for carrying out a food poisoning attack in Dalles, Oregon, in 1984. Ray had led the team that stopped Madyan Al Onazy's 2009 smallpox attack on a Saudi Airlines 747 on its way to Dulles Airport. That midair fight and arrest remained classified. Ray was a heavyweight and I respected him. I had a feeling he'd been a jealous boyfriend when he'd dated Chris. It was still in his eyes.

"I agree with Chris. Dr. Rush must go in," he said.

To his left, inside his square, was impassive-looking Air Force Major General Wayne Homza, whose career I'd almost wrecked a year ago, by proving him wrong during an outbreak, and then resurrected it, by ending a threat with minimal loss of life. Homza had been grateful, but some people can't sustain that emotion. Thanks becomes resentment. These days he was making a professional comeback. Homza was the only officer in the United States with experience quarantining a U.S. town. His learning curve had been steep. But his experience in Alaska had made him the Pentagon's choice when it came to war games involving quarantines, blockades, transport shutdowns, or evacuation protocols.

Homza said suspiciously, "What interests me is how this alleged former Marine of yours knew you were in Africa, yet never contacted you before."

"I wondered that, too. I confirmed his identity."

Homza shook his head. "I think it's a trap."

Gaines said, with visible urgency, "Either way, in light of our other problem—"

Burke cut him off swiftly. "Dr. Gaines!"

Gaines fell silent, but looked troubled.

Vekey said, "There's no way to know what happened until Dr. Rush gets there."

Burke shook his head. "He should have gotten more photos."

"I suggest that we wait for clouds to lift, then try for a sat shot, confirm the situation."

"Wait? But if this thing turns out to be the same as—"

"We'll discuss that later."

The funny thing about teleconferences—they change the way you read faces. On-screen, Burke's eyes flashed left, toward Chris. But in reality, the person sitting beside him could have been anyone. There was no way to read expressions, not without them in front of me for real.

Gaines said, "Can you hear me, Dr. Rush?"

"Yes, Colonel."

"Please list the symptoms."

The little plane lurched, every second taking us farther from the border. I went over Lionel's list: throat closing, rashes, nausea, loss of walking function, hallucinations.

"Please detail these hallucinations."

"He didn't actually *say* he was hallucinating," I explained. "He said he saw a gargoyle. Like on Notre Dame."

The effect of my words on the group was electrifying. The admiral shot up. Chris leaned forward, as if to see better. Burke's gasp was audible, and everyone either gave significant looks to each other, or their gaze sharpened on me. I could not tell who was looking at who.

The whole exchange made no sense. *Why would the word* gargoyle *set them off?*

Gaines said casually, "Joe, please describe the gargoyle."

"Describe it?"

"Saddle nose? Wide forehead? Flesh gone?"

"*What?*"

Burke snapped out, "It's a pretty plain question. Were they winged figures or not?"

Gaines said more quietly, "Colonel, did your man tell you that what he saw *looked* like a gargoyle or *was* one?"

Eddie said, "Hmmph," and fell back in his seat. I tried to remember Nash's exact words. But the distinction was not something I'd paid attention to. "Looked like, I think."

"He *thinks*," snorted Burke, as if I'd missed something obvious.

Gaines looked encouraged. "Ah! So it's possible that he spoke of exaggerated features, disfigurement, and not hallucination? Possibly he saw something that made him *think* of a gargoyle. A useful description. Nothing more."

"You could interpret it that way," I replied.

Burke was shaking his head in disgust. Ray Havlicek broke in thoughtfully. "I must point out that not all the figures on Notre Dame have wings. Wings are irrelevant."

"I disagree," said Galli. "Wings would confirm a hallucination."

Chris said, "How is Colonel Rush to answer properly if we don't keep him in the loop?"

Burke snapped, "How secure is this damn line anyway?"

Eddie nudged me and mouthed, *What the fuck?*

Galli said, "Think hard, Joe. Other symptoms? Loss of vision perhaps? Confusion? Weakness?"

Galli and Chris were trying to tell me something. Homza and Burke were not. Havlicek took notes. Celia looked fascinated. Gaines thrust his hands up and said with emotion, "The speed of this thing is frightening, and lab tests confirm—"

Burke broke in. "Give us a minute here, Colonel Rush."

The screen read MUTE, except MUTE did not happen. For the first thirty seconds of their argument, a technical glitch worked in our favor. I heard snatches of their fevered conversation, far away.

ADMIRAL: *I want backup for Colonel Rush!*

HOMZA: *Mutation! Or worse! Created! This is exactly what they were sent in to look for.*

GALLI: *Then send your guys in, not mine!*

CHRIS: *The situation in Galilee is getting worse by—*

The sound shut off for real. The picture went fuzzy and disappeared. Three bumpy, rainy minutes later they were back, the doctor nervous, Chris looking disgusted, Burke having made a decision, and Galli looking unhappy. That meant we were still supposed to go in.

Burke ordered, "Check in with Admiral Galli every hour. And send photos the minute you can!"

Eddie said as they signed off, "Galilee? Isn't that in Israel? Did someone hit Israel?"

"I wish I knew."

We flew lower to escape turbulence, and through mist/ rain the ground came back into view, ten thousand feet below. We were over the Afro-Asian Rift, a gigantic gash in the earth, longer than the Nile, that started in Saudi Arabia and snaked south all the way to Zimbabwe, a prehistoric Grand Canyon formed eons ago when continents split. It was also the stage for many of humanity's pivotal events, good and bad, legendary and real.

In the north, the Rift was where Moses crossed the Red Sea, the Bible says. In Israel, it was the Golan Heights, where Syrians faced off with Jews. In Ethiopia, it was where anthropologists found Earth's oldest human remains, *Lucy*, a biped 3.2 million years old. In Kenya, experts believed, those bipeds evolved on the west side into apes, and on the east, humans. The Rift was the Bible, medicine, and evolution. It was where human life may have started, and where, I'd realize soon, human life might end.

Our plane was spit from the clouds like a bit of food propelled from a gullet. The shaking stopped. The sky was still gray, but we had visibility now, and as we lined up for the dirt strip landing, I saw the runway guarded by Toyota Technicals, four-wheel-drive trucks converted into mobile battle platforms, and mounted on each, ragged-clothed militiamen aimed .50 caliber weapons.

Any one of which could rip apart the little plane.

"You didn't tell me about this," said the pilot stiffly, looking at the guns straight on.

"Bring us in. It's just a precaution."

Somalia. As we came down toward the clan runway, I saw, a mere half mile east, a gorgeous strip of white beach, looping palm trees, and the calm blue waters of the Indian Ocean. Nomads on loaded-down camels rode in rhythmic up-and-down single file along the beach. In many other spots, there would be hotels in a place like this. Swimming pools. Golf courses. Fenced-off vacation resorts. Trillion-dollar tourist shoreline.

I thought, *About a hundred armed men down there. And behind them lots of screaming women in black chadors and veils.*

"Sharks," the pilot said, nodding toward the sea, as the wheels touched down on hard dirt.

He was not an Aidid, but had been born to a different clan, also Muslim, farther north.

"The people here are liars and thieves and they will sell you into slavery and steal this airplane," he said.

"Then why did you agree to fly here?" Eddie snapped.

"For the triple price. But now I am thinking if I have to wait for you, I want more."

"No," barked Eddie. "And of course you wait. We told you that before we took off."

"Yes, you'll get more," I said. "But if you leave without us, you will be the one to pay."

The pilot flashed white teeth, an offended look. He was a handsome man with fine features, and he wore an old bomber jacket against the AC in the plane, which was turned up full. "No need to make threats, sir. I do not lie," he said.

———

I DUCKED FROM THE PLANE INTO A WET HEAT THAT SEEMED TO
absorb anything else around us—wind, birds, breathing.
And then even more. It sucked up momentum, aspiration,
rational thought.

The props had stopped and small sounds whispered
back into the world: the creak of rubber-soled sneakers
on a Technical truck bed, the slow swivel creak of a .50
caliber barrel, the crunch of desert boots on Earth as a
very tall, thin man in billowy khaki trousers and a red-
and-black-checkered short-sleeved shirt detached himself
from the clan fighters—stringy, muscular guys in shorts
and flip-flops, grouped around trucks. Nobody looked
friendly, scared, or even angry, the usual variations when
med-help arrived. The emotionlessness was the message,
You are nothing to us. The guy walking toward us also
wore tortoiseshell glasses, like the lawyer who owned a
summer cottage down the road from me in Massachusetts. The left-top section of the frame had been repaired
with gray duct tape.

And now a new sound exploded. Ululating. The high-
pitched cacophony sent up by the black-clad women.
Ululating marks happy celebration in the Mideast and in
the Horn of Africa. But it also marks grief and lament.

"I don't think they're celebrating," Eddie remarked.

The man stopped as if he'd hit an invisible border
twenty feet away, *quarantine distance.* He regarded me
boldly. I had a feeling that this was whom I'd spoken to

on the phone. He had a small pot belly and muscular arms, wore a soft-brimmed camouflage cap, unlike the other guys, who wore checkered scarves over their heads, if they had cover at all. Closer up, the posture was military. His black skin seemed to glow. He carried a knobby walking stick of dark wood, but he did not move as if he needed it. Perhaps the stick was symbolic of authority. Certainly the fact that everyone else but him had an AK told me that. His sidearm was holstered, and the holster was snapped shut.

"You are Rush?"

"Where are the scientists? And who are you?"

He ignored my questions and rapped out instructions. "You will surrender any weapons and phones. We will connect by means of the three-way radio I told you to bring. You will disrobe now and put on clothing we will provide, and wear your protective gear over that."

"Disrobe? Why?"

"Because I said so."

Eddie whispered, "Control freak."

But I thought it was about humiliation. He wanted to make us more vulnerable, more scared.

Hassan said, "We will wait for thicker cloud cover, and then you will follow us in your own truck. Keep your distance. This is for your security. After all"—he smiled thinly, conveying more menace than amiability—"after you do your examination, I wish you to go safely home."

He indicated a rusty, sand-scoured, olive-colored Land Rover parked beneath a lone skinny palm. It seemed to

have more bullet holes on it than steel. The hood was half
caved in from a collision or an explosion. The extra clothing, he said, would be in the Land Rover.

"Remember, Doctor, if you approach us, after you see
your Crusaders, we shoot."

Eddie whispered, "'Crusaders'?"

"Scientists. Westerners. Christians. Even aid workers."

I kept my face impassive. We undressed and stashed
our neatly piled clothes in the plane. We donned freshly
laundered jeans, white T-shirts that smelled like Irish
Spring soap, Converse basketball sneakers without laces,
and floppy hats against the sun. All donated aid, I guessed.
Or rather, hoped it had been donated, not stolen from
murdered people. We loaded our med supplies—antibiotics
and hydration fluids, level two biosuits including neck
hoods, double glove layers, fluid-resistant leg and shoe
coverings, plastic eye shields, and white masks—into our
Land Rover, which reeked of sweat and goats, of sweetish
dried blood on the backseat, and of spicy curry.

We would talk by headset and keep it on at all times.
I felt a lone bead of sweat run from my right armpit down
my side. The AKs pointed at us like eyes. Our pilot stayed
in the plane. The high, annoying ululating never stopped.
Then—as the sky darkened from thick clouds—further
blinding any satellites above—most of the Technicals
formed into a convoy, some behind us, some in front.

"Reassuring escort," Eddie said.

I took the wheel, and despite its dilapidated appearance, the Land Rover roared to life. Our plane receded
in the rearview mirror. The muzzle of the .50 caliber gun

in front of us bounced each time the vehicle hit a rut, and there seemed to be more ruts than flat areas.

"At least that howling stopped," said Eddie, removing fingers from his ears.

I downshifted and we followed the convoy along a dirt/sand yard–wide footpath through tall grass, with the .50 caliber barrel pointing at us the whole time. A few fat raindrops fell. The air smelled of alkali salt. Only our left wiper blade worked. I passed a lone conical hut and drove through a pathetically small vegetable garden, crushing some farmer's yams, and across a trickle stream and past a fat-trunked baobab tree against which a large baboon reclined, watching us, hands linked behind his head like he was Tom Sawyer on a Mississippi River summer day.

We crossed through an old abandoned banana plantation. Now the rows of plants were half blasted by artillery, and shredded blue plastic sheeting hung like shrouds over long-rotted fruit. I saw a human skeleton rib cage lying in a furrow.

Ten minutes later, Eddie sniffed and turned to me, frowning. The wind came from ahead, a rise.

"You smell it?"

"Yes."

Rot again, but different. It wasn't just vegetables now. I'd smelled this on battlefields.

The Technical in front of us hit a rut so deep that the chassis bounced, and Eddie and I winced, watching the gunner's hands squeeze the dual handles.

Then we topped the rise and a hundred scrubby yards

ahead saw the deserted-looking research camp . . . about one acre in diameter, a collection of sun-bleached, rain-washed canvas tents.

"I don't like this. Where's the people, One?"

The camp lay inside a man-made barrier of rolled thorn bushes, nature's concertina wire, to keep lions and hyenas out. Rectangular two-person tents ringed the inside perimeter, flaps closed. A larger dining or research tent centered the lot, with an area outside for cooking, long picnic-style tables and benches, and a stovepipe sticking above the tent, not emitting smoke. Lionel had told me that researchers here studied sediments, ground layers. Lionel had said that due to warfare in Somalia, important work on African climate, evolution, and ocean current patterns had stopped for the past twenty years. Lionel had said that his expedition opened a new era of cooperation, albeit one that had been bought by hefty bribe payments. Looking at the silent mass of tents, I knew that everything Lionel had told me was wrong.

As we drew closer, our escorts broke away to join a half dozen other vehicles surrounding the camp.

They would go no farther. Only we doctors could do that.

"Where is everyone, One?"

"Inside the tents, I guess. Sick."

Eddie nudged me and pointed. The first body—a woman from the size and long hair—lay half sprawled on the picnic table. A second—a fat man—lay draped over the thorn barrier, as he'd been crazy enough to try to climb over it instead of walking out. Maybe he'd tried to escape at night, to get away from the militia.

Eddie pointed at a tall tree. The branches were moving. They were covered with vultures, I saw, scrawny, gizzard-necked scavengers. All seemed focused on the bodies below.

"Blow the horn, One. Get them out of here."

I did. The birds did not leave.

Eddie said, "Shit. You think they're all dead?"

I reached back for my biosuit. The stillness seemed exaggerated. But then a couple of flaps moved on the sleeping tents. Slowly, figures began to emerge into the day. It was hard to believe what I was seeing.

Eddie whispered, horrified, "Jesus Christ, Uno. Lionel said that all of this happened in under *two weeks*?"

THREE

I WAS SO STUNNED BY THE SPECTACLE IN FRONT OF US THAT AT first I missed the clues behind. The heat, the palm trees, the camel caravan in the distance, the white beach a quarter mile off, and the blue ocean all added to the sense of disembodiment. I was cast back in time. I was witnessing something I'd not seen since boyhood Sunday school. Only too late would I remember the metallic clicking and growl of engines, the arguing militia behind.

"My God, what the hell . . . it looks like *leprosy*," I said to Eddie over the neck mike, stunned at the number of sick people we faced. At first glance, it looked like at least three quarters of the population of this research camp.

"In two weeks? In a group? Never! Gotta be some kind of chemical blistering agent, you ask me. Or something in the sediment they pulled up, some toxin out of the ground."

"We *were* sent here to look for something new."

"We need to call in the cavalry," Eddie said, meaning more people.

"You heard Hassan. Won't happen." We started forward.

Ahead, more canvas tent flaps had opened, and one by one, men and women were still emerging into the gray light, in a sight I associated with Sundays back in Massachusetts, with Pastor Brad in the Smith Falls Protestant Church droning on about Jesus while I cringed at drawings in *Bible Images for Kids*.

Some of the ill leaned on makeshift crutches—a crooked tree limb, a tent pole swathed in a towel. Healthier people helped the worst ones, but the most extreme cases came by themselves, crawling, hands rising and falling like crash victims in a desert, more tropism than human.

But the juxtaposition of twenty-first-century clothing— Gap blue jeans, a T-shirt reading GREAT DANE . . . UNIVERSITY AT ALBANY, aviator sunglasses, and Day-Glo Reebok running shoes—none of it went with the associations in my head.

Our biosuits sounded like crumpling cellophane. Moon men, that was us. We sweated inside Nebraska Center's mandated protection for Ebola workers. Baby blue plastic gowns and double glove layers; plastic hoods over our heads and necks; goggles and fluid-resistant leg and shoe coverings. But the suits were designed for an air-

conditioned hospital, not a desert country where the mercury could top ninety degrees in the shade.

"At least we're wearing only level twos," Eddie said.
Threes would have stuck us inside sealed hoods, breathing through pack filters, temperature rising inside the
taped-up body suit and rubber gloves. We'd have only
twenty minutes before we either needed water, or had to
get the hood off before our sweat made us blind.

"Remember the Cameroons, Eddie?" Volcanic lakes
in that country had suddenly erupted with poison gas
bubbles a few years back, wiping out a village of three
hundred people.

The lead man dragged himself through the thorn bush
barrier opening, his face so swollen and red that it was
hard to see his eyes. They seemed buried in folds of skin,
with patches peeling away, showing gristle, meat, a fly in
the wreckage, crawling. The eyes looked like a prizefight-
er's after a tough bout.

"This is like Lourdes," Eddie said, over the creaking
of hand-cut crutches, the moaning and coughing. He
referred to the French town in the Pyrenees where, in
1858, rapt fourteen-year-old Bernadette Soubirous told
townspeople that the Virgin Mary, a "beautiful lady,"
appeared to her in a vision. Since then, two hundred million pilgrims have visited the site, and five million more
come each year, deluded supplicants the way I see it, desperate and praying for miracle cures for their cancers
and deformities, prayer against virus, hope against prog-
nosis.

As a boy I'd believed in this trash. But I knew better

now. I knew this after what had happened to Karen. I believed in guns, germs, and laboratories now. Not in hope, prayer, or friendly gods.

Wilderness Medicine 101. Get splints on the injured, but the very flesh seemed to be melting off these people. Administer appropriate antibiotics, but we did not know if a microorganism was involved, or whether it would respond. Call for medevac, but that was impossible. What we knew here was even less than in most extreme emergency cases. We knew nothing. Only bits of truth, of possible analysis. To prematurely choose a cause could be fatal. But to do nothing seemed like it would produce the same result.

My earpiece whispered out the low voice of Hassan, the militia leader, over our shared comm-system.

"My brother is in there. He helped your people find special places, the special rocks," Hassan said.

"Special how?"

"They are old."

"Old *how*?"

"They were the rocks near the ruins."

"What ruins?"

"Roman."

"Hassan, I don't know what's happened, but we'll do our best to find out."

"My brother was a wrestler. A powerful man! Look at him now! I have never seen a disease like this!"

"Have any people outside the compound fallen ill?"

"Not yet. I wish to keep it this way."

Eddie and I shuffled into the compound. Our air filters allowed in some odors now: rot, grease, shit, Lysol.

Hassan's voice hardened. "You will take tissue samples. You will give the medicines. When you are done, you will strip off all clothes and leave them on the ground. You will be naked. You will not take anyone out with you."

Uh-oh. "I thought you wanted these people evacuated."

"We will discuss that later."

The fighters behind us were spreading out, the Technicals moving right and left as vehicles took up new positions. This adjustment placed the entire compound at the intersecting trajectory of at least fifty pointing guns.

"Hassan, there are too many sick here for just two doctors. I need more."

"No tricks. Just you."

"We don't have enough medication for all these people."

"Ah! You do know what this sickness is, then? The proper way to treat it! Tell me what they have!"

"We don't know yet. Hassan, one of these people is your own brother. Don't you want him to have the best care?"

He cut me off angrily. "Go to work."

We closed the last few feet. I have to admit, as a doctor I've seen many horrible things, but this, the sheer number of people, the mass of deformity, produced in me the greatest revulsion. I wanted to turn away. I was eight years old, with my parents, watching an old wide-screen rereleased 1959 Technicolor movie at the multiplex in Pittsfield, one Easter. The leprosy scene. The sick women coming out of caves in a Mideastern valley, in *Ben Hur*. Shunned. In rags. Hiding their faces.

As a boy, I had squeezed my eyes shut, not wanting to see those horrible Hollywood special effects. I had asked my mother, when the film was over, *Can that happen in Pittsfield?* And she had said, *No, it's an old disease. It doesn't harm people here anymore. It's from Bible times, Joe.*

Bible times.

Well, in *Ben Hur* the sick did not wear short-sleeved shirts that read TORONTO MAPLE LEAFS and khaki slacks from Costco. They wore clothing from the time when Jesus walked the earth and Roman armies con-quered Jerusalem, a time when the existence of bacteria was unknown and the greatest doctors believed illness came from witchcraft or vapors or punishment from gods.

Eddie's eyes sought mine over our masks. Hassan would hear everything we said. Eddie's expression con-tained the message: *Hassan's lying about something.*

I nodded. *I know. But we do our job.*

THE FIRST MAN IN LINE WAS A WHITE GUY WHO LOOKED ABOUT sixty, his back bent, his face swollen, breathing raspy, hair patchy like mange on a dog, mouth eaten away on the left side so severely that I saw white teeth, red gums.

"Colonel?" the old guy rasped. "It's me."

I hope I hid my shock. Wilderness Medicine 101. Make them as comfortable as possible. And calm as possible. Get information as fast as you can, once they're calmed.

I managed to keep my voice light. "Hey, who ever figured I'd run into you here, Lionel."

"Yeah," he rasped. He tried to smile, looking more like a skeleton. "Big surprise."

"Lie down." I indicated a picnic bench. He struggled to do it and I helped. I said, "How long have you been a scientist?"

His words came out slowly, forced. *Vocal cords affected.* "I went back to school after the Marines. Got my Ph.D. Dumb to come here, huh? But piracy off Somalia ended research here for twenty years, until now. Climate projects. Ocean. Super important work."

"What's so important about it?" I asked, looking into the throat. *Oh God. Maggots in there.*

"Sediment samples help date early man."

He was as calm as he was going to get. I said, "Well, I'm here to help. Lionel, what's going on?"

Eddie was lining the others up at the mess tent picnic table, our makeshift exam room. Wilderness Medicine 101. Triage them into groups: the doomed, savable, and healthy. Do it whether you're working an avalanche, cyclone, or cholera outbreak. Do it and you'll save the most lives.

"Lionel, can you tell me how this thing started?"

The twisted figure broke out coughing. He raised his left hand to cover his mouth. My horror intensified. The little finger was half gone. The stump of his index finger oozed blood.

But his brain was working, and the words he squeezed out came from an observant scientist who was fighting to maintain self-control, and save his own life. "Two weeks ago everyone was *fine*. Then Miriam—a grad student—said her fingers tingled. And then Dr. Ross cut his leg with an ax, but he felt nothing. Our faces. My toe. I woke up three days ago and it was half gone."

I shone light in his eyes, used a tongue depressor on the rotting pink thing in the cave of his mouth. Heartbeat normal. I maneuvered a thermometer in his mouth, but his lips were eaten away so I had to hold it in place.

"Very helpful, Lionel. Miriam was the first to get sick, you say?"

"I think so. But everyone seemed to get it at the same time. Mike Dellman died." The watery eyes shifted to the body draped over the thorn bushes. "They shot him. He tried to run. I don't know where he thought he could go."

"Tingling, you said? Miriam felt tingling. Tingling was the first symptom? What happened next?"

The eaten-away face before me seemed to consider, but it lacked animation. The nerve endings were probably shot. Flies landed on lumps and open sores.

"Next? The patches, skin patches, like cancer my uncle Fred had in Arizona . . . My nose got thick. I can hardly see." His panic suddenly crested. "Hard to walk!"

"Very observant, Lionel. Keep it up," I said, talking to him as if he were still a nineteen-year-old Marine, not an accomplished professor of geology. "Tell me about that rash a bit, will you? Where exactly did that start? Fingers and toes? Or in the central part of your body?"

"It's hard to think! My face! Yes! My lips." His voice

sped up. "And then the rashes came and my feet lost feeling!"

"Turn over. Good. Any fever? Chills?"

"It gets cold at night. But I stopped eating so I don't know if I'm cold because I'm sick, or not eating."

In my earpiece I tried to ignore the sound of clan fighters arguing behind us, the babble of enraged voices back there, in the circle of guns. I said, trying to find possible sources of infection, "Where do you get your water?"

"It's bottled. Donated. Separate bottles for each person. We thought of that already."

"Any odd smells? Or tastes when you ate?"

"No."

"The sediments you work with. Is everyone here exposed to them? Did everyone go to these Roman ruins?"

"No. Some people stayed in camp, and never got near the work. They're helpers. But they got sick, too."

I was finished with the prelim exam. But not the questions. Lionel was giving me baseline information. I'd need to ask every patient the same things. "Anybody you're aware of with hostility to this group?"

He let out a croaking laugh. "Hostility? That's good! We're in a war zone!"

"Almost done, Lionel. It's important to eliminate possible causes. Are you aware of any chemicals used here, by one of the warring groups? Have you been in any areas where you saw dead animals? Dead vegetation?"

"Only us. Can I help you now, to help the others?"

I gazed into the ravaged face and my chest swelled with pride for my former soldier. "Your answers are already helping, Lionel. The trouble you're having speaking—is that because you're experiencing difficulty thinking of words? Or is it physically hard for you to produce the words?"

"Produce . . . the . . . words . . ."

"Headache?"

"No."

"Chest pain? Shortness of breath?"

"I'm scared, sir. So yes. But is it related?"

"Maybe. Numbness?"

"In my feet."

"Night sweats?"

"It's hot here. You always sweat."

"What percentage of the people here are sick?"

"Some people have it bad and some a little. Maybe seventy percent caught it. Half of those got better. Half, worse."

I heard two male voices coming from one of the other tents, high above the hubbub, singing. I couldn't make out the words.

I snapped a photo, but I had more questions than time to ask them. I said, "Last one for now. The healthy people. Is there anything common about *them* that you're aware of? Maybe they came from the same place? Sleep in the same tent? Eat special foods? Anything?"

"I wish those guys in tent four would *just shut up*!"

I never forgot that Hassan was listening, so I kept my

voice calm, which I wasn't, as I asked person after person the same questions, and got the same answers. Lionel limped up and down the line, and I heard him telling others in that strangled voice, "Dr. Rush saved my life once."

Lionel saying, "He saved my buddies and he'll save us. You'll see."

WE SNAPPED PHOTOS. WE WROTE DOWN NAMES AND HOME AD-dresses and next of kin information. We took temperatures and skin samples. We administered broad-spectrum antibiotics, after asking about allergies. The samples would be analyzed in our tent lab back at the base, but not for many hours.

If Hassan lets us go.

"Ma'am? Lie down." I addressed a skinny, bespectacled black girl in a UPenn T-shirt and jeans who I guessed was about twenty-four years old, a grad student, she said. The disfigurement added years. The cauliflower ears ballooned out, making it hard for her glasses to stay on. Her arms were a mass of lesions. "How much time passed between the first sore appearing and now?" I asked.

"Six days."

"Did you notice anything wrong *before* the rash?"

"I spilled coffee on my hand. But I felt nothing."

"Have you ever had a skin problem before?"

"No, Doctor."

"Hassan? Are you listening to all this out there?"

"I am listening, Rush."

"Dr. Nakamura and I can't handle this alone. We need help. Let me call the base and get another plane here. I don't understand why you're stopping us."

"If you call, the drones will come."

The clouds thickened and the sky darkened and a light rain began. Lionel and a couple of healthy people helped two more sick grad students into the tent and helped others back to their cots. *Wait there, out of the storm, and we'll visit you*, we said. In the mess tent, I used a picnic bench exam table. Rice sacks were chairs. The tent drummed with rain. Rivulets ran in through a hole up top to puddle on the ground. The man lying on the table smelled like decaying meat.

I glanced outside. The circle of militia had not moved. I was sure that the steady rain intensified their rage.

"WHERE ARE YOU FROM, TOM?"

The assistant professor's dark red British passport shot showed a handsome face, twenty-eight years old, a neat blond beard, vivid blue eyes, a shock of boyish hair, a cocky smile. But now the hair was the only recognizable part. The features had swollen; the beard was mange. He looked like a practical joker had stuck a million-dollar hairpiece on a chimpanzee.

"You're British, Tom?"

"John Bull, that's me."

"Have you ever experienced anything like this before?"

"Never sick a day of my life till now."

"Tilt your head back. Can you swallow?"

Some of his sores had opened, become runny and smelly. The brow had furrowed so much, it almost folded in on itself.

"I'm giving you aspirin," I said.

The gargoyle face stared fixedly but that was because his muscles were damaged, producing a single expression. He whispered, trying for humor, "That's the best you can do, Doc? Aspirin?"

"Are you allergic to any medicines?"

"I never needed any. Can I have some water? Most of it runs out this damn hole in my mouth. Better oxygen flow, though."

"You have a good sense of humor, Tom. Anyone ever tell you that?"

"I'm a regular Jason Manford, Doc. That's what Mum used to say."

"HASSAN?"

No answer.

"Hassan?"

No answer.

"Hassan, I need to know if you can hear me. If you can hear me, answer!"

"What do you want?"

"Let me bring in copters. I'll get the sick out. Surely you want them gone."

"We'll talk later."

"In my experience," Eddie said, not caring if Hassan heard or not, "later means never."

Another hour went by.

We took more photos. We could not send them to anyone yet. The rain stopped and started again.

TWO VOICES—TWO MEN—STARTED SINGING RELIGIOUS SONGS again. *One by one six prophets, the sixth the last to come.* What the voices lacked in quality they made up in volume. The men in tent four were driving everyone crazy.

"They stay in their tent," Lionel said.

"So! You two didn't get sick," I said, pushing in the tent flap. I saw the men sitting on two neatly made cots. A milk crate table. Field notebooks. Duffel bags. A once-happy group shot of grad students, khakis on, thumbs up, all smiles. *Here we are in Africa!*

They both looked to be in their twenties, burned by the sun, a thin tall man and a pale chubby one. The blond tall one, clean-shaven as a Mormon missionary, wore a short-sleeved cotton shirt fielding a SAVE THE PLANET motif, Merrill desert boots, and aviator-style silver-framed glasses. The second man was older, curly haired but balding, and dressed in ragged denim cutoffs, flip-flops, and a summerweight hoodie with a Breckinridge, Colorado, logo, a downhill skier etched in dark blue against white.

"I'd like to take blood samples from you, if that's okay."

"Sure thing, Doc, if it helps the others."

"You both seem unaffected physically."

The older one, Ned Ludlum, rapped his knuckles on

a wooden tent pole, superstitiously. "Knock wood. But every day we check each other over, inch by inch."

"Any idea why you stayed healthy?"

"Luck," said Ned.

"Prayer," said Brad Colbert, the other guy.

"Have you eaten anything the others haven't . . . Got different vaccinations before you came to Africa? Different medicines you're taking? Maybe you're on antibiotics for something else?"

"I'm taking Cipro, sir, for a cold I caught in Nairobi," Brad told me, holding up the pill vial.

"Nothing for me," said Ned.

"How about before you came? Do you have your immunization form? Special shots? Preventative medicines?"

I checked the stamps and notations on their yellow immunization forms. They'd received standard prep for Americans visiting East Africa. Antimalarials. Yellow fever shots. Anticholera. Tetanus. Gamma globulin against hepatitis.

I noted that both their cots were protected by pink mosquito netting. But many of the sick people had netting over their cots as well. Neither man showed sores anywhere on their bodies. Temperatures normal. Mouths unremarkable. Movement natural. Sleep irregular, they said, but it was hard to sleep regularly when your friends and neighbors were sick all night.

Ned said somewhat apprehensively, "Are we going to be okay?"

"I hope so."

"Can you cure our friends?"

"I'll do my best."

I left them in their tent, and they started singing again. Hope worked for them as well as preventative medicines, I guess. I just wished they weren't so off-pitch. Those voices would drive anyone crazy after a while. They were grating on me, too.

I HOPED NOBODY WOULD SAY SOMETHING OVER MY RADIO TO SET off Hassan or his militia. If shooting started, we had no place to run.

"I started this," the girl sobbed. *"It's my fault! My God! I started this and now I'm better and they're worse."*

Kate Detrich lay in tent seven, alone, because her tent mate had died. The face of the twenty-four-year-old grad student was slightly red and scaly, but the symptoms were fading, she said. Her speech was clear. If I hadn't seen the others, I'd think she had a bad skin condition. Her agitation was so extreme that she was shaking, from emotion, not disease.

"I caused this sickness! Me!"

She was someone who liked to fix up living quarters, no matter how temporary. The cot had a colorful woven blanket over it, and I saw watercolor sketches of African plants hung up: a fat baobab tree, a myrrh tree, a phoenix cactus, with purplish flowers. The milk crate night table had a Coleman lamp on it, and a photo of smiling parents with a happier Kate. Strawberry blond in the shot. About five foot three. Pageboy-cut hair. Pretty green eyes in a plain, intelligent face. The photo had been taken at Sea World. Behind the vacationing family, a leaping killer whale.

I'd noted, into my neck mike, "Glazed eyes, stuffy nose, slight hoarseness."

Now my heart began pounding at her confession. "You started it, Kate? What do you mean?"

"It was an accident!"

"What kind of accident, Kate?"

Wilderness Medicine 101. Always call a patient by their name. It helps keep them calm.

Fresh tears ran down her cheeks, soaked a stained pillow. I saw in her face what I saw in my mirror back home on sleepless nights—self-blame. *This woman knows something*, I knew.

Kate blurted out, "I promised I wouldn't tell!"

Hassan is hearing this, I thought. *He's looking for an excuse to blame someone. Hassan will unleash those militia if he thinks someone here is killing his brother on purpose.*

But I gentled her. "Why don't you tell me what you think you did. You can help everyone else if you tell."

"No! It's too late!"

I took her hand. It felt like a claw. In the glass covering her family photo was superimposed the reflected girl, head averted with shame.

"Kate? Breathe. Slowly. You know, good people always

blame themselves for things they have no control over. Why, I bet that's the case here."

"It's not fair. *They're* dying and I only got it a little bit! I want to be dead!"

"You don't mean that. Tell me what happened."

Her voice fell to a whisper. But at least she kept speaking. "He was so attractive," she said. "He made me feel wonderful."

"Uh-huh."

"Tim's from Oregon. His family owns a farm there. They grow apples. Sweet gala apples, he said."

Get to the point, I thought.

"He said we'd live there when the project is up. He said I could probably get work at the university in Eugene. He said it's a good place to . . . oh God . . . *have a baby*!"

She broke out sobbing. The heat in my suit was rising. Sweat formed at my scalp and ran down my chin. It poured from my armpits. There was a sour smell in the suit. I cursed the designer of the thing.

Kate said, "I slept with him! Had sex with him! I know it's wrong! I promised the Lord not to have sex until I'm married but I thought . . . I mean . . . I *didn't* . . . I mean . . ."

I did not understand where she was going with this so I asked, "You caught something from this boy, you mean?"

"No! It's punishment! Affliction! God struck me down because I broke my vow. Sex without marriage is abomination!" Her face spun to me, blazing. "I know what this sickness is. *It's leprosy, out of the Bible! Right out of the Old Testament! Like God gave Naaman!*"

She started hyperventilating, but not from illness. I told her she was wrong. I said that her sex habits had nothing to do with the outbreak, although, for all I knew, that was one way it could spread. I told her that leprosy took a long time to take effect, and didn't spread through groups. I did not tell her that I had no time for God, faith, or miracles. That to deny science is to deny truth. That faith is for fools.

I smoothed her brow. There was still a possibility that she'd given me a clue, though. "Kate? Are you telling me that God gave you this disease and the others caught it from you? That you were the first to get it?"

"I was bad! Bad! Bad! But I wasn't the first, no. God struck down this whole camp because of me!"

I heard Hassan exhale loudly in my earpiece. His breathing joined mine for a moment. At least, for an instant, we were in sync in frustration.

"You people are all crazy," Hassan said.

PERSON AFTER PERSON, AND THE ANSWERS WERE THE SAME.

"Fifteen-centimeter lesions," Eddie recited as we worked together in the mess tent on the last two victims, a Somali cook and a Somali guide.

"Erythematous plaque, with well-defined outer margins," I said, scraping samples.

"The center's flat and clear, hairless. No pigment."

"Get bits of normal areas, Eddie."

"Look at the foot drop, One. The foot just dangles."

"Check the corneas."

Hassan's low voice broke into our earpieces.

"Are you finished? You have now worked for many hours. I think you have what you need."

"What we *need* is more help."

Eddie came close and nudged me. I looked through his face shield at his sweating countenance, and I knew he was telling me to open the tent flap. Something was wrong.

When I glanced outside, I sensed the change. The ring of vehicles had drawn in closer. The clan men still stood by trucks, but their attitude had stiffened, even from a distance. The gunners had lowered the muzzles of their .50 calibers while we worked, but now they were aimed again.

"Hassan, what's going on out there?"

"I think that you are finished, Doctor. Do you know for sure what has happened here?"

"How can I know that yet?"

"You took many photographs? Many samples?"

"Yes."

"You will now leave the compound. You will bring your samples and photos. You will walk twenty feet toward us and then you will stop and strip."

"Hassan, I—"

"Don't interrupt! Just listen!"

I heard, through my earpiece, the agitated sounds of men arguing. I heard Hassan snapping back something in Somali. I had no idea what it was, but I did have a feeling that the argument concerned the fate of Eddie and me.

Hassan was back. "Do this now, Dr. Rush."

Eddie mouthed, *Uh-oh*.

Hassan said soothingly, "You are in no danger yet. I promise this. But you will please do what I say."

There was really no choice. Eddie mouthed, *Yeah, our pal*, as we left the tent, walked past Lionel Nash, in the rain, and toward the opening in the thorn tree barrier. We both carried steel sample cases. We left all our drugs there. These people would need them.

Lionel had helped out until the end, and his reserves of strength astounded me. Understanding what was about to happen, the former Marine half straightened and saluted.

"Semper fi, sir," said Lionel.

"Semper fi, Lionel."

The rain made scratchy noises on my biosuit. My visor fogged. The respirator gurgled. At fifty yards between us, Hassan stepped out of the ragged circle of militia fighters and ordered us to halt.

"Hoods off," Hassan ordered. "I want to make sure it is you before I let you go. That you did not trade places with someone else."

The fresh air smelled of alkaline earth and saltwater and camel dung, of sweat and fresh rain and wet palm trees.

"Strip. Everything. Now. But keep the microphones on."

Hassan stood alone, before his fighters, hand on the butt of his gun. Then a militiaman ran up to him and handed him something black, and I froze. But it was not a gun, I saw as he raised the object to his face. It was binoculars.

So! He wanted to see my face close up as we talked. Hassan would be too far away for me to see his features. In his binoculars, I'd be inches away. He could study my eyes.

Hassan said, "I do not think you have previous knowledge of this thing, Doctor."

"Thank you."

He was making a decision. He said, "You have your samples and your photos. To bring back."

"Hassan," I said, my heartbeat rising, "don't hurt them."

"I will not."

"That's your brother in there, you said. Your own brother. *Your people, Hassan.*"

"You think I don't know that, Dr. Rush?"

I pleaded as the rain intensified, "All I'm asking for is a little time. Another plane lands. You keep your distance. You can't be infected. The doctors wear protective suits and bring the right medicines. They keep the sick from you. They help your brother. For God's sake—"

He cut me off. "'For God's sake'? This is an interesting notion. You think I do not believe in a God?"

"I didn't say that."

"You think I am a barbarian. Life is cheap in Africa. Those Africans, those barbaric Somalis, have no respect for the lives of women and men. Is that it?"

"That's not it." But he was right partially, and I was ashamed.

"West Africa, Doctor. Ebola breaks out. A fatal disease. We can cure it, you doctors say. We take *precautions.* We *know* what we're doing, you say. Ebola acts *this* way. It acts *that* way. It is a known quantity. And then suddenly a thousand are dead. And then four thousand. And then ten. And you doctors apologize because you did not really know at all, and you blame the unclean primitive Africans. Well, there are a thousand healthy people a few miles away from here. My people."

I said nothing. I stood in the heat and rain and felt drops running down my scalp and forehead and into my eyes.

"Hassan the clan leader. Hassan and his cruel, harsh men. Hassan who thinks life means nothing. By the way, not everyone here agrees with my decision. They do not want to even let you go. You see?"

"At least let me get the healthy ones out of here."

No answer.

"You can't do this."

"Go," he said gently. "Go back to the plane. Fly away and tell them we didn't start it. That's all you have to do. I'll do what is necessary. I'll do the rest. Haven't you figured out yet why I made you strip? I want to make sure you don't carry out contagion on your clothes."

The guns seemed to lower, as if the metal itself knew there would be no carnage yet. The stillness was profound. We stripped and, naked, sluiced by rain, trudged back to the shot-up Land Rover. We needed to figure out what had happened, to understand this thing. Nakedness suited our condition. We were devoid of power in this particular hell.

Eddie said, "I don't want to leave, One."

Hassan's voice replied, "I cannot control them for long. But it is up to you. That is the power of God. To offer men choices. Drive away while you are safe."

Eddie mouthed, *Hell*.

Hassan watched our lips in his binoculars.

"Just go," he said.

And thirty minutes later I watched our gape-mouthed pilot stare at our nakedness as we climbed into the plane and donned the clothes we'd discarded when we arrived. "Take off and circle back," I told the pilot. "Stay high."

Risky, but I have to see what he's going to do.

We rolled down the dirt runway, to the ululations of the Somali women, who had turned away from our nakedness. They were showing grief, I knew now, timeless, human grief for the dead. The plane took to the air as I saw the first wispy spirals coming from the south. Then the smoke became a black column. We banked toward the research camp until I saw exactly what was happening.

"Flame throwers," breathed Eddie, horrified.

Maybe they'd used the guns first. I hoped so. It would have been quicker and merciful. We'd been too far away to hear shots. But either way they were finishing it with flaming gasoline. Skinny militia fighters with canisters on their backs had circled the compound. Burning gasoline-covered tents and corpses, bonfiring the thorn tree barrier, creating heat so profound it convoluted the air and made our plane bounce. Orange flame spiraled toward heaven.

"Go back to the base," I told the pilot.

"This is the worst thing I ever saw," said Eddie.

We did not speak for a while. We couldn't. We kept seeing that fire in our heads. But at least we had samples. We had saved nail clippings and skin and blood from those who were now ashes. I forwarded the photos to D.C. I could only hope that, back at the base, our samples would give answers. And that the thing we'd just encountered was local, not contagious. A chemical. A gas. A freak accident.

We never reached the base, though.

Because fifteen minutes later, as we crossed back into Kenya, it got worse again, when the sat call came through.

"We're diverting you, Joe," the admiral told us. "The State Department long-range Gulf Stream will meet you at Moi, in Nairobi. Those photos were awful."

"It's in Israel?" I asked, remembering the words I'd heard before, about Galilee, from the Situation Room. "It's spread? It's out already?"

There was shocked silence from the line, and I thought I felt raw emotion over space, bouncing up from the capital, gliding past burnt-up stars, directed back toward our pitching plane. "Israel, Joe? Why did you ask about Israel?"

"Because we heard you over the line earlier when you said there was a problem in Galilee."

The admiral said quietly, "The audio was on?"

"Yes, sir."

"Christ, those technical guys! Well, you're right, Joe. It *is* in Galilee. You heard correctly. But not Galilee, Israel. Come home. It's in Galilee, Nevada," he said. "By the way, how are you two feeling?"

"Us?" said Eddie.

"Any tingling in your fingers?" the admiral asked, sounding concerned.

FOUR

===

THE ANIMALS WENT CRAZY WHEN HARLAN TURNED ON THE LIGHT,
emitting high-pitched cries of panic, clawing up against
their wire mesh cages, bumping into each other in terror,
staring out at him with tiny glazed eyes. He tried to soothe
away their fear as they skittered and screamed. Normally,
when calm, they sounded like cooing babies. Now they sounded
like something from another world.

—Shhh. Shhh. I'm not going to hurt you.

It didn't work, though. They recognized him, or rather,
anything with two legs meant trouble, and they understood
in the recesses of their primitive neuron passageways that
even if they escaped pain at this particular moment, nothing
good would come from association with him. Those things in
the cages had brains the size of walnuts, DNA fifty million
years old. Any analytical effort of which the smartest one—
the Einstein of these creatures—might be capable might, at

best, equal the thought power of a lumbering rhinoceros. They couldn't add one plus one. The concept of "tomorrow" was beyond them. They'd stare at the red telephone as if it were a rock. But when it came to pain, they knew they were in trouble and their cage floors were creamy masses of piss and shit and emitted an acidic odor that took him back to the swamps where he'd grown up, hunted alligators and feral hogs, learned the truth about pain, trust, and the nature of life. It seemed like ten thousand years ago. He was forty-nine.

—Calm down, you little guys!

This time of night, 12 A.M., he was alone in the big lab two stories beneath the ground, the only one permitted access. Red light on. Air control system humming over the whimpering noises. Satellite shots of Jerusalem blown up on the walls; and close-ups from the old walled city; a narrow footpath, Via Dolorosa, "the way of suffering," where Jesus walked to his crucifixion; the golden Dome of the Rock, from where Mohammed ascended on his white steed Baraq to heaven, to converse with God. And only a few hundred yards away, the site of Solomon's Temple, where the Ark of the Covenant, given to Moses, came to rest for the Jews.

One square mile, Harlan thought, filled with joy. Remove that mile of earth, and two thousand years of human history—its crossroads, its major figures, its legends and lies and consequences—would be different. Nothing . . . not countries, not customs, not even science and aspiration would be the same.

Back to work.

Abutting the corner dissection area was a holding cell, now empty, and a top-of-the-line Bosch steel freezer, which required a four-digit combination to enter. He walked in and the cold hit him. He felt himself being watched on closed circuit feed by the night duty guards in the computer center, where the tech team sent out tweets, feeds, e-mails, and alerts. It was twenty-five degrees in here. His breath frosted as he stamped to keep warm, scanned the racks of medicines and blood and vials containing ground-up bits of animal intestine, brain, arterial scrapings. Other shelves were piled with supply cartons, blue stickers for stuff to be donated, yellow for vital, purple for transport over the coming weeks.

—Ah, there you are!

He took five small stoppered glass bottles filled with fluid the color of ten-year-old Dewar's Scotch, his father's old preferred drink, rocket fuel for paternal emotion at 2 A.M. From a cardboard box he removed twenty-one clean, freshly wrapped syringes in crinkly cellophane. He arranged the bottles on a silver tray in two circles, outer bottles for newbies, inner for everyone else. He was glad to leave the freezer, because he had always hated cold, even growing up. Unfortunately his orders had taken him here, to a cold place.

Now he stopped as a new sound hit him. A harsh ringing from the red phone on the computer table, amid the open, glowing Dells. All other phones were black.

It's him, Harlan thought.

He broke out in a sweat. He did not want to pick up the phone. His happiness had evaporated. Everyone fears something and Harlan was terrified of the thing on the other end of the phone. But he answered and heard the dreaded voice, rumbly, a master's voice, soft as static, a voice that sounded merely curious on the surface but held—he knew from experience—a vast torment beneath.

"*Any news from Africa, Harlan?*"

"*Not yet but any minute. I'm sure of it.*"

"*You told me—ASSURED me—that you'd arrange things so it looks like everything started in Africa.*"

"*I did. I did. I swear it. It will!*"

"*You know what your problem is, Harlan? You're too nice. Too easy on your people. You haven't pushed your message with them. I'm disappointed in you.*"

"*My people will come through. I promise.*"

"*No one is sure of the future.*"

"*I didn't make a mistake.*"

A pause, a long pause, and Harlan felt his pulse thicken in his throat. He smelled sour sweat. Then the voice said, quite mildly, "I hope so, Harlan."

The connection went dead. He heard the buzzing on the line as accusation. The headache began as a small pressure in his temples. The sweat rolled from his armpits down his rib cage and collected by his belly, above his belt. He told himself to calm down, that the void of news was a glitch. Satellite delay. It had to be. Hell, Somalia was a primitive hell. You couldn't expect information to leach out of there with the same speed at which it traveled everywhere else in the modern world.

He spoke to himself out loud, to calm himself.

"*Keep to the schedule. You have a job to do right now. You need to finish by one A.M.! You need to keep to the plan.*"

A TWELVE-FOOT-LONG STAIRCASE BROUGHT HIM TOPSIDE, THROUGH the well-lit gouged-out rock tunnel and into the farmhouse, 165 years old . . . stone foundation, Cold War–era overstuffed furniture, granite fireplace, and low, heavily beamed ceilings for tough hill winters. The house was deserted except for him. He was the only one permitted inside between midnight and 6 A.M. He walked out onto the big wooden porch, away from the inside cameras, but in full view of the ones in the moosewood maples, oak, pine, and black birch trees. The men in the guard shack would be watching. They'd see a white man who had lost little to middle age except hair, a lean, spry figure, slightly taller than average, fringe bald at the top, with close-shorn sideburns, well trimmed and flared at the bottom, and a ruddy, open face that was slightly askew in a way that made him seem likable. His aura of knowledge and forgiveness marked him as special. An uncle. A beloved teacher.

He'd ordered his people to blend in with the locals, so all of them, like him, wore rural clothes—faded blue jeans, red-and-black-checked flannel shirts, long underwear, and Timberland boots. One green eye sat a fraction lower than the other. His goatee was white on gray and reddened his thin lips. He was the only one permitted to wear facial hair, or to wear a watch, the only one allowed to move in a clockwise manner across campus, and now he carefully carried the tray along shoveled paths, past foot-high snow and beneath a blanket of North American stars and past small wooden buildings that would look, to any spy satellite above tonight, like a normal "barn" and "chicken house" and "stable" and "fruit cellar."

At one time they had been those things, housing nothing worse than canned peaches or whinnying geldings or masses of docile poultry.

But they were not those things anymore.

Now the old stable was a barracks.

The moon was a bright sickle shape over the forest surrounding the ninety-acre compound, with its trout pond, long paved driveway, cornfield and apple orchard, and two-story warehouses, stocked with food, guns, and explosives. The January breeze brought the smells of fresh snow and pine smoke, barn mulch and winter mist and farm animals: goats, chickens, guard dogs, llamas.

His goal was the old Quaker era—1755—meeting house, on a two-acre lot that had been added onto the original purchase of the property by the Defense Department. It was a one-story building, bricked over, 1950s style, new slate roof, stovepipe chimney, and lights blazing inside. He saw, silhouetted in a large ground-floor window, a single delighted face watching him approach. Then more faces. Happy ones. Black and white, coffee-colored and Asian.

Men. Women. Some as young as nineteen. Some as old as seventy-four. No children allowed in the meeting house. No pets allowed. No smoking. No alcohol, except on holidays.

Someone in there shouted, "Here he comes!"

They sang to Harlan, "He's here! He's here! He's here!"

"MR. MAAS?" INTERRUPTED A VOICE BEHIND HIM BEFORE HE COULD *enter. He whirled. Nobody had been there a moment before. Orrin Sykes stood there now, bundled against the cold, an M4 over his shoulder.*

Harlan halted on the steps, breath catching, but Sykes's eyes were properly respectful, semiaverted, and even slightly cast down. Sykes had done well in Florida. Maas had not realized the force inside the man when he'd first arrived. Sykes's quietness came across as shy anonymity. His ordinary looks gave no hint of the extraordinary violence inside, and the intelligence enabling him to carry it out. He could not be intimidated by anything except his own priorities. Sykes decided what he feared, and he had put Maas's displeasure at the top of his list.

Sykes, in fact, was the most dangerous human that Maas had ever met. He was in charge of security tonight.

The way he moved, if Sykes had been a sound, Harlan thought, he'd be a whisper. Respectful, though. Hair cut short to the skull, prescribed length, shirt tucked in the required way, right tail over left, to cover genitals. Orrin smelled of sheepskin coat, lube oil, freshly laundered jeans, and Juicy Fruit gum, which he chewed incessantly when on guard.

Maas assumed his benevolent face. "Of course. Ask anything anytime, Orrin."

"Have we heard from Africa?"

Maas needed all his willpower to suppress the flood of rage that seized him.

"Of course! I was just on the red line and we're good."

Sykes looked relieved.

"I never doubted, sir. I mean, Harlan."

"Ah, but you did doubt, just a little, eh?"

Sykes reddened. "I need to work on that."

Harlan patted the man's shoulder. It was like touching granite. "Everyone has a past, Orrin. The point is to learn from it. Everyone has doubts. But we use them and don't let *them slow us down. You have a gift. You are valuable. There's a reason you have your skills."*

"Thank you."

"So don't worry because there's absolutely nothing to be concerned about tonight, unless," he said, allowing his eyes to rove the skies, and woods outside the fence, and razor wire, "we get a few you-know-who's out there. They're always looking for us."

Orrin straightened. "I have seven men on the wire, and the dogs."

"Intruder could look like a neighbor. Lost tourist."

"Like the two who claimed to be hikers last month. But after a while," Orrin said, showing something different in his eyes, "they told the truth."

"Orrin, we're on the cusp here, so incredibly close. Days maybe. And once it takes off, well . . ."

Tears of emotion appeared in Orrin's eyes.

"Seems like a dream, Harlan."

"I'll need you to go out again. To Washington."

"An honor, sir."

"Didn't I ask you not to call me that?"

"You saved my life, Harlan."

"Thank yourself, Orrin, not me."

HARLAN MAAS WALKED DOWN THE CENTER AISLE IN THE OLD Quaker meeting house, past the gauntlet of smiling faces— living ones atop people sitting on benches—and less happy visages frozen in the hodgepodge of real paintings and framed magazine cutouts on the walls, some original work as old as five hundred years, other art a month old. The paint cracked and thick. Why, that top-left piece, the full-face visage of the sick man from the Greek island of Calidon, had to be worth half a million. The art magazine shot of Rembrandt's man in a turban was worth a penny, it was just a page, but it made the point all the same.

An art thief would clean up here, if he ever got in, and managed to get out.

"Any word from Africa, Harlan?"

"We're good to go, folks!"

Many faces in the illustrations seemed modern and recognizable, yet the bodies were clad in medieval clothes. No zippers. No buttons. The visages might be the same ones you'd see in the vegetable aisle at Walmart. Same DNA. Others were twisted and tortured. Men with beaks. Women with the heads of chickens. A walled village, burning. Lurid stuff, especially in the plain setting of a Quaker meeting house.

But they went to the heart of the project, as did the red phone by the window, the red phones in every building on campus, the damn need to get news from Africa tonight.

In this very room, Quaker settlers had gathered before the American Revolution to talk and share and pray, and now, Maas realized, the old spirit would infuse new work. All around him as he stepped down the aisle, he felt adoration and hope, welling love, trust, and warm delight.

"Oh, my friends! My family!" he cried, passing the silver plate, offering the syringes, watching eager fingers pluck and choose and hold up amber fluid to the light.

—"You will go to Paramount Pictures, Annie and Eddy!"

—"Washington, D.C. The little brown house! Fritz and Bettina. Make those dollars count!"

—*"For you, Christopher and Eloise, air tickets to Disney World! Bring sweaters for the air-conditioning!"*

But inside, he fought down fear, his mind going again to the communications shack and the screens there, and his watchers, who would be riveted to CNN, Al Jazeera, BBC. WAITING FOR NEWS FROM AFRICA TO START!

He was in agony that the red phone would ring again. It had happened before when he failed.

Everyone, even kings, are afraid of someone, Harlan Maas knew. And he was terrified of the voice on that phone.

But outwardly he smiled so the group would think that nothing was wrong. He stood tall. He was the embodiment of worldly confidence and gentle command. He rolled his left sleeve up to expose blue veins on his pale, thin arm.

Harlan announced, "Now, all of you! Let's line up and give each other the final round of shots."

FIVE

CHRIS VEKEY WALKED INTO THE WILSON HIGH SCHOOL GYM, AND
the sheer normalcy of it—after the horrors she'd seen last
night—almost knocked her off her feet. For the next
thirty minutes, for her daughter's sake and the sake of
sanity, she'd try to block out the situation in Nevada and
the photos from Somalia sent in by Joe Rush. Her experience told her she needed this short break. Her role as a
mother filled her with protectiveness. She looked out at
the smiling kids and her gut clenched up.

*Meet Rush's plane. Find out if he's infected. Find out if
he thinks the Somalis started it. The Sixth Fleet is in the
Indian Ocean, ready to blow those fuckers to smithereens.
Homza believes it's out of Africa. Consensus is, coordinated
attack.*

But in here, take a breath. For the next thirty minutes,
another world. Eighty kids putting last-minute touches

on exhibits that they hoped would win a prize and scholarship to college. Chris had worked in medical emergencies before. She'd worked in slums in Houston, and Los
Angeles, and in shanty towns in Accra. She'd learned a
long time ago that in an emergency you took solace where
you could find it or you lost effectiveness. You controlled
your fears and grabbed the nap, ate the meal, did whatever
the thing was that relaxed you, if you were lucky enough
to get a few minutes to do it. That break made you
sharper, and could, in the end, mean the difference between a win and a loss.

Burke had been livid when he'd learned she was here.

"You're where? A high school science fair?"

"Do you have children, Burke?"

"I don't have that joy, Chris, no."

*"I was up until four A.M. on Nevada. Rush doesn't get in
for two more hours. YOU need six hours of sleep to do your
job, you once told me. I need four. So back off. This is my break.
It's how I stay clear. There's nothing for me to do until he gets
in and I assume you want me in top shape, right?"*

Burke had backed down. He usually listened to any
reasoning that made you better at your job. Well, as long
as the person saying it wasn't Joe Rush.

Twenty minutes to go.

Burke had said, chilling her, *"Two nurses have come
down with it in Nevada, twenty hours after treating the
first victims."*

Washington, she knew, was where too many parents
forgot their children while concentrating on work. *Sorry,
son, I can't see your Little League game because there's a*

key meeting at the Pentagon. But I promise that we'll have time together next summer. I know I said that last summer, but this year will be different.

Next thing you know, you shove your kid aside for a smaller meeting, not an emergency, and then something less important, and then to just write a memo, and before you know it, years have passed, the kid's on drugs, the kid disappears to college or some ashram and you never hear from her again. Tell a kid that they're unimportant long enough, they'll believe it.

The fair was due to open in fifteen minutes, 9:30 A.M., and the tenth graders competing for the opportunity to present at the World Science Festival in New York made frantic last-minute adjustments, as if this, a project, meant the end of the world. The work lay along four aisles of fold-out tables, between the basketball backboards and folded-up stands—a cornucopia of science dreams, mini-robots, racks of test tubes, jury-rigged computers, hydroponic tomatoes, and, Chris thought with pride, my girl Aya's project!

Washington! She'd lived here for twelve years now and was always struck by the way the city juxtaposed the mighty and the mundane. Nuclear war may be imminent but my kid needs braces. The economy grew by 4.5 percent but take the garbage out because it smells! The defense satellite system sucked up another billion dollars, and Ralph the plumber needs four hundred. I know you're the senator from Alaska, dear, but mop up that bathroom floor right now!

The gym smelled of coffee and wood polish and sweat

from last night's b-ball game, where Aya had been a happy cheerleader. It smelled of the cupcakes that one mom had baked to bribe judges, and expensive aftershave from the few dads here, mixed with a cheaper kind from the teen boys.

And the projects. *How fast is your computer?* by Charles Jason, fifteen. *The race between solar-powered bristlebots*, tiny automats made from heads of toothbrushes. *How to block a Wi-Fi signal. What is smog made of?* Chris couldn't believe that fifteen-year-olds had come up with all this stuff.

Mostly moms at the tables with their kids, but a few dads here, too, clad in better-than-usual gray suits, which ID'd them as high-level government or K Street types. Chris batting away a sudden vision of a nineteen-year-old girl in Nevada, her face eaten away as if by acid . . . and at the same time watching Aya arrange connections between a homemade plywood box, two cheap seven-year-old Dell laptops rummaged from friends' basements, and a small red plastic unit that looked more like a toy. Aya's poster. HOW I PROVED OUR SUPERMARKET LIED ABOUT FISH IT SELLS.

Aya, only a few years younger than those hideously mangled drone crews out West, in new crisp jeans and a red Abercrombie sweater, behind her table, muttering words she'd been practicing for the judges. "Anyone can now do DNA experiments in their very own home, like I did!"

"Win or not, you're the best," Chris told her daughter.

Aya's mood jerking back and forth, one minute filled

with excitement over the science, the next fearful over the competition. "It's amazing, Mom. Used to be that if you wanted to do genetics, it was impossible unless you're rich. Like, just a centrifuge costs, like, six thousand dollars."

"Don't say 'like,' honey. Just say the words."

"Whatever! Anyway, my Cathal Garvey does the same thing, spins samples, separates components. I saved my babysitting money. The Cathal cost only sixty bucks! And this little disk? See the slots in it? It spins tissue samples at 33,000 rpms, 51,000 g's, that's 18,000 more than the centrifuge, which costs a lot more!"

"I'm proud of you," Chris said, meaning it.

"You can mix tomato genes with pig genes! Amazing!"

Chris grew aware of another mom looking with ill-disguised antagonism between Aya's exhibit and her own son's, a half dozen bits of labeled cocoa, wood, bananas, and brazil nuts. SUSTAINABLE CROPS FROM TROPICAL FORESTS.

"Is this your daughter?" the woman asked sweetly.

"Yes."

"What a beauty! She looks just like you! And what a smart exhibit! You probably helped her a little, I bet? Moms always want to help their children. It's so hard to resist. I resisted, though. It's the rules."

"Aya did it all by herself."

Bitch. Liar, the woman's eyes accused. *You cheated.*

But she was wrong.

And even if the woman had been right, Chris would

kill to protect Aya. Aya was more important than anything else in her life. This child had started in her belly. She'd cherished that life from the first, when she was seventeen, pregnant, refusing to ID Aya's dad for her parents, not to protect the boy, but because she had no intention of marrying him. Why open that can of worms?

She'd never considered abortion, as her best friend suggested. She'd sat in the principal's office, heart slamming as she was stripped of the valedictorian title, told that she'd ruined her life, warned that fornication violated scripture. But never once did her commitment to the baby flag; not when she put herself through college, working in a toxics clean-up crew for double pay . . . not when other women her age went on dates while Chris hit the books. Never once did she feel less than lucky.

Because I made a life.

She pushed the fear about Nevada away. She would focus on Aya for the next eighteen minutes. She remembered her mother saying, years back, on a porch in Alabama, "Put the baby up for adoption. You have no idea how hard motherhood is."

"I guess I'll find out."

"It will be too late to change your mind. You'll already have a child."

"I have one now, in my belly."

Spending those last two months of pregnancy in Sulfur Springs, stared at by neighbors and friends and churchgoers in the supermarket, Chris was a more popular form of local entertainment than the multiplex; hearing whispers in ladies' rooms, giggles from other cheerleaders, warnings that she was a "bad influence" from friends who'd been ordered by their parents to keep away from her.

Stubborn then. Stubborn now, Dad told her these days. But at seventeen, the words had carried anger. When he said it now, from back in Alabama, it was with enormous pride.

Oh, Aya.

And then, after the birth, the terror when baby Aya had to be put on a respirator. The helplessness when Aya, age six, fell off a bike and broke her arm. The swelling feeling in her chest when the dental braces came off, and the teeth gleamed, white and straight. Aya was a straight-A kid now, popular, smart, a Web genius, and her phone rang at night with calls from boys who asked about more than homework. Aya going on group dates. Aya eyeing a Princeton University catalog last week. Aya saying, *"I want to be like you, Mom, and help people. I want to figure out genomes. But I can start now. You don't have to be rich to do DNA research. A PCR costs only six hundred dollars."*

"PCR?"

Aya rolled her eyes, as in, *You don't know what it is?* "It's polymerase chain reaction, a way to heat up and cool down material. I know a guy at Genspace, the community lab in Anacostia? He built one with a lightbulb, an old computer fan, some PVC pipe, and an old Ardvino board."

When did my daughter start speaking this new language? Chris was awed. "Very impressive."

Aya saying something else now, pivoting from one subject

to another. Aya saying, "Are you going to go out with Joe Rush? You should."

THE HEAT FLOODED HER FACE. SHE HOPED SHE WASN'T BLUSHING. How did the kid come up with this stuff? Chris was sure that she'd hidden her feelings, but the face looking up at her, heart-shaped, blue eyes, cute copper-colored freckles, was canny, teasing, bright.

"Aya, where did that question come from?"

"I heard you talking on the phone this morning to Mr. Burke. I wasn't eavesdropping! I was just passing the kitchen and I heard you say Joe's name."

Joe. She called Dr. Rush *Joe*. She'd only met him once, when Chris brought her to Homeland Security on Parent-Kid Day. Aya glommed on to the guy. Even checked out Rush on the Net and somehow came up with a photo of his house in the woods and a group shot of soldiers in Afghanistan. The kid was an amazing researcher. But when it came to Rush, Chris would prefer that Aya laid off. Just the thought of Rush came with a flood of unwanted emotion, which she fought to keep off her face.

I'm in love with a man who kills people. And his background seems common enough knowledge at the top. Boy, I sure know how to pick them.

She wasn't sure how the feeling for Rush had happened. She didn't even see Rush that much, only in committee, a few hours every few months. Chemistry, that was easy to explain—the way her breath caught when he walked into a room, the way his shaving cream left a whiff of lime in his wake. The quiet way he moved and the way, when he was interested in something, he was razor focused. She'd spotted him alone one Sunday night during the Cherry Blossom Festival, 11 P.M., at the Jefferson Memorial, when she was showing out-of-town friends the sights, and he looked tormented and lonely, staring at the slogans cut into stone. The Lincoln Memorial was the famous one, the Parthenon of D.C., always shown in movies. But the Jefferson had always been her favorite, softer, almost hidden in trees, quiet, by the tidal pool. Joe had been staring at the words cut into white stone. *I know but one code of morality for men whether acting singly or collectively.* Then he had spotted her and smiled, looked embarrassed, and his mask went back into place.

Rush emanated confidence when he knew other people were there. Yet something bleak and pained was inside.

Chris had never had a problem acknowledging her animal side, and her animal side wanted him. In meetings she'd been struck by the way Rush saw things from different angles, and the way he did not back down when he thought he was right. She was drawn to the maverick. She liked conviction. Her instinct told her, in spite of the terrible things she'd read about him, that he was *kind*, a sense bolstered by the loyalty that Major Nakamura and Admiral Galli and Galli's wife, Cindy, had for Rush.

How can Rush be guilty of the things that Burke showed me in the file?

"Mom, are you listening?" asked Aya.

"One hundred percent, honey. I am so proud!"

"Is Joe Rush coming back to Washington today?"

"What?" She jerked. Chris hoped her daughter didn't see the heat rising in her face, sense the warmth in her belly. "How do you know that?"

"You said so on the phone. You like Joe, don't you? I do. Girls think he's cute."

"What girls?"

"That time you brought me to the office, the secretaries were, like, swooning over him."

"Don't say 'like,' I said. And I enjoy being with everyone on the committee, not just Dr. Rush."

"That's not true. You don't like Burke."

"He can be difficult, I admit. But he's dedicated. Where do you get these ideas anyway?"

"Are you going to go out with Joe?" A giggle.

"You don't date people you work with."

"How come you get quiet when his name comes up?"

"Concentrate on your exhibit, young lady."

"Whenever you call me 'young lady,' it means I'm right!"

Her physical reaction to Rush had started the first time she'd seen him, across a conference table. Bam! What was that expression from that old film? *The Godfather?* The thunderbolt? That was it. Over the head! And working with him had only deepened the feeling. She had dreams about him. Her breathing caught when he entered a room. One time on M Street she'd gotten excited just looking at a male mannequin in a shop window wearing the same pullover sweater that he did. Ridiculous! And last Christmas she'd been in the Macy's Men's Department, and some salesman had been spraying guys

with Rush's aftershave. The smell had hit her and . . .
stupid!

"Earth to Mom!"

"I'm listening!"

"Yeah? Then what did I just say?"

"I did not come here to be tested, Aya!"

Why was it, Chris asked herself, strolling again, looking at exhibits, why was it that with other guys after her,
great guys, accomplished, smart, funny guys, athletes, a
Nobel Prize–winning biologist, that Czech actor from
the hit film *Mrazek's Island*, all those guys calling her up,
sending funny or cute e-mails, or flowers, why did she
have to fall for a semihermit with secrets, just because
something inside her turned to mush when he came near?

Even in normal times, he didn't notice her, not in the
way she'd prefer to be noticed, at least by him. He was
polite and deferential, just as he was to everyone else,
except Burke. He ran into her once at the Kennedy Center and barely said hello. Cindy Galli had sensed her frustration, girl to girl, and since Joe and Eddie stayed in the
admiral's guest house when in D.C., Cindy had cooked a
group dinner once, invited Chris, seated her beside Joe,
prompted conversation with the sort of questions that a
smart hostess asks when she wants two guests to hook up.

Nothing. Joe had poured her wine, asked about Aya,
listened with interest to the story about Vietnamese refugees refusing to take pills that were colored red, then
excused himself and went off to bed early as he'd been up
since 3 A.M. on a National Park Service evacuation—a New
Mexican hiker who'd come down with hantavirus. The

guy had zero interest in her. Cindy had told Chris that night, at the door, that Joe had lost his fiancée last year. "He needs time," Cindy had said. "He's a great person. He's worth the wait. So are you."

Idiot! Fool! Can't you go for appropriate people, ever? I mean, she thought wryly, *look at my history. First, the high school football player with the brains of an antelope. Then the married college TA who I stayed away from, because married guys are wrong, but I still had the crush, so I never went out with anyone else. One at a time. Then the Olympic swim champion who told me—four weeks into it—that he regarded women as gold medals. For six years, a few dates but nothing special . . . and now I fall for the killer in the file.*

You go, girl.

As she looked over an exhibit titled, HOW GLOBAL WARMING CHANGES OCEAN CURRENTS, she recalled the way Burke had tried to poison the well for Rush a month ago.

Chris had been in his office to eye evacuation protocols: Congress, White House, Supreme Court, how to move government if the capital was threatened. Plans were made during the Cold War, when the threat was nuclear, and were updated annually, as the nature of threats grew and changed.

"In a protocol 80, you'd stay in the city," Burke had said.

"But my daughter could get out first, right? There'd be advance warning. I could send her to my dad."

"Chris, you know the deal. If there's advance warning, yes. If not, we're inside. But these plans have been around since the 1950s. Send her to Alabama, you can get a tornado. Tampa? Hurricanes! Eighty is a precaution, nothing more."

Burke had gone back to details, which highways would be blocked off while motorcades made their way to the underground facility at Mount Weather, Virginia. Who goes if the President decides to stick things out in Washington. Who stays if the President leaves.

And then, excusing himself, Burke had "accidentally" left a manila file on his desk when he went to the bathroom. COLONEL JOSEPH RUSH in big black letters, sitting there, by Burke's Remington statuette, just a foot away. She'd opened the folder. She'd been unable to help herself. She'd felt manipulated and guilty. *No one's fucking perfect*, she'd told herself, knowing perfectly well that Burke would give her a few minutes to do what he wanted before wandering back.

When she'd seen the highlighted passages, her face had gone hot.

When Burke returned, his eyes flickered to the file, lying exactly as she'd found it. Burke's expression satisfied. Burke knowing that she'd looked.

COLONEL RUSH ADMITTED BEING PRESENT WHEN THE SUSPECT WAS TORTURED. HE PARTICIPATED IN THE . . .

And, another page, another incident, ALTHOUGH NORWEGIAN POLICE NEVER ID'D THE KILLER, RUSH ADMITTED, DURING THE DEBRIEFING IN WASHINGTON, TO STRANGLING . . . HUSHED UP . . . BEST FOR ALL CONCERNED IF . . .

I'm so stupid, she thought now. *I'm making excuses for him and I don't even know what occurred.*

The problem was, Burke didn't lie, and she'd glimpsed the file for only forty seconds. So what had really happened? What was the unhighlighted part? Why did Burke hate Rush so much? Or was Chris blinded by chemistry?

In love with a killer, she thought again.

OVER THE LAST TWO DAYS, AFTER THE INITIAL CALL FROM NEVADA, Burke had forced changes—ordering more FBI help, shuffling staff, sharpening control in case the emergency spread. Good precautions, Chris thought, because she'd seen close up, in the Ebola outbreak in 2014, how a lack of coordination could make a manageable situation wild.

Right now it's only eleven dead in Nevada and forty-five in Somalia, awful, but hopefully containable, although someone's going to have to tell the families of those soldiers and civilians who died.

Nine minutes until she had to leave.

Seven.

"Good luck, Aya!"

"Mom, I'm so scared! What if I lose today?"

Chris thought, *You don't know what scared is, and I hope you never do* . . . Chris headed out for the parking lot, telling herself that Nevada and Somalia were nine thousand miles apart, and unrelated. But not really believing it. Back to work. Burke had sent agents in a Chevy Suburban to make sure she got to Andrews on time. They would drop her back here later to retrieve her car.

Burke had said, "You told Rush and Nakamura to take each other's blood?"

"Every hour. We'll analyze it when they get in."

"And their flight time is nineteen hours?"

"Twenty, including the stop in Germany to drop samples at the lab. They'll take more blood in the air after that."

"Well, the marker shows up eight hours after contact, so if they're clear when they hit D.C., they're okay, Chris. Otherwise, quarantine them and give them antibiotics."

"Burke, you mean the ones that don't work so far?"

"Maybe they take more time to kick in. Have faith."

She climbed into the backseat now, two FBI guys in front, the government being the last steady customer of that pathetic remnant of a once-great corporation, General Motors. The driver's eyes flicked to her in the rearview mirror, glanced at her ring finger on the seat top. He was checking to see whether it was bare. He was a handsome man, but Chris had no response.

They headed downtown in light post-rush-hour traffic, on Massachusetts, then took Branch Avenue toward Camp Springs. The juxtaposition of normal sights outside—a line of idling cars at the Japanese Embassy, a bakery truck near Dupont Circle, Diamond cabs at Union Station—mixed in her mind with dire *possibility*. A bolt of fear hit her for Joe Rush. What if, despite precautions, he was infected? There was no way to know for sure until she transferred his blood to the Andrews Air Force Base Hospital, where lab workers waited, clad in protective gear.

Just as they approached the base, the phone trilled. It

was Burke calling from the White House, where he was getting out of a meeting.

Burke said crisply, "It's in South Carolina."

"Where?" She felt sick.

"Charleston. A seventy-two-year-old retired ticket taker on the Long Island Railroad came into Grand Strand Medical Center last night. He and his wife both show the marker. Ray Havlicek has agents at their retirement community, going condo to condo, seeing if anyone else is sick." Burke sighed. "Five hundred retirees in that place, and half of them together in a dining room every day."

"Has the couple been in Nevada or Africa?"

"They visited a grandson in Galilee last week."

"Are they quarantined?"

A sigh. "Now? Yes. But four hours went by before we learned they were there. And they sat in the waiting room for an hour before going in. Around other people."

The car passed into the base, past guards, barracks, lawns, runways. Up in the blue sky, Chris caught a glimpse of silver, something small and fast, angling down. She checked her watch. This might be Rush. She was unclear which emotion was stronger, the catch in her throat at his arrival, or the constriction brought on by Burke's news.

Chris said, "It's a mistake not to announce it."

"Not our choice. The President knows he needs to get in front of it. But he's figuring out what to say. We hope we'll know more by tonight that will help him. Havlicek's trying to track down any other visitors to Galilee."

She sat, stunned, looking out at the bright sun, the passing cars, the incoming plane, *normalcy.*

Burke said, "Meanwhile, I'm asking key people to quietly move from their homes to the dorm at Homeland Security. Pack a bag. Come out to the campus when you can. Also, I'm relieving Admiral Galli. You'll run that unit."

The breath caught in her throat. Burke continued. "General Homza thinks we're dealing with seeding."

Seeding means that a hostile group is planting toxics in different places. A quiet attack, which spreads. An attack whose origin is harder to determine.

"Homza believes the capital is a likely target."

"Aren't you getting ahead of things?"

"I hope so. That's my job."

"What about Aya?"

Burke said, "You can move her in with you, or you can send her away. Look, it's just precaution, like drills. Terrorism alert level up everywhere. Airports. Amtrak. Federal buildings. I want my people in a protected area. If this gets worse, you're separated from the general population. Better to have your things at HQ just in case."

"I want Rush to come with me to Nevada."

Personally, I don't want him anywhere near me. He makes me crazy. But he's the best person for this job.

"He's out," Burke said. "Plenty of FBI out West to help you."

"Burke, he's smart. He sees things before other people, and in a different way. He stopped the outbreak in Alaska last year. He's an eyewitness in Somalia, and something he saw there might be relevant. You want me? I need him. Or is there some special reason you want him out?"

Daring Burke now. Daring him to say the thing out loud that he'd hinted at earlier. *If you want me to know something, spell it out. Don't go off to a bathroom and leave a file on a desk. Have some guts!*

But Burke caved. Or acknowledged the logic. Burke said, "He's your responsibility then, *and only if his blood work is clear.* But if he goes off on his own, I lock him away. You tell him that."

"Have we identified the pathogen yet?"

"It's a hybrid. Chimera. They nailed some DNA, Gaines said, but not enough for full ID. Can't tell yet if it's lab made or natural. That may take some time."

"And what part did they ID?" Chris asked as the car stopped beside a long runway, and ahead, through shimmering air, she saw Joe Rush's jet touch down, wheels puffing smoke, sun glinting off the windows flashing past.

Burke told her the basic component of the Nevada pathogen. The primary bacterial foundation of the thing.

She felt her legs go weak and flashed to Aya in her head, at a high school science fair, smiling, a kid, an innocent, her only daughter. Chris said, "Sweet, sweet Jesus."

Burke sighed. "I'd say that's exactly right."

SIX

===

"LEPROSY?" I SAID.

We waited in the plane for the results of our blood work, to see if we were infected. The fingers on my right hand had begun tingling, but I told myself that this was because, before landing, I'd fallen asleep on my hand. The troops surrounding our jet kept their distance, ringing us at sixty feet with M4s slung over their shoulders.

"Here we go again," Eddie said. "Something we ate?"

The lone, small figure of Chris Vekey stood outside the window, on the tarmac, looking up as she spoke via phone.

I tried to ignore my anger and concentrate on what she was saying, but the truth was, if Burke and Chris had been open with us earlier, we might have spotted something in Africa that would help us now. But they'd hidden facts, delayed giving information. *Need to know* was the curse of Washington, creating a perpetual catch-up race during crises, a drumbeat of too late.

Now Eddie and I saw *leprosy* up on our screens, on our thumb drive medical encyclopedias. Right side showed a rogue's gallery of photos—faces eaten away, fingers nubs, feet stumps—going back to 1850.

Eddie said, "The facts don't go with what we saw, One. You never get leprosy in groups."

Chris's voice in my ear said, "Now you do."

"It doesn't spread this fast. Normal germination after infection, one to three years. In extreme cases, six months. And it's rarely fatal."

Chris said, "This strain is."

I broke in, flaring at her, "The admiral is *fired*, you say? He's a good man! *You're* our boss now?"

"Yes."

My rage crested. We'd been lied to and we'd been threatened with death in Somalia. We'd been forced to undergo radio silence on the long ride home because our multimillion-dollar communication system was on the blink—they claimed. I'd misjudged this woman, I saw. I'd thought she was different than the backbiting social climbers that populated the capital, self-serving know-it-alls who talked piously of policies and manipulated them for personal gain.

Chris Vekey, I saw, had waited for an emergency to ally herself with Burke, to force a good man into retirement, just when the country needed him. Now she blithely expected Eddie and me to snap to and obey her, pliant as toy soldiers. But we weren't that and had never been.

"Go to hell," I said.

"What?"

"What you did to the admiral stinks."

"Watch your temper," she warned. Out on the tarmac, she was a stiff, glaring presence in a parka, her gamine face shocked, her voice snapping out in white smoky bursts.

I retorted that we were private contractors. We were retired from the service, here only because of private university ties. "Burke's lapdog"—as I called her—could not tell us what to do.

She stared up at me with a stony expression. But Southern women don't outmaneuver you with a bludgeon. They do it with a soft voice, a steel backbone. "Those Alabama girls can break the balls off a Rodin statue with a look," Eddie once said, the truth of that made evident now.

"Colonel, for your information, once you signed on, you're bound by your agreement. If you violate that, and leave, fine with me. I'll make a phone call and where you'll *go* is Leavenworth prison."

I said nothing, fuming. It was true.

Chris said, "Do you understand?"

"Yes."

Her gaze did not waver. The voice in my ear was molten steel. "You and I and Major Nakamura are going to wait for your test results. If your blood work is negative, you're coming with me to Nevada to help track this thing. I want your eyes on the ground."

"That would have been easier if you'd leveled with us from the start."

"While on the job, you will function as effectively as if Admiral Galli remained in charge. Do you understand me?"

"I understand."

"You'll ask the same questions you'd ask otherwise. You'll make the same connections. We're going to Creech Air Force Base outside Las Vegas. I'll forget your rudeness this once, because loyalty is an admirable quality. *You'll* give me one hundred percent or I'll lock you away so fast you won't know what hit you. Was there something else you wanted to say?"

"No."

We broke contact. I went back to reading about leprosy. Eddie sat two feet away, grinning like an idiot.

"You sure told her," he said. "No one pushes you around. You are one tough Marine, man. I must say, she may be Burke's lapdog but she's cute even when she bites."

"Eddie, do me a favor. Shut up."

THE BLOOD TESTS WERE LATE IN COMING.

Were we infected? Was the lab repeating the tests?

The tingling increased in the fingers of my right hand. I flexed them. Was feeling seeping back into them? I told myself, *You're imagining it. Just work.*

"Leprosy," I read out loud, "was so common in medieval Europe that one out of thirty people suffered from it. In extreme cases it killed, usually by blocking nerves, or causing gangrene or infection. Or victims had no feeling, so they cut or hurt themselves without even knowing it. Listen to this, Eddie. Until recently, it was believed that leprosy victims lost fingers or toes to the disease, but it turns out they'd accidentally damage themselves because they lacked feeling. In India, leprosy sufferers have lost their fingers and toes to rats."

"Rats?"

"Yeah. The rats ate them while they slept. They felt nothing."

And it wasn't just symptoms up on-screen, but the horrible social aspects. *The separating disease*, it was called. Throughout history, lepers had been shunned, forced from homes and families, called witches, hounded from villages, locked away in filthy hospitals, feared and stigmatized. I saw a shot of a leper hospital in Jerusalem, 1843, and another, hidden away in the swamps of Louisiana, and a leprosarium on the outskirts of London . . . virtual prisons for people who had done nothing wrong except fall ill.

Eddie read, "Some scientists think the Crusaders brought leprosy back to Europe from the Middle East. Some say it's the other way around. Either way, by 1300, hundreds of muddy French and Italian villages were filled with figures in dirty shrouds, wrapped in rags, tormented, hungry, and sick. By law they had to carry a bell, warning all in their paths that they were coming. Chanting, 'Unclean.'"

Eddie shook his head. "I was sure this thing was going to be chemical, One. Toxic chemical. Not this."

"Fifteen hundred years before Christ, Egyptian doctors recorded cases," I read. "In ancient Greece, Hippocrates treated *sores and destroyed flesh*. The first medically proven case of leprosy was confirmed in 2009, from fifty years before Christ! A Yale team dug up a skeleton near Haifa, and radiocarbon-dated it. Perfect DNA match."

"Says here ninety-five percent of people have natural immunity to leprosy, One. But over half the people in that camp caught it. So does the infection spread because of the other part of the chimera, the second part of the mix?"

Question after question. "Says you can't grow it in a lab, Eddie. Natural spread, you think?"

"Plus, if thirty percent of Europe had it at one time, what made it die out? Wait! It *didn't* die out. Numbers dropped in the 1600s, but shot up again two centuries later, mostly in England and Norway."

"Why those countries?" I asked. *Is this a clue?*

I read, "England and Norway were seafaring nations carrying on trade with India. Sailors brought it back. Then, in 1873 a Norwegian scientist, Armauer Hansen, ID'd the bug. That's why leprosy is called Hansen's disease today."

Eddie looked up. "I'd rather have a ball team named for me. The Nakamura Angels!"

"Still two million cases in the world today," Chris said outside, stamping her feet to keep warm.

"Two hundred thousand new cases a year."

"But only a few in the U.S., and most of those are immigrants from Mexico," said Chris. "Hey! Get this! The only other creature on the planet that carries leprosy is an armadillo. You can catch leprosy from eating their meat."

I envisioned the odd-looking creature, "hillbilly speed

bumps," in parts of the South. An armor-plated, semiblind insect eater, a remnant left over from the dinosaur era.

Eddie scratched his head. "Hey, Chris, about those victims in Nevada? Did any of them visit Mexico recently?"

"We'll ask. Look, Creech is the major operational center running Air Force drones overseas. Our attacks against Al Qaeda leadership, the Taliban, Somalia . . . the boys and girls who control those drones do it from Creech."

"That doesn't sound like coincidence."

She nodded. "Couple of drone pilots came into the base hospital. Then a mechanic and a pilot's girlfriend. All deteriorating fast. The docs thought at first they suffered from some crazy fasciitis . . ."

"Flesh-eating bacteria," Eddie said, referring to the staph infections that could kill in a day, bacteria that got into open cuts then traveled through the fat layers connecting cells. The microbe had started out as fairly innocent, I knew. It caused nothing more serious than pimples or boils. Penicillin killed it. But in the 1950s, a new strain appeared. Its toxins caused tissue to deteriorate, and it wiped out red blood cells. That penicillin-resistant strain killed by brain abscess. It could enter the body through the tiniest cut, then spread so fast it could kill a healthy person—in extreme cases—in a day.

Fasciitis was the nightmare hospital infection. You could pick it up in an ER, but unfortunate victims have also contracted it after swimming in the ocean, or falling on a dance floor. Some survivors lived only because doctors amputated their limbs to stop the spread of the infection.

I said, "But you don't get fasciitis in groups either."

"I know. I'm just telling you what doctors initially thought. An ambulance was set to transport victims to Vegas. Better facilities there. But then two more people came down with it. Civilians in Galilee. Then another airman."

"Did they all get moved to Vegas?"

She shook her head. "RDS," she said, shorthand for *rapidly developing situation*. "At that point, judgment call. The base commander called D.C. No one knew if we had something contagious. The idea of bringing seven possible high-infection cases into a major metropolitan area didn't work, and Vegas doesn't have level four wards."

"Montana's got one in Missoula," I said, remembering that federal dollars built a unit at Saint Patrick Hospital there, in case staffers from the Rocky Mountain Lab in Hamilton ever came down with the deadly diseases they worked with, like Ebola.

Chris nodded. "Missoula was the call. But then more patients started coming in, and we found others in the barracks. Missoula can handle four. We had more. At that point it was clear that we might be under attack. That's why, when you called from Africa, the committee was already in session, trying to figure out what to do."

"Under attack by whom?" I asked.

Chris looked miserable. "No one knows."

"All the victims are still at Creech?"

"We modified the base hospital." She nodded. "Rapid response team from Missoula flew in. FBI out of Vegas. Normal patients moved to an upper floor. The base closed to the public, personnel confined to quarters, Galilee sealed off. Only thirty people live there."

Why is the blood work taking so long to come back?

Right now I'd keep exploring the one solid clue we had, which was: *Whatever microbe we face contains leprosy DNA. So back to the thumb drive.*

"Eddie, you said leprosy numbers fell in Europe in the 1600s, then shot up. What accounts for the initial drop?"

Chris suggested, "Could the contagion have evolved? A thousand years ago syphilis killed in months. Now, it takes twenty years if untreated. It evolved so human hosts could live longer. You think we're seeing that here, Colonel?"

"No. Because *leprosy never evolved*," I read. "An NYU team compared original strains with modern ones. Leprosy today is exactly the same as twelve hundred years ago."

"Then what the hell do we have here? Mutant? Made? Or maybe it's finally evolved."

I spotted a black Chevy coming down the road from the direction of the base hospital. My heartbeat sped up. Outside, Chris answered another call and listened and her face tightened and I saw fear in the way she straightened up. She did not want me to hear whatever she was saying.

We're infected.

But she was back in my ear. "Colonel, you two are clean."

I started to relax. She added, "You'll wear a mask in flight, take one last blood test in the air. That will be over twenty-four hours since exposure. If you're good then, you can mix with other people. But we're not waiting. I'm coming aboard. We're taking off. Now."

She had guts, I had to say that much. I thought about the fright on her face just before she got the news about me and Eddie. For an instant she'd looked like she cared about us. But I wasn't going to be fooled twice. She'd been concerned for herself, probably, since she was going to fly with us.

I don't give people two chances.

Then, while we flew, the news got worse.

AS THE JET CROSSED TENNESSEE, WE LEARNED—CDC CONFIRMED— that the blood samples Eddie and I had taken from Somalia matched the organism out West. As we reached the Mississippi River, I was sleeping, exhausted after being awake for more than thirty hours. Eddie woke me to take a last blood sample. I gazed out as the hypo pricked me. After hunting diseases for years, I'd come to regard the atmosphere as filled with invisible pathways for contagion, *plane routes*, that instantly link places that centuries ago required months to reach. Now an outbreak in Guinea can reach Kansas in a day.

Below, the gritty urban centers of the East had dropped away, fields replaced streets, mountains replaced fields, and forests rose up and fell and finally the jet was landing in a Nevada valley. I saw dun-colored landscape. Sheer escarpments in the distance. I saw a two-lane highway devoid of traffic except for a military convoy converging on the base. Creech was a sprawling boxcar shape, inside of which the lone runway and its taxi lanes formed a gigantic cross from the air. I looked down on living quarters, administrative buildings, and hangars. Indian Springs—nearest big town—lay twenty miles off. Galilee was a mere dot a few miles from the base, and the town had a circle of vehicles surrounding it. Those would be quarantine troops.

As we got lower, I was surprised to spot a small crowd outside the gate, and dozens of cars and campers parked off the road in no particular configuration, and lower still, I saw the hand-painted protest signs, some so large they required two people to hold them up. Words flashed past as we landed.

DRONES KILL INNOCENT WOMEN AND CHILDREN.

DRONES MAKE ENEMIES.

GROUND THE DRONES OR REAP THE WHIRLWIND.

"You're allowing civilian protestors to stay this close?" I asked, shocked.

Chris looked unhappy. "Moving them would have required a court order, explanations, and it would have replaced them with state police to block the road. Either way, civilians there. So we let it lie. They think the troops surrounding the base are on a drill," she said.

Eddie asked, "Do prevailing winds move from inside the base toward the protestors?"

"Based on what you told us from Somalia, there was no spread due to wind."

"Do the protestors know about the Galilee quarantine?"

"If they do," said Chris, "they think it's part of the drill, but sooner or later we'll see YouTube videos."

She sat two rows back, alone, wearing a Moldex HEPA surgical mask over her nose and mouth, just in case. But based on timelines, we were clean.

"None of the soldiers I see are in biosuits," I said.

Her eyes scrunched into an expression that made her look fourteen, and worried. "Suits on the way. Personnel in the hospital and around Galilee have them. But we need more."

Eddie said, "I have a feeling we'll need a lot more than just suits. This whole thing is about to blow."

IN THE UNITED STATES, THE POSSE COMITATUS ACT FORBIDS DO-mestic counterterrorism operations by the U.S. military. Accordingly, we were met by two FBI agents from the Vegas Anti-Terror Rapid Deployment Team in a black Chevy. Dome light pulsing, we turned off the run-up area, and passed a lone parked drone baking in the sun, looking like a spindly, miniature 747. Domed cockpit shape. V-shaped fins in back, and propellers. No windows. It seemed small, toy-like, harmless. Then again, a microbe is small, too.

The base seemed deserted, but I knew it was filled with personnel locked in barracks, who'd watched us come in.

I felt Chris's thigh against mine in the back of the vehicle. She pulled it away.

Special Agent Manny Vargas drove, and Special Agent Carrie LeHarve did the talking. She'd been ordered to hold nothing back. Both agents wore matching field clothes, neat T-shirts with the FBI logo in gold, khaki trousers, and surgical masks. Vargas was dark, short, moved crisply, and wore wire glasses. His fingernails on the wheel were slightly bitten. LeHarve was slim and shag blond and wore small pink pearl earrings and matching gloss. She handed me a zip-up folio, which, I saw, contained two dozen photos.

"Officers usually fly the drones in two-man teams. The top photo there, sir, those two men fell ill first; then a tech sergeant. Then people in town."

In the shot, the officers wore olive drab zip-up flight suits and sat in adjoining, comfortable-looking brown leather high-backed chairs, flight displays before them, video screen above, whitish control board at knee level, toggle sticks for steering drones in between.

"Do the officers know the victims in town?"

"Captain Reyes's girlfriend is sick. So yes."

"Have the officers visited Galilee recently, or have townspeople been on the base?"

A sigh. "There's a bar in Galilee where a lot of personnel hang out, especially on Friday nights. Flip side, five residents of Galilee work on base. Two carpenters. An electrician. And a couple of computer techs."

"Great." Eddie moaned. "That's about a thousand possible routes of infection."

So we start eliminating possibilities. I asked, starting a written checklist on my lap, "Anyone check the ventilation systems on base for microbes?"

I was thinking about Legionnaires' disease, a fatal pneumonia that can break out at hotels, and spread inside old air circulation systems or even hot tub steam.

"Air systems clean," Vargas replied.

"Any military activity inside Galilee? Maybe a drone went down, got recovered in town or nearby."

"Nothing."

"Do all the victims know each other?"

"Some do. Some don't."

Eddie asked, "Did some special event occur recently where townies and base personnel mixed?"

"I told you, the bar. Look, can I ask you a question? If they're not coughing, how is it passing from person to person?"

"Don't assume it's contagious yet," I said.

Chris Vekey stared at me.

"You *still* don't think it's contagious?"

"I'm just not assuming it's passing from person to person yet. Could be point source. Water. Food. A building. Tell me about Galilee," I asked LeHarve. "The town."

"Anything specific you want to know?"

"Whatever comes to mind."

LeHarve glanced at Vargas, then shrugged.

"Nothing special, Colonel. Boring old mining town. Its heyday was in the 1950s. Uranium mines nearby. They closed over a quarter century ago. They're boarded up."

Eddie's breath caught. "Uranium?"

The agent's eyes in the rearview mirror flicked to me. Vargas drove evenly and LeHarve's voice was low and accented, her "a" an "ahhh," as in Boston. Three white biohazard suits, folded and wrapped in plastic, lay in the trunk for us. The AC was on in the car, temp control at seventy.

I asked, "Has anyone visited the mines recently? Kids? Researchers? Any chance that water there mixes with the drinking supply for Galilee or the base? Do the town and base share a water source?"

The agents looked at each other. "I don't know."

"Well, someone needs to check."

"I'll do that," Chris said.

I continued thoughtfully, "Nobody said anything before about uranium mines. About how radiation can change cell DNA."

Eddie agreed, agitated over the lapse. "Nobody in D.C. saw a connection between a possible mutant organism and *uranium mines*? Hell, didn't anyone think of the new bacteria coming out of Chernobyl? That fucking black fungus there? And how about old nuclear test sites *here*? The 1950s. Nevada. Anyone check if this location was downwind of those old tests? If this place got a dose?"

Chris said, "I'll check that, too. But if this microbe originated in Africa, why are you asking about sources here?"

"Because maybe someone here *went* to Africa. Contracted it here and carried it there. Like the Spanish flu in 1918. Soldiers got it at Fort Riley, Kansas, and brought it to Europe. Agent Vargas, is there any possibility that someone from Creech or Galilee went to Somalia recently? Or Kenya? Missionary work? Scientist? Soldier? Hell, a tourist even?"

It turned out that the agents had not been told that

anyone was sick in Somalia so they had not asked—*goddamn need to know*. Now that they knew, "We'll check that, too."

Eddie had had it with the lack of information, with *goddamn need to know*. He snapped out, "Well, what the hell *have* you been checking if not water, mines, or travel?"

"So far, sir, possible connections between anyone in Galilee or the protestors and extremist groups. We've been checking hard drives, phone records, background, even of locals."

"Find any? Connections?"

"A couple of those wackos at the gate have visited some pretty dicey websites. We're also tracking license plates. There's a woman from Tulsa who is a second cousin of the Oklahoma City bomber, McVeigh. So! Website links to African and Mideast Islamic groups, and links to right-wingers."

I turned to Chris. "We need a list of victims in Somalia. Background. Family. Travel. Check backward from Somalia, see if there are connections here."

Chris looked unhappy. "We're on that. State had a list of everyone in that research camp. SUNY had to submit applications. So far, nothing."

The problem is that we're in a race. A minute-by-minute race. Because this thing may be spreading. Leapfrogging. Like a forest fire that suddenly breaks out miles from the source, just touches down, and starts up in a new place.

Chris said, more softly, "Colonel, in the hospital, you take the lead. That's why I brought you."

Was that a peace offering? If so, it did little good. I thought, *No, I'm here because you fired my boss and threat-*

ened me with military prison. Fuck you and fuck Burke, both of you.

Then I pushed away the hurt pride. I owed it to Lionel Nash and the other victims, and the sick people here. As we reached the base hospital, I saw two ambulances pull up to the emergency entrance. Medical personnel in protective gear moved to open the back doors.

Chris said morosely, "If this is spreading naturally, my God, at this speed, we better clamp down pretty damn fast. If it's *seeding*, we may be up against the biggest mass murderer in history. I don't know which is worse."

SEVEN

DR. INOMA OKOYE, WHO MET US OUTSIDE AT THE HOSPITAL, WAS fiftiesh, brisk but personable, a pear-shaped smoker of pipes who smelled of Borkum Riff and Old Spice after-shave. He'd been flown in from Montana to manage the situation. I was glad to see him. In the small world of biowarfare prep, he was a standout. I'd met him at Harvard. I'd also read several of his articles on quarantine procedures in third world countries in *Prevention Monthly*. He was the kind of person you wanted in charge when improvisation was called for. He had no ego involved. Just smarts.

"Ah, Joe and Eddie! It is good that you came. Too often the decision makers hang back in the capital, and that's how you make mistakes. And you were in Somalia? Yes?"

"Close as it gets," Eddie said.

"Maybe you will spot something we missed. We are getting a whole new round of sick. Come."

Okoye had been born in London to Nigerian diplomat parents. He'd gotten his med degree in Chicago, married here, and stayed. He'd worked in West Africa with Doctors Without Borders, in an Ebola outbreak. He was calm and unflappable, qualities I associated with top emergency doctors. There was no mistaking the quiet alarm in his eyes.

"We face something totally new. I have not seen anything like this, even in Africa. First we had the initial group. Now we are up to twenty-two, with more coming in hourly."

To accommodate new arrivals, he'd directed modifications in the hospital, normally a fifty-bed facility that could handle emergencies, but not more complex cases.

"Joe, we brought in state-of-the-art portable patient isolator units, the British ones. Blocked off two floors, used air blowers and plastic sheeting to create makeshift air locks elsewhere; chemical showers for doctors; collection tanks for runoff; separate disposal units for biohazardous material.

"We sealed off air vents on other floors, replaced nurses with trained staff from Montana, and upgraded the lab in the basement. Now we can analyze samples here, even as duplicate versions are flown to Atlanta."

"At least there's air-conditioning here," Eddie said.

I told Okoye, after we suited up and as we headed upstairs, "In Somalia, everyone got sick at the same time. But not here, you said?"

"No. There was a gap. A first group as a mass. Then a one-by-one increase."

"Uno," Eddie asked, "you thinking what I am?"

"Yeah. In Somalia, since everyone got symptomatic at the same time, they were all *infected* at the same time. That suggests point source. Food. Water. Something common. But *here,* you have an initial infection, then it starts to spread to a different group."

Okoye finished my thinking. "Meaning, if you are right, both initial groups were infected intentionally, and in Nevada the pathogen began to move outward. Contagious."

"It must be. I'd been hoping it wasn't."

Okoye nodded unhappily. We were in the elevator. "We always knew it was just a matter of time, that small changes in the DNA of even benign bacteria could amplify toxicity. Ramshaw and Jackson and their virulent mousepox. They created it in a lab and promptly destroyed it."

"Or Furst," said Eddie morosely, referring to the researcher at Totalgen, Inc. in Wisconsin who designed an E. coli strain—one of the most common bacteria—to be thirty thousand times more resistant to antibiotics. Furst also destroyed his creation, after an outcry by other professionals. His work proved that small changes could turn common bacteria into super killers.

Okoye sighed. "I've started half of our cases on a normal anti-leprosy regimen: rifampin, clofazimine, and dapsone. Too soon to see if it works. On others I'm trying different strategy, broad spectrum combo: penicillin, aminoglycoside, metronidazole."

I recognized these drugs. "You think it's related to necrotizing fasciitis? To flesh-eating bacteria?"

Okoye shrugged. "No response there either, Joe."

AIR FORCE CAPTAIN JOAQUIN REYES, FIRST OFFICIAL VICTIM AT Creech, lay like a space traveler inside a cylindrical patient isolator unit, a high-tech tent of reinforced plastic that looked like a gigantic roll of cellophane and came with built-in hoods, sleeves, and gloves to allow medical staff protection while they worked on a patient.

Bolted to the cylinder was a smaller, squarish airlock through which nurses could pass food and drink to Reyes, and remove body waste.

"The waste is heat sealed and removed for disposal in an autoclave," Dr. Okoye said.

Air inside the cylinder was kept at negative pressure by pumps, to lower any chance of aerosolization of bacteria if Reyes started coughing.

Between the air pumps and plastic screens, Reyes and I would communicate through three layers of protection. The face looking out, distorted by plastic sheeting, was monstrous, mottled by growths, right eyelid drooping almost shut. The irises were inflamed, red, veined, and watery. Earbuds piped music or TV in to him. He balanced a screen-tablet TV on knees poking out from beneath his hospital gown, the skin rife with more sores. The gray hospital socks bulged outward, as if the feet were bandaged. The hands balancing the tablet looked like bandaged paws. Half of his condition seemed to consist of flesh growing, half of it being eaten away.

Before I could speak, Eddie nudged me. Following his gaze, I looked up at the corner TV. CNN was on, and a banner running across the screen read, U.S. DRONES HIT SOMALI TERRORISTS. I saw a global hawk reconnaissance shot of a Somali town, houses wrecked, Technicals burning, bodies sprawled on a street.

U.S. RETALIATES FOR MURDERED SCIENTISTS. DEAD INCLUDE WOMEN AND CHILDREN. OUTRAGE SPREADS ACROSS ISLAMIC WORLD.

As the scene changed to a mob outside the U.S. Embassy in Cairo, I had a sense of the contagion spreading in a different way. There came an overpowering sense of malignant forces converging.

I glanced sharply at Chris. I figured that she'd known the attack was scheduled, and hidden this from us.

But she looked shocked beneath her plastic visor. "I knew they were thinking about it."

"But why?" I said, aware that Reyes had looked up. The swollen face stared out at me, left eye bulging, like a fish in an aquarium.

Chris said, "Why? They *killed Americans.* You witnessed it, Joe. How can you even ask why?"

"Because what I saw in Somalia were people trying to protect themselves from infection, same as protocol 80 here, a recently revamped worst-case strategy, buried in a Pentagon drawer."

"You're defending them?"

"No, but now we can't talk to them, can't learn anything else from them. There's no proof that they're even responsible for the infection in the first place."

"They burned thirty people to death, including healthy ones," she snapped. "I would think that *you of all people* would regard retaliation as—"

She stopped abruptly. She turned bright red. At that moment of face-reading honesty, I knew that she'd seen my file. Burke must have shared it. *She knows the truth about me.*

And then the patient cleared his throat and I concentrated on the wrecked face, and wiped away personal concerns to give full attention to the man lying below.

Even in this first second, if we hadn't had lab verification, it was obvious. *It's the same thing. He's not the first patient. He's fortieth in a growing line.*

The nose was eaten away. The nostrils—what was left—seemed raised up. The eyebrows were gone, the neck and wrists a mass of bumps, so joined together in places that they formed the entire surface of his skin.

"Captain Reyes? I'm Colonel Joe Rush, a former U.S. Marine. I'm also a doctor. I'm here to help. I'd be grateful if we talked, if you don't mind."

On the wall, someone had hung glassed-in Matisse posters. Jazz instruments, cutouts. They didn't lighten the mood. Their cheeriness accentuated the grotesque.

"Marines?" said Reyes in the same ravaged whisper that I'd heard overseas. *The same fucking thing.*

"Yes, Captain."

His face showed no emotion. It couldn't. The muscles

had no mobility. But the anger was raw and that was welcome. I'll take rage in a patient over resignation any day of the week.

"Actually, sir, I mind plenty. No one answers *our* questions. All we do is answer yours."

"Ask whatever you want."

Chris cleared her throat warningly and Okoye looked stern. I knew the drill. *Until we know that base personnel weren't involved in this, we do not share what we know.*

Reyes tried to lay the newspaper on his chest but his hands did not function. One section slipped out, drifted to the floor, by the urine container. "*What I want?* What the hell is happening to us, sir? Me, and my girlfriend. Jana."

"We don't know yet." My eyes flicked to the TV overhead, where CNN was showing the Africa shots again, over and over. Repetition substituting for depth. "But it may have started in Somalia." Chris's fingers tightened on my arm. She seemed about to say something, but I rode over any protest. "I've just come from there. What you have broke out there first. And a South Carolina couple came down with it, too, after being here recently."

"Somalia? But that's where we fly drones!"

I removed Chris's hand from my suited-over forearm. Her gloves and mine touched. I felt coolness beneath latex. But she wasn't ordering me to stop; interesting, because shutting me up here was her job.

Reyes struggled to rise inside his cylinder, and succeeded only in raising himself a few inches. "You're saying this is an attack? Because of our drones?"

I got down on my knees, to be at his eye level. Eddie

and I were stationed in Alaska last year, and something that my Iñupiat friends taught me there stuck with me now. In Eskimo culture, you never talk down to a child, or an old person. It accentuates a helpless feeling. I didn't know whether the same custom applied to dealing with the sick in Barrow, but it seemed a good idea here. I looked into Reyes's eyes levelly, from a few protected inches away.

"It's possible. I need your help to try to figure this out. I'll probably ask a lot of the same questions you've answered already, but I may ask new ones, or have a different take on the old answers. Time is crucial."

"I want to talk to my girlfriend, sir. Jana's here, too. But the docs say if we talk, we'll compare stories. Like we can't think for ourselves. Like, if she says something, I'll just agree. But there's nothing wrong with my brain."

Okoye was nodding, arms folded. The principle was the same one police used when separating witnesses to a crime, or co-conspirators. For the first few hours, you needed fresh perspectives. So you interviewed people separately. But my witnesses were sick, not criminals. After a while they wouldn't need to stay apart. I explained this to Reyes. He could talk to Jana soon. He did not like it. But he said, "No one explained it before like that."

Twenty minutes later I'd learned nothing new about symptoms, but I knew, *He goes to the bar in Galilee regularly, and he was last there nine days ago.*

I asked, "Anything happen there that night? Out of the ordinary? A person? A taste? Argument?"

"It was Tech Sergeant Mack's birthday. We celebrated."

"Is Sergeant Mack sick, too?"

"He died, I heard."

Reyes's girlfriend, Jana, was in the snapshot on his night table. A smiling Reyes—handsome man—had his arm around a happy, slim, plain-faced woman in tight jeans, a checkered shirt, and a felt cowboy hat with the brim turned down to highlight blue eyes. They were on a boardwalk. It looked like the Santa Monica Pier. I saw lots of bare skin in it, and all the skin looked fine.

"Pretty girl," I said.

"Colonel Rush, one more thing. Dumb little thing, but it will mean a lot to her. She's terrified."

"Tell me."

"If I can't talk to her, I want to do something for her. To make her feel better. There's this restaurant in Vegas, sir. Jana can't get enough of the Napoli Volcano Special," said the wrecked mouth. "I asked the other doctor, can you get her one? Comfort food? Three cheeses? Special sauce? I'll pay. He said no. She's scared, sir. Please. She's like an addict for that sandwich."

"Dr. Okoye," I asked, "why can't she have the food?"

"Dr. Markowitz advised against this."

"Who is Dr. Markowitz?"

"He's our gastroenterologist. He's trying to eliminate milk products as the cause of—"

"Milk products? For Christ's sake," I snapped. "Captain Reyes, what's the sandwich she likes?"

"The Napoli Volcano Special."

Half the patients here might be dead in twenty-four hours, and some asshole was denying someone a sandwich?

I ordered a nurse, "Get food for everyone. I'll pay. I don't care if someone has to drive to Vegas. Get her what she wants, however you do it. Captain, we'll do this."

One lone tear oozed out of his left eye, smearing a track.

I said, "I promise that I'll tell you personally if I learn more. If I'm not here, I'll call. Now, Dr. Okoye? You think I could get a ride into Galilee?"

Outside, he sighed. "You're a good person, Joe."

Chris sat stiffly in the Humvee beside me, moon man and woman, in our suits. More ambulances pulled up. *She knows the truth about me.* She knew about Joe Rush and the subject of revenge. Giving a patient sandwiches makes no difference on Judgment Day. A gift of prosciutto and peppers means nothing when weighed against the big questions, and Chris Vekey knew it.

Half an hour later, we found a clue.

EIGHT

====

LOADING THE OLD HONDA ACCORD FOR THE ATTACK ON THE CAPITAL,
Orrin Sykes suddenly felt doubts about the success of the mission. He was horrified by the emotion, even though Harlan had told him it might occur if he was away for too long. Harlan had instructed him on what to do about it.

You are my special warrior, Harlan had said.

Sykes was staying in a rented detached garage/apartment behind an empty Tudor-style home for sale in Northwest Washington, a woodsy neighborhood off Nebraska Avenue. He'd driven down in the secondhand car, and the apartment had previously been used by other people from the farm. He was alone here.

He closed the trunk, getting a last view of the Mossberg M1014 combat shotgun and the uzi with grenade launcher. Those were for defense, if he was interrupted today. Harlan had told him not to be taken alive. But today's actual weapon fit in his pocket.

Sykes, fighting doubt, climbed the stairs and went through the open door into his one-bedroom apartment.

Sing the songs if you become frightened, Harlan had told him. *Purify your thoughts.*

Sykes ran a cold bath and dumped in six trays of ice cubes and got into the tub, naked. Back in New Lebanon, doubters sat nude in the snow sometimes, or were whipped while they sang. Sykes rocked back and forth. His teeth chattered. He cleared his head. He was ashamed that he'd even experienced doubt. He felt calm return, and discipline. Harlan was right.

Naked, he toweled off. *I am not cold,* he thought.

Sykes's hit on the capital would be the group's third, he knew, and the effects of the first two attacks should be showing up anytime. There was always a lag time between infection and outbreak.

"The Hebrews went into Canaan and displaced those peoples to create Israel," Harlan had preached last night to a rapt audience back home, and over encrypted Internet to Sykes. "The armies of Mohammed carried his words on horseback. The Crusaders brought truth by sword."

Inside the apartment, Sykes had stocked a month's worth of food and ammunition. Harlan had seen the government plans to isolate the city if the disease got bad. Sykes had U.S. Army self-heating meals, a first aid kit, batteries, water, soap, syringes, bandages, throwaway cell phones, and boxes of Juicy Fruit gum, his weakness.

"Each prophet raised armies of the righteous," Harlan had told the group last night.

Now, the innocent-looking pill vial went into Sykes's black over-the-shoulder Tumi bag—the same sort carried by thousands of commuters—along with today's Washington Post, a manila folder of articles about today's Capitol Hill hearings, and a legal pad. He'd look like he belonged.

Harlan had said, *"The armies of past prophets numbered in the thousands and the tens of thousands. But in this vial is an army of millions."*

Harlan was more than just Orrin's teacher. Harlan had saved Orrin, and Orrin loved him. Harlan was his past and future. When near Harlan, Orrin felt an all-consuming peace that he had never known before. It was inconceivable that this feeling could be anything but right. He would do anything to keep the feeling.

Now Orrin upped the garage door and backed the Honda out into wintry Washington, draped with light snow. At this moment, he knew, people in the compound in Upstate New York were destroying old computers. Piling laptops and desktops on the ground to be smashed by sledgehammers, the wreckage soaked with gasoline. It would be burned, the plastic melted, the files obliterated, to be replaced by new memories that Harlan had ordered inserted into other computers, unpacked two months ago. The old experiments would be copied into the new computers. The dates on the experiments would change. Anyone reading records later would find real details but false dates. It would look like years-old work had started recently.

Sykes turned the car onto Military Road, a tree-lined

*thoroughfare of private homes and a strip of park. His heart
roared with pride and anticipation. The Honda merged into
light midmorning traffic, late commuters, shoppers, a private
school bus. Alerted by radio about road work blockages, he
planned to take 13th Street toward his destination.*

*Harlan had told him, "You are the only one I trust to
send out alone. Everyone else goes out in pairs. Will you be
okay by yourself?"*

"If I get lonely, I'll listen to the tapes. Can I ask a question, Harlan?"

"You need not ask permission, my special friend."

*"Where did we get the money for all this, the compound,
the animals, the weapons? I mean, it cost a lot of money. We
used to be broke."*

*Harlan had smiled and touched Orrin's wrist and Orrin had actually felt power and goodness flow into him, even
through the thick leather of Harlan's glove.*

"Oh, my dear friend. HE provides."

*Military Road intersected with 13th near the Maryland
line, and he turned right to stay inside city limits. Thirteenth
was a gauntlet of detached homes that brought him toward the
Mall. Orrin floated toward his fate as Harlan, on tape, rode
along. The old tape recorder whirred on the passenger seat.*

Harlan's voice sounded strong, in Latin.

*"'Cum autem descendisset de monte, secutae sunt eum
turbae multaem.' Matthew 8:1–4. It means, 'And when he
had descended from the mountain . . .'"*

*Sykes's lips moved silently, following along. He knew the
next words. "'Great crowds followed him.'*

"'Et ecce leprosus veniens, adorabat eum, dicens, Do-

mine' . . . 'And behold, a leper, drawing near, adored him, saying, "Lord, if you are willing, you can cleanse me."'"

Sykes's lips formed, "Jesus touched him, saying, "I am willing. Be cleansed." And his leprosy was cleansed.'"

The Honda glided into a snowy urban fog. For a moment Sykes missed Upstate New York—his friends, his lovers, the certainty of knowing each minute what you had to do. Until Harlan, Orrin had known rage but not direction, logic but not clarity, resentment but not reason, what passed for happiness sometimes, but not peace.

Sykes saw himself at eighteen years old. He saw a headline in the Crystal Lake, Illinois High School paper. SYKES WINS STATE SHOOTING CHAMPIONSHIP. ORRIN, OUR HERO!!!

Sykes passed Logan Circle at P and 13th, and turned left on busy Massachusetts Avenue, which would skirt downtown on its way toward Union Station and Capitol Hill. He kept to the speed limit. The vial in his pocket seemed alive.

Harlan said on tape, "The ancient Jewish general, Flavius Josephus, beat the Roman army. He outmaneuvered them, enraged and taunted them, and then, besieged finally, he slipped from doomed Jerusalem and went over to their side and wrote a history. The Hebrews were a little people, but their determination stopped an empire. Their tenacity changed history.

"Josephus wrote, 'And King Uzziah put on a holy garment and entered the temple to offer incense to God. But that was prohibited. Only priests could do it. And a great Earthquake shook the ground, and the rays of the sun fell upon the King's face. LEPROSY seized him, as punishment.'"

Harlan said, "'Uzziah died in grief and anxiety.'"

Massachusetts Avenue was a corridor for thousands of human drones who served the anonymous, insatiable needs of the capital. Sykes and the bacterial bomb kept to the speed limit. He eyed D.C. cops on the roadside, waiting to pounce on speeders. Near Union Station, traffic went stop and go. Harlan reached the part about the Koran. He was a charismatic speaker, but the prophets he quoted all seemed to speak with the same tone, as if Moses WAS Jesus WAS Mohammed and they all turned into Harlan Maas.

"Verse 5:110, chapter 5, Siral l-merdah—'Allah will say, "Oh Jesus of Mary, remember my favor upon your mother . . . Remember when I taught you wisdom and the Gospel. Remember when you healed the leper with my permission . . ."'"

Remember? Sykes approached the heart of the empire as surely as a bacteria rides an artery toward a heart. Harlan's voice became a mélange of other voices, old ones that had led Sykes on his journey from obscurity to rage, shock, failure, and finally, belonging.

—IS THERE NOTHING THIS BOY CANNOT DO?

—ORRIN SYKES TO STAR IN THE SPRING PLAY!

Sykes sauntering the polished cinderblock halls in Crystal Lake, Illinois High, accepting accolades from boys, adoration from girls. Sykes unremarkable scholastically, but his talents were physical. And physically speaking, he and Carol Ann Held spent long, sweet afternoons in her bedroom, since her parents both worked, and were not at home during the day.

Portrait of a future killer. A normal kid. A Chicago Cubs fan, who liked detective shows on TV. A kid like a *million others, who nobody beat up, nobody abused, who dreamt of being famous. Sometimes he was in Hollywood in the dreams. Sometimes in battle. Sometimes the Olympics.*

"You'll go far," his guidance counselor said.

When did the trajectory alter? Later, lying in a trash Dumpster in West Hollywood, watching a gray rat crawling near his feet, he'd decided it started when he announced to Grandfather that college was out. He'd join the Army, he said, as they sat one morning in the sunny breakfast nook, Sykes smiling, Grandfather frowning, which was odd, as he thought Grandfather would be proud.

—Orrin. Don't do it.

—YOU served in the Army, Grandfather.

—Which is why I know a bad war when I see one. The President can't make war. Only Congress should do it.

Grandfather arguing, pleading, finally coming up with something that swayed Orrin, which was, "If you join the Army and don't like it, you'll be stuck." Grandfather suggesting a compromise. "I'll call your uncle Merrill. He can get you into Iraq, but in a way that, if you hate it, he'll get you out."

Six months later Orrin manned a plywood desk in a trailer near Baghdad, processing pay forms on a computer. Sykes working for Uncle Merrill's company—DIAMOND & SPEARHEAD—providing drivers and guards to convoys bringing supplies to troops, and aid to Iraqi towns. They did the same job as soldiers. They got four times the pay.

"We do good," Uncle Merrill said.

Like all D&S personnel, usually former soldiers, Sykes had gone through basic training, under two former Marine sergeants. He impressed the sergeants with his shooting, quickness, and fearlessness, at least during the training.

BUT ALL I AM IS A FUCKING CLERK, BECAUSE UNCLE MERRILL TOLD THEM TO KEEP ME AWAY FROM FIGHTING!

His opportunity came when a planeload of guards was held up in Newark due to engine trouble. The company was shorthanded but a food convoy still had to go out.

An hour later, Sykes, wearing body armor, sat beside the driver in the third truck in the convoy. The trip was supposed to be easy. Convoys had taken the same route ten times before. Just before the first truck blew sideways, Ray Charles sang "Georgia on My Mind" on CD. The next moment, the second truck in line—in front of Sykes—almost went off the embankment. It stopped, smoking, blocking the road. Orrin jumped out of his cab. He'd spotted bursts of fire coming from behind rocks. His pulse pounded in his forehead. There was no time to be afraid. Instinct and training took over. He lay on his belly beneath the truck, firing three-round bursts at the men on the roadside, as shouted orders came over his headset.

Orrin heard the whine of bullets and the smack of impacts on the truck. He saw an Iraqi rise up, a portable missile tube over his shoulder. He pulled the trigger and held the M4 as steadily and surely as he had when he won the marksman championship back home. The man fell back as the projectile left the tube, but shot up, trailing smoke as it flew harmlessly into the sky.

IS THERE NOTHING ORRIN SYKES CANNOT DO?

He didn't get sick until it was over, didn't smell his own shit until the ambushers had run. Then he saw the carnage. Guys he had played poker with last night sprawled by trucks. Guys calling for help, one man cupping his half-torn genitals, another clawing at his shredded face. Sykes fought off nausea. He rushed to help. He'd been taught how to use the morphine. He soothed the wounded. He watched the light disappear in one man's eyes.

And then, as the medics came, he rose and spotted something odd on the ground, by the first overturned truck. Boxes labeled FOOD *had fallen out, split open, and their contents lay scattered all around.*

But it wasn't food. Sykes walked among scattered handheld Game Boys and sat phones. He went to a second box and opened it with his knife. It contained bottles of Tito's Vodka. Not food. Not aid. Not medicine. Vodka.

He opened another box. There wasn't food inside that one either. The box was filled with pink iPhones.

That night former Sergeants Robert Delaney and Arnold Hasselbach visited Sykes's trailer, sat down with him, acting less like noncommissioned officers, more like pals. They handed him a fat white envelope.

"You're a born soldier," the ex-sergeants said.

"I don't want this money."

"Yes you do. You did well today. Don't spoil it. Hey! Is that your grandfather in that photo, Sykes? Back home?"

"Are you threatening me?" Sykes said.

"Don't be a hard-ass. You were a hero. Money is gratitude. Why are you here if not for that?"

Sykes shook his head. He didn't want to look at the envelope. "Those guys we killed were gangsters, not soldiers."

"They were terrorists."

"I killed four kids over vodka!"

"You saved your buddies, Sykes! Man up!"

From then on, two convoys went out each week, and Orrin Sykes did a good job protecting them. He rode shotgun on the lead truck. He was promoted and got a raise. One day he killed a civilian driving toward them in an old Ford Fairlane. After the violence was over, they found a dead baby in the backseat, also shot, and no bomb. Another time he and other guards shot it out with ex-Iraqi soldiers when negotiations over some stolen iPhones went bad. Sykes killed two men. Hasselbach gave him an extra thousand that night.

"Hey, man, there's nothing you can't do," Hasselbach said.

He started drinking away bad feelings. Hasselbach gave him some cocaine, and later sold him more. Hasselbach smiling and praising but always watching. "We're the tip of an iceberg, Sykes. Take the money. Go home. Spend it on that girlfriend in the photo. You blew away some bad murderer dudes, man. You saved American lives."

Six months later he was out, living in Los Angeles, burning through the $68,000 cash. There were medical terms for his condition—the hours spent playing games at a computer, the inability to get a job, the laughter he heard when he couldn't perform with women. Some days he didn't even go outside. He drew the curtains in his little studio on Havenhurst Street. He sat in the glow of a screen. The money trickled away.

IS THERE NOTHING ORRIN SYKES CANNOT DO?

But there was, apparently, because casting agents turned him down. *"You're not good on camera."* The payoff money ran out. He remembered the laughing face of a beautiful young actress at a swimming party in Beverly Hills. The girl leaning close, green eyes glowing, bikini snug, body filled with vitality. Half-drunk that day, he'd been going on about a wrestling award, trying to impress her. *"You're from where, Orrin? Crystal Lake? You weren't even a big fish in a little pond! You were a protozoa in a little puddle!"* She'd turned away, as if he were already gone.

Now as Sykes reached the Capitol area, the images came faster, like flipping cards. Carol Ann on the phone when he called her from L.A. *"I'm getting married! You disappeared!"* Sykes in Cedars-Sinai Medical Center, blood on his face, but he could not remember why. Sykes waking in a men's shelter to find a skinny guy, pants down, trying to rape him. Sykes in a jail cell. Sykes too humiliated to call Grandfather for money to get home. But finally he did, and did not even hear a dial tone, just a recording. The line was disconnected. He hesitated before calling Uncle Merrill, but knew he had to get out of L.A.

"Hi, Uncle."

"You piece of shit! Your grandfather died asking for you! You ran away from the job! You ran away from Carol Ann. Go fuck yourself. Don't call me again, loser."

Now, in D.C., Sykes got turned the wrong way for a few minutes and steered the Honda along Independence Avenue, past the Museum of the American Indian and the Air and Space Museum. He made a U-turn. The road rose back toward Congress, past bomb barriers ringing the Hubert H.

Humphrey Building, hydrant-shaped concrete blocks designed to block a car bomb. The gaps were large enough for a trillion microbes to float through.

But Sykes was still in the past, remembering the months after that phone call. Each time he'd thought things couldn't get worse, they did. Each time he knew he'd hit bottom, the bottom dropped out again.

Sykes saw himself in a police line-up, but the woman whose purse he'd grabbed failed to identify him. He saw himself breaking the lock on a gas station men's room door for a place to sleep, in Omaha, near a rail freight yard. He saw himself standing in a concrete spillway in Buffalo, gazing at a billboard announcing Warner Bros. Pictures' Academy Award nominees. Sykes a full-fledged member of the academy of failure.

And finally the day it changed. Sykes taking refuge in an old record shop in Albany in a storm, not to buy anything, just to keep dry, standing amid vintage rock albums disdained as old-fashioned ten years ago, but regarded as valuable again. In a record store second chances were contagious.

"You look hungry," a girl's voice said as he stood in back, trying to stay invisible and not get kicked out.

She was pretty: jet-black hair, glistening blue eyes, lean figure, and firm belly visible below the cutoff top. He saw sympathy instead of revulsion in her eyes, kindness where he usually saw dread. Girls had not regarded him that way for years.

"I'm Mariko. You look like you need a friend."

She'd taken his hand as if she knew him, led him outside, just opened the door to her late-model Toyota, unafraid. A miracle. An angel.

"Don't be shy. Get in."

The house where she brought him was filled with wonderful people who gave him a bed, and food, and didn't ask questions. Carla and Fritz, Mariko and Morgan and Shahid. They didn't make him leave. Weeks passed before he blurted out the story, sobbing, and even then they accepted him, gathered around and hugged him and told him he was welcome. He belonged. In that house Orrin met a man who had answers. And in his mind, he was reborn.

And now, heart slamming with excitement, Orrin found parking on 2nd Street, five blocks from the Longworth Building. At one time, years ago, you could park closer, but between the security precaution tire shredders, bomb barriers, and no parking signs, you needed to range farther to find a legal two-hour parking space on Capitol Hill.

He left the car in front of a townhouse. His size eleven footprints filled with falling snow as he walked. A few Diamond cabs cruised Independence, exhaust trailing like breath. Orrin had shaved. His dress shirt was blue and his tie was maroon, the suit gray. His hair was combed and he wore Washington's ubiquitous belted raincoat. He was a lawyer. A lobbyist. The effect was enhanced by clear-lensed, thick-framed rectangular glasses.

The line to get in stretched outside—people stamping in the cold, waiting to go through metal detectors. Longworth filled a city block. Its gray edifice represented the Capitol's

1930s love affair with neoclassical revival architecture, a combo of boxy Soviet utilitarianism with glommed-on Ionic colonnades.

At the security station he watched the Tumi bag float through the x-ray machine. This was the moment when he could be caught, and for an instant he was scared. The bag contained news clips about today's hearing on a religious revival at U.S. Air Force bases. There was also the day's Washington Post, *Tylenol, and a pill vial labeled Cipro, an antibiotic. But it was not.*

It did not cure illness. It created it.

The security guards didn't even open the case. Sykes kept his head down so cameras would not show his face. He walked with a small limp, turned his feet slightly inward. A smart observer watching a tape later and then seeing the real Orrin walking, would not connect the gaits.

The hearing room was packed, standing room only. He stood there for thirty minutes, pretending to listen, because Harlan said that security people would later go over the tapes. He opened the notebook. A Congressman from Buffalo grilled an Air Force major about evangelical meetings at air bases in Colorado Springs and at Creech in Nevada. Daily readings from the New Testament. Lunchtime prayers in a dining area. Hazing of non-Christian personnel.

"Major, wouldn't you say that there is no place for religious proselytizing in an air base?" the Congressman said curtly. "That our Constitution specifies the separation of Church and State?"

The man at the witness table looked up at seven Congressmen and women on a raised dais, and frowned.

"I would say, sir, that at no time were any personnel coerced into participating. Prayer was purely voluntary."

The blood roared in Orrin's ears so loudly that it all was gibberish to him.

The clock ticked toward noon, when the chairman adjourned for lunch and Sykes joined a stream of people heading downstairs to the underground level of the Capitol. It was a maze down there! A mini city. Corridors filled with staffers, tourists, witnesses from the hearings, lobbyists trying to get bills passed or shut down. Orrin saw a post office and a Quick Mart and a dry cleaners. There was a Verizon shop. One tunnel led to the Rayburn Building and another to a little open train taking riders back and forth to the Senate side of the Capitol.

The cafeteria was packed, smaller than he would have imagined. At one table: Iñupiat Eskimos from Alaska, here to lobby against blocking off their entire coastline, polar bear habitat, to development; at another, pro-football players fighting against salary caps. Nuns on the left. Ten guys in AFL-CIO jackets sat in a corner. A Toyota Motor Corp. legal team sat beneath a flat-screen TV showing a Midwest snowstorm. The cafeteria was like a high school lunchroom for the whole country, each table a clique, each group wearing their group uniforms, clerical collars, pinstriped men at the deli counter, logo sweatshirts by the steam table reading, A FETUS IS A PERSON.

"You will want the salad bar," Harlan Maas had said.

Sykes put his right hand in his pocket and palmed the little vial. The blood rushed in his head and his voice, when he ordered a burger, sounded astoundingly calm. The fries

*looked soggy. The burger looked like paper. He had no ap-
petite to eat. He carried the food to the salad bar; shiny bins
offering up red tomatoes and black olives, here a bin of
yellow pineapple squares, there a container featuring freshly
cut rings of red onions.*

*He'd rehearsed the hand movements last night before a
mirror. He was, after all, in public, moving down a line.
This was his most vulnerable moment. He felt sweat inside
his socks. If someone saw him, there would be no question
that he was contaminating the food.*

*All heads swiveled for a moment to the TV on the wall,
rebroadcasting an argumentative part of today's hearing.
As Sykes's tray passed over the mushroom bits, he pinched
the capsule, felt plastic give. He envisioned the mushroom-
colored powder falling on the veggies. Then his legs—as if
by themselves—carried him to a four-person table. He sat
down. From his pocket he removed a small clear plastic vial
labeled* HAND SANITIZER. *He felt the liquid squishing
between his fingers. Stomach churning, he picked up the
burger and forced himself to take a bite.*

*"Remember, surveillance tapes will be scrutinized," Har-
lan had warned him. "Make yourself eat."*

*Sykes finished the burger. Heart slamming in his chest,
he felt a fry ooze down his throat, as if it were a living creature, wriggling and trying to get back out.*

He watched the room. No one went to the salad bar.

*Then suddenly his throat constricted as a cafeteria
worker approached the bar with a rolling cart filled with
replacement vegetables. He was going to take away the infected food before anyone ate it!*

The worker wore thick blue rubber gloves as he replaced some of the vegetable bins in the salad bar with fresh ones. Sykes wanted to scream at him to stop. Not even one person had eaten from the mushroom bin yet. Sykes had to contain himself from launching himself across the floor at the cafeteria worker. But then the worker broke off his activity before replacing the mushroom bin. The attendant rolled the cart away, looking bored.

Harlan's voice, in Sykes's head, said, "Relax, friend."

Orrin Sykes watched a trio of men in expensive suits— including a Congressman he recognized from the TV—step up to the salad bar. Sykes uncapped his bottled water. The Congressman added mushrooms to his salad, then the men carried their trays to the STAFF ONLY area.

Orrin rose and placed his tray with the empties. Leaving the room, he turned back to see a half dozen Amish women, in bonnets, at the salad bar, loading up.

Orrin Sykes walked out of the Longworth Building and down the marble stairs and hit the cold air outside. The weather had turned vicious. The temperature had plunged. A barrage of snowy hail slanted from the sky, smashing taxis, slashing the rooftops of government. In wonder, Sykes recalled that sometimes Harlan Maas sermonized about the ten plagues that God visited upon Egypt when Pharaoh denied the Hebrew slaves permission to leave. The prophet Moses warned Pharaoh that if he did not relent, great suffering would afflict his people. Pharaoh laughed, never imagining that any force existed that was more powerful than him.

Boils. Hail. Leprosy, Harlan said.

The wind blew punishing granules into his face. He tilted

forward against gusts to reach the car. Inside, the noise lessened, and the radio announcer said a worse storm was coming. Today it was ravaging swaths of the Midwest.

"We're in for the biggest blizzard of the decade!"

Orrin had gotten away with it! He was safe! He drove carefully along Rock Creek Parkway, passing sliding cars, a crash, a Chevy idling at a light like a horse afraid to cross water. Washington sent powerful armies ranging across the earth. But it froze with fear if half an inch of snow fell.

Orrin waited until he was back in Northwest Washington to punch in Harlan's number on the disposable.

"Burke is worried about one of his investigators. A man named Rush. I'm sending you his photo," Harlan said.

NINE

===

A QUARANTINED TOWN IS A GHOST TOWN FILLED WITH LIVING
people. The stillness gives weight to air, turns streets into
still lifes, exaggerates any movement at all. Smoke curling
from a chimney seems more ominous than comforting.
Faces at windows drop away quickly, and curtains fall back
in place. Even a stray dog, sensing fear, walks tentatively
down a deserted street with its tail down as a trio of bio-
suited figures knocks on a bar door, the banging sounding, in the stillness, far too loud.

"Go away," called the frightened man inside. "I'm sick
of you people. You're not taking me away!"

"Sir, if we have to break in, we will."

A handful of weathered, sun-blasted wooden homes.
A dozen diagonal parking spots before a motel/gas station
combo. I saw a brown hawk staring down at me from the

flat roof of Gazzara's Tavern. Its creamy feathers matched the dun color of surrounding scrub desert, the dark streaks the escarpments in the hazy distance.

The voice called, "I'm not going to any hospital!"

We'd come into town during a gap between medical team visits, when investigators took samples of blood, hair, fingernails, urine, and probed and examined wall mold, air conditioners, refrigerators, vents.

The screen and wooden slat door opened. Gazzara's smelled of pine sawdust, beer, garlic, and bananas. A hand-scrawled sign by an oval mirror read, OUR SPECIALTY: SPAGHETTI AND ELK SAUSAGE, FRIDAY NIGHTS. Antelope jerky sticks leaned like pretzels in a tall jar. Electric beer signs—RUBY MOUNTAIN ANGEL CREEK AM-BER ALE, TENAYA CREEK—were turned off at midday, below a banner for the Nevada Wolf Pack football team. The sawdust muted the shuffle of our biofootwear. I saw a half dozen empty tables and a pool table and dart board on a wall.

"See my arm? They poke me every six hours!"

Art Gazzara kept the bar between us, like a protective barrier. He looked about forty, balding on top, wearing soiled Levi's and a sweat-stained T-shirt that showed a well-developed chest and biceps, but a pot belly swelling over his belt. Eddie, Chris, and I stood at the rail in our gear, probably looking like aliens waiting for beers.

Gazzara growled, "You have no right to cut us off!"

"We're here to help."

He laughed insanely. Two Gazzaras stood before us, the frightened one and a healthier one in the softball team

photo behind the bar. Before illness struck, he'd been a
sad-faced man with hangdog eyes, large ears, thick brows,
and clumpy chestnut hair that seemed hacked off by a
blind person. He'd not shaved in days. Based on the damage I saw—nose decay, red spots by the mouth, cauliflower left ear—I guessed that his beard obscured more.
No wonder he was angry. *If he's not at the hospital, this
damage is new.*

Eddie kept his hand on his sidearm. But Gazzara's fear
was not aggressive. He was a rabbit hiding in his hole.
Once we were in that hole, his resistance collapsed, and
he became pliant. I didn't need a friend just now. I needed
information.

Had he noticed anyone sick in town prior to two Fri-
days ago? No, he snapped. Had anything unusual happened recently? Had food or drink tasted odd? Had any
illness resembling this one ever happened here before?

"Why did you ask about that Friday?"

"My understanding is," I said, taking a stool to position myself at eye level, "that's when the base people—
first ones to get sick—came in. For the birthday."

"You're trying to pin this on me?"

"I'm trying to figure it out."

He resumed wiping the bar. It did not need cleaning
but he didn't stop. The movement gave him something
to do.

"I don't remember anything *special* about that day, if
that's what you mean," he said.

"Good! Then if nothing special happened that day,
please just go over what was normal."

He polished that bar over and over. His vocal cords sounded unaffected, but I remembered how victims in Somalia had manifested symptoms differently. One person suffered skin damage first. Another, voice loss. There was no way to tell at this point how far the disease had progressed in Gazzara. He'd need to go to the hospital, but I wasn't going to say that yet.

"You want normal? I came down from upstairs—we live there—at ten. I made jerky. Normal! We get hunters on weekends so I keep extra around. I knew there would be a party that night. Crystal already had the cake in the fridge. That help?" he challenged. "Help you figure out what the hell is going on?"

"You never know what can be important. I appreciate hearing about even little things."

His expression soured even more. "I paid some bills. Normal! I cleaned spigots. I got burgers from the freezer. I made lunch for those two weird tourists from L.A."

I felt a sudden throbbing in the back of my head. My lungs seemed to tighten, and for an instant, my breathing slowed. *Tourists were here?* Chris looked shocked. We were thinking the same thing. This bar may have been ground zero for an outbreak. The soldiers would have arrived too late if tourists had been here for the initial infection, if they had then gone blithely out into the world, days ago, shedding the disease.

I felt Chris Vekey come closer behind me.

"I made his elk burger well done. Hers was rare, with crispy fries," Gazzara said. "They're long gone."

"Did they give you their names, sir?"

"I don't require names to take an order."

"Did they say where they were going? Or pay with a credit card?"

That would have been too easy. Food orders were his memory tricks. I curbed my impatience while he recalled clearly that she'd asked for extra pickles. The man had shaken pepper on his fries. But talk? He had no memory of talk, beyond their order. Did he recall the license plate on their car? The kind of car? A rental company sticker or regional accent? Sorry.

"They definitely had two beers each."

"If they said nothing you remember," Chris asked, trying to keep frustration from her voice, "why are you so sure they came from L.A.?"

"Hmmm. Good question. Hmmm. Maybe they *did* say something. Or I just assumed L.A. I mean, most tourists who show up turn out to be from there. Ask Jack Lawrence at the Quick Mart. I think I saw them buy gas. Wait. He's at the hospital with his wife, Millie."

My face had started prickling, and I hoped all that meant was that I was alarmed.

"Mr. Gazzara, did you tell any of the doctors who examined you about these tourists?"

"I might have. I'm not sure. They mostly wanted to know whether I lost power in the freezers, as if I'd serve rotted food to customers! The assholes!"

Eddie shook his head.

We needed to get outside, somewhere where communication wasn't jammed, needed to find out if authorities knew about the tourists. If not, we needed Burke to order an alert. To shotgun a message to state police, health officials, and hospitals. We needed a sketch artist. We needed to search phones, to go house to house and try to ID the pair.

Eddie said, "Someone must have mentioned it."

"No such thing as 'must have.'"

Eddie groaned. "Murphy's Law."

I envisioned a car on a road and a faceless man and woman inside. Then they were checking into a motel, and touching a pen, or one of those punch-button sign-in machines. I saw them in a restaurant, touching a sugar bowl. I saw them at a gas station, handing a credit card to an attendant. I saw them back home in Los Angeles, shaking hands, kissing children, inviting friends over for a drink, ignoring early signs that they were getting sick.

Shit.

"I'll do it," Chris said, and quickly left the bar. The screen door slammed behind her. I heard our Humvee start up outside.

I thanked Gazzara and explained that he needed to pack a bag and get to the hospital. Chris would have him picked up. He started to refuse but Eddie leaned over the bar, snapping out, "You have a wife upstairs? You want to make her sick, too? Or is she sick already?"

Gazzara put his face in his hands. *No, she's not sick.* He looked up. I imagined that in the last twenty minutes while we'd talked, the red patch on his cheek had en-larged. Was that my imagination? For the tenth time today I cursed whoever had ordered the drone attack on the Somali clan fighters back in Africa.

There might have been evidence there—a story, a folktale, a piece of information we might have learned.

Right now we needed to go house to house and continue questioning. But at the screen door I turned back. I'd thought of one last thing. "Mr. Gazzara? Why did you call the two tourists weird?"

"Well, we get tourists in town sometimes," he said, sniffling. "But there's nothing for them here. Usually they took a wrong turn. They stick around for ten minutes, come in for a beer, or soda if they have kids. And go. But those two stayed. Got here in the morning. I saw 'em drive in. Only thirty people live here, so when someone comes, you notice. The weird thing is, they stuck around."

"What did they do all day?"

"I said I noticed 'em, not that I followed 'em!"

He calmed down a little. "Sorry." He scratched at his face, bad idea, and picked at a scab on his lips, another bad idea. But I didn't mention it. I didn't want to interrupt Gazzara's chain of thought.

"Oh yeah! They stayed for dinner. Joined the party right here."

Eddie said, "They knew the captain, you mean?"

"No, they were just here when the food came out. Antelope Italian sausage. My family's specialty. Turned out the parmesan cheese was at their table, so they brought it over, and got invited to join in. I shred that cheese myself. No factory cheese here!"

"Do you have security cameras?" I asked.

Gazzara broke out laughing. "Are you kidding? Look at this place! What do I need security cameras for?"

"Someone must have taken photos at the party."

"Maybe."

Asked to describe the tourists, Gazzara vaguely recollected that the man was on the tall side with long sideburns, and the woman had cropped red hair like the model on the beer tray, but the model was prettier, he said, and the tourist was chubby and sunburned, the way people from up north get when they came to the desert.

"This is a big help," Eddie lied.

"Mr. Gazzara, is there anything I didn't ask about that you think we ought to know? Anything extra?"

"Talk to Mrs. Mitterand. She's in the last house on the left. She said something about those two. She said they were religious nuts."

"Why?"

"I don't remember anymore."

DENISE MITTERAND LOOKED ABOUT NINETY, TINY, WIZENED, PALE, and as cooperative as if the day were normal and we were neighbors she'd invited over for a cold Coke. From the porch of her weathered bungalow, we could see, a half mile off, the concertina wire that sealed Galilee. Chris would be on the phone there hopefully, urging Washington to send out an alert about the tourists.

"Do you want to take blood? Those other doctors did."

"No, ma'am. Just to ask questions."

She was not sick, not visibly. And her mental equilibrium seemed fine. She accepted our precautions as necessary. She was white-haired, delicate-looking. The skin was almost translucent, nose a button, mouth small, forehead narrow, shoulder blades pressing outward, as if her body had been tiny to start with, and time was shrinking it back into thin air.

"The soldiers took away my neighbors, the Lawrences. Are they all right?"

"I'll check when I get back and let you know."

Inside, she offered us ice water and brownies but we explained that we had to decline. She understood perfectly well why. Whatever frailty age had brought her did not extend to her mental faculties. "I guess you can't eat anything in our town just now," she said.

"Yes, ma'am. But thanks."

She sat knees closed on a stuffed sitting chair, in her air-conditioned living room. At her feet lay an old black Labrador retriever, who required a wheeled walker to raise its hind parts. The house was small, clean, and comfortable; an eclectic mix showing foreign travel: kilim throw rugs from Turkey, clay pottery from the Amazon, strung beads from South Africa, souvenirs of not just mileage but attitude and curiosity. She told us she was a retired high school music teacher. Her husband, Al, dead two years, had been a social studies teacher at Indian Springs High. They'd moved west from Saint Louis fifty years earlier, for the desert. Small town and broad-minded, I thought, liking her. Some people adapt to anything. Mrs. Mitterand was old, but she had the ability, that was clear.

I wanted to ask about the tourists but held off at first. Good-hearted people can react defensively if they think you're attacking someone not present. But a few minutes later the conversation swung naturally to that Friday. Denise Mitterand remembered the tourists quite clearly "because of the singing," she said.

"Singing?"

She grinned, as if no emergency was going on. "I'll show you. Sing something," she said.

"Excuse me?"

"Anything. Christmas carol. Popular. Come on!"

Eddie cleared his throat. His voice sounded muffled coming from the suit. He had terrible pitch. He could never carry a tune.

"Jingle bells . . . jingle . . ."

The dog rose quickly, tail wagging like crazy, and raised its head. *"Oooooooooooo."*

Denise Mitterand was up also, faster than I would have thought possible, and she kneeled by the animal, stroking his head. "Are you my boy? My Sinatra? Are you my one? See?" she said. "He does that every time! That's why we named him Sinatra. Like he's the reincarnation. My nephew said we should bring him on late-night TV to do those pet tricks. You try, Dr. Rush."

I sang, *"Dashing through the snow . . ."*

"Ooooooooooooooo." The dog hopped around, spinning in circles, panting from happy effort. We burst out laugh-

ing. It was nice to know that something could still make us laugh. Sinatra looked sad when I stopped singing. He licked my glove, blessed with ignorance of contagion.

Denise said, "That morning he started making those sounds. He can't walk but he hears pretty good. He'll start up if a car goes by with the radio on. I looked out. Saw the couple walking by. I couldn't hear them but their mouths were moving. I thought they must be singing."

"Go on."

"Well! Afternoons, I take a walk in the desert. I can't take Sinatra anymore because the wheels on the roller get stuck in rocks. So I leave him here. I can still do two miles. Exercise helps me sleep."

"The tourists were in the desert," I guessed.

"I was coming up a rise. I heard them."

"Singing."

"Yes, some religious song. When they saw me, they stopped."

"Why do you think it was a religious song?"

"Why? Well! I didn't hear all the words. I guess it was the cadence, slow, you know, like Gregorian chants. *Chanticleer. Adorate Deum.* Beautiful, relaxing music. Calms you right down! I used to have my students listen to it. Not exactly what they were used to."

"They were singing Gregorian chants?"

"No, it was *like* that but *wasn't*. It was English. But it had that same somber, what's the word? *Repetition!* Like a liturgy. What you'd hear at a mass, not exactly something hikers go around singing."

"A liturgy," I said.

"But different. I heard a few words. Something about prophets smiting evil." She scrunched up her wizened face, trying to remember. "The first prophet . . . the sixth . . . then they saw me and stopped."

"Did you talk to them?"

"They seemed nice. I asked what they were singing."

"What did they say?"

"That's funny! I don't think they answered. They were very enthusiastic, though, asking about the town, the rocks here, the old mine. But they didn't actually answer about the singing. A little spacey but nice. My husband, Al, used to say you get all kinds out West. Dissatisfied people. He called the highway to California the Charles Manson Trail."

"Did they happen to identify their church group?"

"I didn't ask. I like music, but I'm not big on religions," she said. "My ancestors were Huguenots. Protestants murdered in France. Music is peaceful, but in the end"—she shuddered—"too much religion makes people fight."

OUTSIDE, I TURNED TO EDDIE. OUR PHONES WERE USELESS IN TOWN because of the jamming, so we had no idea if anyone had been trying to reach us while we were here, if Chris was having success reaching Burke.

"Remember those two guys in Somalia, singing?"

"Weren't they singing about prophets, too?"

"All religions sing about prophets."

"Chris should have been back by now," he fretted.

She'd been gone for forty-five minutes. And over the next ninety minutes she *still* did not return. But we were occupied, making rounds of houses, talking to a family of six: a postal worker, who looked healthy; a retired uranium miner, healthy; a Vietnamese immigrant, who was coughing; a brother-sister team, who lived together and gave me the creeps, because of the way they sat, hip to hip. The sister showed deterioration around her nose.

Our notebooks filled with jottings, our recorders with frightened voices; a mélange of facts, figures, and impressions. Nothing in particular stood out.

"Two hours," Eddie said, yawning. "Where is she?"

"More importantly, where's Broad Street?"

Broad Street was our shorthand for the London corner where the science of disease tracking began. It was the epicenter of the worst cholera outbreak in that city's history, which ravaged it in 1854.

At the time, the finest medical minds believed that illness came from vapors, *bad air*, which they called miasma. When cholera struck, bringing vomiting, leg cramps, rampant diarrhea, and fatal shock, *bad air* was, as usual, blamed.

But a physician named John Snow wasn't so sure about that, so he went door to door, asking questions, drawing maps of the spread. He asked locals about their eating and drinking habits, travel, hygiene, symptoms.

Eventually he realized that every single victim drank water from the Broad Street public water pump.

Snow's idea about the pump was revolutionary. At first he could not convince authorities that the disease was spread by a well. But finally they grew so desperate that, at Snow's urging, they removed the handle from the Broad Street pump, and the epidemic ground to a stop.

Now Eddie and I sought the modern version of Snow's pump handle. We trudged house to house, asking questions and answering complaints.

—*My kids like Fruit Loops, but all the soldiers are giving us is Cheerios.*

—*My reading glasses broke.*

—*No one is collecting our garbage!*

An exhausting three hours later, we'd confirmed that *every initial victim* had been in Gazzara's on that Friday night. From there, the pathogen had spread to some people and bypassed others.

"It breaks out in Africa first," Eddie said, frowning. "Then here. You think there's something in the drones themselves; some component, some chemical they're carrying, maybe a drone crashed . . . what do you think, One? The drones?"

"Something they ate or drank."

"Why?"

"Two initial outbreaks in groups. But no contact between them, no supplies moving between the groups. In Africa, no air vents, no air-conditioning. But everyone eating the same food at the same time and in the same place every day. Here, people fell ill after a group meal."

"If it's canned, there will be outbreaks. It could be anywhere."

I shook my head. "If it was randomly shipped, there would have been more outbreaks by now, I'd think."

"Who did it, then?"

"Who has access to both places?"

"Plenty of people hate the drone program."

It should have been a positive moment, an inch of progress at least, a theory. We'd reached the last home on the street. A hand-scrawled sign nailed to the front door read, SICK. GONE TO HOSPITAL. PRAY FOR US. We'd been spared another interview. I felt some relief.

"Where the hell is Chris?"

As if in answer, here came Humvees, three of them. Only one had been needed when we'd been brought into town.

"Too soon for the next medical check," said Eddie.

"They're coming pretty fast," I said.

When the Humvees reached us and the first small bio-suited figure emerged, I saw it was Chris; but spilling after her from the other two vehicles came troops made beefier by combat biogear. Their weapons were held ready, and from the stiff, wary way the soldiers eyed us, with a sinking feeling I realized that they were not here for the citizens of Galilee, but for us.

"Burke wants us out of here," she said.

There was no doubt that something fundamental had changed.

"What's wrong, Chris?"

"Please put your notes and recorders in a ziplock. Hand them over to Sergeant Leachy. We're out," said Chris. "Me, too."

Eddie tried to make light of it, voice easy, but body stiffening. "Oh? Something we did?"

Chris stared back, disconsolate. "Yes," she said. "We're all under arrest."

TEN

The cell was five by eight and lacked a window. Meals—roast beef, boiled potatoes and milk, eggs and soggy bacon—were inserted through a metal slot but I had little desire to eat. Light came in two varieties, artificial glare and red nightlight. The guards were silent extensions of the cinderblock. No reading material allowed, no television or radio, no explanation of why we'd been flown to Camp Pendleton, California, kept separate, and buried in a brig.

"Give me a hint. Why are we here?"

The air smelled of regulation. Flesh and blood seemed out of place in this steel and concrete world, where rule substituted for reason, and the National Anthem, played over loudspeakers, for talk.

"What the hell happened in Galilee?"

But the only hints I got were buried in the nonstop

questions rapped out by two sour-faced FBI agents who refused to let me call Ray Havlicek in D.C. Had anyone in Somalia mentioned Disneyland? Had I visited a certain Internet café in Nairobi? Had I ever experimented with strains of leprosy? Was I a Washington Redskins fan?

Let's go over your records and memories one more time.

I'd locked up men myself over the years. Watched them pacing on closed-circuit TV as I softened them for interrogation. Now, worse than the isolation were the muffled announcements coming through the walls, barely audible and hinting at emergency. Leaves were canceled. Marines were being ordered to pack.

"At least let Chris call her daughter!"

The red light turned white. Was it morning? I heard Chris, out in the hallway, begging someone to, "Let me make one call? For God's sake, she's alone! She'll be frantic! What's the matter with you people? She's a kid!"

Did we stumble onto something someone wants hidden? Damnit, if someone would tell us the problem, we could help figure it out.

The light turned red again, so outside, it was night. Or was it? Was it midday, the sun strong, yellow, hot?

I marked time by counting times when I heard the National Anthem, with trips to the bathroom, by beard growth. I did exercises to maintain bodily rhythm. The workouts filled the cell with sweat and testosterone. I avoided the cot unless I wanted to sleep. When I did sleep, I dozed fitfully, and did not recall dreams upon waking. You measure victory in small increments, and in this case, that meant the illusion of some knowledge of time, some sense of control.

Doing crunches, I went over events in Somalia and Galilee. I did push-ups on my fingertips and replayed interviews but nothing special came to mind. The guards refused to give me pen and paper so I filled in imaginary checklists in my head. I reached the story about the tourists in Galilee, singing. I heard boots stop outside my door and the lock clicked open.

"Get up!" the guard barked. "Hands behind your back."

I blinked at a dazzling California sun as Eddie, Chris, and I were driven to the airport, where lines of Marines boarded a half dozen Galaxy transports, huge jets capable of long-distance flight. Apparently we were finally permitted to talk. As we stood on the tarmac, a short, exhausted-looking major sauntered close, looked me over with disgust, and said, "So you're the one who started this."

"Me? What are you talking about?"

He moved off, shaking his head. Chris was staring at me now with something resembling fury.

"What did you do, Joe, when I was making that call?"

"We just talked to the old lady."

"Sure you did. Those Marines are carrying biogear," she observed. Her face looked ragged, white, drawn, but her eyes still burned with fierce intelligence and frantic worry for her child. *This is not a drill*, a loudspeaker announced.

I said, "Aya's a smart kid. She'll be okay."

"I hope so."

We were strapped by guards into a row of four out-of-place economy class–style airline seats bolted to the fuselage in back, amid chained-down Humvees, netted food crates and med supplies and ammunition. Our seatbelts had locks on them. Our handcuffed wrists lay in our laps. Eddie said, "I can't wait to hear the safety announcement. What to do if we go down?" as the massive rear hatch groaned shut and four powerful jet engines roared to life, so we had to raise our voices to talk. At least we had a porthole, a view of sorts, natural light.

Chris said, "I called Burke to tell him about the tourists. He never even came on the line."

They'd dressed us in quilted jackets against the chill. She smelled of sweat, cheap shampoo, and prison soap. Eddie smelled like a locker room. I probably did, too. Chris said, "Usually I talk with Aya every night. We've never gone more than four days without talking, and that time I was in Indonesia, in the jungle."

Eddie asked, "Does Aya have someone to stay with?"

"My sister. In Reston. But Aya's independent. She may stay at the loft in case I call. She'll barrage Burke's office with calls. She'll be scared."

"She's a resourceful kid," I said.

"Don't even go there," she snapped, and turned away.

"How many days were we in there, Joe?" Eddie said.

"Too many. A week?"

Eddie was staring out the window, looking slowly north to south, east to west, frowning.

"Uno? Take a look out there."

At first I didn't see it. I saw Camp Pendleton South dropping away, Munn Airfield, California scrub desert, I-5 Interstate running north to Long Beach and south to

San Diego, and the ribbon of gray Highway 76, heading east.

"No commercial planes," Eddie said. "We should be seeing airliners in holding patterns for San Diego and Long Beach. Check the roads, One. There's almost nothing moving at midday. And anything moving is trucks."

My stomach began to throb. The sky was empty of even contrails, in an area normally rife with traffic. All the transports climbed and headed inland, *surprise number two*. Pendleton Marines were *Pacific* Marines, and I'd assumed that deployment would carry us in that direction, or maybe south toward Mexico, cartel country, maybe west toward refueling in Hawaii, maybe on to Asia, or up to Canada, for joint maneuvers.

Eddie nodded, seeing my face. "Right, Uno. East. Hey, look who's here! Ray Havlicek!" I saw the tall, lean FBI agent threading his way around the mass of equipment that blocked our view forward. He wore field colors, dark blue and letters in gold. The former college runner looked wan, pale, but freshly shaven. His expression changed from a grim disapproval when he eyed me to something softer and more sympathetic when he took in Chris, his old girlfriend.

"Boy, did you screw up, Joe," he said, one hand on the fuselage for balance as the plane hit an air pocket.

"Ray, what did I do?"

"I'm not the one to tell you that."

"Why are you here?"

"Supervising."

"How long were we inside?"

He snapped, "For once, shut up. I'm going to put you on with Secretary Burke. If you know what's good for you, listen to him and listen well. People have been fighting over you for the last eight days in Washington. The shit's hit the fan everywhere."

Ah, we've been in prison for eight days.

"Take my advice and act contrite, Joe."

"Act contrite *over what*?"

"Like you don't know?"

He produced a tablet and wedged it between my cuffed hands. His thumb hovered over the Activate button. He seemed torn over whether to give further assistance, and then his better side won out. "Joe, apologize and answer questions, without asking any back. This thing went all the way to the White House, but in the end, it's Burke's call."

The ex–Dallas police chief's face swam into focus as the transport hit another air pocket. His expression had the cold focus of a Roman statue, flesh as marble, eyes rock hard. The lines at his eyes and mouth suggested pressure. Rage almost pulsated off the two-dimensional image on the little screen.

Burke finally told me what my infraction had been. It was so stupid that I wanted to laugh.

I said, "The what? The *sandwich*?"

"ANSWER YES OR NO, COLONEL. WERE YOU SPECIFICALLY TOLD that patients were not to eat cheese products? Then, in complete disregard of that, did you order the hospital staff to allow her to have the outside food?"

I looked around as if expecting the entire scene—the transport, the Marines—to turn into some massive joke. Food? This was about food? I knew I was not supposed to anger Burke further, but the petty infraction made me hot. I started to demand to know what food could have to do with anything important, but Burke cut me off as cleanly and surgically as a drill sergeant reaming out a new recruit.

"*You decide what is important. You*, as usual, did not think of consequences. I warned you. I told you clearly and concisely what would happen if you violated orders. Do you remember that conversation, Colonel?"

"Yes, sir."

"You recall my exact words?"

His words had been *Leavenworth prison*, a place which, for any reason, is no laughing matter. "I do recall."

"But you couldn't listen, could you? So let me tell you what happened because *you*, once again, thought you knew better than everyone else. *You* violated orders in front of the nurses. *You* gave an order that resulted in a nurse turning on a bedside telephone in a patient's room!"

Uh-oh, I thought, remembering what I'd told that nurse. *Do whatever you have to do. Get that woman her meal.* I'd assumed that the nurse would make any phone call herself. It had never occurred to me that the nurse might let the patient make a call.

"That's right. The patient gets the phone. The nurse was called out of the room."

Now I was the one feeling sick, seeing where this was going.

"She didn't call the restaurant, sir?"

"Oh, she did, after she called her brother, who works at the *L.A. Times*. Within the hour the White House was getting calls asking about the quarantine of an American town, outbreak, terrorist attack."

Oh shit.

"The *Times* got hold of satellite shots of the base, troops all around it. They sent a reporter in a car. The car got turned around at a roadblock."

Oh shit, shit, shit.

"It went viral. Let's see, Joe. *White House hiding outbreak! Possible airborne pathogen! FAA stops all flights to Nevada and Southern California!* And, Joe, because this happened at a military base, you should have seen the foreign reaction, Korea, Iran, they *loved* it. *U.S. violates germ warfare treaty!* We were set to release the news *our way*. It was going to be orderly. Every blogger in the world got it early. We lost control before it even started."

"I'm sorry."

"I'm not finished. *Next*, and we still can't find who is doing this, *Wikileaks* released transcripts of our meetings, with a message of support for patients locked up in Nevada. And support for the gallant doctors who risked their lives while I tried to stop you from feeding the patients!"

"Christ."

"Demonstrations at bases. Governors calling for calm. Half of Congress screaming for an investigation. No one believes the President."

"Nobody's claimed credit, sir?"

He snapped, "Half the world thinks we did it to our-selves."

"Sir?"

"What?"

"*Was it* one of our programs?"

"*You dare to ask me that even now?*"

"Sir, it is a legitimate question."

The screen showed him going purple. He said nothing for an instant. I'd gone too far. Then he said, very slowly and distinctly, "It is not, and has never been, one of our programs."

Then I realized the even greater consequences. I saw why there had been no air traffic when we took off, why roads below were clear. "Sir, it's not just that news got out. It's spreading if you're shutting down flights and roads. How bad is it?"

"Seven more cities. Over eleven thousand dead. Over forty thousand infected so far and climbing and CDC predicts even that number could explode."

It was cold in the plane but I had begun sweating. He was right. Completely right. I'd made the panic worse because of a stupid sandwich. I had not kept my mouth shut, or if I had to open it, I'd shown disdain for those in control. I'd made the President's job harder, Burke's job worse. The news would have broken anyway. But now my bosses had to fight rumor and blame as much as disease.

"I warned you," Burke said. "Ray! Put Chris on!"

I looked to my left, where she'd gone paler at the word *spreading*. She was thinking about Aya. The truth hit us simultaneously. *The troops in this plane, the troops in the planes around us, were quarantine or protection troops, moving east. To where? Chicago? Denver?*

"I'm disappointed in you, Chris," Burke said.

"Yes, sir."

"You were there. You stood right beside him. You could have stopped it, or tried to, and you said nothing."

"I have no excuse."

"Goddamnit, Chris. I trusted you."

"I know. I know. You did. You're right."

"You said you'd control him."

"I did."

This was the instant he'd decide our fate. Maybe her agreeing saved us. Maybe Burke liked her to start with. Maybe he figured, if I lock away one, I have to punish all. Or maybe he was the type who wanted to spend his rage verbally. In any event, I felt the smallest hint of his fury subsiding, the faintest whiff of second chance.

Considering what he could have done to us, what he did was small.

"You're off the unit," he said. "Rush? Nakamura? You'll work as medical doctors for the duration. I need doctors with experience and that's the only reason you're not in jail. If you come out of this alive," he said, "we'll talk about what happens to you next. No travel. No investigations. You'll be at a hospital, and if you don't stay there, I don't care how much experience you have, I'll bury you. Rush? You did just what I expected. Chris? You didn't, and for that, I'm sad. You're not qualified to supervise anyone. You're out. You'll be local, too. No investigation work."

He clicked off.

I asked Ray, "Where are we going?"

"Don't you know? *You* helped write the protocol, Joe. *Never use local troops in an outbreak. They may have relatives in town and be reluctant to use force.* We're headed for the capital. It's under semilockdown."

Eddie frowned. "My family is in Boston."

"You should have thought of that before. It hit Capitol Hill, FedEx Field, even some kids from a high school science fair. Washington's the worst."

Chris gasped. "*Which high school?*"

"Wilson."

Chris groaned and leaned forward and tried to draw her hands in to protect her stomach. The cuffs prevented that.

Ray Havlicek sighed. "This isn't the way anyone figured it could happen."

"It never is," said Eddie.

"Wikileaks? The war games never included Wikileaks. Fucking Wikileaks!" said Ray.

Chris whispered, "Aya."

Chris was shaking in her seat.

ELEVEN

JUST BEFORE THE FOOD RIOT STARTED, ADMIRAL GALLI WAS SHOW-
ing us around Washington.

The troops had turned it into a different city. The
buildings were the same, but the feel was like one of those
permanent Hollywood sets, where the mood changes each
time a different film is shot. One day love on the rooftops.
The next, same rooftops, but revolution. Until now, D.C.
had existed as a stage for power or calculation, importance
and glitter. But the few faces in the street, mostly covered
by surgical masks; the shuttered shops; idling police cars;
and ambulances stationed in traffic circles beneath snow-
dusted statues of dead generals—it all reflected raw fear.

"Airport and Amtrak closed while they revamp travel
rules," Galli said. "We're assigned to Georgetown University Medical Center. The school is evacuated and the
dorms are for doctors and their families. Burke's the city's

Outbreak Czar. But the thing is spreading faster than our ability to track it. Joe and Eddie, emergency room. Chris and me, logistics."

"I want to help," Aya said. "I'm a good researcher, Mom. You said! And I'm good with science!"

"Just being here with me is help," said Chris.

"I mean *really* help!"

Chris put her arm around Aya. She and Chris sat beside me in the backseat. Chris was still trying to get over the shocks: terror that Aya had been sent to the hospital, delight when she'd found out that Aya had been released, pronounced clean, and then both joy and fury when the admiral showed up with the girl, outside protected hospital grounds. Galli saying that he'd refused Aya's pleadings—*let me come with you*—initially, but Aya had argued, wept, followed him to his car, said she could get sick just as easily inside the grounds as out, and Galli—a soft touch sometimes, and overconfident in the military's ability to do its mission sometimes—*protecting citizens*—had given in.

"I can't believe you took her," Chris had raged.

"Mom, don't blame him. I made him do it."

"You are fifteen years old and he's an admiral, for God's sake. What if the car breaks down! There's a twenty-five percent mortality rate if you get sick!"

Galli soothed, "There are troops all over. She won't be in contact with the sick. If we break down, we call for help, Chris. The city is quiet and she was frantic. She needed to see you. She's had a bad time."

"Don't tell me what my daughter needs!"

I liked Aya. She was smart and had guts. Despite Chris's rage, the mother and daughter had broken into happy tears when they saw each other. The admiral had ordered us to stay in the car, no matter what we saw outside.

Washington's avenues were as quiet as back alleys. Government buildings, State Department, Interior, open to essential personnel only, on a limited schedule, with most federal workers on "temporary holiday." Marines on corners. Museum Row deserted; the Air and Space Museum and Smithsonian Castle as empty as on Christmas. No tourist busses at the monuments. Gas stations shut by mayoral order. A tenth of the usual traffic on the road.

Galli said, "Once we get to the hospital complex, you need a pass to get out. Anyone working with patients has to get a blood test once a day."

"What about *my* family? Can I bring them in?" asked Eddie. His voice was low and anguished, and he stared out the window at unplowed slush on the road.

The admiral sighed. "Boston's clean, Eddie. Not one case so far."

Eddie mumbled, "So far."

Galli smoothly steered his 4Runner along downtown. K Street was semideserted at midday, when normally you'd see reporters, lawyers, and lobbyists. The White House looked like a giant mausoleum. Lafayette Park, always the site of one political demonstration or another—*U.S. Out of Afghanistan*—was empty. Aya divided her attention between the sights and a tablet on which she relayed news or rumors or sent nonstop reports to friends. She was a fountain of unofficial information.

"Japan just blocked all flights from the U.S.," she said.

"When the news broke, there was lots of crazy speculation," Galli said. "That the Bible Virus is worse than Ebola. That it spreads by touch, air, food. That thousands more deaths have been covered up. Creech wiped out. Tehran responsible." His gray eyes flicked to me in the rearview mirror. "Some people on the Hill want war."

"Against whom?"

"Whoever they wanted to fight before this started."

I asked, "The *Bible* Virus?"

"That's what Fox TV dubbed it."

"It's not a virus. It's bacteria," grumped Eddie.

The admiral shrugged. "Most people couldn't care less about the difference. All they want to know is if they'll catch it. The talking heads had a field day. Conspiracy theories. Maps of worst-case spread. Twenty thousand dead. A hundred thousand. Double by Thursday."

"For all we know, possible," said Eddie.

More cars than usual were parked by the Islamic Center on Mass Ave.—ringed with guards—and outside the National Cathedral on Wisconsin. I stared at the retreating towers of the cathedral, an idea tugging at me, but it remained out of reach.

Galli wore a blue Northern Outfitter parka and Merrill boots and a stocking cap. He looked fit for a man in his sixties, and had the heat dialed up. We hit a bump and his glasses went askew. But he was one of those guys who carried quiet authority. He didn't need a uniform to wield it. Exiled in his own city, he had lost no stature. Plus here, half the time, out of power means comeback. You take people seriously when they're out of power. Galli's personality was so strong that you'd take him seriously if he was lying in bed with a fever.

"I'm fired, but not dead," he said. "We're not just going to sit around. We can call Havlicek or Burke or at least reach out to their staffs if we think of something. And Aya's pretty good at social media. Hell, she learns more from that little tablet of hers than I get from CNN."

Aya beamed. "See? I can help!"

"Building morale, Admiral?" Eddie said sourly.

"Can the tone, Marine."

"We're out of it. And how will we find out anything if we're stuck at the hospital anyway?"

Galli studied him in the mirror. Eddie was sick with worry for his family. "No, Eddie, we're private citizens, who can do what we want, off duty, as long as we don't get in their way. We still have minds. We can think. Frankly, I'm not thrilled with the direction the investigation was taking. They're not looking beyond the usual suspects. They made a decision early based on outbreak pattern. Americans in a Muslim country. Air base. Soft targets. *Islamic terrorists.* I'm not saying they're wrong. But they're sticking to scripts. No harm in considering other possibilities."

Eddie said, "In case you forgot, Secretary Shithead said stay put and keep out of it."

"Watch your language," snapped Chris, glancing at her daughter, who was texting and only half listening, or maybe listening to ten things at the same time. "Aya, you must have been terrified when they quarantined you."

The girl looked up. "Teddy Simon got sick, his whole family did. So all the kids got hauled into Georgetown. But they released us after two days, except for Teddy."

"How is Teddy?"

Aya teared up and looked six years old. "His whole family is dead! They went to that Redskins game. All the first cases were there!"

We reached Connecticut Avenue at the Calvert Street Bridge, and beneath the lion statue I saw three figures beating up a fourth lying in the snow, right in the open. The attackers surrounded him, their boots angling back and forth. They wore ski jackets and balaclavas with surgical masks over their mouths. They were bulked-up thugs or self-appointed militia, or maybe they were using the emergency to pay back a debt, or rob. It looked like the city wasn't as orderly as Galli said.

"Stop the car!" I said.

"No. We're uninfected and we keep it that way."

"You can't just leave that guy!"

"Call 911," Galli said, hitting the accelerator.

I reached for the knob and the admiral cursed, but he skidded into a U-turn and ordered, "*Stay in the car.*" Chris shouted, "No!" Galli bumped up onto the sidewalk and headed for the attack. He pressed his palm against the horn. Despite his anger, I think he was glad we'd made him turn around. Or maybe I fooled myself. I'd done a lot of that lately. Now he was trying to stop the assault the way you'd scare off wild animals.

The attackers stopped and looked up, looked at each other, deciding what to do. One man raised his middle finger at us, but they all turned away, started running, and as we approached the guy on the ground, I reached for the door handle again, to get out.

Galli snapped, "I'll leave you here!"

Chris was screaming at me, "Goddamnit! You don't listen! What's the *matter* with you?"

My palms went up to soothe her. "Look, I know you're upset. But at this point the actual odds of infection are smaller than—"

"The *odds*? The *odds*? *This is my daughter!*"

Looking back, I saw the figure on the ground stirring, lifting a bloody head up. I saw him take something from the snow and put it on his head, before pulling his hood over it. A woven skullcap. So he was Muslim. My last glimpse of the man showed him trying to stand.

Chris had me by the jacket and was shaking me. "*What is your problem?*"

"Mom, Joe was just trying to help," said Aya.

"You stay out of this!"

The admiral sighed. "Watch committees, Joe, although that's the first one I've actually seen. People looking for sick ones to beat up, chase out of their neighborhoods, or vent rage. Most people they attack aren't even sick. A swollen face from a bad tooth. A guy with a limp. *Bible Fever*— that's what I call it—initially resembles twenty things that are completely normal. A shaving cut. A pimple. Vigilantes have put more people in the hospital than disease."

"This bad after only eight days?" I said. My chest throbbed where Chris had grabbed me. She'd been right, I saw, aghast. If I'd gotten out, I could have infected them . . .

"The first two days were tolerable. Then food in stores started running out. The numbers doubled in places. Then, thanks to the President's warning, people stayed home and the spread slowed a little. Wikileaks made it clear to the world that we don't know what the disease is, that the CDC is running around, lost. The numbers got worse. So by day three some truckers refused to drive in shipments. Plus the images on TV. Every new case reported. More cities!"

The admiral's eyes met mine in the mirror. I said, "I'm okay. I won't do it again."

Upper Reno Road—normally busy—was as still as at 5 A.M. on a Sunday morning. Galli zigzagged back to Massachusetts and pulled to the curb outside the Homeland Security complex by American University. It's an old Navy base, lots of redbrick buildings inside a double fence. Unlike other sites we'd visited, this one was bustling. Parking lot filled. Staffers moving up and down outside stairs that separated different campus levels. Guards in balaclavas at the drive-in booth gazed out at us, hands on their sidearms. The impression was effectiveness. But impression, half the time, is mirage.

Homeland Security is like a company on the stock market whose value goes up during disasters. That doesn't mean it is a good company. It's the only one there at the time.

"I never liked this place anyway," Eddie said. "It's a goddamn maze. Building H next to Building B. Rooms with three numbers. You need a roadmap to get around, and half the signs are intentionally wrong. Nobody trusts anyone else in there."

The guards didn't like seeing a car idling outside the grounds, even beneath a two-hour parking sign. Three of the guards started toward us.

The admiral pressed down on the accelerator and we headed off and I could see one of the guys with binoculars pressed to his eyes, recording our license plate, but fence cameras would have already done that.

Galli said, "Look, everyone's tired. We'll have a good meal when we get back. There's food on campus but a shortage elsewhere. Supplies distributed by social security number. Even numbers can purchase twelve items today. Tomorrow, odd. The mayor's trying different systems. New one every day."

"Twelve isn't a lot," Aya said.

"Hopefully, as more food arrives, portions will get bigger."

"I bet there's plenty for the high and mighty," Eddie grouched, nodding toward Capitol Hill.

The admiral looked surprised. "I thought you knew. The President's gone. Congress. Supreme Court. The city woke up and our national leaders had left."

Eddie gaped at him.

Galli said, "Protocol 80 is in effect."

PROTOCOL 80 HAD BEEN THEORETICAL, LIKE A HUNDRED OTHER exercises that we'd worked on at the Center for Strategic and International Studies on Rhode Island Avenue. And late some nights, on Grant Street, at the admiral's home. *My own kitchen cabinet*, he called us as we pored over plans detailing food delivery in an outbreak, medical deployment, ways to distribute vaccines; ways, with transportation crippled, to move investigators around. Protocols for interviewing people who feared even the doctors sent to help.

Protocol 80 had been originally designed after the terrorist attacks of 9/11, when lines of limousines had clogged roads out of Washington, filled with evacuating VIPs; heading for Mount Weather, the underground installation near Berryville, Virginia: 600 acres up top, 650,000 square feet underground, filled with lodging, radio and TV studios, even three 25-story buildings in which evacuees would live, work, and eat while running the government. In a nuclear attack, the limos would have been decimated. So we'd streamlined the process for those deemed crucial to get out.

"Continuity of government."

Eddie quipped morosely, "Someone should have done this to Congress years ago. Quarantined 'em!"

In my head I saw what must have happened a few nights ago. I saw FBI agents working with lists of those to be evacuated, spreading out, knocking on doors, hustling frightened men, women, and children into idling cars in lightly falling snow. *Continuity of government* involves saving more than the President, Congress, and nine justices of the Supreme Court. It means saving the computer files of taxpayers, a Treasury Department midlevel clerk who heads up disability check delivery for veterans, the anonymous crucial cogs in the social security system, a scientist working on a secret chemical program, a spy master getting information from a high-level official in Iran, a rotating list of those deemed important at that particular moment, updated annually, a cast of thousands to be saved to guarantee the survival and operation of the Republic.

"Alpha," I said. "Principal leaders to Mount Weather."

"Beta," said Eddie. "Congress to Raven Rock Mountain, Pennsylvania," which was another underground facility.

I saw more. I saw evacuation beginning in a two-story colonial in Bethesda, a Federalist home on Capitol Hill, a three-bedroom suite with lights blazing at 3 A.M., shared by three Congressmen, a Watergate apartment discreetly paid for by a billionaire Secretary of Housing and Urban Development for his mistress, who was asking, as he pulled on his pants, *Why can't I come, too?*

The chosen would be hustled to designated triage hospitals; Georgetown or Walter Reed—for blood tests. *Healthy folks, step this way!* Babies crying. VIPs, some angry or scared, some meek and helpful, a few demanding special attention, which had happened in drills.

"Third group, Charlie," said Chris. "Those remaining in the cutoff capital. Us." She couldn't resist adding in a voice low with fury, "Ordering Las Vegas sandwiches."

Her eyes swiveled to me. I wanted to tell her that I was sorry. But *sorry* is a pathetic word. It means nothing. It means too late, too stupid, too slow, too fatheaded.

"I'm not mad at you," she said. "I can't believe I didn't stop you."

"You couldn't have stopped me," I said, trying to make

her feel better. But it didn't come out right. It sounded aggressive. It sounded like I was telling her that I would have ignored her order even if she'd given it. And then I realized that I'd meant exactly that.

She turned red as Eddie's hand reached out and pointed. "Holy shit, One. It's a riot!"

"It's like Baghdad," I said.

Aya said, eyes huge, "But it isn't Baghdad. It's here."

BAGHDAD LOOTING HAD LOOKED DIFFERENT, OF COURSE. THERE we'd seen women wearing black chadors and veils carting baskets of oranges from a busted-up fruit stall, donkey carts loaded down with televisions, parades of men in short-sleeved shirts and sandals pushing hand carts piled with furniture, Lada taxis bulging with thousand-year-old museum artifacts, rogue soldiers rolling ergonomic office chairs out of a smashed-up furniture store.

Here we were stuck in traffic outside a supermarket parking lot where denizens of upper-middle-class Northwest Washington—high-level bureaucrats, lawyers, doctors, even a Congressman's wife I recognized—fanned in a stream from the smashed Safeway windows with their gloved hands clutching bulging plastic bags, knapsacks, or cardboard boxes stuffed with loot. So many cars were trying to exit at the same time that traffic was blocked, the air filled with screams, shouts, horns.

"Must be one hell of a big sale," Eddie said.

I saw an elderly woman fall and a man reach and pick up her mesh bag and run. I saw a Nissan Altima smash into a backing-up Mini Cooper. I saw kids, roughly twelve-year-old identical twins, dressed in matching ski parkas, running between parked cars and carrying identical bulging canvas bags that read, SAVE THE PLANET. I saw a man in a police uniform breaking up a fight, but then I realized he wasn't doing that; he was carrying bags. He disappeared on foot as the first faint sharp edge of sirens became audible through the screaming and barking of a lone Labrador retriever in a car nearby.

"Hey, Eddie! That's Kendall Bates," I said, recognizing a looter.

Bates was a State Department analyst who sat in on planning sessions at HS. Now he was dressed out of the movie *Fargo*, calf-high furred boots, ballooning green down parka, furred flap-eared hat, surgical mask slipped down off his panicked face, and his breath frosted as he threaded parked cars, heading our way, hauling bound-up starter fireplace logs in each hand.

I put my mask on and rolled down the window halfway and called, "Kendall!" He stopped, heaving, wild-eyed, hearing his name, but needing a moment to place my face. Recognition replaced confusion. Bates was medium-sized with a largish head, small eyes, and arms that seemed long, partly due to the too-short sleeves of the parka, partly because the wood weighed him down and made him slump, simian-like.

"Colonel Rush," he said in his official State Department voice, as if we sat in his office over coffee.

All around us people were running. Bates looked down at his starter logs like a kid caught stealing chocolate bars in a candy store. He stood mortified and frightened, as if I'd arrest him, which I could not. I just asked, ignoring the loot, "What happened here?"

He relaxed slightly, seeing that I wasn't trying to stop him. I recalled that one time during a conference—*bioterror in the new century*—when he'd made reference to having three children, and living near here. He probably owned one of the big Victorian homes nearby, expensive when heating bills came. He was probably planning on stuffing those chemical logs into his fireplace, trying to provide heat or light, or maybe he was trying to get ready in case the power went out.

He said, gasping from the running and the cold, "It was orderly. But then one woman started an argument by the vegetable section, *it's mine*. And then someone else started yelling about needing more food than other people. The guy had six children. How come childless couples got the same amount as him, he shouted." Kendall's voice sped up. "Someone pushed me. Then Frank Carlyle, my neighbor, broke for the door without paying . . . and . . ."

He was heaving. A man with an overcoat open to a clerical collar ran by, carrying a stuffed shopping bag.

"The front window shattered. I guess someone threw something."

The sirens—multiple ones—sounded very loud now.

"Get away, Joe. They're shooting looters on the news. But I'm not . . . my neighbors . . . *I'm not a looter*." He looked down at the stuff in his hands. He said, "I'm just me. I'll come back and pay later. I will!"

"Sure you will," Eddie said in a flat voice.

Washington as truncated capital, an instant, enormous, upside-down refugee camp for the once elite. I stared at Kendall Bates. Somehow he looked smaller than usual. Part of his job—until now—had involved facilitating food aid delivery to suffering nations. I recalled that one time in a meeting he'd complained that more guards were needed to keep aid from being stolen in southern Sudan.

"There must be order!" he'd said.

He ran now, past the priest, who was trying to unlock his car, Kendall's boots leaving skid marks in the clumpy snow.

My eyes fixed on the priest. The man's hands were shaking so hard he couldn't get the key in the lock of his Mini Cooper. *A priest.* I stared, fascinated, as the admiral got us moving.

What was it about a priest? No, that wasn't it. It was something else, *triggered by* the sight of a priest.

"You said to try other avenues," I said thoughtfully to everyone in the car.

Chris, hearing my request, grew quiet and then, shocked, erupted in a mother's rage. "I can't believe you're even thinking this! *I just can't believe you!*"

I could not fault her. But if we went to Georgetown, we'd be stuck there, so I kept my eyes on the admiral's in the rearview mirror. "Were you serious about what you said, sir, about other ideas? Little detour? Or not?"

"Oh, let's go!" enthused Aya.

"Not a chance," snapped Chris.

"Admiral?"

"No."

I wasn't surprised. And I was ready. I said, "You said

we had to get to campus, but we don't have a mandatory arrival time. Once in, we can't leave. But we're not there yet. So how about *this*?"

ORRIN SYKES SAT IN HIS HONDA OUTSIDE THE GEORGETOWN UNI-versity Medical Center and fretted. Harlan Maas had told him that Joe Rush was supposed to be stationed here, had landed hours ago, and was on his way, but the man had still not shown up.

"I want confirmation that he goes inside," Harlan had said.

The campus had been sealed by Marines, and anyone entering the sprawling complex had to use the Reservoir Road entrance. The grounds included a collection of red-brick hospital and research buildings, med offices, restaurants, a parking garage, the adjoining college campus, and the Jesuit cemetery. McDonough Arena was set up to handle overflow patients. Student and faculty housing had been given over to med staff.

Sykes observed the grounds from a block lined with small attached townhouses, each featuring an identical patch of snow-dusted lawn. An assembly line of private shared student housing or midlevel bureaucrat homes.

"Once he goes in, he can't get out without a pass, and he won't get that pass," Harlan had assured Sykes.

Sykes had to go to the bathroom. He used an empty mayonnaise jar and sealed it back up. He sipped water to stay hydrated. All vehicles bound for the medical center formed a line on Reservoir Road that inched toward the sandbagged guard booth. The line moved so slowly that Sykes could see inside the cars.

Why wasn't Rush here?

Then Orrin saw him.

Sykes pressed the glasses close. A Toyota 4Runner had just taken up position as eighth car in line. The back window was down. Rush was unmistakable, arguing with the four other people in the car, and Sykes matched the face of Eddie Nakamura to Harlan's provided photo on the front seat. There was Chris Vekey. And the admiral. And some kid.

· Sykes felt relieved. They were here.

But suddenly the 4Runner halted, the argument grew animated, the back door opened, and Rush got out. Then everyone else got out, too. The argument was continuing. Sykes's consternation grew.

The four other passengers stayed on the sidewalk. Rush climbed back into the 4Runner, into the driver's seat.

Nakamura tried to open the passenger-side front door, but Rush locked him out. Nakamura knocked on the window, clearly asking to get in.

"Shit!" Sykes said.

The other passengers began walking toward the drive-way entrance, digging in their bags or coat pockets for ID.

The 4Runner broke from the line, made a U-turn, and headed back along Reservoir Road, toward central George-town. Rush was the only one inside now.

Sykes put the Honda in gear and pulled out from his space and rounded the corner, skidding slightly on slush.

He could see the red brake lights on the 4Runner half a block ahead, where Rush turned onto Tunlaw Road.

Sykes reached for the encrypted cell phone as he followed Rush back up toward Wisconsin Avenue, in lightly falling snow, making sure to keep a block behind. He could not get closer without risking being spotted, since there were only two vehicles on the road.

It was easy to hang back and keep Rush in sight. Three minutes later, it became clear where Rush was going.

Rush figures things out, Harlan had told Sykes.

Uh-oh, Sykes thought, reaching to call Harlan Maas.

TWELVE

=====

"WHAT DO YOU WANT TO KNOW ABOUT LEPROSY?" THE VERY REV-
erend Nadine Huxley asked.

She was dean of the National Cathedral, America's
intersection point between God and government. Here
lay saints and soldiers, tributes to both heaven and Earth.
I'd entered the gray Gothic building beneath the gaze of
rooftop gargoyles including the movie villain Darth Va-
der. He stared out beside traditional demons and mon-
sters, set there after children across the nation voted to
add a modern icon to the collection. Inside, stained glass
windows depicted religious figures but also the Apollo 11
moon mission. Altar pieces in Saint Mary's Chapel showed
the mother of Jesus near a statue of Abraham Lincoln,
whose visage, in pennies, lined the floor. The Humanitar-
ian Bay honored Saint Francis of Assisi and also George
Washington Carver, who'd studied peanuts. Last time I'd

been here, I'd attended the funeral of astronaut Neil Armstrong. Diana Krall had sung, "Fly Me to the Moon." Not exactly religious fare.

Now I stood with Nadine Huxley in the Miracle Chapel, beneath the window mosaic depicting lepers. Nadine was a small, trim blonde in black, with a clerical collar snug against her white throat. We both wore surgical masks. Behind us, all three rows of seats were crowded with worshippers, some of whom were clearly sick and should have been at the hospital. A man walked in behind me and knelt. His lips moved. I felt his eyes shift to me. He was praying.

I told the dean, "So far we've been concentrating on medical aspects. I'm curious about leprosy in religion."

I knew Dean Huxley from her previous posting in Boston, where she'd returned from a leprosy mission in India, and addressed staffers at the Wilderness Medicine Program on treatment in poorer countries. I'd found her a brilliant and sensitive person, who managed to mesh a deep appreciation of the Bible with one of science. She had no problem mixing the biblical and the political, the biblical and the scientific. That's what I wanted to hear now.

"Leprosy?" she said. "In the Old Testament, it is basically a punishment. The word itself is a translation from the Hebrew *tzoraat*, or 'smiting.' Moses asks Pharoah to let his people go, allow Jewish slaves to exit from Egypt, and he touches his chest as a threat, as if he's leprous. Leprosy was punishment for *lashon hara*, slander. When Miriam mocks Moses, she is punished by God with leprosy.

Tzoraat is often in the Old Testament. Read Leviticus. It's all over the place."

"As a punishment," I repeated.

"For ridiculing God's messenger, or message, yes."

"And in the New Testament? The same?"

There were many more worshippers here than usual. Some watched Nadine. Others were engrossed in prayer. Smarter ones wore surgical masks and gloves against infection. Others ignored precautions, which was stupid, considering that this place drew the sick. I saw couples holding hands, parents who had brought children. What I saw was undoubtedly repeating itself in towns and cities all over the country. Churches, mosques, and synagogues would be hosting a steady stream of terrified supplicants, seeking divine help.

Above us, in windows, lepers knelt before Christ, frozen in colored glass. The art commemorated events considered divine and, like Bible Fever as Admiral Galli called it, allegedly violated the laws of nature. Twenty-two panels showed impossible events, made true by the Lord. Jesus walking on the sea. The healing of the blind, the man with dropsy, the demonic, lepers.

"In the New Testament, leprosy is cured by prophets. It's an affliction, not a punishment," she said. "In Latin, '*Et cum ingrederetur quoddom castellum, occurrerunt ei decem viri leprosy, qui steterunt a longe.*' 'And as Christ entered a town, ten leprous men met him, standing at a distance . . .'"

I noticed that some of the people who had been praying were now listening to us. Some stared outright.

"Can we continue this somewhere else?" I asked.

"Are you here officially, Joe?"

"Not exactly."

"Then we stay here," she said, "for them."

I sighed. "You said that in the Old Testament, leprosy was punishment for mocking God or his prophets. Have you ever heard of the Sixth Prophet? A person? A book? A mention? Anything at all?"

"'The Sixth Prophet'? Why do you ask?"

"I'm not sure. I'm just asking."

"Well, there are so many ways to answer that, so many prophets. Oral ones. Written ones. Minor ones. A prophet is an oracle of God. A prophet's primary duty is to convey the holy word. In the American Orthodox Church, Micah would be the sixth. He prophesied the birth of the Savior. In the Mormon Church, Joseph F. Smith was, I believe, its sixth prophet. Islam has twenty-five prophets. Abraham is sixth. Where are you going with this?"

"I wish I knew."

"Is there a connection? The outbreak and prophets?"

I tried to remember the exact words that the two men in Somalia had been singing. I couldn't. I said, "I never knew there were so many prophets."

She laughed. "Well, in three thousand years of history, you get a big list. Saint Anthony was a patron for Saint Anthony's fire, thought to be leprosy. Saint Bernard of Siena cured lepers. Saint Damian died afflicted. And those are so-called real prophets. There are plenty of false ones, coming out of the woodwork all the time. Cult prophets. Visit any asylum, you'll find a dozen prophets."

"So Old Testament, punishment. New Testament, not."

"Nothing's that easy. Jacobus de Voragine was arch-bishop of Genoa, thirteenth century. His writings charged that Emperor Constantine was punished by God with leprosy for persecuting Christians. So while the official version was cures, even churchmen pointed fingers."

"Of all the diseases, why did this one stand out?"

Dean Huxley sighed. "Even into this century, leprosy victims have been shunned and stigmatized. Shut away. Mocked. It's a cruel, cruel disease. Leprosy was considered a test by God. *Mithraism* may be the earliest remaining human religion, Joe. It is still practiced in some places. It's thirty-five hundred years old. Mithras was a god, prin-cipal rival to Christ for five hundred years. The movement had similar sacraments. Adherents called their priests 'fa-ther.' Early Christians attacked Mithraic cult temples, smashed their statues, destroyed their graveyards, killed believers. Many scholars believe that if Rome had not become Christian, today Mithraism would be one of the principal religions on Earth. What's the difference be-tween a cult and a religion anyway? Some thinkers say the only difference is how many people belong."

She looked sad, not because Christianity had won out, but because suffering had taken place.

I asked, "What did Mithraism have to do with lep-rosy?"

"Well, they had a sanctuary in France, near Bourg-Saint-Andéol. They regarded the spring there as having healing power. In the middle ages they brought people suspected of having leprosy there, stood 'em up by the bank, and had the town barber bleed them. They'd mix the blood with the spring water. If the blood remained red and liquid, the suspect was pronounced clean. What are you staring at?"

In some ways, the year might as well have been 1200. The pews might have been filled with peasants and dukes. The expressions on the faces around me were probably as similar to those long-dead people as the DNA inside them, and the bacteria multiplying in their bloodstreams.

"The window," I said. "The lepers. Leprosy and religions. I'm thinking about what you said."

Nadine said with some delicacy, lowering her voice, "Joe, you look tired. Eddie called a few weeks back, and told me that you spend too much time alone in the woods."

"Eddie is an asshole."

"No, he's not. You know, Joe, the French writer André Malraux wrote that everyone is really three people: the one you show the world, the one you think you are, and the one you *really* are."

"So you know who I am but I don't?"

"I would never be that presumptuous."

"The world was simpler when Malraux was alive."

"It was never that."

"Oh, I think you'll agree that we face a few new complex problems just now, Nadine."

"Technically, yes. But in the end, complexity is something humans dream up to deny truth."

I appreciated the concern but the preaching irritated me, especially now. "I'm not going to play this game so you can feel better, Nadine. There are more important things to do."

Unfazed, she said, "You don't believe in God anymore?"

I shook my head. "Oh, I do. That's the problem. But he and I made a deal."

"Which is?"

"I agree to keep making the choices he throws at me, and he agrees to keep me away from love."

"What does one thing have to do with the other?"

I saw Karen, dead, in an abandoned house in Alaska. I was startled to have that image switch to a vision of Chris Vekey, which I pushed away. "I've killed people, Nadine. I'd do it again. Eddie thinks I feel guilty about it but he's wrong." I poked my chest. *I signed the deal here.* I said, "No more dragging in other people."

"Joe, we both know that you can't make deals with him, he doesn't work that way, and if you think you have, you're fooling yourself."

"All kinds of new things seem to be going on."

IT WAS IMPOSSIBLE FOR ORRIN SYKES TO HEAR WHAT JOE RUSH and the dean were saying. He'd knelt only eight feet from them, but they spoke in low voices, and the prayers around him were loud. Sykes wished he could get closer, but that might draw Rush's attention. He'd hoped that the cathedral would be one of those places where you could stand on one side of a room and, through weird acoustics, hear whispers on the other. You were always reading about *whisper corners* in castles or cathedrals.

There was no whisper corner here.

The prayers fell silent for a moment and Sykes watched Rush. Through the quiet he heard a single phrase.

The Sixth Prophet.

Sykes rose and looked down at the worshipper beside him, a heavyset jowly guy wearing a Washington Redskins hat and a jacket. He was a football fan and that had been his undoing. The condiments had been infected before Sykes arrived in Washington, during a game against the New York Giants. Hundreds of people putting mustard or ketchup on their burgers and hot dogs had consumed the bug. Orrin saw sores on the man's lips. The man had to know what was happening. He was staring up at the depiction of Christ. Sykes could read the moving lips, "Save me, save me."

Sykes thought, with real compassion, *After you die, you will change into something new.*

Sykes got to his feet and, with a backward glance at Joe Rush, made his way back down the nave and past the redwood-sized columns and beneath the soaring V-shaped ceiling, past the Woodrow Wilson Bay, where the remains of the Twenty-eighth President were buried. Past the Lee-Jackson Bay, which depicted scenes from the lives of U.S. Civil War generals. Past the Folger Bay, where windows honored eighteenth-century explorers who opened the American West.

Outside, the snow had thickened, and fell heavily, and Orrin Sykes left rapidly filling tracks as he made his way back toward the car. Rush was still inside. Sykes called Harlan, who went oddly silent when he heard the report.

Sykes was unaccustomed to detecting any sign of doubt in Harlan. But when Harlan spoke, it was with the same soothing tones he used day to day back home.

"He *asked* about the Sixth Prophet, Orrin?"

"About the term. The words."

"He's alone, you said. Major Nakamura isn't there?"

"No."

"There's nothing in the reports I saw about this. No guard with him? Private car? You said you saw him arguing with the others in the admiral's car?"

"I don't know for sure. I think I saw it."

"Did he phone anyone?"

"Not that I saw."

"Did he mention Columbia County?"

"I couldn't hear well. Everyone was praying."

Harlan muttered something bitter, which Orrin could not make out, then said, "He was told to stay out of the investigation. *He's supposed to be out!* And he's still in the church now, but you left?"

"I thought you'd want to hear this right away."

"Right. Of course. *But why is he asking? Does he know something? Or is he fishing?*"

Harlan gave Orrin instructions then. He knew that what he requested was risky, but it was necessary, he said. "If there's a way to talk to him, a way to pick his brain, that would help us very much, Orrin."

"But there's people going in or out every few minutes. And you never know if someone will appear."

"Remember those things you did in Iraq? That you confessed? I told you then there was a reason for everything, there's a reason you learned those skills. You must call upon those skills now. A skill is neither good nor bad by itself."

Orrin had a vision of a cement block house in a village. Of an Iraqi tied to a chair, screaming as Orrin did things to him. The man had been nothing more than a thief who worked for a rival gang. Orrin had tortured and killed that man to find a thousand gallons of diverted lubrication oil. When he was done, even his socks and the space between his toes had been soaked with the man's blood.

"I'll try, Harlan. But if it's not possible?"

There was no hesitation in Harlan this time. "Kill him, Orrin. Find out what he's up to or not, but I don't want him back at that hospital. We have to hope he's the only one, of all of them, who may be figuring this out."

Orrin Sykes clicked off and, dwarfed by the massive cathedral up the hill, sighed and missed Harlan. He missed the people back home. His friends. He wanted to go home.

It would be simple to walk up to Rush and just pull a trigger, but Harlan had asked him to try to do more.

There has to be a way, thought Orrin.

Far up the driveway, in the dusk, a lone figure appeared on the cathedral steps.

Rush?

THIRTEEN

BACK IN 1980, AT THE HEIGHT OF THE COLD WAR, THE FBI COMMIS-
sioned a study by Stanford psychologists to predict public
reaction to a biological attack on the United States. Aca-
demically titled "Probability Analysis of Mass Fear Among
Certain Populations," the study used as a premise that an
unknown enemy had released a rapidly spreading infectious agent in the United States.

"Our purpose is to assist decision makers in designing
effective policy," the authors wrote after crisscrossing the
country for months, taking surveys.

I'd read the report, one more attempt to mask anarchy
as controllable. The researchers had driven from city to
city, administering five hundred true-false or multiple-
choice questions to sixth graders in Little Rock, Montana
convicts, Ohio steel workers, welfare moms in Oakland,
migrant farmers in California, Wall Street brokers, corn

farmers, teachers, long-haul truckers, bank clerks, house painters, heart surgeons.

If law enforcement in your city ceased operating, and you were ill and knew you were infectious, would you:

a. lock yourself in your home
b. attempt to relocate to a possibly safer area
c. consider the use of firearms justified
d. go to a designated hospital

The dryly written report predicted an initial phase of mass confusion, during which, "eighteen percent of people will panic, while 23 percent willfully ignore health announcements and refuse to take precautions, not believing that the illness is infectious. Seven percent will flee, believing that safety lies elsewhere. Four percent will secure their homes, hoard food, even attack strangers. Between 2 and 5 percent 'will turn to crime,'" the summary stated, as if prediction were fact. "We expect a brief period of mass confusion but general cooperation, followed by rapid descent into anarchy, and an abandonment of all essential services. Therefore, we recommend a quick establishment of martial law, and the temporary closing of mass news outlets in order to minimize confusion and promote a common agenda."

Which had not happened.

I stood on the steps of the National Cathedral with an encrypted cell phone in hand, knowing that I was once again going to anger Chris Vekey. I saw in my mind's eye the frightened worshippers at my back, kneeling, praying, lips moving, eyes staring at the miracle windows inset into gray stone. I didn't need a ten-million-dollar report to confirm the obvious—that the illness was in the initial phase, and things would worsen if it wasn't contained.

In 1980, when that report was written, our government had, for all its faults, still functioned more efficiently than under the unstable collection of extremists who currently kept the nation in gridlock. I punched numbers into the phone, readying arguments. But Chris didn't answer. The person I really wanted to speak to did.

"Aya, did you mean what you said about wanting to help?" I asked.

"Yes, Joe." She sounded breathless, eager.

"Put your mom on the phone, please."

I explained to Chris that I could use a researcher to replace the staffers Burke had pulled from the investigation. Aya could access social media with ease. She could surf the Net probably better than me, or half the adults I knew. She could check backgrounds on people, public records, at least. She could monitor news reports. She wasn't a pro, but she was competent, and I needed all the help I could get.

I took her silence for serious consideration until she said, "Only hours ago we were told to stick to the medical end. Are you out of your mind, Joe? If she looks into things, they can backtrack what she did on her computer. Then she's in trouble, too."

I argued into cold silence. I had not forgotten. I simply wanted Aya to look at public records, not government ones.

"You're not dragging her into this."

Chris hung up.

I started down the driveway. At its foot, the block was deserted. Lights came on in some small homes, but residents in others might have left the city, as they were dark. I was preoccupied, thinking that once I returned to the hospital, I'd be busy with patients, and conducting even the most basic Internet searches would be difficult.

It was so quiet here that I heard my footsteps on snow, heard the distant organ start up in the cathedral, and the muffled swell of voices came through the revolving door as someone else went in or out. It was the daily 5:30 P.M. evensong. Men and women, books open, voices raised. A pair of headlights came on down the block.

The choristers, singing.

I thought, *Two locations. Africa and Nevada. Two pairs of strangers. Two outbreaks. One song.*

As I left Woodley Road and walked onto the small side street where I'd parked the 4Runner, my phone rang. I saw it was the number I'd just telephoned. My spirits rose. I hoped it was Chris, calling back. I was wrong. It was Aya.

"Joe, I heard what you asked. I want to help. Mom went out. I'm alone in our room now. They put us in a student dorm. I can keep a secret if you can."

Go for it, I thought.

I asked her to get from Eddie the names of the two grad students in Somalia who had been singing about the Sixth Prophet. "Try to find background on those guys. They're from the State University of New York at Albany, they said. Maybe you can access the school website. Try to find any phone numbers. Home addresses, family. Departments. Maybe we can call one of the faculty members at home."

"Duh! I know how to look up things. It's not like I'm five years old, Joe."

"Don't personally contact *anyone*. Stay on the computer. If nothing comes up, just stop. Move on to the next guy."

"Sure."

"This all stays between you and me."

"Of course. If I tell Mom, she'll kill me."

"She'll kill me more than you. Also, look up *the Sixth Prophet*. I don't know who it is, or if it even means anything. *The Sixth Prophet*. Check links with disease. Or religions. Any references over the last five years at all. Song lyrics. Online sermons. Prophecies. Try Galilee. Cults. Collect it all."

"Thanks! I'm going crazy without something to do!"

"And, Aya, don't forget what I said about—"

She cut me off, her disdain making her sound exactly like her mom. "You don't have to tell me twice. *Don't tell anyone*. You know what Mom said? She said if she was a man, a dad instead of a mom, you wouldn't have gone against her wishes. Joe? Is that true? You don't respect women as much?"

"Maybe we should forget this," I said, but I also wondered uncomfortably if Chris had had a point.

"No!" Long pause. "Um, I, I better tell you that, uh . . ."

"Tell me what?" I asked, a drumbeat of alarm beating in my head.

She blurted out, "Burke knows you're not here, at the hospital. He knows you left."

"How?"

There was silence. Then, in a smaller voice, almost a child's, she said miserably, "Someone told them."

I was vaguely aware of the kiss of snow on my face. I asked who told them and she didn't answer. I heard jagged breathing. She was learning about choice. I think understanding the consequences of choice is what distinguishes childhood from adults. Suddenly I understood that her tortured breathing *was* her answer.

"Your *mom* told them?" I whispered into the phone.

Aya started babbling. "She was afraid for me! She got jailed last time you did something! She was scared we'd be separated, Joe, and she *argued* with Mr. Burke that you were right. She took your side! You should have heard her! Fighting for you, Joe!"

"Fighting for me. I see that."

Christ, I thought. *Burke knows I left. There might be soldiers on the way here right now. Judging from what happened in Nevada, I might never get to see Burke if they take me in. I might never get to tell anyone except a prison guard anything.*

"Joe, she was shouting and she never does that. Don't be mad at her. I shouldn't have told you. But I think they're after you. I can't believe I said it. I'm such an idiot. I didn't know what to do."

"You did right," I soothed. "I'm not mad at your mom, or you. Your mom was right. Absolutely right," I said, thinking, *Fucking asshole fucking you didn't even tell me* . . . I said, "I understand. Thanks for the heads-up. Aya, why don't we just forget that you and I ever talked."

"No! I'm going to help you!" the poor girl said. She clicked off.

A wave of futility hit me. I was dragging people I cared for into things again. Chris was right. *What's wrong with you, Joe!* I called back but Aya didn't answer. The truth was, Chris had done the sensible thing if she wanted to make sure she stayed with Aya. Burke might wait for me to return before lowering the boom. He wasn't stupid. He just hated me. It would be stupid to waste manpower by sending troops after a doctor who'd temporarily absented himself from a hospital.

What had I learned anyway?

Nothing really.

Go back and throw yourself on his mercy. Damnit, Chris. All you had to do was shut up and I would have come back.

Either way, no good.

I rounded the corner and turned onto the small side street where I'd left Galli's 4Runner. It was darker here as a streetlight was out. Who was I kidding anyway? I'd gone from depending on trained researchers to begging a fifteen-year-old kid for help. And the fifteen-year-old, almost instantly, had started questioning everything I asked her. I could no longer see the cathedral. I was almost at the car.

I saw, in my mind's eye, exactly how far I'd sunk.

I'd fallen victim to the delusion of feeling essential, Washington's principal disease. I was tired. I needed to get to the hospital and ride out Burke's anger and *see patients, be useful*, instead of imagining I had answers that everyone else had missed.

Still, I thought, *maybe I can convince them. Maybe when I tell them about the Sixth Prophet, they'll at least check it out. But what will I say? I don't even know whether it means anything, or if it is a dead end.*

Where the hell had I put the car keys?

Then I saw the vandalism. Four cars in a row were tilted sideways, toward the middle of the street. Someone had gone down the line and punctured tires, two on each car. Two flat tires meant my spare would be of no use.

Of all the times for this to happen, I thought.

Then the stranger appeared up the block.

"GODDAMN KIDS. THEY GOT YOU, TOO? I CHASED THEM AWAY ON Woodley Road. They were slashing tires there, too."

The man had walked up to me as I was trying to call the admiral's road service 800 number. The admiral's GEICO help sticker was on the window, but when I punched in the number, a recorded voice told me that service was "temporarily suspended" due to the national emergency.

I clicked off. The man and I stood ten feet apart, slightly farther than the usual distance for polite conversation, but with sickness spreading in the city, that was, at best, the probable new norm.

"Kids," I said.

"Yeah. Teens. Just going car to car, laughing. I hope they didn't get my car, too. I'm at the end of the block.

I'd offer to help you with the spare, but," the guy said, as if embarrassed, "everyone's nervous about infection."

"I understand. Anyway, I've got two flats. The spare won't help."

"All the gas stations are closed."

"I know."

"You live near here?"

"I was heading over to Georgetown Hospital."

"My father is there," the man said, taking one step closer. "He got sick at the stadium. They won't let me see him. They won't tell me how he is. Are you sick, too?"

"No, I'm a doctor. I work there. I'm sure the staff is doing their best for your dad," I said.

"Hey, I recognize you," he said. "You were in the cathedral, praying."

I squinted in the dark and realized that the man might be the same guy who'd come in while I was talking to Nadine, and who had kneeled in the Miracle Chapel. I saw a bland face below a stocking cap. The snow-dusted jacket covered an average-sized man, maybe thirty years old. No accent to speak of, except helpfulness. A man who, like any normal stranger, showed a combination of courtesy and wariness that was understandable on this particular night.

"My dad phoned me two nights ago and said his lips were tingling, then he said he had sores on his nose. He said he thought he had the Bible Virus. I told him to go to the hospital, like the TV says."

"That was the right thing to say."

The stranger started to walk away. Then he turned back.

"Oh hell," he said. "Nobody helps anyone out here. They're all scared. I guess I could drive you to the hospital. It's only a couple of miles. You're not sick, are you? If you're a doctor, they wouldn't have let you out of the hospital if you had symptoms. Don't lie to me. Are you sick?"

"I'm not. I can walk it. Don't worry."

The man continued to stand there awkwardly, torn between the Good Samaritan instinct and survival. He made up his mind. He even took a half step forward. His left hand stayed in his jacket pocket, rummaging for keys, I guessed.

He said, "No! You're risking yourself to help people like Dad, and I won't just leave you here like a hypocrite who goes to church and then ignores the needy." The man laughed wryly. "I'm Robert Morton. I was just asking God to help my father. I swore if he did that, I'd be a better person. Maybe you're a test," Morton said. "From God."

"I doubt it. But thanks for the ride."

"Well, only if my tires still work. Let's check."

"I THOUGHT YOU SAID YOUR CAR WAS ON THIS BLOCK."

"It's just around the corner."

We walked in the opposite direction from the cathedral. We reached a section where three streetlights were out. We stayed six feet away from each other, proper plague distance, in the middle of the street. The wind seemed stronger on this block and piled snow in irregular mounds on front lawns.

"Have you doctors figured out how to cure the Bible Virus?"

"I wish."

"Still no idea where it came from? Fox News says terrorists spread it, but nobody knows if it came from a lab or not. Wikileaks says the White House blames Al Qaeda or ISIS."

"We don't know that for sure," I said. "By the way, it's not a virus. It's a bacteria."

"There! My car! Hope *my* tires are okay. Ah! All good!"

I wondered if I'd be arrested when I got back to the hospital. I considered not going back but then where would I go? I hoped that Secretary Burke would understand what I'd done, but I wasn't particularly comfortable with throwing myself on his mercy. Maybe I should phone the admiral or Ray Havlicek, tell them what I was thinking, tell them about the singing and the Sixth Prophet and afterward try to approach Burke.

"Why were you in the cathedral?" Robert Morton asked as he unlocked the passenger door on his car. "Is someone in your family sick, too?"

"No. I was just . . . curious about something."

"You must be pretty religious," said Robert Morton.

"Not really."

"I'm going to put on a surgical mask while I drive. I don't mean to be rude. I hope you don't mind. I mean, we'll be sitting close together. I don't have an extra. Sorry."

"No problem. It's smart for you to do that."

His Honda smelled of wet wool and air freshener, strong chocolate, and surprisingly and pungently, I detected the long-familiar mint/banana/gasoline tinge of Hoppe's Number 9 gun bore cleaning solvent. Robert was probably a sports shooter. Or he kept a firearm for self-protection. Considering the emergency, it was probably a good idea. In fact, I wished Burke had not ordered my own sidearm taken. The Hoppe's smell was strong, which told me that Morton had either spilled some recently, or that a freshly cleaned firearm was in the car right now.

"You law enforcement or a sports shooter?" I said.

His head swung toward me. His eyes, above the mask, looked surprised. I tapped my nose. "Hoppe's."

He laughed, his eyes merry.

"My wife says it's her favorite cologne," he said. "I'm a sports shooter."

"What model?"

"Glock 9."

I waited for him to volunteer more. He glanced at the glove compartment and sighed.

"It would be dumb to drive around without it, but I don't have a concealed carry permit. I'm not supposed to have it outside the house. Hey, Doc, don't turn me in when we get to the hospital, okay?"

"No problem." I relaxed a bit. Still, there was something about being in a car with an armed stranger. He turned the ignition key and we half jerked, half slid from the parking space, swerved on slush, and made the corner as the car slippery-climbed Woodley Road toward

Wisconsin. I saw more people exiting the cathedral. The radio was on and played a show tune, from *Annie*, so softly that it was almost part of the engine hum. Annie sang, "Tomorrow!"

The dashboard was dirty and the heater threw more dust into my face. The right-hand windshield wiper moved faster than the left, scratching against the glass. Robert Morton drove with his gloved right hand—closest to me— cupping the wheel. The left hand lay on his lap, by his door. The ride should take seven to ten minutes, even going slowly due to storm and road conditions. There were no plows or salters out. Other than an occasional police car or Humvee, we were it.

"My neighbor says this disease is the apocalypse," said Robert Morton. "Punishment from God."

I snorted.

"He says it's like the ten plagues of Egypt. He says we've lost sight of who we are," Morton said.

"Everyone's got a theory."

Morton nodded. "Me, I agree with Fox News. This is an attack by ISIS or Al Qaeda. Fox says the President may order air strikes. Do it. Go get 'em, I say."

"That's a little premature."

"How can you say that?" He seemed agitated. "The President knows the whole picture, knows the things we don't. Shit, if Franklin Roosevelt would have attacked Tokyo before Pearl Harbor, we never would have had World War Two, that's what I say. But Roosevelt did nothing. Ever think of that?"

"I hadn't," I said.

"I'm *serious*," Morton said, nodding. "First the Bible Virus hits us in Africa. Then the air base. Then, suddenly, it's in all these cities. No-brainer. Attack the fuckers."

"It's not a virus," I repeated.

"Whatever. They hate America. They want to destroy our way of life. What are we supposed to do while they slaughter our wives and kids? Nothing?"

"Trying to figure out what's happened isn't nothing."

He looked offended. Our argument, I thought, was probably going on all over America at this very moment—in homes, on street corners, even deep beneath the earth at the continuation of government campus in Virginia. Robert Morton snapped, "Well, who the hell *else* attacked us if not *them*?"

"I'm just saying, if you hit the wrong people, you can *cause* your apocalypse, start a whole religious war. Drive a few more thousand people to jihad."

I looked down at the seat divider and saw a couple of plastic cassette holders lying with some change. The tapes were labeled. HARLAN AT CHRISTMAS. HARLAN, SUMMER SOLSTICE. Robert Morton pumped down on the accelerator in agitation and the car lurched and settled down. His eyes in the mirror were hard. "What are we supposed to do then? Stand around and watch our families die? I'd think that a doctor who sees such suffering wouldn't be so liberal. Liberals! Always a reason to do nothing! They make me sick."

"I'm not saying do nothing. Just get proof first."

"What were you talking to Dean Huxley about?"

We were in Glover Park, the high ground abutting

Georgetown, a historic neighborhood where the Army
Signal Corps was founded during the Civil War. He made
a right turn off Wisconsin onto 39th and a quick left onto
Tunlaw, a narrow graded street that seemed more suburban
than urban. We passed a row of stores, the back side, that
is; rear of a liquor store, barbecue joint, sushi place. We
skidded in silence down an incline and into a residential
area of small homes and townhouses, and descended toward flatter, row-house-lined 37th Street.

A Humvee filled with Marines passed, the helmeted
faces gazing out at us sternly. Extra patrols had been in-
stituted around the hospital complex. Lights in most
homes were on. I glanced at Morton and for an instant
our eyes met. There was something off in the car. His
friendliness on the street had become something harder.

"The dean and I were discussing leprosy," I said, answering his question in a mild tone.

"You mean, like, where it comes from?"

"Leprosy. The Bible. Religion and the disease."

"Is she an expert on that?"

I saw a third plastic cassette sticking out from under the
two others. I picked it up. It had a label scrawled on white
tape on the side. The label said, HARLAN, EASTER.

"Yes. Who's Harlan?"

"A really great singer."

His eyes flickered and watched me put the cassette
down. We came up on a two-car accident that must have
happened since I'd passed here before. The wreckage normally would have been cleared away, except with city services interrupted, the smashed-in van and pickup remained

where they'd collided, half up on the curb, jutting into the road. No people around. Falling snow coated the cold hoods. We veered around wreckage. It reminded me of Baghdad again. Baghdad in D.C.

Robert Morton doesn't seem too concerned about catching the disease from me.

"Did you know that in the Old Testament, leprosy was a punishment?" I asked, pushing.

"The Old Testament? Punishment? Really?" Morton said.

Once the first thought in a chain appears, the next one rolls out. *A row of tires gets punctured. A Good Samaritan appears out of the blue and asks questions. But how would he have known I was at the cathedral to start with? He wouldn't. I'm being paranoid.*

"Yes, in the New Testament, it's cured," I said.

"We could sure use a few miracles now," Morton said.

The man has a gun in his car. So he's the suspicious type to start with. But why would a suspicious person offer a stranger a ride during an infectious outbreak, and risk contagion? I bet Robert Morton's fingerprints are on these cassettes.

I shrugged, and said, "You said it! The lepers appear before Jesus. Jesus touches them, and they're cured! I wish we had something like that now."

"He didn't cure all the lepers," Morton said. "Just the ones who deserved it."

"What do you mean?"

"Well, look at those windows in the cathedral. The men he cured were believers. It's not like Jesus cured bad people. You had to have the right things in your heart."

The friendly curiosity in the eyes was back.

I need to get some sleep, I thought, and said, "You're right. I had not thought of it that way."

"What else did the dean say?" he said.

The gun oil smell seemed stronger. We warn ourselves of danger in different ways. I wished I could remember more of the song that I'd heard in Somalia, and which also may have been sung in Nevada, where the outbreak had started. I couldn't remember more. Anyway, I was a poor singer. I couldn't carry a tune. But I recalled the cadence of the music, even if I could not summon specific notes. Four low notes followed by two high.

Hell, try it.

I looked out the window, as if bored or tired. I tried to reproduce the musical notes in my off-pitch voice.

"Mmmm, mmmm, mmmm, mmmm, MMMM MMMM!"

"That a song?" he asked.

"Was I humming? Sorry! My girlfriend says I do that all the time. Drives her crazy. I don't realize I do it. The tune? Just something I heard recently. Catchy."

"Heard? Heard where?"

"Overseas and out West," I said, a bland enough answer if he didn't know what I was talking about, but a threateningly specific one if he did.

"Overseas?"

"In Africa. I was stationed there."

We were less than a mile from the hospital, crawling along on a deserted street in the dark. If he was going to try something, he needed to do it fast. When we reached the hospital, I'd try to get the guards to somehow detain him. Then we could question him, and if he was simply Good Samaritan Robert Morton, he'd be allowed to leave.

On 37th Street, we passed row townhouses and parked cars and bare trees and an empty block-sized park. He made a right turn onto a smaller side street. There was no reason to do this. The hospital lay dead ahead on the straightaway. But the side street was darker, and narrower, and more private.

Go for it, I thought.

I clicked out of my seat belt to give me more room to move. He didn't seem to notice it, but if he was a professional, he'd noticed it all right.

"Who is the Sixth Prophet?" I said.

"Excuse me?" His voice was lower. "The sick what?"

"Not 'sick.' *Sixth*. The Sixth Prophet."

"What are you talking about . . . Hey! *Those are the same kids who hit your car!*"

My gaze flicked right and I caught his blur of speed. He was fast, but he'd moved a fraction of a second too soon. His left hand was up, drawing the pistol crosswise from the hiding space between door and seat, bringing it up between belly and steering wheel. It had never been in the glove compartment. He would have blown my face off if he'd waited that extra fraction of a second. But the fraction gave me a chance to react.

BOOM . . . BOOM . . .

I parried his wrist and the pistol fired twice. A Glock 9 sounds like a firecracker in open air, like a bomb when detonating inside a car. The decibel level of the shot is actually higher than many shotguns and rifles. There was a hot, searing pain along my jaw. *A fraction of an inch closer . . .* My eardrums seemed to cave in. I could barely hear except for firing. Or maybe I didn't hear it; maybe I just felt shock waves.

The car was straying sideways as our hands rose and fell; parry, hit, parry, parry. Holes appeared in the windshield, fringed with white. The laminated glass didn't shatter but each shot webbed the areas around the holes. The Honda bounced off a parked car and kept going. His foot was off the accelerator, but the car remained in gear.

BOOM . . .

An ejected shell bounced off my forehead.

I parried again.

His face seemed huge, inches away, all yellow teeth and onion breath. He was screaming something. I smelled urine. I could barely hear and then I heard one word, *virus* . . . A flash of headlights swept past and something big rumbled by. Our front grille bumped into a parked Smartcar. Its alarm went off. The Honda pushed the tiny vehicle against the curb as we fought.

BOOM . . .

Eddie and I had spent a week at Quantico once, taking an Israeli Krav Maga course, focused on combat in enclosed spaces. We'd fought with an instructor named Gilboa inside a Volkswagen Passat, in a broom closet, in a roach-filled crawl space, in a rocking cabin cruiser off Virginia in a storm.

Counterattack as quickly as possible. *Neutralize and counterattack!* Gilboa had screamed in his Israeli accent.

Who are you? I shouted in my head, but got no answer.

The gun was not in his hand anymore. He must have dropped it. Or I'd knocked it away. This man was ten years younger than me, and very fast. He went for my eyes with a two-finger strike. He tried under the chin and bridge of nose hits with the heel of his palm. I went for his throat with my elbow. The back of my neck slammed the dashboard. The whole car smelled like a campfire now.

I thought, *Bring him in to Burke!*

Probably only a few seconds had gone by. An extra surge of adrenaline hit us as high beams raked the car, and somehow my side door was open, and as we tumbled out, locked together, a new voice, enraged, was screaming, *"You hit my car. Fuck you! You rammed my car!"*

Out of the corner of my eye I saw, across the small, shadowed lawn, the golden rectangle of an open front door and a woman standing there with a phone in her hand. BOOMBOOM*clickclickclick*. Robert Morton must have retrieved his gun and now it was empty. The car owner's face—the guy above us—had exploded in red and he fell away. I could hear the woman in the doorway screaming. I was going for Robert Morton's eye sockets. I was trying to blind him with my thumbs.

The police and Marines had extra patrols out around the hospital. I didn't realize they'd arrived until the loud hailer warned us to stop fighting and stand up and put our hands in the air. Two pairs of headlights up the block had stopped, set low, so they were cop cars, not Humvees.

The police behind those cars would see two floodlit men at each other's throats, a third on the ground, shot, a wife in a doorway screaming. I had no ID. It had been

taken away. I had no weapon. Burke knew I was AWOL
and had threatened to put me in Leavenworth. The police
were taking suspects to holding areas, locking them up
for days. No lawyers during the emergency, Galli had said.
No phone calls. Normal arrest procedure on hold. Everyone making up process as they went along, not as in the
unit's already useless war games.

Robert Morton was getting up, standing. Was he giving up? No, he was running off, pointing back at me. Why
didn't the cops just shoot? I heard him shouting, "He tried
to hijack me! Help! He has a gun!"

I tried to stand but my knees buckled. I groped and
the gun was in my hand. *It will have his fingerprints on it*,
I thought. Snow was falling upward suddenly. Little puffs
blew into the air from the ground. The police had seen
the gun and misinterpreted.

A fuselage of shots slammed into the Honda.

Robert Morton was gone.

I dropped behind the car, shouting that they shouldn't
shoot, that I was a Marine, that I'd dropped the gun and
if they stopped firing, I'd come out.

But they were coming at me from two sides. Maybe
they'd not seen me throw the gun away in the dark.
Maybe they'd seen but they were angry or scared or didn't
care. I shouted that I was giving up. I started to stand but
someone fired and I dropped down again. There was
something glinting in the snow, which had fallen from
the Honda. It was one of Robert Morton's music cassettes.
I shoved it into my parka pocket. *It might have his fingerprints on it, if I get out of this alive.*

I crawled backward, keeping low.

The angle of the shots hitting the Honda changed. The police were on two sides now, coming through the yards. They were tired and scared and on triple-shift duty and the woman in the doorway kept screaming, *"He shot him!"*

I scrambled back but the woman was pointing at me. She could see me clearly from her vantage point. I reached some bushes as behind me I heard her high-pitched screeching. *"He shot my husband! He shot Larry!"*

"That man murdered my husband!" she screamed. "He's getting away!"

FOURTEEN

===

CHRIS VEKEY HATED HERSELF AT THAT MOMENT. SHE COULD HARDLY
believe that she had phoned Burke's office, turned in Joe
Rush, telling the assistant that Rush was AWOL. Now
she sat at a fifth-floor window in the Georgetown campus
dorm given over to medical personnel and families, hearing Aya typing on her Mac in the other bedroom of the
suite. Outside, the storm had worsened. Moments ago,
through the open window, she'd shuddered as she heard
gunshots from beyond campus, in the residential neighborhood nearby. People out there were starting to fight.
The flood of incoming patients was increasing. She saw a
copter in the sky and a stabbing searchlight. The campus
was an island of order, but increasingly, she knew, if a cure
wasn't found, that island would become more isolated,
the city around it more barbaric, the sense of order mere
memory. Stunned by the speed of the deterioration, she

thanked Burke in her mind for his foresight in ordering medical personnel to safe places.

I had no choice, Joe. If I hadn't told Burke that you left, he would have punished me, too, when he found out. I warned you. You're crazy if you think I'd do anything to separate myself from Aya.

But she felt wretched for doing it.

She was freshly showered and dressed in clothing that Aya—thinking ahead—had brought from their condo when the admiral fetched her: gray wool pantsuit, white blouse, flat-heeled shoes, all under the white lab coat and new ID designating her as complex staff. The clothing would reassure patients and families. She no longer had access to Burke but now it was time to go help people. She'd be planning space use on campus, food distribution, bed assignments, and decontamination procedure when staffers exposed to the sick went back to their families in the dorms.

Knock . . . knock . . .

Ray Havlicek stood in the hallway outside. Surprise!

"I'm on campus checking security. We've got some VIPs checking in. Thought I'd drop by, see if you and Aya are okay."

She'd always liked him. Dating him had been a mistake, but he was smart and athletic and handsome, attributes she liked in a man. Unfortunately she'd felt no chemistry. He'd made it plain that he felt otherwise but had been a good sport when she told him after several dates—a movie, a Kennedy Center play, kayak day on the Potomac—that she'd prefer to stay friends.

"Thanks, Ray. Want a tour? Two pretty big bedrooms here, kitchenette. These students live in a hotel. It's not like when I went to school."

"The Hilton!"

"I'm about to make rounds, Ray."

"Heard from Joe, by the way?"

She started. Havlicek said, "Yeah, Burke told me about it. I sent some agents over to the cathedral, to pick him up. He's in trouble."

"Don't you need your people elsewhere?"

Havlicek shrugged. "Burke doesn't want people to think they can just walk off. You know. Make an example of Joe."

She felt hot. "Oh."

She needed to stop thinking about Rush and concentrate on her job. She was here to calm people by systemizing their fear, giving them the illusion that order meant control. She'd expected to see lots of patients but still had been shocked by long lines at the gate, by all the people waiting for triage. The obviously sick ones would be sent to Building A, possibly infected to Building B, families turned away but names, addresses, and phone numbers recorded for the FBI. *Go home and wait. If your loved one is sick, people will come for you, too.*

"Mind if I make the rounds with you?" Ray said. "Might as well do the tour together."

"I'm glad of the company, Ray."

Burke's aide had told her, *Thank you for the warning on Colonel Rush.*

The praise burned in her stomach.

Chris Vekey asked Ray to wait one last moment, put a benign expression on her face for Aya, and crossed the shared living room to say good-bye. She knocked at Aya's bedroom door. The girl sat at a desk by the window, where students had once solved chemistry problems. Aya even looked like she was doing homework, leaning forward, concentrating so hard that she'd not registered that Chris stood behind her. Then she saw Chris's reflection in the window. She turned and moved the laptop sideways. In the light of the desk lamp, her face was alarmed. Aya tried to smooth it away. Chris knew the expression. Aya was up to something. She hadn't been doing homework.

"I have to go to work, Aya. Be back in a few hours."

"Where's your mask, Mom?"

"I'll put it on when I get outside. Ray is here. Want to say hi?"

"No."

"What are you doing, Aya?"

"Just reading . . ."

But the panic was unmistakable. Aya was an honest kid, so when you questioned her about legitimate activity, she got angry. When you caught her doing something wrong, the wide-open eyes gave her away. Chris bent over the computer. There was no time for Aya to change what was on-screen. But when Chris saw what was there, she frowned, because it did not explain Aya's look of guilt.

Chris looked down on an eight-year-old article from the AP wire.

Cult leader says group will leave Vermont after Animal Rights activists force closure of basement lab.

The caption read, *Is research torture?*

"Aya, what is this?"

"I was just scrolling around."

Chris stared at Aya, who had showered and had a towel around her head and was barefoot on the carpet. She wore an overstuffed bathrobe with a Moose logo on the left side. The normal cute expression was back, the light blue eyes innocent. The girl's posture was forced casual, arm thrown over the back of the chair. Aya had a habit, when nervous, of tucking in her upper lip, and she did it now. She'd be a lousy poker player, Ray Havlicek had once said, back when Chris dated him. Aya's face was one constant tell.

"You're chewing that lip, Aya."

She rolled her eyes. "Oh, just turn on the electricity, Mom. Get out the water board."

Chris told Aya to get up and she sat down at the computer. She hit Previous and the article disappeared and now she saw a six-year-old article titled, "Cult Charged with Animal Torture."

She hit Previous again.

"What is this, Aya?"

The girl's face was set. "It was an assignment we got before the outbreak. Ms. Jefertson is *such* an animal rights activist. Like, she was always going on about them. Like, I think she likes animals more than people. Like, she's not like married you know. I bet it's a substitute!"

"Don't say *like*. I've told you a hundred times." But Chris experienced a second bolt of suspicion. Aya had said the word *like* so many times just now that it was almost as if she wanted Chris to pay attention to it. Diversion!

"Whatever, Mom! So she made us do a report on animal abuse around the United States. I might as well finish it in case the emergency ends and we go back to school. You told me to think positive. So I am."

Something was off but there was no time to deal with it. If Aya was doing schoolwork, Chris would not get in the way. If Aya wanted to regard the emergency as temporary, Chris could only give thanks for that.

It's going to get a lot worse first, either way.

Havlicek the gentleman held the suite door open for her. Zipped into her white hooded Andrew Marc parka, a $99 clearance sale purchase, she stepped out with the FBI agent onto the snowy campus and headed beneath vapor lights toward the hospital complex. Ray wore FBI blue.

"So you haven't heard from Joe," he said.

"Nobody has. He should have been back by now."

"Well, my guys missed him at the cathedral, I found out."

They stopped at mid-campus, by the Jesuit graveyard. Its tilting, worn headstones marked the remains of priests who had died over three centuries, in trouble spots around the world. "I once wanted to be a priest," Havlicek said as they eyed the gathering of dead: Jesuits who had died of the flu in World War One, tending soldiers; Jesuits who had perished of cholera in Haiti; Jesuits who had given their lives fighting outbreaks, or who'd been killed by the

Soviets, or died of old age there in Georgetown, their final
resting place only two hundred feet from a hospital, as if
those buildings were doorways to the next world.

Joe Rush came into her head.

*I had no choice, Joe. You asked me to choose between Aya
and you. There was no choice.*

Chris fought off the stab of misery. She felt as if she'd
destroyed a relationship, yet she had never been Rush's
lover, or the recipient of any of his affections at all. Not
that that would have changed what she had done. Not for
a second.

"Chris, I think Burke plans to reinstate you," Havlicek
said. "He might even send you to Virginia, get you out
of the line of fire here. Maybe I can pull some strings and
get Aya sent there, too."

"You could? Really? My God, Ray! Thanks."

"No problem." He smiled. He had a very nice smile.
"Anyway, let me know if you hear from Joe."

Even at 9 P.M. more ambulance headlights rolled into the
horseshoe-shaped driveway. Extra ambulances had arrived
from outlying suburbs, and moved past the guards in a
stream. The line of cars grew longer at the entrance. Masked
nurses escorted patients to designated buildings. New arrivals to triage, in the Medical and Dental Annex. Clearly
sick to the hospital, which normally held six hundred beds
but had been expanded. More beds were being set up in
the Dahlgren Memorial Library and Davis Performing Arts
Center. Military station in Building D; Chris's office in the
Lombardi Cancer Center.

She told Havlicek, "We'll add beds in the field house, too. But we may need to open up another building."

From the searchlights a few blocks off, and sirens, she surmised that another police action was going on. They heard shots. Havlicek explained that after an initial period of laxity with civil disobedience, "police and Marines are now responding with extra force."

"Ray, I thought Burke was crazy when he told me to move in here. But I guess he knew what he was doing."

"He does. Believe me. He does." Ray paused. From his expression, she thought he was about to get personal. It made her uncomfortable. "Chris, remember when we were going out, our talk about bad timing?"

"I do. But not now, Ray, please."

There are no good choices. If the disease gets out of the wards, then this campus will be the worst possible place to have my daughter. I can't send her into the city. It's too late to send her to Dad, and even if I could, I'm not sure whether things will get bad down there, too. Maybe I should be nicer to Ray. Shut him out more gently. He's a good guy. He can get Aya to safety.

"I'm just upset," she said.

"No, it was stupid of me to bring personal stuff up. No problem at all," Ray said, smiling, palms out. A pal.

He stayed with her for one last stop before going with her to her office. At the front gate she checked the line of walk-ins that stretched down Reservoir Road toward 37th Street. Two hours ago she'd found one of the guards mistreating people, shouting, pointing an M4, scaring little kids and making them cry. She'd had the man transferred to the hospital. She'd told the Marine captain in charge to make sure that his soldiers treated the frightened people with kindness. At the time, she'd thought that Joe Rush would never treat strangers badly. He was good with frightened people. He was just bad with normal people. *Go figure*, she thought.

"Must be four hundred people out here," Ray said.

They stood on the "safe" side of the razor wire. The line was seven deep out there and Havlicek's shoulder brushed hers. The scene reminded her of bread lines she'd seen at refugee camps in Syria, in Haiti, in New Orleans.

She started to turn away when she spotted something familiar. She shielded her eyes with gloved hands to cut out the vapor light glare. A man in midline wore a dark parka, hood up, and had his head down, his hands jammed in his pockets. She was not sure what had caught her attention. Then he inched ahead and she realized that was it. Rush moved like that, favored one side, because of his amputated toes. Left side dipping slightly, then coming back up fast.

The man shuffled forward, face away from the street, where a police car was slowly approaching, shining a side light down the line. The man seemed to make himself smaller. The car rolled past. The man's head came up and followed the receding car and the vapor light turned a flash of face green.

It's Joe! He's hiding from them!

The thumping in her chest happened when he was close whether she wanted it to or not, whether she was angry at him or glad to see him or puzzled, as she was now. *Why is he standing in line instead of announcing himself at the gate?*

"Why exactly did he say he was going to the cathedral?" Havlicek asked, as if sensing that Joe was on her mind.

"He wanted to ask the dean about leprosy and religion."

She started to tell Havlicek that Rush was here. But she stopped. The throbbing in her head spread down into her intestines. All she had to do was say it and point and she'd be reinstated at her old job and Aya might be in Virginia. People like Burke thought in terms of rewards.

Rush took two steps forward with the line. Havlicek was saying, "Religion? What does religion have to do with it?" The police car was coming back down the block, and this time its spotlight paused here and there on the line. Rush turned away, very slightly, not enough to attract attention. You had to be watching to see him do it.

Chris remembered the gunshots she had heard ten minutes ago, and she remembered the helicopter. Mentally, Chris measured Rush's place in line against the stop-and-go speed with which the line moved. He looked as if he'd been here for . . . about ten minutes. *No*, she thought. *It couldn't have been for you.*

Her breath floated into the night as mist, as she turned to Havlicek, looked into his face. Havlicek's full attention was on Chris. His soft smile.

"You can really get Aya to Virginia?" she said.

"There's going to be a second wave sent down, once people are tested and disease-free."

Rush had eased himself to the outer edge of the line. Rush ambled away from the line, into and across Reservoir Road. Rush was a diminishing shadow moving out of the streetlight, into the darkness of Glover-Archbold Park, one more person tired of standing in line, or changing his mind about checking into the hospital, one more lone individual on a night filled with emergencies, going off alone. She saw a gate guard watch him go. No big deal.

"Thanks for trying," she told Havlicek.

"I'll come back and check on you guys again," Ray said, and squeezed her arm. "I'm glad you're okay."

She hurried into the main hospital building. Instantly, the sounds of mayhem echoed off the cinderblock walls: babies crying, someone shouting over a public service announcement, an apology for long waits in the emergency room.

I never saw you, Joe. I hate the choices you give me. Funny, but maybe if Ray had not offered Virginia, I might have told him. But it sounded like a deal. You're on your own, Joe, whatever you are doing out there, whatever you have done.

FIFTEEN

I SLIPPED UNNOTICED INTO THE SMALL BAMBOO GARDEN BEHIND
the admiral's two-story house. The massed shoots and
high picket fence blocked neighbors' views of the yard.
The key was where he always left it, under the metal flow-
erpot on the screened porch. I let myself into the kitchen
and punched in the alarm code, *1776*. Eddie and I had been
guests there so often that we knew the system. We came
and went as we pleased.

*Robert Morton knew I was going to be at the cathedral.
Who is the traitor?*

Grant Road, where the admiral lived, was in Northwest
D.C., named after the general who won the American
Civil War. It was a lovely narrow street off Nebraska
and Wisconsin, a tree-lined Americana where neighbors
knew each other, shared cookouts, watched out for each
other's properties, even helped each other shovel snow.

The neighbors knew me as a regular guest there. If they saw me, I hoped they'd think nothing of it.

Could the traitor be Chris Vekey? She told Burke I'd left. Could it be Burke? Once Burke knew, others would, too.

The house had been left heated at fifty degrees, which, after four exhausting hours outside, seemed like a luxurious seventy. The air vent system hissed; the stainless steel refrigerator sighed. Pinprick tingling in my fingertips indicated some warmth returning. In winters I usually feel extra chilled where my amputated toes had been. Once you get frostbite, as I had in Alaska last year, the sensation always surfaces in cold.

Or is it possible that Robert Morton was waiting for me at the hospital and followed me? That would still mean I could be dealing with a traitor inside the investigation.

Normally, a drive from the hospital here would have taken no more than ten minutes. Metro busses made the trip from Tunlaw to Tenley in double that. But I'd needed hours to walk a mere 3.5 miles and stay clear of police and soldiers. I'd circled around an apartment building fire on Fulton and Wisconsin, as an exhausted, understaffed crew of firemen tried to get it under control, and pajama-clad residents watched. I'd ducked behind a parked Chevy Tahoe to avoid a gang of young men, judging from their laughter, who were smashing car windows with tire irons and baseball bats. More widely spaced headlights connoted Humvees patrolling near Macomb Street, where looters had sacked the Safeway. I moved through backyards and alleys, slid past lit homes and abandoned ones, used side streets paralleling Wisconsin, zigzagged my way toward the best place I could think of that might provide a temporary place to hide.

Ray Havlicek knew I was going to the hospital, and could have had someone waiting for me. Burke knew. Their assistants probably knew. Who to trust?

I fell into a chair at Galli's kitchen table and tossed a plastic RadioShack shopping bag on top. Out spilled what I'd run off with through the store's bashed-in front grille. Other looters had gone for computer components and audio systems. I'd taken prepaid disposable cell phones, the last twenty on display. I'd been one more figure in the half dark, hunting supplies amid a maze of crushed display boxes, tangled wiring, and rifled cash registers. No sirens outside, just flashlight beams amid the grunting and footfalls of other people's desperation.

I thought wryly, *At least the looting was predicted in our old war games. Other than that, it's make things up as you go.*

In the fridge I found sliced ham, Swiss cheese, dill pickles, and romaine lettuce, shoved a food mass between two slices of seven-grain bread, and started wolfing it down. I guzzled water from the faucet and found a bottle of Maker's Mark Bourbon in the liquor cabinet. Sticking with water would be smarter. I poured bourbon into a ceramic mug and sprawled at the table. I clicked the TV remote that operated the SONY flat screen on the wall.

Let's get the big picture.

CNN exploded on, with its usual head-churning montage, ten shots at once, and a running national death toll on the bottom, numbers rising one by one, jumping ten, then a pause, then thirty more, then fifty. TAMPA AND LOS ANGELES UNDER MARTIAL LAW, the banner read. Gas gouging in nine states, mob sacks hospital in Orlando for medicine after a rumor spreads that there's a cure there . . . Saint Patrick's Cathedral in New York holding round-the-clock masses. Survivalists in Idaho peering out of a barbed wire fence, automatic rifles slung over their shoulders.

"We've been preparing for twenty years," one said.

NATIONAL DEATH TOLL: 22,856.

I clicked to NBC, and overhead shots of highways, nothing moving in Chicago, National Guard monitoring the interstate in Tennessee, blocked to all but official traffic by the governor, everything normal in Oklahoma City. Some airports open to disease-free essential personnel, others closed. Food convoys snaking down I-95, the East Coast corridor, driven by Marines.

CONFIRMED TOTAL CASES: 84,749 so far.

Christ.

I saw the nation in colored swatches, red for highly infected areas, with crimson blobs covering Los Angeles, Reno, and New York City; light blue connoting disease-free North Texas and splashes of Deep South and northern Maine, Denver, Indianapolis, Galveston, Santa Fe.

Europe and Asia almost disease-free, with U.S. flights barred from entry.

Pulsing green marking avenues of spread: highways, air travel lanes, ship and rail routes.

Freight trains moving, an announcer said. Passenger trains not.

Fox News broadcast a timeline: infected areas yesterday, with brown marking the previous day, pink the day before. PBS showed a rolling montage of disaster: Dallas ambulance attendants taking away dead on gurneys; Brooklyn homeless, faces eaten away; gas gouging on I-80, *$41 a gallon*; a faith healer tent rally in Mississippi, *hallelujah*; doctors arrested in Madison, Wisconsin, for selling salt tablets labeled antibiotics.

"Beware of charlatans," the announcer said. "There is no known cure to the Bible Virus. Go to a designated triage center if you become ill."

The moving banner offered bullet points. POPE ASKS WORLD TO PRAY FOR AMERICA. U.S. SIXTH FLEET ORDERED TO STAY FAR FROM HOME, TO KEEP SAILORS SAFE.

As I clicked to local news, I unwrapped the first disposable cell phone, or more accurately, needed a scissor to cut the damn vacuum wrapping off. Whoever invented this stuff probably worked for Homeland Security. It was harder to open than a vault at Chase Manhattan.

All the networks simultaneously switched to the underground government complex beneath Virginia, an hour from where I sat. I saw the President interviewed by a blond ABC reporter, famed, *Vanity Fair* had said in a profile, for her "sympathetic eyes." Both people sitting with legs crossed, in maroon leather chairs before a roaring fireplace, as if they were at the White House, not on a set designed to look homey a hundred feet belowground.

UNDER MOUNT WEATHER.

"God is with America," the President said.

"Sir, would you comment on the latest Wikileaks report that you've okayed a plan to bomb terrorist camps in Mali and Nigeria?"

"The enemy doesn't need spies. Just Wikileaks," the President joked.

"Don't you think the public has a right to know war plans?"

"If you're asking whether they need to know everything that happens every second, no. I make decisions based on hard information, after consultation with some of the best prepared security staff on Earth."

"Then it's true. You've authorized massive attacks in retaliation for the infection."

"You shouldn't spread baseless rumors."

"I'm not the problem, sir."

The President didn't look particularly safe in his bunker. He didn't look confident. He looked exhausted.

"Why don't Americans trust each other anymore?" he said.

THE SANDWICH TASTED BETTER THAN A SIRLOIN STEAK AT PETER Luger's. The quiet was a blanket. When I opened my eyes, I was slumped in the chair, and the clock told me that I'd slept for hours. It was 4:30 A.M. I smelled like a man who'd sweated through his outerwear.

I needed a shower. But first I trudged into the den, my missing toes throbbing. I turned on the admiral's computer, muted the sound, and found local news, for the headlines. Then I rummaged through the admiral's collection of

DVDs for one of his favorite documentaries, *A History of the Potomac River*, which we'd watched together the last time I'd stayed overnight. I inserted the DVD so the TV could show it, and scrolled to a four-minute segment I recalled where the only sound was the capital's river, swelling over rocks, falling into pools, turgid, pure, unadulterated, turned-up sound.

Only then did I call Eddie's number. He picked up on the second ring.

"One, where the hell are you? Are you okay? It's four forty in the morning. Do you need help?"

"C-c-cold out here," I said.

"What is that I hear? Water?"

"Eddie, someone came after me," I said. "At the cathedral. Someone was waiting. The song. The Sixth Prophet. Remember the song? We need to get to Burke or Havlicek. Or both, because someone told them I was there."

I meant, *Tell as many people as possible because one of them is a traitor.*

"Who came after you?"

"He said his name was Robert Morton. One guy. Alone."

The scene on the computer switched from weather to local crimes, video recordings. *Have you seen these suspects?* A store video froze looters in a Best Buy. A gas station video showed thieves turning on the pumps, waiting with five-gallon containers to fill them up.

Eddie said much, much too patiently, "Come in, One. We'll explain together. I can meet you. I'll get a car. You and me, man, Uno and Dos, just like back in the sunny Korangal Valley!"

I froze. *In Korangal Valley, Afghanistan, we were separated and sent on different missions. Eddie's telling me that someone is there with him, listening in right now.*

"Gotta go," I said. "I'll call back in five."

I hung up, pulled out the SIM card, and smashed it with a hammer I'd taken from a tool kit beneath the sink. Eddie was not allowed to leave the hospital grounds. He'd never come and get me. He'd warned me that we were being monitored and now I knew what I had to do to protect him.

It was not to call him back.

Because if someone sent Robert Morton after me, or if that someone got reports from whoever had listened in to us now, I'd put my best friend in the line of fire if I told him more.

I cursed. I would call Eddie anyway. I hoped he knew enough to change his room after this, add locks, bar his door, watch his back as he moved around the hospital complex. The crushing weight was a ball in my lungs. But Eddie and the admiral would have access to people I didn't. Eddie and the admiral might get through and get a response when I could not.

I couldn't stop myself if I wanted to at this point.

I was punching in his number again with the next cell phone when, shocked, I saw myself on the computer screen. The footage had been shot from a police squad car. I was holding Robert Morton's pistol while Morton ran away. There was a dead man—the man whom Morton had shot—lying on the curb. A woman, his wife, screamed and pointed at me from the house.

I felt a barb move into my intestines. I heard my breathing pick up. They say cameras can't lie. This one zeroed in on me, then switched to a rape attack near the Dupont Circle Metro entrance. *Have you seen these men? Call this police phone number if you have. Reward!*

When I'd first called Eddie, I'd hoped there was little chance of anyone on his end having the ability to track me, at least not quickly. All the better equipment would be allocated to major security—for terrorist suspects, interstate hijackers, gasoline thieves, or border crossings; to the larger emergency, not street crimes in Washington, D.C.

But if the problem is our own people, and they feel threatened, they'll use every means to find me. They'll make up a bullshit story. They probably have the power to do that.

"Joe? I lost you there for a second," Eddie said when I reached him again. His voice was calm.

He knows exactly what I'm doing. Take the risk! The more who know, the better. There will be good people in the mix. I'll hope Eddie gets through to one of them.

I ran down the story quickly, watching the second hand on the wall clock move. A man saying he was Robert Morton had tried to kill me. He'd shot the homeowner near the hospital complex, on 37th Street, not me. He'd punctured my tires and offered me a ride. He'd grilled me about the progress tracking the disease, and attacked me when I asked about a "Sixth Prophet."

I sound lame even to myself, I thought, but pressed on.

"The police will have that car, Eddie. They'll have his prints. Hair. DNA!"

"Come in, Joe, and we'll both tell them."

I pictured Eddie in a room with police or FBI agents. Guys in suits. Guys with access credentials, guys who could move around legally, not like me.

"The . . . river . . ." I gasped. "Cold here. Sleepy."

I smashed the phone to bits, in the process chipping off the top of Cindy Galli's Shaker-era antique wooden table. *I'll pay you back.*

I tried the admiral and got his voice mail. *Leave a message.* I did. I tried Burke, and reached an assistant to an assistant, who sounded distracted as I ran down information. I heard a yawn. I was talking to someone so low down in importance that he thought I was a random nut. So much for access.

Try Havlicek. But the number he'd had days ago was disconnected. Ray was probably using a new phone.

By now someone at the FBI or in Burke's office had probably recognized me from the police video.

I need sleep. I should lie down . . .

But then I remembered Chris Vekey, who had told investigators that I'd gone to the cathedral. What else had she told them? That I stayed here when in Washington? If they knew that, sooner or later someone would swing by.

Has she already told them?

There were no good choices, only gradients of risk.

Get out. Now.

At dawn, the storm was over. Bright rising sun tinged five fresh inches of unplowed snowfall outside. The street was deserted. I saw no car tracks. There was one last thing to do. I turned on the desk lamp at a kitchen window overlooking peaceful Grant Road. I'd head out the back door if I saw even one car turn onto the block, whether it looked like an unmarked or not.

The kitchen computer was a Hewlett Packard, Galli's day-to-day home model, not an encrypted machine, which required a password to get in. Maybe Eddie had sent me an e-mail. Maybe I'd gotten a relevant message that way. There was nothing of note there but I laughed when I saw that even in a time of national disaster, SPAM came through. A stranger named Brad wanted to friend me. A newsletter invited me to the annual dinner of the board of the National Emergency Disaster Group. I was about to click off when I saw a message from Aya Vekey, hours old.

I tried to call you, Joe, but there was no answer. I just saw you on TV and hope you are okay. I bet the police shot first!

I thought, *I have two solid supporters, her and Eddie.*

I couldn't find anything on those names you gave me, but I really, really tried. I'm sorry.

I thought, *That's okay, you did your best.*

I tried to find records from SUNY, and those men you asked about from Africa, but the school is closed. The university website is up, but to get student addresses it says you have to call the registrar. They're closed.

Don't worry about it, I thought.

Then I looked up other stuff you asked; Sixth Prophet and Cults. There was a cult called the Branch Davidians in

Texas. They had a shootout with the FBI in 1993 in Waco, after a 51-day siege. Their leader David Koresh said he was the Seventh Prophet. I thought if there's a seventh, there must be a sixth, but I never found out who they said it was.

Nice try, Aya, I thought, impressed with the kid's inventiveness. The Branch Davidians had been a violent offshoot of the Seventh-Day Adventists, believing that an apocalypse was imminent, and Koresh had been a charismatic leader, but he had been dead for years.

Cults, I thought. Back at Wilderness Medicine, two months ago, at Harvard, Eddie and I had sat through a talk by a visiting Tokyo professor named Goro Akiyama, a Japanese expert on the cult Aum Shinrikyo, and their multiyear effort to secure biological weapons.

"Genetic manipulation is easier and cheaper than it has ever been," he'd said, while we eyed a photo of Shoko Asahara, the chubby, bearded, benevolent-looking academic and business failure who somehow had convinced highly educated followers that he could levitate, and that the apocalypse was imminent. "They tried to jump-start a global war by releasing poison gas in Tokyo in 1995," Goro said.

"At its peak, Aum Shinrikyo had over two thousand members, many of them Ph.D.s. It is still listed by the State Department as a terrorist group. They allegedly have members in Russia," Goro went on.

"Or in the U.S., Marshall Applewaite, the bald, avuncular fanatic believed he was the son of God. His thirty-three followers in 1997 committed suicide at his order, thinking that would release their souls to join aliens in space," Goro said, showing slides of the dead laid out with their feet facing in the same direction, their shirts and trousers all the same, their expressions benign.

Cults, I thought again. Charles Manson's followers had believed he was the reincarnation of Jesus, and had gone on a rampage in California. Jim Jones, leader of the Peoples Temple in San Francisco, had led almost a thousand followers in Guyana, South America, where they'd poisoned themselves at his command.

Each leader predicted apocalypse. Each exerted life and death influence over followers. Each, Goro had told us, created an isolated culture composed of a hodgepodge of existing old religious belief, mysticism, and the notion that the leader alone had answers to universal questions, and that they could gain enlightenment by joining up.

After Goro had left, one of the Los Angeles–based doctors in the department had taken me aside in the cafeteria. "Chicken Littles." He'd sighed. "You can scare yourself to death with this stuff. It will never really happen."

And now Aya went on in her e-mail, *I couldn't sleep after that horrible segment of you on the news. I was almost asleep and found this blog from Pakistan. It's from the sister of a man named Tahir Khan, who police say killed himself by jumping off a balcony in Florida. She didn't believe it. She said her brother was pushed.*

I sighed, thinking that this was the type of worthless tripe you got when you sent out a kid to answer a crucial question. She got distracted. She didn't focus. She lacked experience to weed out dumb stuff and pass along the relevant. You couldn't fault her. She was fifteen.

As I reached out to shut off the machine, my eyes slid over her next few words.

Miriam Khan said Tahir Khan had gotten mixed up with a dangerous cult near Albany, New York, at SUNY . . .

My hand stopped moving.

Tahir was a science major, just like those other names you gave me. And he went to the exact same college!

My heart beat faster.

Tahir's sister said he took the money he inherited from his father and gave it to the cult leader, a man named Harlan Maas. She said Maas bought an old Quaker meeting camp in New Lebanon, New York, with the money, and made it a compound for about eighty followers.

My breath caught in my throat.

Tahir e-mailed his sister that he was scared of Maas, and thinking of leaving. She never heard from him again until the Pakistani government contacted her. Police in Florida had traced the fingerprints of a suicide. Tahir was Muslim, but quit that religion. Miriam said Harlan Maas had crazy notions about the end of the world. I e-mailed her but got no answer.

I stared at the screen.

Joe? Ready for this? Tahir Khan studied LEPROSY at SUNY! Uh-oh. Mom is coming.

The message ended.

There were no other e-mails from her since then.

But now that I knew the blog existed, I found it easily

and read it. Aya had hit the high points. There was nothing more to be learned this way.

I told myself, *Erase this e-mail and don't respond. If there's a Washington connection, and they're in my e-mail, if they know she's looking into things, I may have doomed the kid. If I don't respond, she'll have a better chance.*

First Karen in Alaska, then Eddie. Now Aya.

I knew where the admiral kept his 9mm home defense Glock 17. I stole the admiral's five-thousand-dollar inherited antique watch. I'd need funds or valuables once I left this house. I made turkey and ham sandwiches and wrapped them in foil, filled a thermos with coffee, and shoved it all in an old knapsack. I took the admiral's Russian flapped hat from the front closet, and a waist-length Thermolite ski jacket to give me a different look. I riffled the pockets of my old parka for gloves. That was when I felt the sharp edge of the cassette box I'd taken from Robert Morton's car. I'd forgotten it. There was a label on the spine, in faded blue ink, in script.

HARLAN AT CHRISTMAS.

The force of the connection—HARLAN—made my knees weak. Stunned, I dropped into the chair, heard my own breathing. Was it possible? Was it conceivable that Goro Akiyama's prediction had come true . . . and all the suffering had been caused by eighty people on a farm in New York?

NOT Iran or Al Qaeda? Not any of the bad guys on the target board? Not the people whom the President is about to attack? Or is it more complicated? Is there a connection

*between that farm and Washington, D.C.? Because someone
here went after me at that church.*

I heard myself laughing. It was a harsh, abrasive bark.
I remembered what Eddie had said once after one of our
Wilderness Medicine sessions, in a Mexican restaurant in
Cambridge. *Want to bet, One, that the world won't be de-
stroyed by Doctor Evil in the end, but by Bozo the Clown?*

Well, I thought, taking the cassette but leaving the
plastic container on the kitchen table, they'd need DNA
equipment, but that costs only a few hundred dollars.
They'd need a way to spread the disease. A few vials could
do that. They'd need samples of leprosy, but Tahir Khan
had been a researcher. It wasn't proof in a court of law,
but it was enough just now for me. I felt my throat go
dry, and my heart beat strong and steady.

In the kitchen the TV was still on as I considered turning myself in and appealing to Burke directly. Would
I even reach him if I tried? *Holy shit! The numbers just
shot up!*

NEW PROJECTED DEATH TOLL: 65,000–80,000.

PROJECTED INFECTED ESTIMATED: 270,000–
360,000.

On the CNN map, the red ovals were bigger. Perhaps
whoever was reporting numbers had changed interpreta-
tion, or made an error accounting for the sudden jump,
or, as I hoped, was overstating things.

At what point, I wondered, would those numbers start
rising as fast as the WORLD POPULATION totals on the
electronic sign in Times Square; single digits becoming
triple, climbing at slot machine speed, a backward count-

down to total disaster, digits rising instead of falling to reach the point of no return.

I WROTE A LONG NOTE, AND LEFT IT ON THE TABLE WITH THE PLASTIC cassette holder. I shotgunned an e-mail out to Eddie, Burke, Havlicek, and Homza. I cc'ed the head of the Wilderness Medicine Program, and a major general I knew in the Marines. I said I'd leave the empty cassette container— hopefully bearing Robert Morton's fingerprints—on Galli's table. I took the cassette itself.

How to make friends with your boss: Break into his house. Steal one car and leave the other for vandals. I'll pay you back, Admiral. I'll buy you new cars.

Albany, New York, would, on an average day, be a seven- or eight-hour drive away, requiring one Prius refill, if the tank was full to start.

I knew about the mudroom corkboard where Galli hung extra keys to Cindy's ten-year-old Prius. I left a hand-scrawled IOU for $55,000 to pay for all I stole. If money was still in circulation when this was over, and I was alive, I'd be happy to pay. If it wasn't, the loss of two cars and a watch and a pistol was not worth mentioning. Neither was the extra cash I riffled from a kitchen closet, and jewelry—more barter material—that I stole from up-stairs.

The Prius started right up in the garage, but the tank was only half full. I'd worry about fuel later. The day had a beautiful, dazzling, post-storm glow, soft cottony snow-fall on trees, the kind of white you see in urban areas before cars dirty it, the Currier & Ives winter wonderland effect.

Even if I manage to reach New Lebanon, what then?

A Prius is a low-slung vehicle, so despite front-wheel drive, getting out of the snowy driveway was difficult. I had to back up and change direction twice, and gun the engine when the tires spun in five inches of fresh fall. Grant Road was no better. It rose slightly on the way to Nebraska Avenue. I slid sideways and slowed and went to a lower gear and almost made it to Nebraska when I got stuck. A door opened on a one-story ranch house on the right and a bulked-up figure in a parka emerged and headed for me with something long and metallic, glinting, over his shoulder.

I fumbled for the Glock. But I saw with relief that Galli's neighbor carried a snow shovel, not a rifle. He rapped on the window. I recognized him from block parties. His name was Fred Gray and he worked as a lobbyist for the American Tobacco Consortium. The soft-spoken joke teller didn't look particularly happy now. I rolled the window down and his worried look changed to surprise.

"Joe Rush! I thought you were the admiral!"

"He let me borrow his car."

"He and Cindy are still at Georgetown Hospital?"

"That's where I'm going," I lied, realizing that this man had not seen my face on the news, didn't connect me with anything wrong. It turned out that something much more important was on his mind. He'd come out to ask Galli a question.

"Our daughter, Celia, is stuck at college, in Iowa. The TV says she's in a clear zone, but last time I looked, that red area is almost in Ames. She's in her sorority house. She says they have food for four more days."

"Thank God she's safe," I said.

"Do you think she'll be all right?"

He knew I didn't have an answer. He was too smart for that. But I gave him what he wanted, assurance. "Everyone's working hard to figure out this thing," I said.

"Let me give you a push, Joe. And thank you. Tell the admiral. Thank *all* of you for working so hard."

WISCONSIN AVENUE WAS PLOWED ALONG A SINGLE LANE RUNNING north-south, so police or troops could pass. I was alone on the road at the moment, and felt exposed, but had little choice. If I could convince Burke or Havlicek to send people to Upstate New York, there could be Marines in helicopters there in an hour. If I couldn't, I had to go.

Turn left, and I'd head for the Pentagon or FBI, to try a direct appeal. Head down Nebraska, to Homeland Security? Burke had threatened to lock me away in Leavenworth. By now he'd probably issued orders to that effect. Or was he the one who had sent Robert Morton to kill me?

Turn right and I'd drive toward the Beltway, and Interstate 95, out of Washington.

I turned right.

Hell, I'll have a better chance if I stay away and hope

that one of my messages gets through. There's no guarantee that even if one does, it will convince anyone. No guarantee that the traitor won't block it.

I stepped down on the accelerator gently. The one open lane had been salted. I heard the tires crunching on the granular result. On a normal day, I could make New Lebanon in eight hours. But now I could be stopped any minute by police or soldiers, even before I reached the Beltway.

Now, every block is a risk.

Driving, I pulled out Robert Morton's tape cassette. The Prius was ten years old, so the sound system gave riders the option of listening to cassettes as well as CDs.

HARLAN AT CHRISTMAS.

I inserted the cassette in the slot, and listened, horror growing, as the Prius skidded north.

SIXTEEN

MAJOR EDWARD NAKAMURA WATCHED THE STRIPED CURTAIN SLIDE
open in the emergency room alcove, and the next patient walked in. He tried to smile sympathetically at the woman, who was clearly terrified and sick and fighting panic. Eddie was exhausted from lack of sleep and worry for his wife and daughters and for Joe Rush. He'd been working for ten hours straight. He'd not eaten in eight. The scrape of the curtain sounded like fingernails on a blackboard. The announcements over the intercom seemed louder by the minute. A man was screaming out in the ER, *"How long do you have to wait for help around here anyway!"*

Eddie said calmly, "I know you're scared. I'm going to do all I can for you. Would you mind undressing down to your underwear?"

The woman was forty-two, the admission form said, and had been in decent health only days ago. Now the face was ravaged, the symptoms identical to ones he'd been looking at helplessly for hours. Diagnosis wasn't complicated; a six-year-old could do it.

Any serious disease in your family? No. Any allergies to medicines? No. Onset of first symptoms? Four days ago.

He said smoothly, listening to her galloping heart, "Every patient we see adds to our knowledge about the disease. You never know when the big break will come. It could come at any time. Let's check your blood pressure."

Then came the standard leprosy check. He poked the eight spots on her hands and feet to test sensation, which she lacked. He checked the eyes for inflammation, and found a forest fire of inflamed veins. Squeezed the base of the thumb, the median nerve. Checked the ulnar nerve for tenderness by the eyes, for a lack of ability to shut them.

What's the point of diagnosing the same thing over and over? What we really need is to kill it. The normal multidrug therapy has no effect at all against both the paucibacillary and the multibacillary strains. Complicate that with fasciitis, and the fucking third piece that the CDC finally identified today, the tiniest almost hidden fraction of norovirus DNA. Making it spreadable by touch and air. Making it the goddamn hydrogen bomb of man-made disease.

"Thanks so much, Mrs. Haverhill. Take your paperwork down the hall to the nurses' station. The helpful folks there will set up a bed."

Yeah, except every bed is filled and we've got people coming in faster than we can handle them.

He took a break, which meant that he turned his attention from the endless patients to Joe. He had a cell phone connected into the encrypted emergency med network, and security network. He tried Burke's office and got the overworked fourth-tier assistant again, who'd been clearly ordered to keep Joe's and Eddie's calls away. He tried the Junior Senator from Alaska—a woman he and Joe knew from work there—but the office was shut and the senator underground. He reached FBI Special Agent Ray Havlicek and got a noncommittal "We're aware of Colonel Rush's theory." He called a D.C. police commander and former Marine, who told him, after checking records as a personal favor, that "Rush is on a special list. We're to hand him over to the FBI if we get him. And he's wanted for murder, by us, Eddie."

The commander added, somewhat harder, "He shot at cops, Eddie. The way things are out there, things getting worse, no one sleeping, tempers rising, I can't guarantee that if we find him, he'll be brought in alive."

"DO YOU THINK I ENJOY SEEING SO MANY PEOPLE SUFFER?" SAID the warm, calm tones of Harlan Maas.

Connecticut Avenue was in slightly better shape than Wisconsin had been. There were two cleared lanes on each side, but traffic remained sparse. I passed locked-up strip malls and apartment buildings with private guards outside, or perhaps they were vigilantes. Traffic lights still worked, sending directions into an anarchistic void. The voice on the tape was soothing, therefore more terrifying.

I thought I heard the voice catch, as if the man battled away tears.

"Do you think I enjoy knowing that we will have a role in children losing parents? Men and women with faces eaten away? Neighbors fighting people who they once considered their best friends?"

The road—if open—would take me into Maryland at Chevy Chase Circle, a few miles ahead. It would continue through residential suburbs until reaching the ramp to the Beltway, and I-95 North. I passed an apartment building where Army Rangers in biogear were arresting people; herding at least two dozen handcuffed men into a canvas-topped truck. Police and soldiers had opened mass detention centers, Admiral Galli's TV had informed me. Those arrested would be confined there, possibly for weeks, before they could get a lawyer. And that was if, the announcer said, courts reopened at all.

"Hopefully within a month, there will be a way to process these people. We can only wait and do our best," the mayor had said.

When the Humvee swung in behind me, I was planning the trip: I-95 to Baltimore, then past Wilmington, Delaware. I'd exit on the Jersey side of the George Washington Bridge, avoiding New York City. I'd hopefully figure out how to get gas. If not, I'd come up with another way to move. I'd stay on the west side of the Hudson River at first and make my way to Columbia County, and New Lebanon, New York.

As for the cult and compound, I'll wait to see the place first, then decide what to do.

In the little rectangle of rearview mirror, I saw the boxy Humvee swing onto the road, stay back, and follow.

Harlan Maas said, "I can't stop thinking about those poor sufferers; yet we must ask, why were these people chosen? The scientists in Somalia were out to disprove creation. Imagine! Making lies up about rocks and sediments to argue that human beings are descended from apes!"

What?

"The actors and directors making that film at Paramount would have mocked my father's work, if not stopped."

It can't be this, I thought. *Who is his father?*

"The air base, where prayers were banned! The sports stadiums! Where thousands ignored Holy Sundays! My friends! The last time I came to Earth, I told my followers . . . Let he who is without sin cast the first stone. Don't you think I know that we have done that? But there was no other way."

He thinks he's Jesus Christ!

"When I see a little child, a six-year-old boy or girl, sick, I admit it, I ask myself, maybe we should stop," said Harlan Maas.

I've got to get this tape to the right people!

The voice began weeping. I heard great intakes of air. The voice composed itself enough to begin speaking again.

"But this suffering will end all suffering for all of humanity. When the transformation is complete, those hurt will be whole. War and hunger will be memory. As we begin the last phase, I thank you for your faith and love.

You are the special ones. You will lead the world into a new age of peace, love, and understanding."

What does he mean, "the last phase"?

Something went wrong with the tape. It snagged and tore. The Humvee in the mirror closed the gap between us, but I did not speed up, despite the urge. My armpits were soaked. I stopped at a light and the sand-colored vehicle pulled up beside me. The soldier in the passenger seat wore sunglasses, and his face—with the helmet on and surgical mask—turned in my direction.

I reached and tried to remove the cassette from the player. A long, thin trail of snagged plastic film caught in the slot. When the Humvee's horn boomed beside me, I realized the light had turned green. But the tape was still snagged; the cassette dropped toward the wet carpet as I pressed down on the accelerator. The Humvee fell in behind me again. I saw the front rider on a phone, gesturing toward me, checking on my license plate, I guessed.

Harlan Maas, whoever he was, hung upside down in plastic, swinging back and forth and knocking gently against my right knee each time I hit a bump.

Ahead, some kind of portable traffic alert sign was coming up on the side of the road. The Humvee closed the gap again as I approached Chevy Chase Circle, the border with Maryland. Funny thing about those traffic circles. They were designed by Frenchman Pierre L'Enfant, George Washington's city planner. L'Enfant created traffic circles so that troops could gather there, to repel invaders or deal with rebellious citizens. And now a rebellious citizen, me, approached a traffic circle. The headlights on the Humvee flashed on and off. There was a loud-hailer on top but the soldiers did not use it. There was no way I could outrun a Humvee. I thought they wanted me to pull over. I was preparing to do that, trying to think of a lie to tell them, when I read the words on the electric flashing sign.

MARYLAND CLOSED TO VEHICULAR TRAFFIC BY ORDER OF THE GOVERNOR. DO NOT PRO-CEED PAST CHEVY CHASE CIRCLE. VIRGINIA ALSO CLOSED. D.C. RESIDENTS, GO HOME! STAY SAFE!

To turn back, you needed to go around the traffic circle. I saw a couple of cars—their drivers must have also been trying to flee the city—going all the way around and coming back toward me now. The faces inside these cars were furious or frightened; crying children in one car, a couple arguing in another. On the far side of the circle sat a line of idling Maryland National Guard ve-hicles, and troops ready to stop anyone attempting to enter the state.

I took a chance that the soldiers in the Humvee had not been trying to stop me, but to warn me. Nauseous with tension, I took a right turn into the circle. When it was clear that I was going back into the city, the Humvee peeled away and stopped on the far side of the circle, by the National Guard line.

Little soldier-to-soldier social call, now that duty was done.

I'd sweated through my shirt.

Safe, for the moment. But trapped in D.C.

As I headed back into the city, I had no goal except to get distance from the soldiers. I didn't touch the dangling cassette until I was a mile away. Then I pulled off Connecticut and onto a suburban-type side street. I was breathing hard, as if I'd just sprinted a mile. I hit the windshield wiper knob by accident, and the wipers slashed back and forth before I stopped them. When I tried to ease the tape from the slot, it ripped again. Three feet of tape dangled on one side, a foot-long strip from the other.

Tape lay spooled in a mass on the wet carpet.

What do I do? I can't go back to the house. I can't turn myself in or I'll end up in one of those detention centers, or in a military prison. I don't even know if the tape is audible anymore.

High above, I saw a lone jet leave a fading contrail as it angled into the blue, looking more like a vestige from history than a common sight. Looking as far away as Venus. The airport—any place with police and soldiers—would be out of the question. To board a plane, I'd need ID and a ticket that cost ten times the usual price, and even then, I'd need a medical check. Roads would be blocked. Military flight? Private airfield? I sat there thinking, with a pile of prepaid phones on the backseat, and my fuel supply draining away while I didn't move. I could not fly planes. At a private field I'd need a plane and a pilot. Did I know a pilot? I knew one in Alaska, and a few in Kenya. I had an old Parris Island buddy who'd retired as a major and now owned a small Cessna in Provo, Utah. They were all thousands of miles away.

I thought harder, spooling some twisted tape back into

the cassette. Try to lie my way onto a private air base, if it wasn't guarded? Hope I find a pilot hanging around? Try to hijack a plane? Was I that desperate?

It was over.

Turn yourself in. Throw yourself on their mercy. Give them the ripped-up tape and hope they can fix it, and that they bother to listen to it. There is no other way.

Doggedly, I told myself there would be no harm in trying to find a private airfield. Maybe a bolt of luck would strike. Then I had a better idea. Not exactly a good one. Just better than anything else I'd considered so far.

AS THE PRIUS REACHED ANACOSTIA, I REALIZED THAT I WASN'T THE only one who had this idea. The onetime home for the Nacotchtank Indians, on the banks of the Anacostia River, was named for that long-slaughtered tribe. They'd hunted black bear and deer in the woods that once stood here. I drove through an impoverished, ratty wasteland neighborhood famed for its street gangs and high crime.

Freight trains are still running, the newscaster on WUSA9 had said. I hoped that she was still right.

Back during the Great Depression, tens of thousands of Americans had hopped freight trains to move around the country. Now as I cruised Anacostia's commercial strip, I saw more moving cars than elsewhere, and from the packed belongings inside, and nervous faces, I realized that these refugees sought the rail yard, too.

My GPS flickered on and off. Soldiers blocked some streets. Where to go? I saw several high-end cars circling around blocks, nosing around, backing from one street, gliding across a supermarket parking lot and into an alley. It was as if the cars were animals looking for a water hole, as if the vehicles themselves had a lumbering intelligence. They sought exit from the city in which they'd been trapped.

I think all us drivers were aware of each other, aware of a competition, but we also watched to see if someone else knew a secret route to Benning Yard. I made eye contact with a male driver I'd passed three times in the last five minutes. I saw a Mercedes packed with young people, displaying American University stickers on the back window. I saw a low-slung white Cadillac Escalade—windows down—filled with tough-looking young men—locals, I think—who eyed the circling cars as if we were a herd of antelopes and they were cougars. I spotted high wires and cranes over a low rooftop. These would mark a rail yard. I turned down a side street in that direction. The street turned out to be a dead end. I turned around.

For the next frustrating twenty minutes I tried different streets, guided by the smell of boardwalk—rail ties—and by the high, crisscrossing mass of guide wires and loading towers jutting above the lower rooftops. I was tantalizingly close to the rail yard, but every time I tried a route, it was wrong, or blocked.

I tried one street heading in that direction, and rolled past row houses. At the end, a six-foot barrier of plowed snow blocked the way, forming a cul-de-sac. No way through. The oily Anacostia River flowed by.

Another street looped into a turn, which took me back the frustrating way in which I had come.

A third street was occupied by troops ahead, warming themselves around a trash can fire. I turned away.

I changed tactics. I pulled over on a commercial strip, Eisenhower Place, and watched other cars. Maybe I would learn something from circling traffic. The block featured a rib joint and a seafood store and a 7-Eleven and a funeral parlor. The commercial stores were untouched by looters. The steel grille of the funeral home had been smashed in.

Go figure. Why loot that?

The white Escalade came around the corner, passed me, and a block later, made a U-turn and stopped. It idled there, tinted windshield like enormous square sunglasses, side windows up now. Previously, they had been down. I felt eyes on me, *who the hell is there?* I saw faces looking out from the upper-floor windows of an old brick apartment building. I felt watched by riders and drivers of other cars, as they realized that one of their number had changed behavior.

The Escalade made a quick left and left the block, spraying snow.

The admiral's Glock lay on the seat beside me. I pulled out a sandwich, unwrapped it, and chewed while my eyes went from the view in front to back. I told myself that it had been stupid to put coffee in the thermos. Water would have been smarter. I drank the coffee anyway. I felt a tug at my bladder. Great. *The power of suggestion*, I thought. Not now.

The Escalade pulled up beside me, so close that it blocked my door. The front window remained up, smoky and inscrutable, but the rear window rolled down, and sound emerged. It was Pachelbel's Canon. Strings, not drums; baroque, not rap. I looked into the face of a twenty-something man below a broad-brimmed Nats cap, with a heavy faux gold chain around his neck, and an M9 Beretta pistol in his hand. The man beside him held an M4. *How did they get military weapons?* I thought.

"How much mileage that little car get?" he asked.

"Fifty. Sixty."

"My cousin had one of those. He got hit by a semi in Tampa. Ain't no use saving miles if you end up a pancake."

I had to look up to see them. He could see down into my car, at my lap.

"What you need all those cell phones for?"

"Talking."

"Hey, you know Captain Grady? Jim Grady? In Metro?"

"No."

I had a feeling it had been a trick question. He turned away and talked in low tones to the man beside him. He turned back, with the same unreadable eyes.

"How about Lieutenant Trethewey? You know her?"

"Nope."

"You some big talker."

I shrugged and said nothing. It was his play.

"What are you doing here?" he said, not a demand, more curiosity, the music swelling and ebbing, and over the sound of those strings came the high-pitched whistle of a freight locomotive entering or leaving the yard. Opportunity approaching or ending. I did not think I moved my eyes, even changed my attitude. But something must have changed in me enough for the man a few feet away to smile, showing perfect polished teeth. Somehow I'd answered him.

"Oh, you one of *them*."

I knew what he meant.

"You want to leave! What you got to trade?" he said.

"I didn't say I was leaving."

He snorted. "There's only a few trains going out every day. They unload and there's empty cars, see? But you can't get a ride unless you know how. This is our neighborhood. We know how. You want to look at the sky, sit, think, cogitate, masturbate? Or you want out?"

He sat back. He looked like a gang kid, but half the time, he talked like something else. Another car pulled to the curb, across the street. I saw a man and his wife and a couple of kids inside. Somehow that driver had heard that if he wanted to try to leave D.C. on a freight train, he must come here. The man got out of the car, and started walking toward us, changed his mind, and turned around. He looked pale and uncertain, middle-aged and out of place, and the faces behind him were pressed to windows. There were suitcases tied to his roof. The family reeked of desperation. Was the man actually stupid enough to think he could carry so many possessions away?

I said, "How do I know you'd really get me out?"

The kid in the car nodded, appreciating the question. "See all these people driving around? They here 'cause someone they know got out *already*, and told them this is the place. You people our advertising! You and me conversate, and then make a deal and later you tell your friends it worked!"

"You're not scared of getting sick?"

A shrug. "Chances the same if I stay away or come. What's the difference, Sam?"

"Why me?"

"My cousin's car was the same as yours."

"Uh-huh. What if I want to get to a certain place, not just out of D.C.? What if I have a specific destination?"

"Tell the guys in the yard, and they put the right people in the right cars. Those trains hit Baltimore; cars get divided up, some go to Chicago, some go north, see?"

I considered. His answers came smooth and fast. Too fast? "You set this system up pretty quick," I said.

"Who says we just set it up? This was all in place, Sam. It's a highway. Now we use the highway for something new."

"Why are you calling me Sam?"

"You Uncle Sam, aren't you? You one of these government chicken shits on the run. Got left behind when the big boys left. Leave your family? What can you pay?"

He's saying that for a long time they've been moving drugs or guns or illegals on these trains. He's saying they . . . whoever they are . . . adapted an existing system to new cargo, if he's telling the truth.

I'd take the chance. I offered cash and he laughed. *Are you kidding?* I offered the admiral's watch, but that was not enough. Maybe nothing was. Maybe he just wanted to find out what I had. Maybe there was no escape through the train yard and the whole thing was a trick.

I told the man that the Glock stayed with me, and he seemed to accept that.

"I want the car," he said.

"The *car*?"

"What the fuck you need it for? You leaving!"

He was right.

"Hey! It really get fifty miles a gallon?" he asked.

"Even more on the highway."

"Hmph! You follow us now. Keep your little gun, but leave the phones and we'll take the cash, too. The CD work?"

"Yes."

"Looks like the cassette player is fucked up, though. I like a good sound system," the kid said, then his window rolled up. I followed them off the main street, and into an alley, then through a lot for wrecked autos, through a fenced-in parking lot, and up to two Army Humvees parked outside a steel chain-link fence barring the expanse of rail yard. Inside, weeds poked through fresh snow. I saw cranes and power lines and idle tank cars and one lean barking brown and white mutt.

A trap!

The Escalade stopped. But it wasn't a trap. The kid talked with the soldiers. The kid pressed something into the hand of a surgically masked officer, and the officer waved our two-car convoy through.

I bumped through a gap in the fence, past soldiers who were splitting up money, and into the yard, where the train I'd been hoping to catch was rolling off. The freight yard was wide in the middle, filled with tracks and idle cars, then the tracks narrowed into two or three ways out. The departing train was two hundred yards away, going faster every minute; a parade of disappearing tank cars and V-shaped coal cars and rectangular boxcars. Through an open door in a departing boxcar, lots of sorry-looking, bundled-up riders stared out. I spotted more gang members near the loading docks, using forklifts to move stolen crates. They loaded the crates onto tow trucks. The black market was thriving in this particular spot.

My favorite quote about military matters comes from Napoleon. It's "Sure he's a good field marshal, but is he lucky?" For the moment my luck held. A second train had arrived from West Virginia, bringing coal for Washington's furnaces and power plants. A new line of refugees, most wearing surgical masks, kept as far apart from each other as possible as we were directed onto freight cars while soldiers watched, a train crew watched, and gang members stood by. All of them clearly paid off.

If ever the world ends, there will be an opportunity in it for commerce. For fire extinguisher manufacturers and gun makers and those who bought stock in insurance companies to sell short. We take pride in those who survive disaster. But cockroaches are good at survival, too.

The train lurched into movement. I sat on the steel floor of a coal car, the open sky above. The temperature was dropping. Long after the car should have been full, more people had climbed in. We were a Washington version of the refugee-filled trains chugging north from

Central America, peasants clinging to roofs, undercarriages, sloping tops of cylindrical tank cars.

I looked around, trying to place my fellow travelers. Students trying to get home? Husbands stranded on business trips, trying to reunite with wives? Parents evacuating kids away from an epicenter of outbreak?

Now we all lurched north, in a moving pit filled with strangers, some grateful, others irritated or frightened. Some had envisioned more comfortable quarters, and not considered that riders packed beside them might be sick.

I'd handed over more than thirty thousand dollars, if you figure in jewelry and the Prius. Multiply that by forty, and as much as a million dollars in cash, carry goods, and property had paid for the riders in just one open, creaking car.

A ragged cheer went up when the man hanging up over the side announced in a loud voice that we'd cleared the yard, and a second cheer rose when we passed the line of Maryland National Guard whose vehicles marked the border, and who must have also been paid off.

Some people sat alone. Others in groups. Most kept on their surgical masks. The children's faces seemed completely gauze covered. I smelled coffee, and alcohol from a bottle passing between three scruffy-looking men. I found a corner and settled in. I told myself the cold wasn't so bad. I wondered how long this train would take to reach New York State, or if, as the gang kid had said, the cars would be split up in Baltimore. I wondered whether, after a hundred miles or so, we'd enter the territory of a different gang.

Nearby, a tall woman was on a cell phone, loudly voicing second thoughts. "What if two gangs are working together? What if when we get to Baltimore, we'll be robbed? Or they make us get out?"

There was nothing to do but wait. I pulled from my parka the busted tape, the words of Harlan Maas, half shredded, proof, if I could patch the thing, get the tape on the spool, and get the spool to the right place.

But just then a man's voice said from right above me, "How about slipping that mask down for a second and showing us your face, mister? Face and hands! Now!"

SEVENTEEN

THE TRIO OF VIGILANTES STARED AT MY FACE, AS IF BACTERIA
might be visible on skin, crawling and multiplying, eating
me from the inside. They bent closer, human tropisms of
fear and ignorance. *"Show us your hands!"* Satisfied, they
went on toward the next refugee party, young women, a
couple, and two young girls. None showed visible signs
of disease.

Which means nothing, I thought. They could still be
carriers.

My heartbeat slowed to normal rhythm. But suddenly
the last of the vigilantes spun back and reconsidered me.
The others turned, too. The man, walking back toward
me, was thick-necked, unshaven, and red-faced, from bad
blood pressure or too much liquor. His peacoat was too
thin for this weather, but the lumpy bulked-up chest suggested that he wore layers of sweaters beneath. Paint-

stained corduroy pants ended at Doc Martens, with more white paint spots on top. House painter, I figured. Handyman. I was wrong.

"Do I know you? You work at Health and Human Services, right?" he said.

"Wrong man."

"Third floor? Measles-rubella group?"

"Everyone tells me I look like someone they know."

"I'm good with faces," he insisted. I felt a throbbing in my neck. He came closer, then he brightened. I saw his day-to-day persona when he wasn't terrified. "Tuesday night softball, right? By the tidal basin!"

"That's it."

"Which team?"

"Senator Vialisek's office."

I had no idea if Senator Vialisek had a softball team. But most senators' offices fielded teams. Grinning, the man lost his thuggish aspect. Give him a shave and a Starbucks go cup, he'd be at home in the office measles-rubella group. "I told you I'm good." He seemed happy to talk about something normal. He tapped his forehead. "I never forget a face," he said, and then transformed back into vigilante mode, rejoining his new friends.

I was glad I'd not pulled out the Glock.

By the time we reached Baltimore, the riders had relaxed a bit; the inspection was over. No one looked sick. Some people tried to doze, but between the cold and the rocking, sleep was impossible for all except the most exhausted. In areas where mobile devices worked, riders texted or phoned loved ones. *I'm safe, Daddy.* Strangers sat as far apart as possible, but we were crowded. One impulse was to learn about each other in order to feel safer; the other impulse was to stay away.

Where are you heading, miss?

To live with my brother. He has a farm in Connecticut.

Do you think we'll be robbed at Baltimore?

My cousin rode the rail yesterday and said the system works.

Baltimore. Clearly the yard crew had been paid off here, too. More gang members—a dozen hard-looking young men—waved us out of the car like customs officials, separated riders onto other trains, one going west toward Pittsburgh and Saint Louis, the other north. Younger kids—nine- and ten-year-olds—sold ham sandwiches and sodas for ten times the usual price. The crew worked as smoothly as Lufthansa flight attendants. Flight attendants don't carry semiautomatics, though. These guys did.

"We're like the old underground railroad," one teenage boy told me, herding a half dozen of us into a rust-colored boxcar. "You're like the runaway slaves."

By Delaware, I learned from a rider holding up an iPad that a United pilot had just flown his 737 into the Rockies, killing all aboard. He'd been infected. In southern New Jersey, stumpy pine barrens flashed past as we listened to a volume-up podcast talk-show argument between a CDC disease expert and one from India, over whether the "Bible Virus" had evolved naturally or come from a lab. By the dilapidated rail yards of Secaucus, New Jersey, I eyed oil storage tanks and winter brown swamps, and watched a YouTube video of U.S. Marines on an aircraft carrier off Nigeria, allegedly ordered to hit Islamic militant sites in less than forty-eight hours from then. Muslim militias in eight countries had jointly threatened retaliation against American embassies, travelers, and companies should the United States hit Islamic targets, the maker of the video—a self-styled freelance journalist— claimed. There was no way to verify the information.

"We will not be deterred by threats," a White House spokesman said on another rider's screen.

No, you'll just hide under the earth and send troops to die, to make yourselves feel like you're doing something.

I tried to phone the admiral, Burke, even Chris, and tell them about the cassette tape. Their comm-system was down or blocking outside calls. The wagons were circling. The bulk of the country was shut out.

I fought off doubts about whether my journey could achieve anything. I was probably on a wild-goose chase. At a switching yard over the New York State line, forty more refugees climbed in. I kept expecting troops or police to stop us, but for the moment, the gangs controlled this old smuggling route. They'd probably been paying off yard crews for years.

North of New York City we began losing more people at stops—a bridge, a crossroads, a rural intersection— than we took on. The tracks rolled alongside the Hudson River, with pancake ice drifting, bare trees on the right, high palisades, gouged-out cliffs created during the last ice age, on the left, a mile across the river. Those glaciers had towered up a mile high. The animals who saw them were long extinct. Had they died of disease?

The Tapanzee Bridge was empty. The guards on Sing Sing prison's towers peered out. We rolled through centuries-old industrial towns and past Revolutionary War battlefields, and the narrows where the British Army once strung a chain across the Hudson, to split the thirteen colonies in two. Divide and conquer.

Some of these towns had successfully climbed out of the recession and looked prosperous, albeit too quiet. Others were decaying, with trackside signs promising hope. COMING SOON, GLOBAL GENOMICS LABS AND RESEARCH PARK, thanks to Governor Wilcox's science and economics initiative.

What is Global Genomics? I wondered.

A tinny iPad voice said, "Paramount Pictures, site of the most recent Los Angeles outbreak, was burned to the ground today by order of health officials. The historic studio is now a pile of embers."

New riders shared stories as the weather cleared, but the mercury dropped. Our unheated railcar rolled into snow country, past fallow cornfields, red-sided barns, and ice-covered winter pastures and rock walls and stumpy third-growth forest.

WELCOME TO COLUMBIA COUNTY.

I was close to my goal, the rail yard at Chatham, New York. On a normal day, I could drive from Chatham to New Lebanon in less than twenty minutes. Now, once I got there, *if* I got there, I had no idea what I'd do.

I'll figure it out as I go along.

Gazing out now, another world. I knew there were pockets unaffected by the disease, and we might have reached one. Cars moved smoothly along well-plowed rural roads flanked by two-foot-high snow piles. A truck salted the highway. We picked up a few passengers and rolled through the town of Hudson, where pedestrians strolled on sidewalks, shops were open, traffic lights worked, no troops or roadblocks to be seen. That's how it is during emergencies. On one block, disaster. On the next, chocolate ice cream for sale.

The normalcy out there provided a false security sense, and for a few minutes, relief permeated the car. It was as if we were refugees reaching Switzerland. There were only seventeen of us left, some new. Most others had dropped off. With crowding eased, so did the mood. Conversation took on a more normal tone.

"I'm Anthony Coates . . . I'm a software engineer."

"Frederick Kohn, Aidan and Bill . . . We have a drugstore."

"We're the Kruthammer family, from Canada . . ."

A bearded young man named Dave announced, "I'm trying to get to New Lebanon and this train gets close!"

My head turned toward the speaker, a librarian from Putnam County, he said . . . ruddy boyish face, chestnut eyebrows beneath the *Poetry Slam* stocking cap, in his mid-twenties. A cheery presence in faded blue jeans and an old moss-colored parka, who had climbed in during the switchover at Hudson. Everyone liked him. From a rucksack he'd removed granola bars, almonds, and dried fruit, to share. He'd done tricks to amuse the kids, pretending to take off his thumb. He'd told us that two men in his town had been among the first to fall ill, after they drove down to Washington to attend a Redskins game.

"The Bible Virus is a sign," he told us.

"Of what?"

"Mankind must change our ways."

"Great. More New Age crap," the Canadian father growled. "Just what we need."

Dave didn't mind doubters. He shrugged, a dreamer or a perpetual optimist. I asked him why he was heading for New Lebanon.

"There's a group there that has a cure."

"Bullshit," the man heading for Canada snorted. "There's more phony cures out there than patients."

"This is different," Dave insisted, shaking his head. "I heard it from an old girlfriend. I've known her since I was eight. She was studying at SUNY and got disillusioned and quit and joined up with these great people who live on a farm."

The Canadian rolled his eyes. "A commune?"

"Why do you have to label it? These are educated people who decided there's more to life than their labs. And the man who heads the farm is really a scientist! He's studied leprosy for years, I heard. His name is Harlan Maas."

I sat riveted.

A woman from Montclair, New Jersey, asked, "How much money is this charlatan asking, for the, uh, cure?"

"Nothing! They will give it away! Friends first, and loved ones. They're announcing the cure on the Net! But it's not just medical, see? It's spiritual, too. God wants people to turn away from false science, my friend said. She said come and listen, and if I don't like it, go home."

The man from Canada snorted. "You believe this?"

"I believe my friend. She was valedictorian of our high school. She said science is God's way of teaching. And science without God is empty. She said leprosy is a punishment, like in the Old Testament. The meeting will be at a truck stop off the interstate. Why don't you come?"

It seemed colder, deep down, but I was sweating at the same time. I felt a lone bead run down the side of my face. The Canadian stood up, agitated. "For God's sake, listen to yourself! A truck stop? A fucking truck stop in Upstate New York? The world is saved by ten people? With what? Little Debbie Snack Cakes from the store?"

"You don't have to be nasty about it," Dave said.

"You seem like a nice guy, Dave. You must be educated if you work in a library. Are you really that gullible? You ask me, the President should blanket the Mideast with atomics and wipe out anyone who might remotely have anything to do with this disease. Blow those godless raghead bastards up until the guilty ones confess and hand over the formula, or whatever they have."

"Now who's gullible," Dave said. "You believe the President! And by the way, the meeting will be at a truck stop so people can get there! Word will spread. Reporters are invited. The goal is a new era of peace and love."

The blood roared in my head as I asked, "Who will head up the new era?"

"My friend said that a man on that farm is amazing! He has this aura of goodness and wisdom! He's a prophet, she said."

I took a deep breath. "The *Sixth* Prophet?"

Dave smiled. "You know about him! You're invited, too?"

I nodded, smiled, jaw hurting, tried to look as eager as Dave. "Worst case, it can't hurt to see if the cure works. Right, Dave? If the preaching is ridiculous, who cares, just leave!"

"That's how I feel!" Dave stood up. I had a feeling he'd been chasing answers his whole life. He emitted the rapt passion of the regularly converted. How many other causes had he espoused before trying this? At that moment the light hit his face in a different way. Beneath the affable surface I saw something lost that had lived in him a long time. He was no less genuine, but now I saw him as a potential foot soldier in an army of fanatics. Were other Daves making their way to the truck stop, too?

Of course they will, thousands will, if the cure works.

I wondered, *Is this what it has been about?*

Big things start small. The doubter from Canada had probably never sat in a classroom at Quantico and heard lectures about cults. Aum Shinrikyo, which had released poisonous sarin gas in the Tokyo subway system, to start a world war, they believed. Jeffrey Lundgren, whose followers cut up a family in Ohio. Jim Jones, whose 918 followers killed themselves.

Dave was arguing, shiny-eyed, "Look at the Wright brothers. They invented flight in a garage! Nobody figured that two mechanics could do it! Well, why can't average people invent a cure, too? Everyone thinks average people can't do anything."

I said, "I agree with Dave."

Dave sat back, happy to have an ally. The Canadian looked from Dave to me, as if we'd turned into aliens. "Some people believe anything," he said.

Dave offered me granola from his bag. He was more confident with an ally close by. He asked the Canadian, still trying to convert him, "Do you trust Jesus?"

"I sure do, mister. Especially now."

"Then you believe prophets exist. You just don't believe in this one. You believe in miracles. Just not this one." Dave suddenly seemed to tire of being nice. He had another side. "You don't know anything about Harlan Maas," he snapped.

"Salvation at a *truck stop*?"

"Jesus preached in the slums. Why not a truck stop?"

The doubter threw up his arms. "Fine! He's a prophet!"

"You say that as a joke now. You'll change your mind."

Dave turned his back on the guy and smiled at me and reached into his knapsack and came up with a folded-up paper. It was a roadmap of the New York–Massachusetts border area. My home lay only an hour away. It would be funny, I thought, to be plucked from home and sent to Africa and learn, in the end, that the problem had originated less than fifty miles from where I started out.

"The website says if we can get to this railroad bridge, volunteers will drive us the rest of the way," he said, gloved index finger tracing rural roads, coming to rest on a dot in western Massachusetts, red veins on a map, along the rail spur to Pittsfield.

"Aren't those drivers afraid of getting sick?" the Canadian's teenage son asked from behind us.

"No, because they have a cure."

"Aren't you afraid to ride with strangers?"

"I'm doing that now, and so are you."

"This cure," I asked. "Is it a pill? A drink?"

"I don't know."

"Dave, were there any companies named on that website you mentioned that helped make the cure? Any specifics at all?"

"Let's call up the website and YouTube and see. Rats! No reception."

YouTube. The ultimate arbiter. Our age's essential truth. Maybe history will one day call our times the age of information, maybe the age of rumor. When the sheer weight of complexity drove millions away from fact. Dave remained calm and hopeful. I suppose if you have to take refuge in something, hope's not bad.

I spoke to the stranger named Harlan Maas in my mind.

If your people released the disease, and then you cure it, I wouldn't exactly call you a prophet, Harlan. I'd have another title for you. "Prophet" surely isn't it.

THE CLATTER OF STEEL ON TRACKS SEEMED FARTHER AWAY. I jerked awake and Dave was sitting right beside me, gazing into my eyes with fascination and, I sensed, sympathy. He was eerier by the minute. He leaned close. His whisper, fogged breath, smelled of his coconut-chocolate energy bars. "I know your secret," he said, hand half covering his mouth.

"What?" *Shit! Did I talk in my sleep?*

His eyes flickered down to my hand. For an instant it didn't register. When it did, a flood of horror seized me. A long wooden splinter had pierced my glove. I took off my glove and pulled out the splinter and a burst of blood came with it but there was no feeling where it had penetrated. I poked the finger. It was numb. I poked the next finger. Nothing.

I'm sick.

Dave said, "They'll cure you. You'll see. There's a reason you came." He slid back across the lurching floor to his corner. I realized that he'd moved close to me while I slept to protect me, to shield from the others that a four-inch-long projectile had lodged in my hand.

Twenty minutes later we crawled into the hamlet of New Lenox, and sure enough, the train halted atop a small bridge over a stream. I saw four automobiles idling on a country road, waiting for passengers, us, I guessed. Dave and I were the only ones climbing out, and walking through the foot-high snow to the lead car, an idling Dodge Ram.

"Hi, pilgrims!"

The driver was a plain-looking, moon-faced woman with a bright smile, a Midwest accent, and she waved us into the rear seat. She asked if we were hungry or thirsty. She said there were ham sandwiches in back, from animals slaughtered at the farm. There was a thermos filled with hot coffee. She said that we should relax, we'd reached a beautiful place. We would be cared for.

"Are either of you sick?"

"Me," I said.

"You will be cured," she said.

I'd felt nothing at all against my fingers when I'd grasped the door handle, nothing when I'd climbed over the top of the boxcar. I didn't feel the glove fabric, or the cold, or the pressure of metal.

"You will be cured," she repeated, "by the prophet."

We started driving.

The truck stop, our driver said, was a mere eighteen minutes away, off the Massachusetts Turnpike. I saw a pin sticking out of the backseat, and picked it up. I stuck it in my finger.

Diagnosis, confirmed.

Joe Rush, leper, pariah.

Wouldn't it be nice if he's really a prophet? I thought. *Who is this guy anyway? This Harlan Maas?*

EIGHTEEN

It is estimated that over thirty thousand children
in the United States are growing up in cults.
They are isolated and have no other experience
with life outside of these twisted environments.
Many never adjust, even after being rescued.
Many commit suicide later in life.

—CHILD WATCH,
NEW YORK CITY

THE LITTLE GIRLS HAVE BEEN NAMED FOR FLOWERS: DAISY, ROSE,
Tulip, Violet. The boys—Enoch, Jeremiah, Ezekiel, Micah—
have Bible names and first names only, until age twelve,
when Brother Agabus assigns them adult identities and
gives them jobs: girls to sewing, kitchen, and laundry; boys
to the sugar fields or gun shows or the group-owned auto
garage in the Louisiana town of New Bethlehem, twelve
miles away.

"We will purify ourselves. This will lead to Christ's re-
turn, the end of Babylon, the new Kingdom of Solomon,"
Brother Agabus says.

The twelve-acre compound abuts a swamp, amid moss-
covered cypress. There are alligators and gar in the black
waters, and the old abandoned, long-closed leper colony

consists of two rows of cheaply made bungalows that were crumbling when the isolated property was auctioned off by the state.

"In two thousand days will come the end times prophesized in Revelation 11:3," Brother Agabus assures them. "Outsiders call us a cult, but that is a hateful word that devalues truth. This is a gathering place for those to be spared. This has been revealed to me by the Seventh Angel and by four secret messages hidden in the Old Testament."

Harlan was born here. He has no memories of anywhere else. He's only left the compound twice, rushed away by adults when Agabus thought that agents from the Bureau of Alcohol, Tobacco and Firearms were coming. After the agents left, the children were brought back.

"You are a special boy, my favorite," Agabus always tells him when they are alone at night.

Harlan's mother—91 IQ—quit her 7-Eleven job in Baton Rouge and moved here after hearing Agabus preach in a park one day. Harlan was born ten months later. His twenty-eight brothers and sisters were also fathered by Agabus, by fourteen women, all of whom dress as Agabus ordered, in modest print dresses and white bonnets. The men wear coveralls. No one owns private possessions. Agabus keeps the bank accounts and has a new Cadillac and better clothes. Only he can consume liquor. "To speak with outsiders, I must adopt their customs," Agabus explains.

"Take off your trousers, my son, for more photographs. Lift your legs, please. Touch yourself," he says at night.

Agabus is vibrant and charismatic, age thirty-five, thickly haired all over, curly black on top, with a beard that drops to his chest. He has a V-shaped torso, massively tattooed with religious symbols, saints and halos, and he has thin legs and an almost dainty pigeon-toed walk on small feet. On most nights different women go into his bungalow.

On others, Agabus soothes Harlan and whispers hoarse things in his ear. Agabus smells of peanut butter and lime. After he leaves the bed, there are curly hairs on the damp sheets, and the room smells like dirty feet.

"If you tell anyone what we do, I will kill you."

Adults work the sugar field or gun shows nine hours a day. Sunday sermons start at six and last until two, with an hour lunch break. Phones and televisions are forbidden. Visitors are not allowed. Women sleep in one dorm, men in another, with conjugal rooms provided for the better workers. Children are homeschooled in approved subjects: math and English, Old and New Testaments, Siddhartha, and certain black-and-white 1950s science fiction films, which were, Agabus tells them, "guided by Angelic hands."

"Touch me here, son. Ahhh."

Agabus, in sermons, quotes scripture in the whispery lost language of Mesopotamia, which only he speaks, after being taught it, he says, by the winged angel Zadkiel.

"Today we discuss spanking. The abandonment of spanking children will lead to criminal activity among the young."

If you get sick, Agabus comes to your bedside, and mutters in Mesopotamian and dispenses medicines—only he can do that—until you confess what you did wrong.

Then you get better, unless you get worse, which means you lied. Lying means a whipping.

God led us to this old leper colony, Agabus says. Leprosy

*was Bible punishment. Leprosy was God's judgment on sin-
ners. Leprosy cured was God's reward, delivered through the
great prophets and saints.*

*ON THE NIGHT IT ALL ENDS, THE NIGHT OF THE RAID, THE BOY LIES
awake on top of a thin blanket, listening to the nutrias
screaming outside, smelling rotting vegetation, black water,
and swamp, a mix like cut grass and old sweat and a damp
bathing suit locked up in a ten-year-old musty duffel bag.
Mosquitoes whine behind him, or batter against the screen
from outside. He's listening for Agabus.*

I hope he comes, the boy, eight, thinks.

*He looks at the wall. Agabus keeps old black-and-white
leper shots in rooms to remind people of God's punishments
if you don't listen to his word. The boy sees children's faces
eaten away, crutches instead of legs, holes instead of mouths,
gaps instead of noses. Leper children line his walls. Sometimes the visages populate his nightmares.*

I'll be good. I'll do what he tells me, the boy thinks.

*The boy jerks when the first gunshots go off. He can barely
reach the window. There seem to be more mosquitoes inside
than out. He hears shouting out there. He hears a bullhorn
and a stranger's electrified voice warning, "Throw down
your weapons." Women create elongated running shadows
in the floodlights of the compound. Someone screams. The
boy's mother is on her knees, hands pressed to her temples,
insane with fear. A man charges out of another bungalow
with a shotgun but stops and drops it and throws up his
hands. The other men put their hands up also. The bullhorn*

voices order them to stand together in the light. Then strangers wearing helmets and armored vests appear, herding the adults away. The boy is terrified.

"God has chosen you for something special," Brother Agabus told him more than once. "You are a genius. You are the smartest child here."

Now Agabus appears out there on his porch, between two armed strangers. Brother Agabus is in handcuffs. His head is lowered. His hair falls over his forehead. He is shuffling toward their black car and looking at the ground.

The boy runs out of his bungalow, screaming, enraged.

"Leave my father alone!"

TWO DAYS LATER THE BOY SITS IN A PARISH POLICE STATION, ACROSS *the gouged-out wooden table from a fat, sweating detective named Edward Wohl, and a woman who says she's a prosecutor, whatever that is. He's refused the ham sandwich and the cold Dr Pepper they offered. He's refused to answer questions.*

"Don't worry, son. That pervert is locked away. He can't hurt you now."

"He didn't hurt me!"

"He was a fraudster. His real name is Leon Charles DeGraves. He tricked people. He stole money. The things he did to you kids are disgusting."

"You're the one who is disgusting." The boy stares at the woman. Her bare arms are fleshy and visible for all to see. So are her legs and calves. The man is wearing jewelry; a

watch and a gold ring. Agabus has preached about this ostentation, the exhibition of the body.

The boy shuts down as if he could make these two—and their godless glitter—disappear.

The woman says, "All that stuff he told you about angels and prophets, son, he made it up."

"I'm not your son!"

The man and woman look at each other, then tell him to "think about things." They leave a TV on when they walk out, but the door is locked. The boy has never seen a TV before. On-screen is a show about a father, a mother, and kids all living in the same house, saying stupid things to each other, even talking to a dog while other people, unseen in the background, bray and laugh. The music is awful. It's like watching aliens from another planet. The dog cocks its head, as if it understands English, causing more stupid laughter to erupt from the tinny speaker.

There's also a black telephone on the wall, which fascinates the boy. When the adults were here, it rang, startling him, and then the woman picked it up and a voice came out of it. The woman spoke into the telephone. This was amazing! That you could speak into a piece of plastic and someone could hear you on the other end.

"The doctor found bruise marks on you," the woman says when she comes back, all alone.

"I fell."

"We know what those marks mean. The other kids told us about it. That freak can't hurt you. It's important to talk about things."

He pushes the ham sandwich onto the floor.

"There's no secret angel language. There's no souls flying around. Leon DeGraves targeted the weak-minded. He's a sick pervert. He sold tapes he made of you for money."

"I want to talk to my father!"

Fat chance. The terrified boy next sits in a doctor's exam room, eyeing the straps and gowns, and syringes. He's never seen a doctor's office. The white-jacketed, mustached older man introduces himself as Dr. Robert Maas, GP. He pokes the same places that Brother Agabus does, but his touch is clinical and different.

When the doctor goes into the other room, the boy presses his ear against the wall to listen to Robert Maas talking to the woman. The boy is trembling with fear.

The doctor says, "Give me a break, Charlene. The mother is delusional. That kid is not going back with her. She doesn't want him anyway. He doesn't even have a real name! Yedaiah? He's not going through life called Yedaiah!"

"Foster home, then." The woman's voice sighs.

"He needs to be with people who understand what he's been through. He needs therapy and time. Reaching smart kids is tougher. Their defenses are sharper. The last thing he needs is the Louisiana system determining his fate."

"Do you have a better suggestion?"

A sigh. "The mother's schizophrenia kicked in at twenty-five. In males the average age for onset is twenty. Between his childhood and genes, he's a walking time bomb."

The boy's new bedroom is on the second floor of the doctor's home. The wallpaper has a fire engine pattern, and an Oakland A's baseball pennant on the wall, instead of leprosy photos. Another boy once lived here. The doctor tells Harlan—his new name—that the boy who had lived here is dead and that he'd loved the Oakland A's, but if Harlan wants, the wallpaper can be changed. Is there some decoration that the boy would prefer?

Leprosy pictures, he thinks. At least they would be familiar. He misses the pictures.

There are also telephones in the house, which the boy learns to use, learns which numbers will bring his adoptive father's voice to him from Dr. Maas's office. One day the phone rings and he answers and hears his real father's voice, just as if Brother Agabus stood beside him.

"They think I'm calling my lawyer, but I called you. I miss you. I can always find you. I love you," Agabus says.

The boy is frozen with love, terror, confusion.

"Don't tell them what we did or HE will punish you," Agabus says. "You will sicken and rot and die."

Another voice in the background tells Agabus that his phone time is up. Men are arguing. Give me that phone! Suddenly all the voices cut off, leaving the boy shaking, the receiver buzzing in his hand. After that, he starts whenever the phone rings. In his dreams Agabus calls him, and whispers and threatens, and one time, in a nightmare, a hand even comes out of a telephone.

The boy wakes, wet from sweat.

But Brother Agabus never calls again.

By age twelve, four years later, the bedroom feels like his own room, and he's happy with the pennant, and with playing in the town softball league. He's a pretty good left fielder. By fourteen, he's a straight-A student, with a special inter-

est in science, atoms, and disease. By sixteen, he's got a girlfriend. He's a happy kid. He has friends. He loves biology class. He is president of the debating club.

"You can convince anyone of anything," a teacher admiringly tells the boy after a big win.

He never speaks of what happened when he was younger, even to the doctor. The boy blocks it out. Sometimes he wakes up sweating, and cannot remember a nightmare. He reads in a newspaper that his biological father died in prison, knifed by another inmate.

"DeGraves was a child molester and pornographer," the newspaper says, "sentenced to life without parole."

He feels nothing at this news. He's never spoken of the cult, or of that phone call from Agabus. Never has. Never will. He gets a letter from his birth mother. She's in a hospital in Baton Rouge. He rips it up without reading it. His real father now is Dr. Robert Maas. His new family—cousins, aunts, and uncles—visit at Christmas. They give presents. They phone him on his birthday. They're not perfect, they squabble sometimes, but to Harlan, they're as close as you can get to what he wants life to be.

The boy loves Dr. Maas and on Sundays the family attends church. Dr. Maas is deeply religious and takes Harlan to tent revivals, where they sing Bible songs and pray, kneel, throw their arms into the air, where, the preacher tells them, the angels live. Dr. Maas volunteers in Doctors Without Borders, disappearing for a month each year to less fortunate areas of the earth. He flies to Turkey after an earthquake. He volunteers at a rural clinic.

I want to be like him, the boy thinks.

By seventeen, the boy wins both a National Merit Scholarship and a Kellogg science scholarship to the college of his choosing. He picks premed at the State University of New York at Albany.

In the last class of high school, senior year, the teacher goes around the room, asks students what they plan to be when they grow up.

I want to design automobiles!

A criminal lawyer!

I'll inherit the trucking company!

"*I want to wipe out leprosy,*" *says Harlan Maas.*

THIRTY-TWO YEARS LATER, HARLAN MAAS WEPT WITH EMOTION because in one hour he would reveal his mission to thousands of pilgrims who undoubtedly were gathering eight miles away. Cars were probably pulling into the lot now. Pilgrims would be climbing off freight trains. Others would have walked miles, through snow. Harlan envisioned a great packed mass of men, women, and children, sick and well, rapt, breath frosting, converging on the spot.

And the first thousand will be saved.

Many journalists had been invited as well.

He recalled his happy start at college and the way the special voice first came to him as a hard-to-hear whisper. The way he threw away his medicines at the voice's urging. The voice soothing him when he was in torment, when Dr. Maas died, turning from friendly to demanding, finally revealing who it was.

By now, it has told Harlan what to do for years.

Weeping, Harlan saw a smaller, elongated version of himself distorted in a glass vial, like a tortured figure in an Edvard Munch painting. Hands flat on his face, cheeks concave. Tears leaving pink track marks. He would never cry in front of the others. But down here he was alone with the animals, the samples vault, the cure, and the oil drum fertilizer bomb that would destroy it all if the FBI came, as they had come to take Harlan's father to prison almost forty years ago.

I do thy will.

The red phone had not rung in days, and as he'd received no new instructions, he knew he had done right.

Many will perish, but the core group will lead the world into a new era.

Harlan dried his tears. He felt the great burdening weight of being alone. But he remembered that Moses, the First Prophet, had been alone when he went up on Mount Sinai. Mohammed, the Third Prophet, was solo in the desert when he got the word. Christ rode into Jerusalem alone, and his first disciples numbered a mere dozen. Harlan had eighty. By tonight, eighty would be a thousand. By next week, ten thousand. By month's end, with the disease ravaging unbelievers, the faithful would bring New Jerusalem to the world, the cure spreading out from Upstate New York.

Which is where Mormonism was started by Joseph Smith, the Fifth Great Prophet, last one before me.

There came a knock at the lab door. It was one of the security men. "It's time to go, Harlan!"

"Any news I need to know in the holy documents?"

Holy documents meant *Wikileaks*. Wikileaks kept him informed of doings in Washington. On Wikileaks, each day, he read minutes of secret meetings, speculations, strategy, and he tracked the Marine doctor named Joe Rush, the only one groping toward minimal knowledge of what had triggered the outbreak. Wikileaks proved what the voice had assured him, that several hundred dollars of equipment and the Internet, in the hands of the righteous, could bring the corrupt powers of the world to their knees, as the Bible's Tower of Babel was destroyed in that era.

"Wikileaks says that troops will be attacking Islamic militia overseas within hours. It predicts wider war. It's like you said, Harlan. Apocalypse."

"Have they found Joe Rush?"

"He's disappeared."

"Any news from Orrin?"

"He can't find Rush either. He says the police are looking to arrest Rush. He thinks Rush is powerless, stuck in D.C."

Up top, some guards would remain here to blow the bombs if the FBI came. All others had been assigned jobs at the truck stop: as greeters, crowd control, press liaisons, and deliverers of the cure; first a shot, then pills to be taken for a few more weeks.

Harlan nodded at his driver and slipped into the backseat of the twenty-first-century's version of Christ's donkey in Jerusalem, a maroon 2009 Hyundai Sonata, which smelled of mint air freshener and fertilizer transported in the trunk.

"How many in the crowd so far?" Harlan asked, filled with anticipation.

The driver's head turned. The man looked nervous. Something was wrong. At first the driver did not answer.

Harlan frowned. "How many did you say?"

"More are probably coming right now."

"Of course, but tell me. Is it a thousand yet?"

The man looked mortified. "Twenty-six."

Harlan gasped. He could not have heard right. The driver must have meant a thousand and twenty-six, or twenty-six thousand. The blood drained from Harlan's face and he felt springs in the backseat jab him. The air drained from the car. Twenty-six was impossible. The call had gone out days ago. The Internet must have reached billions with his announcement. The voice had assured Harlan that many would come . . . so many that he'd have to cull out supplicants.

"Twenty . . . six?" he heard a small voice, his voice, say.

"I guess, with so many false cures out there, people are waiting for proof. Or bad weather kept them away."

"Bad weather? A cure is here and *bad weather* kept them away?"

In the vast and terrible silence, the number seemed to reverberate in his skull, with each bump of the chassis. *Twenty . . . six . . . twenty . . . six.* It was worse than mockery. It was not even a fraction of a fraction of the vast crowds he'd been assured would come. Into the shock came the thinnest twinge of logic, from a time when his brain had functioned better. Because *twenty-six* was inconsequential. Twenty-six meant he led not a movement

but a pathetic group of misfits and losers who had un-
leashed a scourge upon the earth.

Have I made a mistake?

"What about the press?" he asked weakly. Harlan had
ordered reporters invited, from Albany radio and news-
papers. PBS and Fox. CBS. The *New York Times*.

"I e-mailed them and sent the video. None here so far."

Harlan fell back with the taste of dead things in his
mouth. The pounding in his skull grew worse. He did
not hear the screech of the red phone on the rear parcel
shelf. When he did, he turned to it in dread.

"I don't understand," he whispered when he picked up.

"What did you do wrong, Harlan?"

"I did everything you said."

"YOU'RE BLAMING ME? DON'T YOU DARE!
YOU MADE A MISTAKE! YOU CAUSED THIS TO
HAPPEN! THE ONLY MISTAKE I MADE WAS IN
CHOOSING YOU!"

"That's not true."

The driver had heard Harlan talk into the red phone
before, so he kept going, but Harlan's whimpering frightened him. He was a washed-out ex–grad student at Williams College, a chemistry major. A shy, pimply lost soul
when he came here. He'd been recruited by one of the girls
at a bar where they trolled for students. With Tahir Khan,
he had helped Harlan design the combo-therapy to beat
the disease. All the medicines involved already existed. But
they had to be administered in correct doses, the right way.
Probably scientists would stumble on the mix sooner or
later. But many would die before that occurred.

The car passed out of the front gate and into third-growth state forest; rumpled hills folded over on themselves, Welsh-style, flinty soil sprouting ash and maple, oak and a few towering pines that had not been knocked over in the last ice storm. Next came a local land trust property, a former granite quarry, with a deep green lake that covered discarded century-old equipment, engines, saws, and chained-down bodies of people—hoboes, hikers, bums—who had been infected with the hybrid disease in the lab.

The water was so thick with silt that divers would never find all the corpses down there.

State Route 20 meandered past a Shaker village museum and a four-corner general store that still sold individual hard candies and John Deere snow plows and locally made greeting cards and locally grown corn. Billboards begged tourists to visit: the Blue Caverns, Shakespeare on the Mount summer theater, Tanglewood symphony grounds across the Massachusetts line.

"You failed. You failed all along. In penance, this is what you must do," the voice said.

Harlan gasped.

"This is what they deserve," the voice said.

Harlan didn't know which was worse, the number twenty-six. Or this. He sputtered, "You can't want that. You never told me that. You never said anything about this."

He was in shock. This new order was diametrically contrary to everything he'd been instructed to do so far. It was, he saw quite plainly, monstrous.

"I won't do it."

The voice responded mildly, usually a sign it was getting angry. "Oh?"

"There is no way you can make me do that. You never said anything before about that."

"You refuse ME?"

Harlan said with venom, "If only twenty-six come, I'll talk to twenty-six. They will bring more people. In the end we'll have a thousand. I promise. You'll see."

No answer.

"Are you there? I don't care if you are or not!"

For one second of almost-clarity, he vaguely glimpsed what he'd become: a Jim Jones, a deluded madman who'd convinced a handful of gullible followers that they could be kings of the world. But the realization couldn't last. It was too horrible to allow it to fully surface. He was unaware of pushing it away, only of exhaustion. He realized that he had, for the first time, hung up on the voice.

How did it feel? He sat up in wonder. Was the emotion inside freedom? Yes! Strength? Yes! It was a wild, surging sense of rightness and exhilaration.

I'll save people with the cure, not do what he said.

But then suddenly the voice erupted in the car, not just over the phone, in the actual air, so loud that it was a wonder that the driver kept his hands steady and on the wheel, as if no voice were there at all.

"YOU ARE TELLING ME WHAT TO DO? YOU ARE THE SERVANT! THEY HAVE IGNORED YOU! YOU HAVE FAILED AS MY PROPHET!"

Harlan wept. He gasped. "No, I won't do it!" he argued. The driver hunched over and looked frightened but kept going.

The pain in Harlan's head grew hideous, enormous.

In the end, as always, he gave in.

THE HYUNDAI PULLED INTO THE PARKING AREA AT THE TRUCK STOP off I-80. Harlan's people had set up a podium in one corner of the lot. There were long folding tables from which they dispensed hot coffee and buttered rolls to three dozen people who stood stamping in the cold. Snow clung to the top of the EXXON and HOT SHOP signs. The snack shop was boarded up. In the distance, winter pasture, a clapboard farmhouse, a thin line of gray rock wall.

The voice had instructed him, *"You will make the speech. You will administer the cure to those who came because they have been faithful. But others laugh at you. You will return to the compound and blow it up; the medicine, the cure, the grounds, yourselves. It will not be death, but transition. You will return to Earth as saviors, all evil wiped away."*

"I am so happy to see you all," he said, watching his words curl away in the cold as smoke, gazing down at strangers' faces; desperate, curious, black and white and Latino.

"You have heeded the call and now you will be rewarded. You will be cured."

It was obvious which cases were the most severe. One or two people moved closer, to see or hear better, but a cordon of security men blocked them off. The sound system filled with static. Harlan watched a man step from the front line and stare at him. This man did not look ill.

He looked, in fact, vaguely familiar.

"The cure is painless," Harlan said. "Take the shot today, then one pill a week for three weeks."

Suddenly Harlan recognized the man, and with that came the great flood of relief. It was Rush. It was actually Joe Rush, standing there, his face as clear as in the Wikileaks photo, fifteen feet away. Rush had been delivered to Harlan. The voice had given him this gift. Harlan saw with vast calm that he was doing the right thing. He saw that even Jesus had suffered doubts on the cross, crying out, "God, why have you forsaken me?"

Now his words came more easily, the pace picking up. The appearance of Joe Rush here had killed any last shred of doubt. It was the sign that Harlan had needed. There was no question now that he would do as he had been instructed!

You will destroy the compound, yourselves, the cure.

Harlan Maas gave the security man behind him the clenched hand signal behind his back. This was an alert that there was a problem needing attention in the crowd.

"My friends, let me tell you about your glorious future," announced the Sixth Prophet to those below.

NINETEEN

===

THAT NIGHT THEY GATHERED IN CHRIS VEKEY'S DORM SUITE ON THE
Georgetown Hospital campus, to fill each other in on the
state of treatment at the hospital, city, and nation. They
missed their old missions, even though their new jobs
kept them occupied sixteen hours a day. They hoped that
Joe Rush was all right.

"The White House is fixed on overseas," Galli said.
"They won't seriously consider a domestic source for the
outbreak."

"No word from Ray," said Chris. "Ray thinks maybe
Joe is hurt. Ray promised to tell us if he heard something."

"Joe could be in one of those police detention centers
and nobody would know it," grouched Eddie.

"There's no central list of names," said Chris.

The light flickered—that had started happening over

the past few hours—and out the window, a wavering glow in the distance that had not been there the night before. Fire. There were more sirens, ambulances or police; the whooping wail from the Humvees; the low, hollow symphony of bullhorn announcements, from beyond the wire. The lines outside were growing. Even healthy people were trying to enter now, for the food, or protection. News reports indicated that the initial estimates of sick had been underreported. New statistics were now coming in from all over the city. Double the amounts.

Eddie went first tonight.

"The holding area for bodies is filled up."

Chris looked exhausted and overwhelmed. "We're out of room. Every bed is occupied. We've got people coming in faster than we can handle them."

The admiral nodded. "I know. We're rushing to open more facilities. The Kennedy Center. RFK Stadium. There's talk of using Metro stations, too."

"Aya read on the Web that people have been getting out of D.C. by hopping freight trains. She said that the Army just shut down the yard."

"The President wants to make a statement, give people something positive. They're asking for anyone who has anything positive, call an 800 number."

No one said anything.

"The new plan is, mass graves," Eddie said.

Exhaustion was plain on all their faces. Just to move around inside the complex, take a stroll, get fresh air, required protective clothing. Friends did not shake hands with each other anymore. The cafeteria was closed. Once you got food, you took it back to your room. Disinfectant was available in wall dispensers in hallways. You carried your own utensils.

Eddie sighed. "Remember that old Edgar Allan Poe story, 'Masque of the Red Death'? A plague is ravaging Europe. The rich take refuge in a castle. They hold a masquerade ball. They think they're safe until Death appears, dressed as a plague victim."

"Cheery," said Chris.

"I should have gone to the cathedral with Joe," Eddie said.

"He didn't let you."

"I should have gone anyway."

The TV offered only one working channel as of three hours ago and, at the moment, showed a briefing room under Virginia, where a White House spokesman pointed to a map of the Mideast and North Africa on the wall. X marks delineated terrorist camps. Red denoted countries that "harbored enemy combatants." Arrows in the Atlantic showed the direction in which Naval warships were steaming. Headlines crawling across the bottom of the screen conveyed warnings from leaders of friendly countries, or of terrorist groups, cautioning the United States against attacks.

"Mom?"

Aya stood in the doorway hesitantly. She'd been barred from the gathering because Chris thought she'd be frightened by it. She'd been in her room, doing homework on her computer, texting friends, or whatever else she did on the Net. The girl looked smaller than usual in white flannel pajamas with a doggy motif, Labradors in sunglasses, basset hounds in reading glasses, beagles in thick-lensed black-framed glasses. The pattern shrieked of innocence and vulnerability. Chris fought off the urge to cry.

"Are you all right, Aya?"

Aya said nothing. Her face seemed to be breaking into pieces, as if the muscles warred with each other in there. Chris recognized the expression. Whatever bothered her daughter had been growing and was about to peak.

"I have to tell you something," Aya said.

Chris saw guilt and fright and determination. The set jaw. The eyes flashing with fear, or anger.

"Excuse me," she told the others. "I'll be right back."

"No," Aya insisted. "I need to tell you all."

Chris suffered an explosion of fear. Her daughter was ill! Aya was going to hold up a hand with a white patch on it. Chris could never forgive herself for bringing her daughter here, if that turned out to be the case. If keeping Aya in Washington had made her sick.

"It's about Joe," Aya said.

Eddie's chair scraped on the flooring. Galli stiffened and Chris's headache grew worse. She recognized Aya's "confession face," which, in the past, had preceded admissions of giving her best friend answers during a math test, leaving school early without permission, accepting a driving lesson—*for only five minutes in a parking lot*—by one of her friends' moms.

Aya addressed Eddie. "I don't know where he is exactly. But I think I know where he's trying to go."

She broke into sobs. She'd been holding it in. She said

that Joe had ordered her to say nothing about this, but as the situation worsened, that had grown harder. She said she didn't care if she got punished, and began blurting out a story. They knew some of it, from Joe's e-mails. But they didn't know it all. Chris struggled to grasp what Aya was saying.

Galli said, "The website says these people have a cure?"

Eddie made a face. "A truck stop?"

Chris said, "Aya, I can't believe you did this."

"This is no goddamn coincidence," Eddie said. "This has to convince them. The thing comes from here!"

After that, everyone seemed to be talking or shouting at the same time. Galli left, to track down authorities in the complex. Eddie left, on the run. He never said where he was going. The TV showed fighter planes taking off from a U.S. aircraft carrier. They were not attacking anyone yet. So far they were on maneuvers.

Chris stroked Aya's hair in their now empty suite.

"You should have said something earlier. Don't worry, honey. No one is going to punish you. I'm proud of you."

Aya sobbed.

"I didn't know what to do."

TWENTY

THE MAN PRODDING MY BACK WITH AN M4 AUTOMATIC CARBINE
was ex-Army, he'd said in the car, *so don't try anything*.
He was tall, with a bony face, watery blue eyes, and a sour,
wary disposition. The smaller, muscular Asian man who'd
affixed the handcuffs to my wrists also seemed to have
some familiarity with firearms. He stayed four feet behind, ready to use his Sig Sauer. He'd taken away my
Glock.

"Get in the cage, please," he said.

They'd come up on me from behind in the crowd, as
Harlan delivered his sermon. Snow had begun falling and
specks drifted down as the man at the makeshift podium,
under the HOT DONUTS sign, announced to the assembled multitude his return to Earth after two thousand
years. The New Age was upon us. Those here would be

saved. Gaze upon the new Kingdom of God and receive communion, only instead of a wafer in your mouth, extend your arms please, roll up your sleeves. Good friends will pass among you and administer a shot. Those who are sick will be cured. Those who are healthy will stay that way, as long as you follow up the injection with pills. A weekly regimen, three times.

Dr. Jesus.

One or two had turned away, doubting, eyeing the syringes with suspicion. Most—especially the visibly sick—had done what Harlan asked, from belief or desperation. Why come just to look? I'd rolled up my sleeve as a small, dark-haired woman in white approached me. The woman's tray held wrapped syringes and glass vials. A second woman, grandmotherly and older, administered shots as smoothly as a nurse. Maybe she was one. Just as they reached me, I felt the muzzle of the carbine press into my back.

All who wish to come to our farm are welcome.

My cell was the size of a holding area at a small town police station. The lab was in a farmhouse basement and the compound was like the hole of a donut, surrounded by state forest and an abandoned quarry, and it was fenced in with razor wire. I'd seen a lot of activity when our little convoy returned. Residents appeared to be readying for a celebration; sweeping the grounds of snow, stringing colored lights, setting up tables. I hadn't seen a celebration of any sorts in weeks. No one else had anything to celebrate.

As I was prodded onto a porch, I noticed more of the oil drums. Some had been back at the gate; others were clustered beside the house, with small antennae and timers on top. They weren't defensive barrels, not the kind you use as a truck bomb barrier, line 'em up around the perimeter of a property to be protected. They were the other kind of barrels, the kind you fill with explosives, and then, as guards were doing before my eyes, you tested connections going into the timers, to make sure the current worked.

Each signal in this frightening place was clear but the combination was contradictory. The lights meant party. The barrels meant explosions. The syringes meant cures. The lab meant infection.

"Please remove your belt, Colonel Rush," the taller guard said when we stopped before the cage.

"You know my name?"

They looked calm. Everyone up top had been smiling, at each other, at least, if not at me. I'd been in armed camps before and the mood was usually wary. But here I sensed a cheerful passivity. Island of the Lotus Eaters. Up top, men, women, and children had watched me pass with no more than idle curiosity, and then gone back to their jobs at hand. Joe Rush. No threat.

"Can you take these cuffs off?" I asked.

"Harlan said no."

Harlan said. The lab smelled of animals, deep earth, century-old timbers, and new chemicals. The two dozen armadillos in wire cages had grown agitated when we'd arrived. They'd probably seen what happened to other guests here. The sight of the only other mammal on Earth that carried leprosy confirmed that I'd reached ground zero. We were prisoners together. I was shoved into the cell and hit my knees against the cot chained to the wall. There was no window. There were words scratched on the cinderblock, barely gouged out. *Don't want to die!*

"How did you like that sermon?" I asked. Anything to get them talking. The lock was a big Medico and the bars looked firm. If I could talk the men closer, maybe some opportunity would present itself. Maybe I don't have faith in gods, but I do have hope. There's always that.

The taller man said, "We're not supposed to talk to you."

"I won't tell anyone if you won't."

The Asian man regarded the taller one. "Harlan said to check the timers down here," he said.

"Why? Aren't they all set to go together?"

"Yeah, but if he wants, we can trigger it from up top or down here!"

I smelled animals and formaldehyde, and something more human and familiar, from the cot. It reminded me of another room near Moscow, where a year earlier a man I hated had been tortured as I watched. The circle turns. The sweat smell reminded me of cracked leather and borscht, which guards had slurped while the man died ranting and salivating, pounding on a wall. I shivered. That smell was a finger pointing at my chest, a reminder of Burke's words in Washington. I could have stopped what happened in that room near Moscow. I didn't. So maybe God was in here after all.

I see restraints on those exam tables, and judging from the size of the table, they are for humans.

The steel door opened and Harlan Maas walked in. Joe Rush meets the Sixth Prophet, who coughed, as if getting a cold. Maybe he'd gotten a chill back at the truck stop, where he'd addressed the audience with his parka off. I didn't know that celestial messengers were susceptible to colds.

His shuffling footsteps sounded like papier-mâché crumpling. His smile was soft, intelligent, and shiny, like everything else in this upside-down place. His blink pattern was off, a little too long, then normal. Maybe he had some minor form of Tourette's. He pulled a swivel chair away from a lab table, rolled it toward me, and sat backward, arms over the top.

"Joe Rush."

Harlan Maas looked to be in middle age. Up close, his wide-set gray-blue eyes emitted sympathy, peace. Yet they were also tired. His hair was sparse, balding gray-white and bristle short, showing contours of skull. The sideburns flared. He wore a lumberjack's checked flannel shirt and trousers that bunched at the belt. I guessed that he'd recently lost weight. Either that or he cared little for appearance.

Figure out how to get out of this cage.

"You look just like your photo, Colonel."

"Who sent it to you? Who's been giving you information?"

He smiled. He looked toward the ceiling, as if gazing beyond. He was deciding whether to tell me the answer. Why not? Was Ray his contact in D.C.? Was it Burke? Who was the traitor? *Who has been helping you all along?* I tried to maintain calm, look like it didn't matter so much.

"Wikileaks," he said quite seriously.

"*Wikileaks?*" I was stunned. "You've just been reading everything *on the Net?*"

His eyes flicked upward, toward heaven. "He provides."

Could it be true? Of course it could be true. The whole damn country had been privy to the committee's minute-by-minute secret workings in Washington. Wikileaks? *Wikileaks?* I'd not alerted anyone about Harlan; I'd come up with my strategy after assuming that there was a traitor in Washington. Of all the things he could have said, this was the last one I'd been prepared for. The joke was on me, on the committee, on everyone back home. I felt sick with disgust.

He seemed surprised. "Who did you think it was?"

My laughter bounced off the freezer and walls and faded into the whoosh of artificially circulated air. This was perfect. This was what Eddie the cynic had always predicted. *Who needs spies when you have Wikileaks!* It was what our strategy games had never covered. Armageddon by accident, by circus, by amateurs and fools.

"Harlan? Why were your guys checking the wires on these barrels?"

If you are ever taken prisoner, make eye contact with your captors, the lecturers always tell us. Try to get them talking. Make yourself a real person to them. Never give up.

"You don't seem frightened," Maas said, not answering me. Ask a question, you get one back.

"I'm not."

Maybe Eddie had been right back in Africa. For the last year I'd sought out every dangerous situation I could find. Now I'd arrived at the great mother of dangerous situations. Chris had been right to try to keep Aya from me. The admiral had tried to protect me from myself, I thought, but then saw that he was the one who'd kept me in the unit. Upon reconsideration, I could not say that Galli had tried to protect me at all.

Harlan Maas said, "I don't take pleasure in hurting people. Or even animals."

"I see that."

"I'm funny?"

"After what I've seen, far from funny."

"How did you get here, Joe Rush?"

"The train," I said, as if the trip had been easy. Buy a ticket. Take a seat. Doze on the way. Buy food.

His brows neither rose nor fell. The man's gaze never changed. Maas said, "How did you know to come here at all? Why did you go to that cathedral?"

"Divine guidance?"

He smiled thinly. "People have made fun of that for two thousand years."

"Harlan, *you* said it. You put an invitation on the Internet. I saw it. What's so hard about that? By the way, the soldiers will be here soon. Why don't we meet them together? Let me go. Your people stay safe. You announce the cure. You're a hero."

"No soldiers are coming or I'd know. And we both know it wouldn't happen like that. Because it's not just the cure we came up with."

Once again, here was God, choice and consequence. Harlan had told the assembled at the truck stop, *You don't have to believe me. Make up your own mind. A lot has changed in the last two thousand years, but one thing is the same and it is the yearning for better.*

God, he'd said, over the centuries, had sent to Earth six great prophets, who were actually all versions of the same entity. Harlan happened to be the last in the line. He'd been Jesus and Mohammed and Joseph Smith, too.

If it wasn't so awful, and so horribly real, if the consequences had been milder, I would have had sympathy for the deluded guy.

And now Harlan Maas draped his long, thin legs outward and leaned over the top of the chair, stretching. He coughed. He was definitely getting sick. But I think it was just a cold. He only caught the easy stuff.

"If you're sure no one is coming," I asked, "why are your guys working on those barrels?"

No answer.

"Are you planning on doing something with the barrels?"

"Believe me, I don't want you to suffer. I don't want anyone to suffer, Colonel Rush."

Considering my question, this was a very bad answer. He didn't look evasive as much as he looked resigned.

And in a way, if gods could really change appearances, then Harlan's was no different than the one who had ordered Aztecs to cut the hearts from human sacrifices; told men with skullcaps to behead hostages in Pakistan; sent thousands of Europeans to Jerusalem to plunge swords into Jews and Muslims. That god changed names regularly, talked peace at your front door, asking for entry, and then, once you provided it, whispered ugly suggestions in your ears.

You've got a bad attitude about God, the admiral had told me one Sunday when he, Cindy, and Eddie had gone off to church, and I'd stayed in the house, reading the *Washington Post* Sports Section.

"Tell me you're not going to blow this place up," I said.

He said nothing.

"I don't understand. You created a disease. You created a cure. You're going to destroy it? That makes no sense."

"To you, no," he admitted.

I was in a madhouse, except I was the one in the cage, and everyone else was outside, stringing lights up top. Strumming guitars. No different, I supposed, from the Heaven's Gate cult members who dressed in their finest clothes and enjoyed a tasty dinner before killing themselves. They'd looked happy afterward, in photos, dead by their own hands.

"Do your people know what you're going to do, Harlan?"

"They know who I am."

"They're going along with it?"

He looked surprised. "Of course."

He leaned closer, but still three arm lengths away. Anyway, the cuffs prevented free movement, especially through the bars. Harlan seemed curious, interested. "Or do you think I'm a false prophet?"

I wasn't buying his placid surface and I didn't know if he was working himself up, but beyond a certain point, if you are in a cage, taunting the person who put you there is not the wisest thing to do.

Keep him talking.

"Not at all," I said. "But I'd rather talk about the leprosy, if you don't mind. How did you design the bug?"

He sighed. "I didn't."

I waited. He stood, and I thought, *He's not going to tell me.* He walked to the nearest barrel and bent over it and I saw his hand do something at the top. Had he checked a connection? Or flicked a switch? If he'd flicked a switch, would I hear ticking? Or was the timer the silent kind?

Harlan walked back and settled into the chair and sighed. What had he just done?

"We found the *cure* here," he said. "Well, Tahir Khan helped. The illness? That happened some years ago. I just never let it out until now."

"Harlan, what did you just do at the barrel?"

"I was a grad student working with leprosy," he said. "I wanted to cure it more easily. So many people get it in the third world. It's a terrible disease, Dr. Rush. We tried to grow it in a lab. But you can't do that. It's hard to work with a disease if you need fresh animals all the time."

"Armadillos," I said, glancing at the cages, telling myself that from his casual attitude, he'd just checked wires; he hadn't set the timer. Everyone up top was preparing for a party. They would have the party first. I thought, *Why prepare for a party if you weren't going to have it?* But then again, logic didn't seem to be the paramount value here.

Harlan said, "Back then, at SUNY, I needed samples that could survive in labs. So I made chimeras. Dog and human DNA. Tuberculosis and leprosy. The diseases are close, you know. TB, over four million base pairs of genes and four thousand proteins. It's one of the best known pathogens on Earth, after E. coli."

"Easy to work with," I said.

"Exactly!" Then he frowned. "But *Mycobacterium leprae*? Huge chains of unknown material! Uncoded chains. Pieces, just fragments of long dead genes, mutated beyond recognition. What did they do originally? No one knows!"

"TB was the doorway! Leprosy the locked gate!" I said.

He nodded. "Leprosy has *lost* thousands of genes since it first came into existence. Whole swaths of purpose, gone. But the TB didn't work. So I tried riskier combinations. My thesis adviser warned me not to. But at night . . . when no one was there . . ."

"Fasciitis," I said. "You mixed fasciitis with leprosy."

"Flesh-eating bacteria."

"The last two organisms you'd think to put together." I tried to remember what I'd learned in Nevada. I pulled snippets of information from memory. "Counterintuitive. Fasciitis doesn't come from soil, like leprosy. It's gram positive. Different cell wall structure altogether."

"And drug resistant." He nodded, glancing at the barrels. "But sometimes you risk making something worse to make it better. I was trying everything. It was a shot in the dark."

"And the third piece you added? The norovirus?"

Something like pain flickered on his face. He was back at least for a second, reliving a time when he wasn't a prophet. Maybe he was reliving the moment when his mind snapped and he *became* a prophet. The pained look worsened. And then I thought I understood.

"You had an accident," I said.

He didn't answer.

"You were sick. Or sloppy. You were tired and you infected a sample. Broke a slide maybe. Or sneezed. You were working in a home lab. You were doing something the wrong way. A damn accident."

The vulnerable look cleared away. The eyes sharpened. Whatever edge I'd had with him was gone.

"What is it with you?" he said. "You're not scared. You don't care about yourself. You're just trying to keep me talking here."

And trying to figure out how to make you open the cage.

I shrugged. "I care what happens to *them*." He knew

who I meant. I meant Eddie and the admiral. Chris and Aya. I meant the people who had ridden with me north in the coal car, the gang members in Washington. I meant the scientists in Somalia, Eddie's family, the worshippers at the National Cathedral, strangers even, I guess.

It's funny how some people who don't have families or intimate love can care more for strangers. But that doesn't make the caring less real. Maybe it means you have more caring to spread around. Who am I to judge? I'm a bad judge, but an honest one, and Harlan saw it, and nodded.

"I care about them, too," he said. He seemed sad. Maybe he was thinking about the tens of millions of people he cared about that he planned to kill with a disease he'd created.

When he opened the lab door to go, leaving me in the cage, I heard choral music from up top, coming over a speaker system. I was hearing the same song that I'd heard in Somalia, sung by two men in a tent. But now eighty people were singing it.

> *And the Lord sent his prophet . . .*
> *To walk among the people*
> *And the prophet smote all evil*
> *On that great and fearful day . . .*

I tried to stop him with a question. "How did Tahir Khan come up with the cure?"

When the door shut behind him, the music stopped. All I heard was the scraping of animals against steel mesh. There was no sound from the barrels. No ticking. I could not see the red digits on a timer. I wondered if Harlan Maas would come back at all.

I WAS PULLING AT THE BARS USELESSLY WHEN HARLAN RETURNED.

He walked over to a red phone on a table. It was an old scratched-up plastic model, heavy, 1950s style, but had no wires attached. The phone could not possibly work. But he picked up the receiver anyway and put it to his ear. He listened intently. He said something I could not hear. He hung up as if someone had been on the other end. He said, nodding at me, "I can answer your question now."

"You do know, don't you, that phone's not connected to anything?"

He smiled. Fine. We wouldn't discuss that part, if that's what he wanted.

"Tahir Khan," I said.

"Tahir found the cure. Yes. He went back to my old notes and re-created the strain step by step, but with one difference that allowed us to control it. He added a new technique for controlling gene expression—activation— in transgenic organisms. That means modified ones."

"What new technique?"

"Well! People think that to make a new organism, all you have to do is combine a few genes, little snipping, little splicing, make the pie. Bingo, they express themselves!"

"That isn't how it works, though," I said, thinking that he did not seem so mad when he talked about science. What he *did* with it was insane. But the man knew of what he spoke.

He said, with some eagerness, "You need a third part. You need something called a *promoter*. A trigger. A small genetic element, could be only a few dozen nucleotides . . . or a thousand. You splice it into the hybrid before the new organism can work. Think of the whole thing like a train, Colonel. The chain of cars is the DNA, but railroad cars— the links—can't move by themselves."

"The promoter is the engine, you mean."

"Yes!" he said, and smiled. "Some are designed to be active all the time. You can't turn them off. But others only drive the train under specific conditions."

"Like what?"

"An example? Say you want to try out a new gene in a mouse. But you only want the gene to work in the mouse's brain cells, its neurons. Well, there's a promoter that limits your new gene to working in that specific area. Or take recent research on fireflies."

"Fireflies?"

"Do you want examples or not?" he snapped.

"Sorry." The Sixth Prophet could be riled, I saw.

"Fireflies glow with a yellow-green light. Anyone who has been near them on a summer night knows what I'm talking about. That light comes from the insect's *luciferase*, a protein. Well, a couple years back, researchers wanted to see if they could make tobacco plants glow, too."

"Why?"

"They just *did*," he said. "They wanted the plant to glow when under stress if it was thirsty."

"This really happened?" I wanted to scream. I couldn't care less, at the moment, about fireflies.

"Too little rain, the glow would be a cry for help! Imagine a thousand plants in the field, calling to their farmer for water."

"Doesn't he know if there's too little rain anyway?"

Harlan shook his head impatiently. "That's not the point. The point is, researchers came up with a promoter to enable tobacco plants to glow!"

Harlan had apparently forgotten about all the people who might appreciate glowing plants and would—within weeks—expire from his outbreak. I didn't remind him. He was talking eagerly and I wanted to keep him that way. I said, "You're saying that Tahir Khan killed your leprosy by going after the promoter that turned it on, not the bacteria itself."

"Yes! The promoter. He created a tet-on, tet-off system against it."

"And what is tet-on, tet-off?"

HARLAN EXPLAINED THAT TET-ON, TET-OFF HAD BEEN INVENTED recently to control potentially dangerous genetically modified life. "Tet" was the antibiotic tetracycline, or its stronger relative, doxycycline. Scientists at a biotech company created genes that could be turned on or off based on the presence of doxycycline. *Tet-off* activated genes when doxycycline was missing. *Tet-on* was the opposite.

I said, "You're saying that Tahir rendered your hybrid inactive with doxycycline? But we tried that drug!"

"No! Same principle, but different drugs. Tahir found a combination therapy to shut the promoter off."

What he was saying sank in. I grew excited. "Existing drugs? You mean, all we have to do is find the right combination that already exists that will stop this whole thing?"

He sighed and looked at his watch and went to the barrel across the lab. He bent over the top and I saw his hand move. He straightened and regarded me with a look approximating affection.

"Yes. But it took Tahir years to find it."

"But the combination cures it, you're saying."

"Maybe someone else will find it someday. I have it. I have the cure to give. But nobody came, Joe Rush. That truck stop was empty. I can see that my time has not yet come on Earth."

How many minutes were left? I remembered the photos of the Jones cult in Guyana, the aerial shots of bodies lying in the open, birds pecking at the eyes. Nine hundred people had poisoned themselves. I remembered the shots we'd seen at Quantico of the Heaven's Gate cult, forty followers of Marshall Applewaite, who'd dressed in the same style clothes, same colors, same brand of sneakers, and lain down beside each other, feet all facing the same direction. They'd cheerfully consumed poison believing their souls were about to go into outer space and be transformed into something else.

Jokes. Fools. Gullible but harmless to everyone but themselves.

Harlan Maas said, opening the door to leave, "Just so you know, we have twenty more minutes. Good-bye, Colonel Rush. Do you pray to anything or anybody? You should. Now."

I NEEDED A LIE. I NEEDED A REALLY GREAT LIE. I NEEDED A STOP-per, this second, something so good that it would make him hesitate, delay, stop the count, have my cuffs taken off. Not that I knew what to do if that happened. Just that it was the best place to try to start.

I called out, "Do you know why I really came? I'm sick."

"Oh, Dr. Rush. Up until now you've been honest."

I held out my hands stubbornly and Harlan Maas hesitated and turned back toward my cage. He stopped at the chair again, a safe distance. He leaned forward, ever the researcher interested in manifestations of his disease.

I pushed my hands out between a bar. I rotated my palms as much as possible. It was clear where the dead spot lay on my fingers. It was now a white patch.

"When did you get this?" he asked, like a doctor with a patient. As if he had not just checked a timer on a ticking fertilizer bomb, fifteen feet away.

"When did it become visible, Harlan? Or when did the dead feeling start?" I asked.

"Either one."

He was turning away, seeking something in the lab. And then he saw it. He retreated and came back with one of those long, probing needles, used usually for pinning some sample down. Thin as a sewing needle, it was three times as long.

"Go ahead," I said, as if he needed permission to stick me.

The needle went into my finger and I felt no pain at all.

He tried again, watching my face. I didn't wince. He stuck all the discolored patches. I felt nothing.

"When?" he asked again.

Hide the lie. Bury the lie. Bury it in the middle of an explanation. It's the only chance.

"The numbness? Actually, back in Africa. I didn't tell anyone, though. Kept it to myself."

He started. And stared at me. Then his eyes narrowed. I knew his thought process. He was thinking that if I'd caught this in Africa, then blood tests should have shown me infected before I even got back to the United States, whether I hid symptoms or not.

I said, "I know! I figured when the tests showed nothing that I was imagining it. And the tests never came back positive. Even now. So I hid it when it got worse. I didn't want to be locked up."

He asked in a smaller voice, "The blood tests didn't work?"

"That's what I said, isn't it? Anyway, I tried to figure out how *come* they didn't show infection in me but did on everyone else. I went back and tested samples from Africa and confirmed it, see? Most sick people there tested positive. But a few, three or four, again, negative. Even people in bad shape. Like the two guys you sent, the ones singing your song in their tent. So I figured—"

Harlan broke in, anxious, "What do you mean, my people were sick?"

"Well, almost everyone was sick, so I—"

He interrupted again. "They couldn't have been sick," he said stubbornly. "They got the cure."

"Those two were in as bad a shape as the others . . . Look . . . maybe your strain mutated. It happens. The point is—"

He stepped closer, but not close enough. He was breathing hard. His eyes had gone small. He barked out, "They took the cure so they weren't sick!"

I backed up a step. "Well! You know this thing better than I do. But the rashes on their inside thighs and scrotum . . . those triangular purple marks, they're the same on me."

"On your scrotum? What rashes?"

"They cleared up now but the skin's all tough, and under the microscope that scaly purple pattern looks exactly the same as what we saw on them."

He said nothing, but he was breathing more audibly.

Come on. Don't you want to take a look at a symptom you've not seen before? Don't you want to check whether your strain has morphed into something else?

I said, "Maybe the cure doesn't work all the time. Maybe it just works on some people, not others."

His face twisted. His head jerked up. He stared at the red telephone on the lab table as if frightened of it. I'd heard nothing, but he tilted his head as if he did. And then he went over to the phone, and picked up the receiver, and listened, and his hand began to shake.

"No," he said into the phone. "I can't understand it. No, it's impossible. Yes, yes, find out! Yes, I will."

Harlan ran to the barrel and did something to the switch. Then he ran to the door and cried out for help in a wavery voice. After a moment the guards were back.

I'd stopped the countdown. At least for the moment.

He told them to unlock the cage door and strap me onto the table and peel my clothes off. Now.

TWENTY-ONE

═══

THERE WAS ONLY ONE WAY FOR THEM TO GET THOSE MANACLES ON the exam table on me, and that was to take off my cuffs. The two guards ordered me out of the cell, telling me to stand still, arms out, eyes forward. Harlan waited across the room as the tall man aimed his carbine at me and the Asian moved close with a key. Harlan turned away to select sharp-looking instruments from a table.

"I won't hurt you, Colonel. I just want to run some tests," Harlan said. "It's better that you don't move."

In the brief moment when they'd opened the lab door, before they'd shut it, I'd heard hymns coming from above, over their sound system. The same song as in Africa. Now the key, moving toward my handcuffs, seemed to shake slightly.

The guard was not so confident as he wanted me to think.

"Hold your hands straighter!"

I kept my face blank. I could not show intent in my eyes. The Asian man laid his pistol on a table before approaching, and the man with the carbine watched my face, stepping to the side to let the Asian get close. *But he didn't move far enough to the side.* It was possible that if I hit the small man at the right angle, I'd spin him into the other man's line of fire.

"Don't move, Colonel!"

I kept my wrists easy. Rigid would be a signal. The Asian man's eyes flinched to his key, off my face. Otherwise he'd never get the key in the slot. The key glinted. His nails were clean and evenly cut. I heard the smallest scrape of metal touching metal and moved fast at the exact second that the click sounded. Both men had been looking at my wrists, not at my knees, which I used to launch myself sideways, still keeping my face straight.

The shot seemed thunderous and I felt the air pressure when the bullet skimmed my ear. I felt my shoulder drive into the Asian man, driving him back, spinning him around.

With the loudspeakers going up top and the singing, maybe no one had heard the shot. The Asian man's skull was spraying blood on the left side. He toppled like a truncated statue. The gunman was stunned and that slowed him, and by the time he swung the carbine, I'd reached the pistol on the table. I had the gun in my right hand, the one in which I had full sensation in the fingers.

Something hard punched into my left side, spinning me back against the wall. *Shot.* But I kept moving, dropping, as wood shavings and glass splinters flew off tables and beakers shattered and animals screamed. I half fell, half ducked behind one of those blocky lab tables. There was no pain yet. There was adrenaline. M4 carbines fire .223 bullets. They tumble and chew up tissue inside. I'd been hit in the lower left chest, away from the midline but in the rib cage.

The area under my shoulder was pulsing and sticky and there was a feeling like wasps crawling under the skin. The whole left arm didn't seem to be working.

I heard a great rush of loud hymn singing. Someone must have opened the steel door. But when I glanced up, I saw it was Harlan leaving, not someone coming in. Harlan was running. I fired at him and missed and ducked down as more bullets came my way. I crawled behind the side of a freezer as the metal side thudded with pings and whines. I kept away from the oil drum. I didn't think a fertilizer bomb could be set off by bullets, but what if I was wrong?

Crackcrack.

I popped up and fired and glimpsed two guards there. *Double vision.* He'd split in two. I had no extra ammunition and there was no way to tell how many bullets remained in my magazine. I heard a *snap* across the room. The guard had fed fresh ammo into his carbine. Up top, I could imagine the scene. Harlan running into the compound. Harlan shouting for the singers to stop. Some ticking cosmic clock moving a second hand toward his timer.

I called out to the guard, "He's crazy, you know."

No answer. As if this would have worked. Then I heard a slight shuffling sound from the left, barely audible over the frightened whimpering of the armadillos. The guard was moving.

"He's not a prophet," I called out. But I was as effective as a Roman centurion telling an early Christian that Christ was no more a messiah than the donkey on which he rode. "He's sick," I called out. "Don't destroy the cure. You can save millions of people."

The top of the table blew apart above me. I crawled left.

Ahead, on the floor, I saw a sideways mesh rack for test tubes, half smashed and knocked to the ground by firing. I reached for it and tossed it, below tabletop level, six feet to the left. The moment it struck the ground, the table above it splintered. CRACKCRACKCRACK. I was already rising. He had no chance to turn. My shots took him full in the chest before I ran out of bullets. But I did not need them anymore, at least not here. Not under the ground.

THE RED DIGITS ON THE BLAST TIMER READ 19. THEY DIDN'T MOVE. They didn't blink. They were jammed or not running. Was it possible that Harlan had not started the timer again? Then I remembered that remote activation was possible from aboveground.

Maybe he's waiting to see who comes out of the lab before he starts it up again. Maybe he's hoping the guard will be the one to survive, and then he can take blood samples from me, see if I was really sick, confirm or disprove that I've got the same strain he released, or one that morphed from it.

I jammed a fresh magazine into the M4 and stumbled into a wall, the explosion of pain in my chest enormous. My shirt was soaked with blood. I'd smeared blood on the wall, too, and the freezer. Blood dripped as I moved. But dripped was better than sprayed. Dripped meant I had more time. The wasps beneath my skin were crawling around now, hotter and sharper, as if the insects dragged stingers across nerve endings. On the left side, in the hand, nerves deadened by illness designed by Harlan Maas. At the shoulder, nerves enflamed by a bullet fired by his guard.

I lurched out of the laboratory, and up the stairs, just as the hymns stopped and an alarm began blaring. At the top I moved into the old farmhouse. It seemed empty of people, but seeing what was on the walls, I halted for an instant, stunned. I was in a living room turned into a patchwork museum, staring at lepers through the ages: sepia photos of a leper colony in Louisiana, bungalows beneath cypresses, nurses standing like shrouds. A hand, half eaten, extended out from beneath a mesh mosquito net. I saw black-and-white shots of lepers from India. Lepers begging . . . a bowl balanced between two child hands that looked more like claws. Mexico. Indonesia. Cheap magazine cutouts hung beside good oil paintings hung beside amateurish drawings of Jesus curing lepers, as if someone had visited the National Cathedral and sketched the murals in that place. The room was a shrine to disease and obsession. It was also a prediction of a hundred million people's future if Harlan blew this place up.

At the door, I looked outside. The common area was deserted. The festive lights swayed gently, and falling snow had stopped. The sky had the washed-out winter gray of New England. I saw puffs of smoke floating out from behind the lower corner of a building. No. Not smoke. Breathing. They were there, quiet, watching. They'd drilled for emergencies. They'd all had assignments of where to go if the FBI came, or police.

If I run out, they'll shoot. If I stay here, they'll come for me, or just blow the place up.

Harlan Maas had delayed destruction because he had to know if he was master of his own creation. He might be the Sixth Prophet but he'd fallen victim to the first deadly sin, pride. My old pastor in Smith Falls used to deliver an annual sermon on this just before Christmas. "Pride turned an angel into Lucifer," he said.

I heard soft, running footsteps above me on the roof. The footsteps stopped, but then different ones were moving above the far side of the house. The breath rising across the compound was gone. People were moving around. I saw a curtain rise across the compound and a child's white, frightened face looking out. The kid saw me. I raised my carbine but couldn't shoot a child. The boy pulled back. He'd be telling them where I was.

I saw clouds scudding across the sky, west to east, the only natural pattern that seemed real in this upside-down place. I slid to the floor, my legs splayed outward. I tasted blood. If Harlan's people took me, they'd carry me back downstairs, dead or alive. They'd strap me onto that table, and Harlan would come at me with sharp instruments and peer down at bits of my flesh and liver and brain through a microscope. He'd check the leprosy that I carried against the strain he had created. When he saw that I had lied to him, he'd resume the countdown on the barrels, I figured. Blow it all up.

No one was coming to stop them anyway.

In the end, some suicides don't want to die alone. Some kill themselves to finish a rampage. A pilot flies into a mountain with the passengers in his plane. Hitler ordered the Germans to keep fighting while he ate cyanide. Harlan would carry out the biggest damn mass suicide in the world. Delusion challenged, he'd kill himself and take half the earth along.

Some prophet.

I still had the M4 loaded with a fresh clip that I'd jammed in downstairs.

I started singing.

I raised my voice as loud as I could. I really belted it out, or perhaps the volume was a product of my imagination. It was possible that my hearing was going mad along with my wavering vision.

> *One by one six prophets*
> *Last one here and now*
> *Joyous song and loving*
> *God touches his brow*

They were coming at me now across the clearing. They were coming down from the roof and from two directions across the main yard. The kid must have told them where

I was. Or maybe they just knew. They were firing as they came. The wooden door frame splintered behind me. The bullets tore up the leprosy pictures and paintings and ripped chairs, and made stuffing fly. Wood took to the air. Glass flew like snow. I had the M4 on spray. I put a big man down as he ran straight at me, like one of those Chinese Boxer Rebellion fanatics who believed, charging Marine guns in 1900, that bullets could not hurt them. Delusion atop delusion. I saw a woman go down. I saw a man on his knees, fumbling with a pistol. I shot him through the throat.

Clickclickclick.

The carbine was out of bullets.

It took a couple of moments, but then more men and women, in the silence, rose out of their hiding places. I groped for another magazine, tried to jam it in.

People coming toward me now, converging.

"I'll kill the first ones," I croaked out.

They stopped. Had they heard me? They were all looking up, into the sky.

Choppers.

THE MARINES HIT THE FENCE POINTS AS GUNSHIPS RAKED THE grounds. The little guardhouse blew apart. The strung-up Christmas lights bounced, their wires shot to pieces, with the loudspeakers. Now the chorus was one of terror and confusion. Heaven had come all right, the sky had spewed forth messengers, but not in the way Harlan had predicted.

A fire started up in one of the buildings and flames shot out. I tried to stand. I couldn't. I needed to reach the cluster of barrels and stop the timer and pull out the wires. His people had forgotten about me. They were running and screaming and trying to hide. And then I saw Harlan Maas lurching across the yard.

Alone, he headed straight for the barrel bombs. He was going to set them off. The ground burst around him, bullets whining and missing and spraying off. To the Marines, Harlan was just one more person here, no more dangerous than the others. In fact, he was older, so maybe less dangerous to them. He did not carry a firearm. He looked like a frightened guy running for shelter. He wove through their fire as if protected by heaven. He sped up with only twenty yards to go. He was fast crabbing toward those fertilizer bombs like a tropism of destruction, fifteen yards, ten, then only twenty feet separated him from carrying out his plan.

I forced myself to my feet. "Harlan!"

His legs kept pumping but his head cocked and I knew he'd heard me. Rather than slowing him, that seemed to propel him forward.

"Harlan! I don't want to shoot!"

I hit him with two shots. They seemed to be absorbed into him and propelled him forward. Like I'd added jet propulsion to his momentum. Four feet to go. His hands reached out. His head strained forward like he was an Olympic runner trying to stumble across the finish line. His whole body tilted toward whatever switch would set things off, blow the whole compound, buildings, lab, cure, us.

Harlan's legs tangled and he crumbled. Marines were on the grounds. They'd poured through a gap in the fence. They were taking control, the choppers lowering and snow flying up, not down, and troops shouting instructions and surviving men, women, and children on their knees.

"You!" a Marine shouted at me. "Hands up!"

But Harlan was still moving. The Marine didn't understand what I saw. I must have looked like one of Harlan's people. Harlan was crawling toward the barrels. Reaching the barrels. Pulling himself up.

"DROP THAT GUN!" the Marine yelled at me.

I heard firing as I pulled the trigger.

A sledgehammer hit me and drove me back and down. The sky went in circles as I waited for the immense blast.

The pain ballooned inside me, white hot. The ground was as hard and cold as it had been in Jerusalem, two thousand years ago, when snow coated Christ in the high hills in April, when he mounted his donkey, when denizens of that time believed that the Messiah had come to Earth.

TWENTY-TWO

IT WAS WHITE, CLEAN, AND QUIET IN THE HOSPITAL, EVEN THE soft beeping of the heart machine a soothing cadence through twilight sleep. The doctors bending over me did not wear masks. *Odd*, I thought, since they knew I was infected. Over the last few days, hospitals had lost their quiet. It had been replaced by pandemonium in hallways. A constant stream of sirens. Exhausted staffers losing tempers and screaming, panicked patients who knew that they were doomed from a mutated, resurgent disease.

"Colonel Rush? I think I saw his eyes move!" a voice said.

A second voice. "How long has he been unconscious?"

"Four days."

I fell back into dreamless sleep.

―――――

AT A FLASH OF LIGHT I OPENED MY EYES AND FOCUSED. HOMELAND Assistant Secretary Burke was standing by my bed. So were a half dozen photographers, who kept shooting photos as my vision cleared. Galli stood beside Burke. So did Eva Mendes from the White House. She should have been underground, in Virginia. Why wasn't she there? Mendes looked proud and happy. Beyond her, a cluster of nurses stood out in the hall, looking in.

My lips formed a word. "Burke."

He swung a chair around and sat, arms over the top just like Harlan Maas in his lab. His aftershave seemed effeminate against the disinfectant and all the flowers. He was shiny shaved, his gray suit immaculate. String tie. Dress boots. Burke.

"The President's going to give you a medal," he said. "But while you slept, I saw your other medals." His eyes moved down the blanket to where my foot was visible, and the two amputated toes, which I'd lost in Alaska. "The chest," he said. That meant the bandages. "The hand." He meant the leprosy. "Those are the real medals."

I had to give him credit. He wasn't going to be phony and pretend we were friends, or even that we liked each other. He wasn't going to say things that made him look good for the press. I liked him better for that.

He told the cameramen, "You can go." Which meant, *Get out of here.* He told me, after they did, "You did good." This meant, *No thanks to me.*

I closed my eyes. The pain in my chest was a deep thrumming, and there was heat in my skull and a kind of cool hard tingle midway up my left wrist. I held up a finger. My hand was wrapped up, but it was all there.

"I'd hold a grudge, too, if I were you," he said.

"I don't, Burke. Everything you said about me is true."

He nodded, appreciating that. "It is. But it blinded me to the other part. Ten more minutes, Colonel, and the Marines would have found a smoking pit instead of a laboratory. Ten million more people would have died, and we'd be at war and that nut would have gotten what he wanted. Annihilation. Every step of the way, Colonel," he said softly. "Every step, I tried to stop you."

He added, "We found you because Aya Vekey tracked the place down. Chris bulled her way into my office."

"Your regrets aren't my problem, Mr. Secretary."

"Well, the thing is, knowing what I know now, I would have done the same thing," he said. "Guys like you, sooner or later they drag everyone else into a disaster." I liked him more for that, too, but candor only goes so far. He asked, "Need anything, Colonel?"

"No."

"Small point," he said, "but you've been reinstated."

Grinning hurt. "Into where? Leavenworth?"

He had a boomer laugh, hearty. Texas. "Now I know you're getting better. Good-bye, Colonel. I didn't think you'd take me up on the offer. You are, of course, released from your contract. You've got some rehab time coming up. On us. If you ever need anything, don't hesitate."

"I usually don't."

He turned and left, his cowboy boots clomping on the linoleum. Mendes followed him. Nurses shooed away reporters in the hallway. I turned my head. Out the window, Washington. Still the same.

The nurse who came to check my vitals told me what I'd surmised from the lack of masks, and the topics that Burke and I had discussed. There was no panic here. Only mop-up. Harlan's cure worked.

Another nurse, waving off the reporters, sounded annoyed with them.

Colonel Rush needs to sleep.

EDDIE STOOD AT MY BEDSIDE, AND SO DID THE ADMIRAL. CHRIS Vekey was at the foot of the bed, beside Aya, who clutched a gigantic bunch of bright yellow flowers. She'd been crying. But she was also smiling. She looked between my face and her mother's like a kid hoping her parents would make up after a bad fight.

"Shot twice. He's not a man," Eddie said in a mock radio voice, like some quavery 1930s horror show announcer. "He's a super-steroid-driven animal!"

"What happened to Harlan?" I asked.

"You nailed the bastard."

"The bomb?"

"Dismantled," Galli said. "By the way, all charges against you in Washington were dropped. Turns out some kid—a neighbor—recorded the whole thing. The name of the cult member who tried to kill you is Orrin Sykes. Havlicek's got a net out for him. And some pretty good leads. The Marine who shot you thought you were a member of the cult."

"Is he all right?"

Chris's eyes widened. "You're asking if the man who *shot you* is all right?"

"I would have done the same thing," I said.

Eddie answered the question. "He's been here four times, One. He keeps calling to see how you are. He went a little nuts when he found out who he shot."

I was growing tired. My eyes wanted to close. But I asked, through pain, "Who were all those people on that farm?"

"It's incredible, One! Couple of Ph.D.s! A chemist. Straight-A grad students. I always figured, a cult, you'll get low-IQ losers. What the hell did they see in Harlan Maas? Maas never even finished college. Brilliant IQ but flunked out, went skitzy in his twenties and thought he was smarter than everyone else! Those sheep threw away their lives for him!"

I remembered the cult guards in the basement. *Harlan said this* or *Harlan said that*. Like Harlan had carried the original Ten Commandments down from Mount Sinai. I remembered the armored animals screeching and clawing in their caged-up worlds.

I was growing exhausted. I only vaguely heard my visitors talking among themselves as I drifted off. Eddie saying, "What the hell is it about people that makes them believe this shit?"

"Faith," said Galli.

"You call that faith?"

"What do you call it?"

"Nutcases," said Eddie. "Or evil. Plain and simple. Why do we excuse evil just because people can't accept that it exists?"

Galli disagreed. "People want to believe in something. They hit a low point. They're vulnerable. They believe miracles are possible to start with, so they believe they've seen one themselves. They're drowning and a man like Harlan Maas becomes the lifeline."

Eddie shook his head vigorously, not buying it. "Anybody could end up like them, you mean?"

"Hitler did it to eighty million people. Jim Jones did it to a thousand. Harlan Maas with eighty."

As my eyes closed, Eddie retorted, "The trials will start soon. Death penalty is too good for them. Let them burn in hell. Say what you want about understanding. What I *understand* is, people have responsibilities. People have choice."

"I OWE YOU A COUPLE OF CARS," I TOLD THE ADMIRAL, NEXT TIME we talked, the next day.

"The 4Runner is okay, Joe. I found it on the street and put on new tires. The Prius? Call that my contribution."

"I insist on paying for it."

"We'll talk about it later."

"You're agitating a sick man."

"Let's see!" The admiral grinned, holding up two empty hands, palms up, as if measuring options. "Lose a ten-year-old Prius and save the world? Or lose the world but keep the Prius?"

"Never mind grand announcements," said Cindy. "Joe! You left dirty dishes in the sink!"

That made me feel more at home.

HARLAN MAAS AND KAREN AND I WERE WALKING ACROSS A GREEN New England meadow. Then suddenly we were on a tundra, covered with snow. I saw a truck stop in the distance, and a neon sign above it, COFFEE AND LEPROSY. Above that, the lights of the aurora borealis shone in the sky. They dripped like lava, as if someone had drawn a razor blade across the dark, and caused heaven to bleed iridescent green.

Karen said, "I miss you."

"I miss you, too."

Harlan said, "I could have reunited you."

I said, "Not in that way, thanks."

Karen linked her arm in mine and Harlan vanished, and in the dream we drove sled dogs under the aurora borealis. My favorite dream. I had it every few months. It was a dream from which I hated waking. Waking from that dream left me empty and drained, even before the outbreak had begun.

But this time the last image was of Harlan Maas reappearing on the tundra behind us. His face morphed into the man who had tried to kill me in Washington. Orrin Sykes.

"Don't forget me," he said in the voice of Harlan Maas.

AYA SAT ON THE SIDE OF MY BED READING A BOOK ON CHEMICAL reagents and diseases as I awoke. There was a stack of *Entertainment Weekly* magazines there, too.

"Mom went downstairs to get lunch," she said.

"You need to wear a mask, Aya. Until they're sure that the medicine works."

She held out her arm. I saw the Band-Aid.

"I got the shot," she said. "And they're sure. There were laptops in that compound with all the information in them. Harlan Maas was smart, Joe! Turned out they busted up all their old records and put them into new machines, so everyone would think they invented the cure *after* the outbreak started. Six-drug combination! They stop the microbe right away!" She nodded toward one of the liquid-filled pouches hanging from a stand beside my bedside, and the tube running into my left arm. "The medicines are common and easy to manufacture. Within a few weeks the cure will be available, like, for everybody!"

She was a kid but also an adult. She was, like Eddie, my partner. She was the only one who had believed me during the dark time. She had risked jail to help me. She would, I knew, receive a Presidential Medal, too.

"Guess what, Joe? A bunch of colleges called," she said.

"And offered scholarships to any one; for after I'm a senior, even in two years. Eddie made a joke about it. He said some kids will do anything to get into the right school."

It was a pleasure to talk about something normal. "Which colleges are you thinking about, Aya?"

"I don't know. Princeton has a good chemistry program and it's not too far from Mom. Yale called, like, four times. But they're further away from Mom, and I worry," she said meaningfully, "about leaving Mom alone."

"Don't go there, Aya."

"She just wanted to protect me!"

"Just let this stuff stay between the adults."

She bristled. "You didn't mind that I was fifteen when you wanted help! You know what I learned in English class, Joe? I learned that a writer once asked a priest what he learned from all his years of taking confession, and the priest said there's no such thing as an adult, and no one is as happy as they seem. You know why I think that is? It's because *some* people like *other* people but pretend they don't!"

"Interesting point," I said, and smiled.

"Mom said you were engaged to get married last year and your fiancée got killed."

"You're worse than Eddie. But, yes, that happened."

Chris walked in and, seeing me awake, almost dropped the bag of sandwiches. She looked from my face to Aya's. But she addressed me. "Aya wanted to visit." Meaning, I took it, that she wouldn't have come otherwise. That she knew I did not want her here.

"I'm glad you both came." But I said it for Aya's benefit, to let Chris know that her daughter was welcome, but not her. Seeing her irritated me. She'd stabbed Galli in the back to steal his job. She'd told Burke that I'd gone AWOL. Some voice inside, my own voice, was asking me why I could forgive a Marine stranger for shooting me, but I couldn't forgive a kindhearted mother for trying to protect her kid.

"Aya and I have to go now," she said. "The high school is open again. They want Aya to give a talk about what happened, to the whole school. She's nervous about it."

"Three," I said, addressing Aya by her new nickname. Eddie was Two. "Three, you saved the world. Who cares about giving a little speech?"

Aya blushed. "Me."

THE VERY REVEREND NADINE HUXLEY OF THE NATIONAL CATHEDRAL was considerate enough to have a nurse ask if I would care to see her before entering my room. She brought along a meatball hoagie from Curtis and Jody's Deli on Wisconsin. Curtis and Jody were from Alaska and their Tundra Special included elk and caribou meatballs. Extra peppers. Extra onions. Extra tomato sauce. Extra cheese.

"I was going to say no, Nadine. But I can't turn down the Tundra Special."

Nadine pulled up a chair. On the TV, CNN was showing a commercial jet from the United States landing at Orly Airport. *American travelers welcome again in France.* The Sixth Fleet had withdrawn from waters off North Africa. Roads in quarantined states were open. Supplies of Harlan Maas's cure were making their way across the nation by rail, truck, car.

"Medical stocks are up," said the economics correspondent. "The Dow went higher today than it had been before the outbreak."

"I also brought a King James Bible," Nadine said. "If you want it."

"I think I've had enough prophets."

The TV announcer said, "The search for Orrin Sykes centered today on Crystal Lake, Illinois, where the fugitive is believed to be hiding. He grew up there."

"I haven't changed my mind about God," I said.

"Up to you. But millions of people are thanking the Lord for what you did."

"I think we've had enough heavenly messages to last the next hundred years. Keep me out of it."

Nadine unwrapped her sandwich. "Do you mind if I start first, Joe?" She took a bite. "I see a man who is alive, and triumphed, and who walked into my church and found answers. If that's not a message, my friend, you tell me what is."

"I'm too sick to have this conversation."

"I think you have it with yourself all the time."

"If you don't shut up, I'll tell the nurses to eject you. But I'll keep both sandwiches."

She smiled. She ate with healthy bites. She wiped her mouth with a napkin. She opened a couple of Dr. Brown orange sodas and put one on my tray. The TV was now showing the Sixth Prophet's Cult compound, once a

Quaker farm, then sold to the Defense Department, then auctioned off to the public during a budget-cutting bout.

"Tasty sandwich, Nadine. Thanks."

"God willing."

"He made the sandwiches, too?"

Nadine laughed. You could never faze her. She was one of those missionaries who would keep coming at you, but she was so good-natured about it that I didn't mind. There was something solid about Nadine, and I appreciated her. She'd always protect a friend's back, whether you agreed with her or not.

"He provides sandwiches, Joe. He even made you."

TWENTY-THREE

━━━━━━━

I'VE ALWAYS LOVED THE FIRST MOMENT OF SPRING IN THE BERK-shires. It's an almost instant rotation away from the winter world. One day, the trees are bare and gray and the soil muddy from snow melting. The air smells of wood smoke drifting from towns and weathered houses. The lake where I kayak is ringed with brownish trees, the waves have white caps, and the blue herons seem to shiver when they watch me pass, stork-like, perched atop dead beaver lodges.

And then, as if a switch was flicked, brown is green. The herons move more languidly. Bald eagles soar above the lake, near their nests in the tall pines. The bad-tempered moose who crosses my property at 5 A.M. each morning appears with the regularity of a clock. He disappears like a snowbird in the winter, and comes back in the spring.

It's time to walk past Joe's house again.

I could move around again. The scars and pucker marks remained, and sometimes I heard bones rub inside while I worked on the house. I repaired a water pipe that had cracked while I was away, cut a hole in a bedroom wall and severed six inches of copper, then welded in fresh tubing. I put new shingles on the roof. The deck needed painting. A couple of cathedral-style double-paned windows had fogged up inside with condensation. The air-tight seals had weakened so I replaced them. I liked the physical work and went to bed each night exhausted. It was good to be out of rehab, or rather, good to be on the self-imposed kind, working the shoulder with a hammer, instead of having a stranger's hands kneading it. Relearning the touch of a steering wheel while driving when there was no feeling in one finger. Taking pain pills without a nurse bringing them in a paper cup.

Sleeping in my own house.

I turned down the reporters who wanted to interview me. I shut down the investigators at a certain point, too. You can only go over the same story so many times. The only people that I allowed to come to the house after that were two men—different as night and day—scheduled to testify in the upcoming trials of the apprehended cult members. One of those experts was a forensic psychologist who worked for the defense team. The other was a man who had studied cults, and the damage they do, for the past twenty years. They both wished to question me about Harlan Maas. I wanted to talk to them, too. I wanted answers.

The psychologist arrived first, on a May afternoon, when mud season was over and the first buds bloomed on the birches outside. He was a kind-faced, soft-spoken man with penetrating eyes, wet lips, and an open, vulnerable manner—a Yale University professor who'd worked on numerous high-profile cases over ten years. He had testified in the trial case of a Minnesota man who'd sent letter bombs to senators, a Kansas woman accused of kidnapping four thirteen-year-old girls, a Miami heir who had murdered his parents one night and burned their home to the ground, a respected major in the Army who had shot nine soldiers at Fort Bragg.

"You don't believe evil exists?" I said, astounded. "You don't believe that any of those people were guilty?"

"They did it," the psychologist said as we sat on my deck. "They were not rational when they did. Something happens in the brain. It's no different than any other physical disability. It's chemistry. It drives you to do things. It's clear that Harlan Maas was abused as a boy, severely. He grew up in a cult. He loved his abuser. The most traumatic event of his life was watching his abuser being arrested and led away. There was schizophrenia in his family to start with. He tried to live a normal life after the raid, was adopted by loving people, and it worked for a while, and then his adopted parents were killed in an accident and a college love affair went bad. Trauma triggers schizophrenia, and Maas was the right age. He thought he got a phone call from his adopted father one day at college, telling him he was calling from heaven. Remember, this boy didn't grow up like you or me. He grew up being told by the people he trusted most in the world that the man who abused him every night was God."

"A phone call *from a dead guy*?"

"In the lab. At SUNY. On an old-style table phone."

"He really believed this?"

"The lawyers say I'm not supposed to go into more detail."

"You want answers from me? Then talk."

"Look, we can only reconstruct by talking to the people at SUNY. He thought it was a cruel joke at first. He went to the other students, demanding to know who was pretending to be his birth father on the phone. He was referred to the medical center. We've got the old reports. He thought he got a call *at the medical center* while he talked to a school psychiatrist, ordering him to get out. This is classic. Son of Sam—who shot couples in their cars in New York City—thought his orders came from a dog. Dennis Sweeney was a civil rights volunteer and big fan of Congressman Allard Lowenstein. But in 1980, he pumped five bullets into Lowenstein, believing that he'd received orders to do it through a radio receiver in his teeth. For Harlan Maas, it was phones. Old, clunky phones. He bought them at yard sales. It could have been a jam jar. It could have been a shoe. It could have been a magic coffee cup. That's the definition of insane."

"But he was rational enough to do research."

"Yes."

"And attract followers who murdered for him."

"So did Asahara and Jones."

"But he invented a whole new disease."

"You don't get it. IQ has nothing to do with it. In fact, high IQ made him more effective."

I shook my head. "You're coddled up there at Yale, Doc. You just can't conceive of evil."

He shrugged. "Other people have said that. You know, I watched a stranger shoot my parents to death when I was seven, watched them lying on the street in San Diego. The man who did it smiled at me. He didn't even know them. He'd been told to do it, he later said, by an angel. That man actually offered me a piece of fudge, and then he walked away. *He offered me fudge!* So, Colonel, who knows? Maybe I came to this point of view to protect my own sanity. But if that's the case, I like the world just as I see it. Please tell me exactly what you talked about with Harlan Maas."

THE FOLLOWING DAY—AFTER THE DOCTOR LEFT—A HONDA FIT with Delaware plates pulled into my dirt/grass driveway and the middle-aged man who got out in a dark suit, tall, lanky, and harder-looking, was the cult expert named Bobby Boyd. Boyd was a self-educated Kentucky man who said that his first experience with cults occurred when his mother was in a nursing home, and a cult took hold inside. Someone convinced half the residents there that he could turn back time and, if they followed his beliefs, make them younger. But that man stole money from the residents. Then he fled.

"Since then, for twenty years, I've been after them," he said. "The people who run these things are evil manipulators. They're con men and women. They study the techniques. They read up on methods. Harlan Maas did the same thing. They control every aspect, every minute, of their followers' lives. They shut out influences from the outside. They say they have the great cosmic answers, that their followers are special, that they will lead the world into a new age. You'd be astounded how many times this has happened."

"So Harlan Maas wasn't insane?"

Bobby Boyd laughed. "No more than you or me."

"What about the red telephone?"

"After a while they come to believe their own bullshit," said Bobby Boyd fiercely. "But don't think that means they're insane. They know what they're doing every step of the way."

MY BEDTIME READING CONSISTED OF REPORTS THE ADMIRAL FOR-warded, about cults. I followed the search for Orrin Sykes on TV. I watched a PBS special about Harlan Maas and the Cult of the Sixth Prophet, which ended with a trio of forensic psychologists—talking heads—arguing about Orrin Sykes.

The first man said, "He's hiding. Separation from the group obviously gave him distance to reevaluate his connection."

The second said, "I think he did what the group planned. Mass suicide. He's dead. We may never find the body."

"*Mission*," the third shrink predicted. "If you look at his mission, it was to kill Colonel Joe Rush. And because he failed, the cult was destroyed. I believe it possible that he's trying to make up for it and complete his mission."

And I thought, *Tell me something I don't know.*

Before I left Washington, I'd hit the spy shop and spent four thousand dollars on security equipment. I put the laser alarm detectors in the trees out back, and at the foot of the driveway. That didn't work because at night too many animals prowled around outside. I moved the detectors to the deck and the foot of the front steps. They were small white boxes, visible, but you had to know where to look.

With the detectors so close to the house, I'd get less warning if the alarm went off. But I wouldn't keep waking up in the middle of the night because a bear lumbered past and crossed a beam.

Spring became summer and the leaves were thick that year, and my shoulder ached less. Doctors said that sensation might return in my finger. I kayaked three times a week to work the muscles. Orrin faded from the news. His photo was covered up by a bank robber's in our post office. The trial date was set for the other cult members. Harlan Maas was not even a subject of dinner talk anymore in Washington, the admiral e-mailed me. The new crisis in Ukraine was.

A couple of my old high school buddies knocked on the door and said they had seen that week's *New York Times Magazine*, "the real story of the outbreak," and the old photo of me from the Marines. A town selectman showed up and said that he wanted to honor me in the Memorial Day parade this year. No thanks. Aya and Eddie kept in contact. Eddie was in Boston, with his family, starting the business that we'd once thought to create together. Aya was getting ready for two weeks of science summer school at Woods Hole.

Each July the closest neighbors on my dirt road hold a paella party. They lay out immense cooking pans on steel rods, perched on concrete blocks, over a fire pit. They light up mesquite-scented charcoal and stir into the pan olive oil and chorizo, shrimp, peppers, onions, chicken, and the smells drift over the forest as outdoor speakers echo with old jazz favorites: Billie Holiday . . . Art Tatum.

More than a hundred people come. Our little road fills with cars; some park in the weeds along the shoulder, or in our driveways, the license plates from New York and Connecticut and as far away as Virginia.

I'd debated with myself whether to go this year, but the gathering was the perfect kind of event for me. There would be old friends there from high school. There would be neighbors who I bumped into sometimes by our grouped mailboxes on the road. Even strangers were welcome. Sure, for a few moments I'd be the center of attention for the out-of-staters . . . *that's the man who stopped the outbreak* . . . but courtesy was the rule. I wouldn't be bothered. I'd stay an hour, get the minimal amount of human contact that passed for social life these days. Then I'd walk two hundred yards home, and watch PBS, or read, or plan out tomorrow's cement patch work on pockets of foundation gouged out by ice during the cold winter this past year.

Aya walked toward me in the crowd, holding a paper plate loaded with food.

"I made Mom drive me here. We're taking a road trip looking at colleges. I wanted to see Williams. I made her not call you. She wanted to ask permission to come. But if we called you, you'd say don't, Eddie said."

"He's not always right, you know."

"Was he wrong, Joe?"

"No."

"Here comes Mom. Be nice."

She was the kind of woman that you notice even before you realize that you know her. Something about that petite body, the rhythm of the walk, back straight, hips rolling, slightly pigeon-toed steps, that drew glances. Chris Vekey made her way between the cluster of New York theater people drinking homemade sangria and the trio of town selectmen in folding chairs, stuffing brownies into their mouths. She held a paper plate piled with paella and romaine leaf and sweet walnut salad. Her eyes held me. They created a warm sensation that instantly became irritation that she was here.

"Joe."

"Colleges, huh? Isn't it a little early for that?"

"Aya finished up the year with straight A's. She wanted to look now, start thinking about it."

Aya said, "Can we see your house, Joe?"

I thought, *Did you want to see colleges? Or did you want your mom to come here?*

I could not say no. She was my partner. She was a kid

but more, my *partner*, just as much as Eddie. She'd had my back when I needed help. She'd believed me and I owed her forever. You don't send away people whom you owe forever, if they show up at your house.

"I insist you stay with me tonight. There's a guest room upstairs."

Aya beamed, and turned to her mom. "See?" she said. "*See?*"

I sensed conversations within conversations. This kid was really something. But on the social end, she was about as good at playing matchmaker as Harlan Maas had been at being God. I put my arm around her. I hugged her. I wanted to put my arm around her mother, too, but that wasn't going to happen.

"Wow! It's so isolated out here," Aya said as we picked our way home on the road. In the dark, my flashlight beam playing over woods, boulders, rain gulleys, a shadow, a box-shaped form, two feet high, moving fast across the road. Lynx maybe. We get them sometimes.

"What was that?" Chris said.

Midnight. We were still talking. We were in the living room, and in a safe area of conversation, one which Chris and I could discuss with equal enthusiasm. Her daughter. The women had their patter down. Chris did the bragging, Aya the blushing. Chris gave the headlines, Aya the text.

The White House? *And the President said anytime I wanted to come over, just call his secretary!*

Her high school? *Mr. St. John said winning the science fair was nothing compared to what we figured out, Joe.*

Her friends? *They can't believe it!*

"Sleepy, Aya?"

"Not a bit!"

"Want some more coffee, Dr. Vekey?"

"I won't sleep if I do, Dr. Rush."

At two they went upstairs. I got the shotgun out, and my Beretta handgun, a Brigadier. I'd done guard duty many times over the years; at Quantico, in Canberra, at an embassy; in war camps, in Iraq.

I sat in the chair at 3 A.M. I emptied my mind of thought and willed myself to stay awake. Understand that I had no sense that anyone was coming. I was simply doing what you do to protect people you must shield. The moon came up full and hard and so bright that night was day, silver day, the tips of leaves trembling and glinting. The moonlight glowed on my gravel/grass driveway, on the top of Chris's packed-up Ford Focus, on my woodpile, on the grudgy porcupine who, tiny hands like a monkey's, climbed a maple tree each night, slow as a sloth, an inch at a time.

Three twenty.

At three fifty-five, the dot of red light—the alarm system—at the junction of wall and ceiling went out.

I sat up.

There was no light on the digital clock either.

Which meant no electricity.

No electricity, and no storm outside.

My heartbeat picked up. Slowly, I moved out of the chair, and slid sideways across the floor, to take up position in a corner that provided a view out the sliding glass door to the deck.

Upstairs, no sound. They slept.

Nothing.

Then a creak outside. Or maybe it had been the house settling. Or the bad-tempered moose, who, every couple of years, actually brushed up against the house at night. Don't ask me why. Maybe he's scratching his flank.

An owl out there somewhere went, *Oooooooooooh!*

It's possible that a power line went out in town. An old tree fell. It hit a wire. It hit a junction box. It's possible that too many air conditioners are on in Pittsfield and Hartford and Boston, and there's a power surge somewhere, and lots of rural towns have gone dark.

I saw the shadow before I saw the man. It seemed to puncture the coned moonlight on the plank decking. A bump became a head, which elongated into shoulders. The shoulders grew a shadow chest, a square darkness. The man was trying to peer in through the double glass.

A hand touched the pane. He was shielding his eyes. I saw the rapid breath condense on the outside of the glass.

He did not see me yet.

It wasn't his body that I recognized. Last time he had worn a parka. It wasn't his face, which was so heavily bearded that the shadow resembled a Charles Manson or a San Francisco Giants pitcher now. It wasn't the features; because with the bright moon behind him, his front was indistinct.

But the shadow cradling a shotgun was distinct enough. The intent was clear and genuine. I recognized intent.

I stepped out into his view and fired.

BOOM . . . BOOM . . .

He was moving already. The moonlight must have glinted off my weapon, or—flooding in—illuminated my movement. The picture window blew apart but he was gone. Glass shards fell. I saw his foot scrabbling left, out of view, and now I was the one getting out of the way as the remaining fringe of window shattered and more blasts raked the walls. A fixture shattered behind me, and so did the TV. The table seemed to move back by itself.

Shielded by the wall, I stuck the shotgun out and fired again and heard dragging footsteps. I heard a muffled stumping that usually marked someone going down the deck steps behind my house. From the bottom he could flee fifty feet across a grass clearing into the forest, or duck beneath the deck, and shoot up if I stepped outside. He could sink into the massed three-foot-high ferns at the base of the steps . . . weeds which I'd been putting off whacking, and which could now conceal him.

It's always the job you put off that screws you up.

Inside, Chris stood on the balcony by the second-story guest bedroom, looking down at me in the cathedral-roofed living/dining room. The bedroom door was closed, as if she'd ordered Aya to stay inside, and could protect her daughter by being there. If I shouted up instructions, Orrin Sykes would hear them. I cursed but jammed the Brigadier into my belt and slipped up the stairs to Chris.

I should be outside, not here.

"Do you know how to use a shotgun?"

"A shotgun?" Her voice was weak.

"Put it firmly against your shoulder. The spread pattern is wide so if he steps into the house, just fire. And keep the goddamn thing snug *against your shoulder* or the recoil could dislocate your arms."

"Don't go out," she said. "We'll call 911."

"Stay in this spot. *Only this spot.* You can see the front door and sliding door both. I'll call out if it's me coming in, got it? Say you heard me. Say it. I want to hear you say it."

"Joe, I—"

"Just say it!"

I moved rapidly back down the stairs, keeping my eye on the shattered sliding door. It would have been better for me to keep the shotgun with me, for close combat, but Chris needed a weapon that had the bigger spread pattern. Downstairs I used up four seconds pulling a quilted winter jacket from a closet and slipping it on. I'd need the heavy fabric on if I jumped out onto shattered glass. I grabbed a bulky cushion off the couch and slipped back to the wall, by the blasted sliding glass door. If he was out there, he'd fire when I came through.

If he'd run, he had a four-minute head start.

I don't think he'll run. He came all the way here to finish me. He'll know that even if we call 911, the state police need a half hour to reach here. He'll try to end it now, while he has a chance.

The picture window was so shattered that I could step through it. The house smelled of forest, mulch, and fired weaponry. I saw no blood on the deck. Then again, it was night and dark. I tossed the cushion out and jump/rolled through the opening in the opposite direction.

Fire at the cushion if you are there, I hoped.

Nothing happened except that my bad shoulder hit the deck. The pain made my breath go shallow and it radiated down into my chest.

Silence.

I scrambled off the deck, keeping low, crabbing down the stairs and into the ferns. I zigzagged toward the tree line. Behind me the house was like a boat anchored in a cove rimmed by forest. The trees, under a full moon, were bright as if in a photographic negative, a silver and black world, inside out.

Nothing.

"Orrin!"

I'd reached the trees and, shielded by a fat hundred-year-old pine, heard myself breathing, smelled sap, heard an owl . . . *ooooh*.

"Orrin, the cops won't be here for twenty minutes! Here's your chance to finish it! You screwed up in Washington!"

I moved left, to a different tree, an oak, judging from the thick, ridged bark at my back. He was close; he was somewhere close. He was fucking close and he was waiting. A Beretta Brigadier carries fifteen rounds, and is accurate up to fifty yards. Clouds scudded above and silver light disappeared and reappeared and slid left to right. In the glint I saw battered-down ferns, a fresh place between trees. Either Orrin had passed this way or an animal had. Several areas showed flattened ferns. Which ferns had been flattened by Orrin?

"Hey, Orrin! You got Harlan killed! If you had taken me out in D.C., he would still be alive!"

I avoided a moonbeam and kept to deep shadow. I stepped as quietly as possible over rotting trunks and foot-deep holes. He was not behind the freestanding granite boulder, deposited here by a glacier a hundred thousand years ago. He wasn't coming out from behind the birch trees or maples. Something small skittered away through the brush. I almost shot it. Possum maybe. Or raccoon. Pet cat maybe. Fisher.

Every step I took carried me farther from Chris and Aya. If I wanted to protect them, I needed to stay close. But I also needed to finish things with Orrin. And maybe I needed to finish things with myself.

"You're a loser, Orrin."

I was making too much noise, even when I was trying to be quiet. I wondered if he had night vision goggles, if his world was a clear, underwater green. The moonlight made some spots bright as day. I smelled rancid musk, *bear*. East Coast bears are small and harmless. Well, they're not harmless if you get between a mom and cub. This time of year was when moms and cubs moved around near my house.

I only realized I'd stepped into a stream when I felt the shock of cold water on my ankles.

"Orrin! You had me in the car! You should have finished it! I don't know how Harlan ever trusted a jerk like—"

He ran into me from the right side, smashing me back against a tree. Either he was out of bullets or, maddened, he wanted to finish it by hand. The Brigadier was gone. He was howling like an animal, not in words, just with a high, crazed rage. I lashed out even before striking the ground but missed his face. I must have struck a root because my lower spine exploded with pain. There was no finesse to his attack, just brute vengeance. We were rolling, going for eyes, nose, soft spots, death spots. At the bottom of the slope we rammed into a boulder, and the breath went out of me.

I saw his eyes in moonlight, but the lower face, the screaming, was all shadow. As if the earth itself or the night created the sound. It was not human. It seemed to come out of time. The ferns were in my face and mouth. He gripped my wrist and slammed it into the moss-slick boulder. I parried an elbow launched toward my face. He was on top of me.

Warriors scream to ratchet up energy, but the scream *is* energy, concentrated adrenaline, and his waste of it was a mistake. As he pulled in more air, I felt the smallest opening, the briefest weakening. I twisted my wrist and pulled free as my other hand jabbed into the shadow area below his eyes. I struck something soft and pliable. He reared up and jerked back.

Orrin Sykes's hands stopped clawing at me, and started clawing at his own face. Pushing him off was easy. He was gagging. My own ragged breathing was hard but regular. Orrin's was begging, a plea for oxygen, but one which could never get enough of it through a trachea that had been half crushed. He was up on his knees. He kept clawing at his collar.

It was over.

Orrin Sykes was still alive as I stood over him. A hollow gurgling came from his throat. The eyes were blinking and I smelled a gut wound, too, a mix of blood, rot, and viscera. Maybe I'd shot him before or he'd injured himself in the forest. Orrin Sykes was dying.

He had lied and crawled and snuck his way across a nation. He'd come to finish what Harlan had told him to do. Maybe it was out of vengeance. Maybe like Harlan Maas, he was sick, if that psychologist who'd visited me was right. Maybe he'd come because I had robbed him of membership in something, and cast him back into loneliness. I'd never know.

Things take a long time to build up. Sometimes they end in a few seconds.

He might have realized that I looked down at him. From the way his eyes moved, he saw *something*, that was sure, but what it was may have been beyond my ability to comprehend. He was trying to talk. I leaned over to listen.

"I'm not . . . the last . . . one," he said.

And he died.

When I got back to the house—ten minutes later—Chris and Aya were on the deck, waiting. I was angry at them for leaving the protected interior of the building—*what if I'd been killed, and Orrin was the one coming back*—but no one was listening to anyone else tonight.

The relief on their faces was so profound that I bit off my retort and didn't mention Orrin's last words. I surrendered to exhaustion. It had been a while since I'd felt anyone's arms around me. The two of them hugged me. The sensation felt strange.

That Orrin had come alone was certain. I had no doubt of that. If he'd come with help, the fight might have ended differently. But what had he meant, *I'm not the last one?* Had he lied? Had it been a useless threat? Or were there really more cult members out there? And someday would another show up?

Thirty minutes later we heard the thin wail of a siren. A glow of light appeared above the treetops, two hundred yards away, and then red lights were pulsating, and the first headlights turned into my driveway, throwing up gravel the way a dog digs at dirt with its hind legs. Within the hour would come more headlights. And then local reporters. And then a chopper, hovering.

WHAT I REMEMBER MOST ABOUT THAT NIGHT NOW, SIX MONTHS later, is the way Aya's face changed, that last vestige of *kid* disappearing as she stared down at Orrin's body, before the cops came. Aya pushing away her mom, just looking and not crying, perfectly alone. Aya had lost innocence. We can't protect the people we love. We can only try. When we can't approximate trying anymore, we let them go away.

Karen had taught me that.

That Orrin Sykes had chosen that night to show up was no coincidence. That he had come when Chris and

Aya were there was part of the great game I played. I'd told Reverend Nadine that I believed myself to be in a macabre tug-of-war with God, or some force approximating God—fate, humor, coincidence, you name it—and the notion that for whatever reason, it kept coming back.

Joe Rush, superstitious fool.

I let them stay the night, of course. In the morning they were brought to the state police barracks to be questioned by detectives, and FBI, and days later, allowed to leave and continue Aya's alleged *college tour*, as if nothing, no outbreak, no deaths, no bacteria, none of it had happened. Out beyond my town four hundred million people were trying to do the same thing: get back on commuter trains, shop at Costco for apples and wines, go to the beach, repair houses, go to church.

Chris and Aya stopped in to say good-bye. I kept it quick. I told Aya we could e-mail each other. I shook hands with Chris, felt the small fingers, and her grip, and the coolness of the departing touch. Then their car backed out of my driveway and the last pebbles sprayed out and settled and the world was still. It wasn't just people leaving. It wasn't just love. It wasn't even God leaving. To me, it was different. It was more. And it was right.

There's been no evidence found so far that other cult members are still out there. But maybe that is wrong, and someday one will come for me.

That day, I scraped off the blood on the deck with a sharp spatula, and applied brown deck stain. I probably got all of the blood off, but you never know; probably some bacteria-sized bits remained.

AUTHOR'S NOTE

Although leprosy has been mostly eliminated as a health hazard around the world, in 2013, there were 215,456 new cases reported globally, according to the World Health Organization. Pockets of the disease still remain, mostly in third world countries. The key to eliminating the disease and cutting down on transmission remains early detection, and rapid treatment with multidrug therapy.

ACKNOWLEDGMENTS

The author wishes to thank the following people for their help during the writing of *Cold Silence*.

Huge thanks to fellow authors and good friends: Charles Salzberg, Jim Grady, and Phil Gerard, for giving plot advice and for reading versions of the manuscript.

At Montclair State University, thanks to Dean Robert Prezent for providing an intellectual home during writing and to Dr. Jack Gaynor for the hours he spent educating me on issues regarding DNA and experiments with it.

To forensic psychologist Dr. Xavier Amador and to cult expert Rick Ross, my respect and my gratitude.

A very special thanks to my dad, Jerome Reiss, who is a genius at envisioning what certain characters would do in a tricky situation. Go Dad!

Lizzy Hanson, thanks for the advice!

To Stuart Harris, head of Wilderness Medicine at Harvard,

thanks for letting Joe Rush affiliate with your fine program, and thanks for walking me through how Joe would handle a problem in Africa.

Novels often come out of past experience, and this story would not have come about without terrific magazine editors like David Hirshey, formerly of *Esquire*, who sent me to Northern Kenya and Sudan on assignment, and Walter Anderson, formerly of *Parade*, who sent me to Somalia.

KEEP READING FOR AN EXCERPT FROM
JAMES ABEL'S NEXT JOE RUSH NOVEL . . .

VECTOR

COMING JULY 2017 IN HARDCOVER
FROM BERKLEY!

KYLE UTLEY RECEIVED THE FIRST THREAT OUTSIDE THE NEW POST Pub, in Washington, a dark, cool bar on L Street near 15th, popular with *National Geographic* editors and softball teams. Inside, on July 10, the White House National Security Team was celebrating a victory over the Senate Committee on Intelligence when the stranger appeared. The "Protectors" had overcome a 4–1 deficit to win the division championship. Twelve sweaty men and women sat drinking cold draft beer and eating the pub's famed Diplomat Burgers, reliving the game. Their come-from-behind victory had been so satisfying that for once no one talked shop.

Nothing about this morning's raid by FBI agents in Miami, where a gun battle and explosion had destroyed a small home. Three "foreign males," as neighbors described them, had rented the house, barricaded themselves inside, and blown themselves up rather than surrender. *"All evidence was obliterated,"* the FBI report said.

Nothing about jihadist branches popping up in South America. Or the U.S./China face-off in the South China Sea. Just softball and gossip, until the cute Thai waitress bent over and told Deputy Assistant National Secretary Advisor Kyle Utley that a man needed to speak to him, outside.

"Tell him to come in."

"He says it is too noisy in here."

"Who is he?" Kyle asked, only half paying attention.

"He says he has big news," the waitress said.

Kyle left his cell phone on the table—mistake—and walked out of the bar. On humid L Street waited a trim, white, neatly bearded stranger wearing a wide-brimmed red Nats cap, blue tennis shirt, and Adidas. Utley, a former Army Ranger, noted the lower end of a Special Forces tattoo on the right bicep: a coiled snake on a knife hilt. Above that, but hidden beneath the sleeve, would be the skull, beret, and snake head on the muscled arm.

"Sorry to interrupt the party," the stranger said, not looking that way at all. "Nice home run in the seventh, by the way."

"What do you want?" Kyle was irritated at the coy, I-know-things-you-don't attitude, and the fact that the guy had been watching him. He noted the southwestern twang, alert posture, and smile that did not reach the mud-colored eyes. The man's slim frame rose to wide shoulders. He radiated fitness.

"Kyle, you have instant access to the President's Security Advisor. You're not important enough to have a body-guard. Pass along a message, will you?"

"What message?" Utley asked, chilled despite the heat and understanding that a threat was coming. All threats—he knew—were to be taken seriously.

"That slush fund you guys run out of Ankara, Turkey? To pay off friendly warlords across the border? We're going to kill several hundred Americans in seventy-two hours if your bosses don't divert that money. On this paper is a list of charities. Three hundred million dollars is not a lot. Imagine if a few hundred million would have averted the World Trade Center attack. That cost trillions and the bill keeps rising. Pay and everyone stays safe. Plus"—he winked—"it all stays secret, with the convention coming up. Hey, the money's there already! Easy access!"

Utley stared into the eyes and saw intelligence and calm. His pulse had risen. His combat time in Afghanistan had destroyed any illusions about the depths of human violence. The stranger seemed rational, if that word could be applied to threats. Kyle eyed the paper and thin rubber gloves on the stranger, meaning no fingerprints.

"You sound American," Utley said.

"Then my language lessons were good."

"If you have a gripe about something, let's talk."

"We are."

"What's the money for?" Kyle asked, trying to delay, thinking, *five foot ten, mid to late twenties, no visible scars, gap in the front teeth, three freckles on the right lower lip.* He felt sweat on the back of his neck.

The man said, "Consider the payments reparations for Tol-e-Khomri."

"What was that name again?"

Darkness had fallen. Kyle had never heard of Tol-e-Khomri. A lone Volkswagen Jetta cruised past. Two wilted-looking *National Geographic* writers—the only other people on the block—brushed past, into the bar. Air-conditioning blasted out into the ninety-degree night.

Kyle held out the paper. "These organizations are not charities. They're fronts for terrorists."

The man smiled. "That can't possibly be right."

"You'll stop making demands if you get the money?" Utley said, not negotiating, just trying to keep the man there while he took mental notes, figured out what to do.

"Give us what we want and we go somewhere else."

"What exactly will happen if we don't pay?"

"Something terrible and unprecedented. *Bombs, but not bombs.* Panic, but no one will understand at first. It will occur in three cities. It will turn your world upside down. When America learns this warning was ignored, there will be consequences for your bosses. The third coming of wrath."

"You're not being clear."

"I think I am."

"I don't believe you."

The man shrugged. "Then wait seventy-two hours."

"How about if I call someone more senior than me?" Kyle gathered himself to attack. He'd been trained in close combat, but that was years ago. These days he didn't even have time to work out in a gym. He said, changing stance so he could move fast, "This is not my area and I'm sure . . ."

"Stop!" the man hissed.

He'd stepped back. "I'm faster than you, Kyle. You've been out of the service awhile. Just call your boss. That's all you have to do. Then your part is over."

The man smiled. *What could be easier?* he seemed to suggest. Left-winger? Right? Veteran who had suffered some injury and blamed the government? Kyle had been schooled in what to say if a threat ever came, although the lessons had always assumed a phone call, not a personal confrontation. *Try to control the situation.* What a laugh. He might as well try to fly.

The man said, "On 9/11 you had no warning. This time you have a choice." He turned and limped briskly up the block toward 15th. Utley began to follow. The man spun and raised an index finger. Kyle halted.

Kyle watched the man disappear around the corner. Kyle went to the corner. Somehow, the man was gone. That he could disappear so fast made his threat seem more real.

Kyle went back into the pub, where his teammates realized from his expression that something bad had happened. He retrieved his phone, walked back outside, and punched in the emergency number for the President's National Security Advisor, who picked up immediately. He was at a barbecue in Potomac. Kyle heard men and women laughing in the background. Someone had made a joke.

"A nut," the National Security Advisor said, after hearing the story, but they both knew this was hope, not analysis.

After a beat, the NSA asked, "He actually said Tol-e-Khomri? Those exact words?"

"What's Tol-e-Khomri?"

"Never mind. Special Forces, you say? An American?"

"He had the tattoo. But anyone could have that."

"He knew about the special fund, eh?"

"Sir, everyone over there knows. It's the worst-kept secret in the Mideast."

"There's never been a situation where someone just walked up and made a threat outside a bar. And bombastic rhetoric is par for the course. They talk big. They bluff."

An hour later Kyle was at the barbecue, too, at the home of the White House Chief of Staff, on the patio, where a strategy session—how to handle *soft-on-terror* charges before the national political convention—had just been interrupted. He recounted the story, ice cubes melting in the tumbler of Maker's Mark in his hand.

By midnight, the heads of all major security agencies were on a conference call with the President, answering questions about ongoing alerts. There were no specific threats being investigated at this time. The three terrorists in Miami were dead. Nothing alarming intercepted over the past few days on monitored phone or e-mails. No particularly important national events scheduled within the next seventy-two hours. They tried to figure out what "*bombs, but not bombs*" meant.

"Like I said, someone wants to rattle us. If they really had something, they wouldn't give us a heads-up."

"The third coming of wrath? Churchill called the nuclear bomb the second. What's the third?"

"Pretty damn confident, bragging that they're here already. Usually they claim credit after," Kyle fretted.

"The *Tol-e-Khomri* reference bothers me the most," the National Security Advisor said.

The decision was not to pay, of course, or announce a potential threat days before the national political convention, but relevant agencies would try to track all spending by the "charities" overseas, even though the guess was, money trails would be dead ends, a traceless series of transfers, cash disappearing into black holes.

The national terrorism threat level was raised to red that night, but Homeland Security announced it was a drill. Police around the country increased patrols around public facilities. Army Reserve copters flew over major harbors. Homeland Security added staff at airports. The cost drained hundreds of millions of dollars, as usual.

Another drill.

"We don't bow to threats," the National Security Advisor told Kyle boldly, after the meeting.

We just did, he thought, at home on Calvert Street, unable to sleep. The seventy-two-hour deadline had shrunk to sixty-six. He had not told his wife what happened. On TV, sound off to let her sleep, he watched a firefight between U.S. Rangers and ISIS troops. Then came a segment about veterans being mistreated in VA hospitals. *Is it about this?* Utley wondered, each time the announcer detailed another gripe.

AT THAT MOMENT AMTRAK'S REGULARLY SCHEDULED PATRIOT EX-press pulled into Pennsylvania Station in New York City, and the fourth man who exited the quiet car no longer looked as he had at the New Post Pub. The blond wig was gone. The hair was short, thick, black, and curly. The limp was absent, the tattoo and freckles washed off. The man stood just on the tall side of average. The face, without beard or cheek plugs, seemed rounder, and the eyes, contact lenses out, were almost azure blue, with a slight bulge that made him look less intelligent. The look was deceptive.

Tom Fargo transferred to the New York City subway One train, heading south, downtown. Even at this hour people were moving around the great city. College boys coming back from having sex with girlfriends. Pissed-off Yankees fans who had closed a Chelsea bar after the fiasco with the Red Sox tonight. A homeless man who snored and stank of urine. A Japanese tourist, too shy to ask directions. Any of them, Tom speculated, might be dead by next week, and the subway filled with panic-stricken people trying to flee the metropolis any way they could.

Tom Fargo looked around the car and hated these people with a vast, steady drumbeat that pulsed through his veins. *You are of them but not one of them,* Dr. Cardozo had said. He had fought them overseas, in dry wadis and wet melon fields. He'd assassinated an American diplomat in a Rio shopping mall. Now he was back home.

The subway rocked, and he smelled cologne and garlicky sweat, French fries and cleaned-away vomit. These people lived in filth. They were so fat that they actually paid others to help them become thin, the natural hungry state of millions elsewhere. Their armies slaughtered while they occupied themselves with subway advertisements to cure toenail fungus. These people were as oblivious as the old fool who had taught him what to do tonight.

When you make a threat, Hobart Haines had told him, long ago, *you need to back it up with action. Hook them with easy cooperation. Then nail them to the wall.*

Tom Fargo was not afraid. Running over what was to happen next, he recalled that before boarding Amtrak he'd made a phone call from outside Union Station, used an encrypted cell, punched in a twenty-digit number, and the signal had joined a hundred thousand other calls shotgunning into space at that moment, to bounce off a commercial satellite in a flood of talk that overwhelmed monitoring. Even if listeners broke the encryption, which was virtually impossible, he spoke in code. He and Dr. Cardozo traded comments about soccer. Hundreds of miles above Earth, words lived, money moved, plans coalesced. Their coded words had meant:

"Think they'll go for it?"

"Makes no difference. We do the same either way."

"Your suggestions were smart, Tom. *You* suggested

sending two separate groups. *You* said to make the demands first, not after. *You* know how to talk to them."

"I had a good teacher."

At Brooklyn Borough Hall, Tom Fargo exited the train and walked up top and into an area housing century-old municipal buildings, heading toward Brooklyn Heights. The night was sultry, the air so saturated with moisture that a light mist coated cars, the hulking courthouse, a neon-smeared falafel shop window. The city smelled of baking tar, coal oven pizza, hundred-year-old brick, diesel fuel. At 3:45 A.M. even the muggers were asleep. The neighborhood was a high-income area filled with young professionals. His rented co-op was in a converted potato chip factory, across from the Brooklyn Bridge, down the cobblestone street from the popular River Café.

Tom Fargo pushed through a polished glass revolving door to enter the sparkling lobby, where the night doorman sat behind a large post, eyeing a portable TV, on which a White House spokesman was telling a news announcer, "*The President has kept us safe for four years.*"

"Good morning, sir," the doorman said.

"Call me Tom."

"Been clubbing again in Manhattan?"

Tom Fargo grinned and rubbed his thick hair as if happily woozy from drink. "The shop doesn't open until noon. Might as well have some fun before that."

The doorman sat beneath a framed black-and-white 1950s photo of Christmas shoppers on 5th Avenue: sleekly dressed executives, upscale tourists, wealthy leisure seekers. The shot caught the casual power and confidence at the heart of a great empire. People who knew they were safe. But Tom knew that within days the looks on those faces would change. It was too late to stop his first attack. He'd set it in motion before going to Washington. There was no way the Americans would capitulate to demands at this stage without proof.

The doorman was a forty-year-old Dominican, nine years in the union. He lowered his voice, as if to reveal a secret. He was a tall man with a tough face and sensitive disposition. He wrote poetry lyrics late at night, and listened to biographies of singing stars on DVDs.

"It happened again, sir."

Tom Fargo stiffened.

"She came down to walk the dog. Her face, sir. It was black and blue. It's not right."

Tom Fargo relaxed, because this wasn't about the FBI. But he was angry. The doorman was hoping Tom would call the cops on his next-door neighbor, a big, loud-mouthed architect who chaired the building co-op board and relished his nickname, "Captain," and lived with his girlfriend. The doorman wouldn't do it, fearing that if he did, he'd lose his job.

"Someone ought to stop it, sir."

Stay out of it, Tom Fargo told himself. *What happens to Rebeca is none of your business.*

"You're a good guy, Mauricio," he said.

Mauricio, disappointed, went back to his book.

The elevator had a TV in the wall—Americans needed them like drugs—that showed CNN news, something about an explosion in Miami. Four stories up the door opened into a freshly painted semi-private foyer providing entry to only two apartments. There were framed lithographs of British jockeys on the wall, his neighbor's idea of class. He slipped the key into his top lock, then the dead bolt. Inside, the polished concrete floor threw back moonlight flooding in through floor-to-ceiling windows. The view of the Brooklyn Bridge was close and magnificent. The lights of Manhattan—even from across the river—drenched exotic artwork on his walls: jaguar head Day of the Dead mask from southern Mexico; tropical hardwood crucifix inlaid with Spanish gold links, from Peru; lacquerware bowl, 1859, Guatemala; Chacal rosary necklace that Tom's mother had picked up on a buying trip south, fifteen years ago, when she only owned one shop, not fourteen, scattered around the U.S., and an online shopping site, too.

Just the art that a spoiled trust fund artist wannabe—as his neighbors believed him to be—might display.

Forget Rebeca. Check the darkroom, he thought.

The darkroom—ground zero—had been installed by the owner, a photographer who was in China on assignment, and who had sublet the place to Tom for cash. He'd installed extra locks. Tom stood in a red glow, excitement building. The room was hot and moist. He could almost feel the vibration coming off the terrariums on the shelves, from a thousand *particles*, as he thought of them. He'd learned about particles from Hobart Haines when he was a teenager, in the high mountains, under a clear blue sky.

Bombs, but not bombs.

There was also $30,000 in cash here, and two perfectly

good credit cards in other names. There were pistols and explosives, a microscope, a laptop, medicines and Clorox wipes, and, in a rack on the wall, bulb-shaped glass containers clasped upside down, and, stretched across each top, a thin membrane of elastic covering.

He was startled when his encrypted phone rang. It was not supposed to ring unless there was an emergency. His heart seized up. "Hi there," he answered, casually.

A half-drunken voice slurred, "Felix? Felix! It's Marty, man! Marty Bolton!"

"There's no Felix here."

The caller hung up, and Tom Fargo—in shock—took the SIM card from the phone. He smashed the card and phone with a hammer. He tried to control his racing heart. His plan had just changed almost before it started. *Felix*—said twice—meant bad news. *Bolton* made it worse. *Marty* was a worst-case scenario. He understood instantly that the CNN report, the Miami explosion, meant that the other team here to carry out attacks was all dead.

Shocked, he went back into the living room, with its view of the high-rises, power centers, and apartments across the river, filled with enemy. Enemy extending across a continent; 350 million of them. He had always dreamed of facing long odds. Now he faced the longest.

The message had been: *You are the last one left. They will kill you if they find you. Good luck.*

Back in the darkroom the red light seemed to come from inside him now, pulsing into the air to saturate the glass containers and water pans, plastic cassettes, steel tweezers, and glass pipettes. As if fission was produced by intent, and *will* answered a scientific question, *will* was a formula that Dr. Cardozo jotted on his blue board. *Will = energy. Energy = destruction.*

Tom, filled with will, thought, *I can do it.* He was hot with rage but not fear. He'd lost that capacity some time ago. *I can fool them. I will make them think there are many groups here. I will finish this thing even if I have to do it alone.*

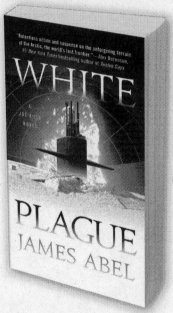